Charming!

or

if the glass slipper fits...

First published by O Books, 2010
O Books is an imprint of John Hunt Publishing Ltd., The Bothy, Deershot Lodge, Park Lane, Ropley, Hants, SO24 0BE, UK
office1@o-books.net
www.o-books.net

Distribution in:

UK and Europe
Orca Book Services
orders@orcabookservices.co.uk
Tel: 01202 665432 Fax: 01202 666219
Int. code (44)

USA and Canada
NBN
custserv@nbnbooks.com
Tel: 1 800 462 6420 Fax: 1 800 338 4550

Australia and New Zealand
Brumby Books
sales@brumbybooks.com.au
Tel: 61 3 9761 5535 Fax: 61 3 9761 7095

Far East (offices in Singapore, Thailand, Hong Kong, Taiwan)
Pansing Distribution Pte Ltd
kemal@pansing.com
Tel: 65 6319 9939 Fax: 65 6462 5761

South Africa
Stephan Phillips (pty) Ltd
Email: orders@stephanphillips.com
Tel: 27 21 4489839 Telefax: 27 21 4479879

Design: Stuart Davies

ISBN: 978 1 84694 383 6

A CIP catalogue record for this book is available from the British Library.

Printed by Digital Book Print

O Books operates a distinctive and ethical publishing philosophy in all areas of its business, from its global network of authors to production and worldwide distribution.

Charming!

or

if the glass slipper fits...

Gregory Dark

BOOKS

Winchester, UK
Washington, USA

Dedication

To my nephews and nieces, all of them special, and all (in their very different ways) charming!

To: **Simone Best** and **Richard Larder;**

Rebecca and **Tom Dark;**

Grace and **George Lane;**

y tambien a: **Augusto, Anita** y **Tuti Fajardo;**

Miguel y **Juan Carlos Pastor.**

Acknowledgements

Three colleagues who are also dear friends: **Bruce Crowther**, **John Hunt** and **Anne Piper**. Bruce proof-read it; John published it; Anne publicised it. To all of them I owe a debt that cannot be repaid.

Jodi Mudd's illustrations do not appear in this edition. I shall try to ensure they do so in future ones. Without the help of **Stuart Davies** and my brother, **Daniel**, I would never have mastered even the basic technology required of today's writers. My thanks also to the three of them.

There will also be others whom I will need to thank in subsequent editions. The exigencies of the publishing world are such that many who will have helped at the vital stage of publicising and promotion will have done their work too late for that work publicly to be acknowledged.

The idea of 'Charming!' took shape within a conversation I had with my daughter, **Lyubov**. I am *always* in debt to Lyubov.

I also want to thank the first three young people who read the book: **William Ashton**, **Charlotte Findlay** and **Oliver Dickinson**. Their appreciation was ... appreciated. As were their admonitions! The work benefited from the subsequent editing. (I also appreciate the later appreciation of **John Ashton** and **Louise Findlay**, too young to have read the book before its submission.)

A writer's life is famously lonely. I seem to be blessed, though, in the quality of people who enter my life. So many people, so lovely and loving. In the list of acknowledgements in other books, I have already made mention of some of these people. Here are a few more, whom I remember often, always with the greatest of affection. This list likewise is far from complete. I have, for instance, deliberately not made mention of any actor friends. I panicked that this rota may read like a wish-list of an Equity groupie!

The influence of these friends on either my life or my work may not be overt, but it is none the less real for its subtlety. They have all made my world a happier place. I certainly owe them a public vote of thanks.

Bobbye Aaron; Jo Bergerstrom; John Bernard; Tony Blechner; Harry Booth; Kristine, Manuel, Matthias and **Michaela Bronisch-Holtze; Tracy Byers; Michael Bywater; Harriet Carpenter; Malcolm Cockren; Tim Coddington; Ron Davies; Lesley Faux; Ron Fry; Rosa-Maria Gonzalez; Linda Graeme; Andrew Gritten; Russ Hill; Barbara Lynn; Stephen Long; Maeve** and **Robert McLean; Szuszanna Mills; Chris Munro; Robert Oakley; Terry Pierce; Krystina Plater; Margaret Porter; Gordon Roberts; Catherine Sherlock; John S. Smith; Katja Steiner; Arthur Tarry; Malcolm Vinson; Martin Weddell; Camilla** and **Norval Whyte; Zivko Zalar.**

Chapter 1

"Balls!" the king replied. And then he chuckled. But it was a chuckle lined with sadness. "It was all balls then, just one after a-damn-nother.

"They called me 'Charming' then, you know. When I was still a prince, that is. Well, of course you know. It seems to be the only thing anyone does know about me. 'Charming'. Hard to credit today, I know," he said, tapping his gouty and bandaged foot with his walking-stick. "Not too many, my dear, call me 'Charming' today."

I tried to ignore his condescension.

"Cinderella? She came at the end of it. At the end, at least, of so much of it, the first part of it. The first part, that was all BC: Before Cinderella," he explained. "A lot happened BC."

I looked surprised.

"Oh, I know what's been reported. The official version. All the biographies to date. I was at school in the South, in San Pedito. If you choose to believe that …" He left the hypothesis to dangle. "There's been too much distortion, too much deception. 'Enough, no more. 'Tis not so sweet now as it was before.'" Again that sadness. His rheumy eyes misted over. His gaze wandered over to some abstract place in the middle-distance.

"Will I be able to remember it all? There's so much to remember. And it is *so* long ago," he repeated. "It belongs, *all* of BC, to that time which was 'once upon a'. And sometimes," the king added with a wry smile, "it's as close as yesterday."

"The first time they tried to kill me, I was still in my pram."

We were talking in Parsifal palace, about twenty leagues from Wodinton, the Belgic capital then as it is today. Prince 'Charming' had become King Sebastian on his coronation.

Parsifal is, appropriately, a fairy-tale palace, all coned towers and thick forests and portcullised moats. Damsels, you feel, should be distressing out of its leaded windows.

Appropriately too we were ensconced in the infinity room. 'Appropriately' in this case because the room seemed to contain many of the riddles of the man himself.

It had been furnished some five years previously to his very specific design. It was hung with dozens of gilded mirrors, so arranged that their mutual reflection was apparently endless. Was this, I wondered, the work of a mystic or a madman? Was it poetry or pottiness?

Beneath the wrinkles, the young man still sinewed in him. And I thought even as that young man he had probably also been a combination of all those things: mystic and madman, poet and crackpot.

He was seated on a crimson wingchair, embossed with golden fleur-de-lis, fringed too with gold. A huge fire roared toastingly from a stone grate. It exuded, lusciously, the smell of pinecones. The flames, reflected a thousand times in the mirrors, gave the impression you were immersed in fire. But that immersion somehow was not threatening. It was calming, in fact; even soothing. The infinity room – though it was rather reluctantly that I admitted it – imbued those inside it with an almost womb-like security.

The king brushed away a tear. I wasn't sure I was supposed to have seen this.

"Sorry," he said. His liquid eyes darted at me. "It still hurts. Philly, my twin sister, and my cousin, Horatio, both killed. So many others. *So* many dead. And for what?

"They say, don't they?," the king continued, "that the truth shall set you free. Maybe I need to set them free, the ghosts of Philomena and Horatio. Maybe by telling the truth, that shall set *them* free, at least. I can't get my head around the idea that they should have died for nothing. *Still* can't. Not even after all these years." He wiped away another tear. A liveried flunkey appeared ostentatiously at his side, ostentatiously proffering a silk handkerchief.

"Thank you, Elton," the king said. It was, I thought, touching that he should know the names of his servants. "And if it *was* for nothing," he continued, tracing his finger along the edges of the silk square, "then it's important that they should, at least, be *remembered.*

"*Will* you remember them?" he asked me with a directness which, because of its suddenness, was almost intimidating.

"It's your story, sire," I replied, aghast at the way I was almost fawning before the man. "I'll tell it as you tell it to me. I'll just ghost-write it for you. The best ghosts are those you don't know are there." And smirked in the glow of what I thought was my excellent turn of phrase.

"Those are phantoms, my dear," he told me all but sharply, the schoolteacher exasperated by a careless answer. "Ghosts you *always* know are there. Ghosts neither sleep nor let you sleep. That's why I have to speak. I have to sleep. And so do they."

I said nothing. There was nothing to say. He wouldn't have heard. He was hurtling back through the decades, a journey of lightning speed. Far faster than the speed of sound.

"That King Cole was called a 'merry old soul'," the king started, "is indicative only of the way sarcasm can, over time, turn in on itself. He was a cantankerous old codger, my father. He smoked a hookah, you know: the much-vaunted 'pipe'. And the 'bowl'? Yes, a rather greater fondness for the grape than was altogether good for him – or the country. As for the fiddlers three, well, we'll get to them soon enough.

"As I said before, the first time they tried to kill me, I was still in my pram." ...

***

King Cole already had three daughters. Finally he had a son. And the entire of Belgiss celebrated for him and with him. Ox was roasted on the frozen streets, fireworks sparkled in the night sky, the February wind seemed to bite less and kiss more.

In those days only male descendants could succeed to the throne. Four marriages had been needed for the king to acquire a son. That his mother had died bearing him and his twin sister, Philomena, was certainly sad – the more so as the king's previous wife had died in similar circumstances. But it was not considered a tragedy of sufficient sadness to mute the celebrations.

The Crown Prince was three months' old. The twins' nanny – a pretty but immature flirt, Miranda – was walking them in their pram through the grounds of Wodinton Castle. Her fiancé histed at her from behind a bush topiaried as a cockrel. Her fiancé was a dashing young cavalry officer whose ambition to grow a man-size moustache was proving more problematic than he'd imagined. Miranda had been gone – oh, for no more than a minute or two – just enough time for a quick kiss-and-a-cuddle.

Princess Cordelia, fortunately, was also in the grounds at that time. *Not*, to her not inconsiderable displeasure, being kissed and cuddled. She was then also being courted – and by her future husband, Antonio, the Duke of Azrac.

Cordelia was the youngest of the prince's half-sisters. And the nicest. Physically she was tiny. Her hands and feet were the size of a child's. But she was perfectly proportioned, and thought of as something of a beauty. One of those 'best things' that 'come in small packages'.

She had been coquetting around the paths of the royal park. This adjoined the almost forbidding forest which then stretched all the way to Parsifal palace. She was hoping that Antonio would find the courage sufficient to try and kiss her. She had, of course, rehearsed in her head her abashment at such a turn of events. And she would, of course, have had to scold him severely – not *so* severely, however, as to have discouraged him from trying again!

To her horror, she had come across the unattended pram. To her considerably greater horror, she had found that within it the prince's face was covered with a pillow. As she hurled it from him, already, she noticed, his tiny face had adopted a bluish tinge. Away in the distance her eyes caught the flick – just the merest flick – of something black.

"Miranda and her fiancé," Sebastian interjected, "were told to consider themselves extremely lucky to have avoided the headman's axe."

The lovers' future also was to prove merciful: They were to live out their lives far away from the Court and Wodinton, in the far reaches of Belgiss. With a clutch of children. For the most part happily. He died having fulfilled his ambition of attaining a man-size moustache.

History would prove to be less kind to Cordelia.

A lot less kind.

Chapter 2

Later that day Baron Naitly was talking to the king in the latter's office. "There are evil forces abroad, Your Majesty," he told him.

"If they're *abroad*, Lord Chancellor, they're not our problem," quipped the king's jester, Mandy, "We only have to worry about the evil forces at home."

"Yes, very funny, HM," Naitly told the jester.

Baron Naitly was Lord Chancellor of Belgiss.

He knew himself to be, in all things, a cut above the average. He was of above average height; his hair was thicker than average and was swept back, above averagely, from a brow *higher* than average. The ermine-trimmed smock he wore, and his pointed shoes, proclaimed him to be *way* above the *social* average, to be indeed of the highest social order. His boudoir included a socks' drawer and a smiles' one. He only owned black woollen socks. Smiles, though, he had for all seasons. Indeed he was famous for them: He was known nationally to own smiles of all shapes, sizes and sincerities.

After the king, Naitly was the country's most powerful man. Some said he was, in fact, *more* powerful than the king. Naitly ached for the day when that would be true – and when the whole world would *know* it to be true.

Twice a week Naitly and the king would meet, usually in this office, to discuss policy.

It irked Naitly – and not a little – that the king would insist his jester, Mandy, should also attend. But the king found the meetings tedious. The only way to mollify such tedium was with a laugh or two. Not, surely, too much to ask?

It irked Naitly too – also not a little – that this jester, whilst being debarred the ermine-trimmed smock, *was* allowed the pointed shoes. Pointed shoes were a privilege, a recognition of accomplishment and importance. What had this ... jackanapes ever done to deserve them?

It was in those days extremely rare, probably unprecedented, that a king should have a woman as a jester. But Mandy was no ordinary jester – nor ordinary as a woman.

She was the king's closest adviser and best friend. Together they would go hunting in the nearby forest – something of a passion with the king. Mandy was an expert tracker. Rarely did the day end without the king having made some kind of spectacular kill.

Added to which, Mandy made the king laugh; and she spared him the tiresome job of thinking. In short, she had made herself indispensable to His Majesty. So much so that she had dubbed herself 'Handy-Mandy', a nickname which had both stuck and which had – to the confusion of the entire Court – been shortened to HM. No-one was ever quite sure, therefore, whether the HM alluded to was Handy-Mandy or His Majesty. There were many who opined there was essentially no difference.

This was not one of their regular meetings, but an extra one – an emergency one. The attempted assassination of the heir to the throne is, after all, a cataclysmic event.

"We have reason to believe foreign insurgents are responsible," Naitly continued, the accompanying grin adding, he thought, compassion to concern.

"Insurgents?" asked the king, a trifle blearily. He'd had a hard day, a nasty shock. He needed time to recover from both. "One does not know what that means, 'insurgents'?"

"It's an abbreviation, sire," said HM, "for *insur*ance a*gents*. And the Lord Chancellor is right: Insurance agents – trust me, sire – *are* the most deadly enemy known to Belgiss." The king had started to giggle. HM liked giggles from any quarter. Royal giggles she liked royally. She therefore continued, "They have the cruellest form of execution, sire, known on this planet: They *bore* their enemies to death."

"Them and Lord Chancellors, eh, HM?" the king guffawed.

Mandy and Naitly exchanged a look that was partly venom ...

and partly (curiously) ... well, almost collusion. "As Your Majesty so wittily says," said the jester.

They were in the king's private office. It was a room only king, Lord Chancellor and jester were allowed to enter – oh, and the cleaning lady, of course, but no-one counted her. No other minister of state, none of his wives or children was ever allowed even a peek into this inner sanctum. It had assumed, therefore, an aura of being the 'holy of holies'.

Which was to exaggerate its importance. It was simply the place where the king would go to escape from the rest of the world; where in peace he could smoke his hookah, and drink, liberally, from his bowl. Where he could cogitate on the affairs of his state – and the state of his affairs.

Apart from its book-shelved walls, its décor was almost that of a sheikh's tent: dozens of ornately embroidered and differently shaped cushions cascaded across intricately woven rugs. Lengths of fabric gushed from the ceiling, not all of which were curtains. The only pieces of traditional furniture were a Louis XIV desk, and the chair which belonged to it. The room smelled pleasantly of wool and velvet and unopened books.

"I cannot stress too much," said Naitly, "just how serious, sire, is this threat. Your son's very life could be in danger."

"What are you suggesting, Naitly?" asked the king.

"He needs round-the-clock protection, sire," Naitly told him. "With Your Majesty's permission, I should like to appoint two men – specialists, professionals – Krantz and Stern, to look after him." There was again the merest flicker of collusion in the glance between him and HM.

"One has no choice," said Cole 'philosophically'. "When the entire future of the realm is at stake there is no cost that is too high. No, HM?"

"As Your Majesty so wisely says," said the latter.

"One *will* be called *wise* King Cole when one is dead," the king said, indulging in a sort of pre-emptive nostalgia.

"May it therefore be many years," toadied Naitly, adopting a grin of exaggerated humility, "before Your Majesty is called wise." He'd got that one wrong! And he knew it. The king shrivelled him with a glance. "What I mean, sire, is ..."

"What the Lord Chancellor meant to say, sire," said HM quickly, "is that you have no need of *death* to be called 'wise'. Already there is enough wisdom in your kingdom for you to be known as such."

"You're such a comfort, HM," said the king 'confidentially'. "One has made another decision," he continued. "One hopes it is a wise one." He shot a look at Naitly, defying him not to agree.

"If it is yours, sire," said the Lord Chancellor, attaching a smile of extreme subservience, "it would of necessity be wise." He flicked a glance to HM, again almost of collusion. There were certain things they *could* agree on. The wisdom of the king's decisions, for instance, often required ... archaeology before it was uncovered.

"Alas, one seems unable to remember what that decision was," said the king, and let the goblet dangle limply from his hand. This was his favourite drinking vessel, his 'bowl'. It was a silver goblet, its stem studded with rubies.

"But of course Your Majesty cannot. Your goblet is empty," said HM. "Memory is a thirsty beast. It can't be expected to work without ... irrigation." She filled the king's goblet from a crystal decanter. She passed the king his recharged goblet. He drank deeply.

"Ah," sighed the king, "*now* one remembers. One has indeed had a *brilliant* idea."

"Your Majesty is too modest," HM 'admonished' him. "An idea, trust me, Lord Chancellor, of *genius*."

"One's modesty forbids, HM. However ... One is going to have the prince tattooed."

"Sire?" asked Naitly, wondering whether he'd heard correctly.

"Makes sense, doesn't it?" asked the king.

"So very much more, sire," said HM, "than mere sense. Sense is common. This is not a decision, Your Majesty, of *common* sense. *Its* sense is extraordinary."

"Extraordinary, sire," Naitly agreed.

"The castle's crockery – correct one if one is wrong – is embossed, is it not, with the royal coat-of-arms?" asked the king.

"Not quite the same thing, sire," laughed Naitly.

"Exactly," said HM in a tone of indignation, the sincerity of which was impossible to gauge. "You are not seriously trying to suggest, Lord Chancellor, that you consider the Crown Prince less important than a *plate*?!"

"Don't be preposterous, jester," Naitly replied crossly.

"That's my job, Lord Chancellor, to be preposterous. Yours is to protect and honour the king. And therefore the king's family. And therefore," continued the jester, "you will feel yourself obliged, will you not, to find such a tattooist for the king?"

"Alas, Your Majesty," Naitly replied, side-stepping the jester, "the ship of state does not steer itself."

"But without the full attention, Baron Naitly, of the *captain*, without him not being distracted by side-issues, like – I don't know – finding tattooists, for example, the ship – trust me – is liable to collide with an iceberg. Which is why the captain has a First Mate – in you, Lord Chancellor, a first rate First Mate, I might add. Could a First Mate have a greater responsibility than the safety of the Crown Prince?"

"Naitly?" the king asked.

"Of course not, sire. The jester, sire, is putting words ..."

"Then, Lord Chancellor, His Majesty will be delighted," crowed HM, "to leave in your very capable hands the job of finding of such a tattooist."

"Whilst you, madam, I suppose, enjoy yourself hunting?" Naitly's grin was finding it hard not to hide itself in the nearest corner.

"To the contrary. Whilst I, Lord Chancellor, perform the

equally demanding job of finding a replacement for the prince's nanny."

"That is my job," Naitly protested. "Your Majesty, I cannot stress too much that finding the royal nursemaid is a job which should be the Lord Chancellor's alone. There are security implications ..."

"But you will already be so busy, Lord Chancellor," HM interrupted him, "finding a tattooist, steering the ship of state ..."

"Naitly?" the king asked again.

"Oh no," quipped in HM quickly, "I don't think Naitly would make a good nanny." Naitly was not amused.

"I don't have time for this, Your Majesty." Naitly's grin remained fixed, but his eyes steeled into resentment and their icy glare promised future retribution. HM noted the look. She even acknowledged it. "I will appoint Krantz and Stern. The nursery arrangements I leave to those," he looked pointedly at HM, "more suited to tending the nursery."

"Are you calling me a vegetable?" HM asked in jestered dudgeon.

"If it please Your Majesty ..."

"Surely you mean, if it *peas* Your Majesty," HM quipped. The king cuffed her lightly, but laughed nevertheless. He took another swallow from his goblet.

Naitly bowed, took four backward steps, then turned on his heel and, his grin now no longer necessary, frowned his way from the office.

When *he* ruled Belgiss. When *he* was in charge ...

Chapter 3

The famous 'fiddlers three' was a soubriquet (nothing as common as a 'nickname') given by the Court to the triumvirate deemed, not without reason, to be the 'power-behind-the-throne'. The soubriquet didn't leave the Court's confines for some time after the king's death.

Naitly and HM were two of that triumvirate. The third was the king's eldest daughter, Goneril.

She was waiting in the corridor outside.

Goneril hated this sanctum of her father's. *Hated* it. It was there that he had signed her mother's death warrant.

"Well?" she asked, scurrying away from the study. She waddled rather more than she walked, and stooped slightly as she did so. Her frame appeared fragile, but it housed an iron constitution.

"Do you have any idea, pumpkin," asked the Lord Chancellor, "how galling I find it, playing second fiddle to that jackanapes?"

"And do *you* have any idea, LC," asked Goneril, "how galling *I* find it playing third fiddle to the two of you?"

Naitly ignored the question. Naitly was an expert at ignoring questions. "Our first act as queen and consort," seethed the baron, "the very first, will be to have the last laugh on that jester. Preferably by beheading her."

"Don't tell me, LC! She persuaded the king into letting *her* choose the nanny!" Goneril was not happy.

"She just twisted my words, pumpkin," said Naitly. "I cannot stress ..."

"Beheaded? We'll have her hanged, drawn and quartered," said Goneril, who, in addition to being vengeful, was also somewhat pedantic about her grammar. "As for you, LC!" she added scornfully, without adding anything further.

As well as one of the fiddlers, Goneril was referred to by the Court cognoscenti as 'The Hatcher' – in recognition of her prowess at intrigue. She was *forever* hatching plots. Often when there was no reason to do so; often quite brazenly. It was, for instance, a 'secret' (known to everyone but the king) that she and Naitly would marry just as soon as the old king had died.

Which marriage, both of its 'intendeds' knew but kept secret from each other, was ... well, certainly a love match, but not one where the love concerned was between the two people concerned. The object of both their affections – of both their *loves* – was power.

The marriage would enable both to acquire a level of power that, without the other, would be denied them.

Well, such, anyway, *had* been the plan ... And then, Enter from left field the Crown Prince. To put it extremely mildly, this was a severe setback to this plan. Neither Naitly nor Goneril was a big fan of set-backs, least of all to plans which were their own.

The proposed wedding had been kept secret because, at HM's suggestion, the king had expressly forbidden any romantic liaison between his eldest daughter and his Lord Chancellor.

The reason cited had been that Naitly was a mere baron, whose blood therefore lacked the requisite blue cell-count. This had never cut much ice either with the couple themselves, or with the slightly larger public who had got to hear of it. And had cut even less when Goneril's half-sister, Nancy, had married a commoner.

HM, though, had urged the king to remain firm. As a team, she told the king, Naitly and Goneril would be so invincible as effectively to rob him (and thus her) of any real power. The king had therefore resorted to the rarely used 'it is not the king's pleasure' to stop any attachment from developing.

The corridors leading from the king's office were as cheerless as the stone from which they were made. Their walls seemed designed to keep out all comers – including sunlight. A few flambeaux threw a desultory light in wobbly pools. These emitted a burnt toast smell, musty and unpleasant.

"And the other thing?" Goneril asked. Her chin jutted at him – she used this chin-jutting in the way others wag their fingers – and she replaced a loosened strand of hair behind her ear. Goneril was a blonde – though one whose colour had rather less to do with genetics than with the skill of her hairdresser. She always wore black and loved nothing better than being underestimated.

"Done deal," said Naitly. He allowed a grin to seep from one ear to the other. This was a real grin and was as close to that he'd adopted before the king as granite is to pomegranate.

Goneril stopped him, mid-stride. She looked both ways along the corridor. It was deserted. Even of soldiers. But it also echoed. Thus it was that she whispered, "Krantz and Stern, all agreed?"

"Done deal," Naitly confirmed and smiled again.

"And this time they will … make sure?"

"Oh yes."

"You know what it is I'm trying to say: This time they will …?"

"Kill the prince?"

"Yes."

"Done deal," Naitly said again. And again he grinned.

Again a real grin.

Chapter 4

The prince was only a few months' old when he was tattooed. Throughout his life he could never so much as see a tattoo without wincing. It wasn't that his conscious could find a memory; but his subconscious was as engraved with the pain as his toe was with the insignia. The toe was immediately sealed within a waterproof cover. Almost no-one who wasn't present at the actual tattooing got to see it.

It had taken Naitly's staff some little time to find a tattooist capable of etching something as detailed as a royal crest onto something as tiny, and wriggly, as a baby's small toe. HM was the only person the king would trust to hold his precious son during this procedure. It was another tie in the bond that was developing. HM brought the twins' new nanny, Gretel, along with her. HM also wanted to develop the bond between the prince and Gretel.

Before he started with the procedure, the tattooist, very sensibly, demanded a written amnesty for any pain he might inflict on the prince.

Which, at his trial, availed him ... nothing.

Lord Nelris was a judge whom Naitly had appointed precisely because he could be relied on to come up with what Naitly considered to be correct verdicts. The king told Naitly he wanted there to be no-one at large who had knowledge of the tattoo's detail. Naitly imparted this to Lord Nelris, who therefore deemed the written amnesty a forgery. He found the tattooist guilty of causing grievous bodily harm to a member of the royal family. This in Belgiss was treason.

And for treason there was only one punishment possible.

No-one had been executed in Belgiss ...oh, for some time. The axemen's duties were, of late, mostly ceremonial. Any time, though, the (deeply monarchist) population started murmuring a mite too critically or republicanly, these headmen would be returned to a more conspicuous duty – just to remind the (deeply monarchist) population of their presence.

Naitly showed surprising clemency in selecting for this job the very best of these executioners.

The tattooist was still protesting his innocence as – mercifully with one blow – his head rattled from his shoulders into the basket set to receive it. The crowd hooted its disbelief of his protests.

Goneril and Naitly watched the grisly spectacle from the balcony which adjoined the Cabinet office. This was housed in the Decagon, the Prime Minister's official residence, dubbed by HM the 'Decadence'.

Unlike Wodinton Castle, whose exterior exuded power and invincibility, the outside of the Decadence was almost remarkably *un*impressive. It was a dumpy, overtly symmetrical building, with an almost Quaker aspect.

It lay to the right of the royal residence, to the left of which was the barracks, home to the king's guards. The fourth side of the square was defined by railings. Through these the general public (or 'hoi-polloi' as they were known by the square's residents) could catch a glimpse in the square beyond of important occasions: the receiving of visiting heads of state, for instance, or the severing of heads deemed hostile.

Goneril and Naitly waved to the throng which had gathered. And returned within.

Inside, the Decadence was considerably more sumptuous than its humble outside. The Cabinet office was painted in a lush lemon yellow. A neo-Grecian frieze ran along its walls, about three feet from the ceiling. This, along with its cornices and columns, was painted a dazzling white. The room was dominated by the central table, huge and of oak. It had been carved from a single trunk. To get it into the room had required the demolition of part of the wall – since, obviously, rebuilt. The table was polished daily and now gleamed in an agony of elbow-grease.

Standing awkwardly before it were Messers Krantz and Stern, the prince's 'bodyguards'.

Krantz was, to use Naitlyspeak, 'dentally challenged'. What was visible to other than his (unfortunate) dentist was only two teeth, and these showed signs of profound decay: there was one on the top, and another skewiffly below. Apart from being unsightly and the cause of a halitosis which was considered by many Belgiss's secret weapon, this (in Naitlyspeak) 'incisorial deficiency' was the cause of a pronounced lisp.

Stern had a limp.

"And?" Naitly asked them.

"'*And*, Lord Chancellor?" asked Stern eagerly. "You want an 'and, does you? 'Appy to oblige, de-lighted. You just tells us what you want an 'and *with*, sort of thing." Stern's hobby was to make himself useful to Lord Chancellors.

Naitly groaned, and sat down on one of the chairs adjoining the central table. There was only one couch in the office and that was already occupied by Goneril. It was of a red damask, with off-white stripes. It almost framed the blackly dressed figure of the princess.

"You were recommended to us," she said with deliberation, "as men who could despatch with subtlety, discretion and expedition."

Stern and Krantz looked at each other wondering whether the other had understood. What they thought of as 'posh' words was not the forte of either one of them. Goneril might as well have been talking a foreign language.

"Ecthpedition?" Krantz asked, latching onto one of the few words familiar to him. "No, ma'am, we're not going on no ecthpedition, ma'am. We've thaid we'll do the job, and we'll thtay right here till it'th done!"

"The prince continues to live," she said slowly and evenly.

"It wath *you* who thaid we had to be careful!" protested Krantz.

"Beyond a certain point, Mr Krantz, caution becomes cowardice." Stern intuited what it was she was trying to tell them.

"I'ss the nanny, ma'am," he complained. "That bloody nanny found by bloody HM, ma'am, pardonin' my French. She don't never leave 'im for, like, long enough for ... you know ... us to do our business, type of thing."

"Mith oh tho thnooty Gretel, there'th the problem, ma'am."

"She's a girl," Goneril reminded them. "You are fully-grown men."

"You want us to kill 'er too?" asked Stern.

"Don't be childish," said Naitly – unhelpfully, the men felt. "I thought I had stressed the urgency of the matter."

"Whilst legion," said Goneril, "our patience *is* finite."

"Well, we wish 'em continued recov'ry, your 'Ighness."

"What are you talking about, Mr Stern?"

"Your patients, ma'am. We's glad they's fine ... finite, whatever. We 'opes they continues to get better." He shrugged a 'what-have-I-said-now?' shrug at Krantz when the princess let out a low growl and seized her head in an attitude of despair.

***

As far as HM was concerned, her relationship with the prince's 'bodyguards' was one of hate at first sight. She knew they were Naitly's men, answerable to him and Goneril, and this compounded both her dislike and suspicion of them. She nicknamed them Cross-Bones: Krantz seemed to be in a permanently bad temper – which, because of his permanent tooth-ache, he was; and Stern was so skeletally thin he was only a 'bag of bones'.

As for the skull which usually accompanied Cross-Bones, well, there wasn't one. Not really, not one worthy of the name. Not unless '*numb*skull' qualified. Cross-Bones, it seemed to the jester, had less brain-cells between them than a rather dim-witted earthworm.

Later the prince was to acknowledge, though, that it was precisely this dim-wittedness that was one of three things which kept him alive.

The second was the watchfulness of his new nanny, Gretel. Whom he grew to love. She cuddled him almost as warmly as Cordelia. And she tickled him almost as raucously as HM.

The third was HM's sharpness. She was as quick as Cross-Bones were slow.

Well, her sharpness, that is, combined with her hankering for an ermine-trimmed smock!

Chapter 5

In a toffee shortage the luckiest person is the one who has never eaten one. That person is unaware of any hardship. By that token, the young prince wasn't unhappy. Not consciously. It would be truer to say that he'd never known happiness. He'd never eaten that particular toffee. Not the toffee of *real* happiness.

And, no, it wasn't either that his father mistreated him. Not directly. It was a king's burden, that was all, that first of all he *was* a king. Only secondly could he be a father.

The king thought it "sissy" to hold his son or – perish even the thought – cuddle him. Such cuddling as the prince got was exclusively from women: fulsomely from Cordelia and (latterly) Gretel, raucously from HM, and tentatively from the usual plethora of Court goo-gooers. Who seemed to be unsure whether royal babies should not be cooed over differently to those of less lofty birth.

HM did her best to entertain the prince and to make him laugh. But the king was wont to grow fractious if his jester were too long from his side. And HM's first responsibility, of course, was to HM – however you cared to elongate the abbreviation.

Neither was it that Gretel failed in her concern for the prince. If anything, to the contrary. It was just that her concern had to be informed by a royal protocol which stretched back generations.

The young man, for instance, just could not get 'caught short' publicly. He couldn't suddenly stop the carriage and rush behind a bush. There would be onlookers by the townful to witness such a royal wee.

If he were travel sick, the whole country would be talking about it. The manufacturers of whatever conveyance he was in would probably go bankrupt. The consequences of even his most inconsequential actions took on a dynamic almost as a consequence of their *in*consequence. And, whilst the prince was not conscious of this, it became as ingrained as the tattoo on his toe.

Of the king's adult daughters only Nancy was married. She, as it were, was the middle daughter: younger than Goneril, older than Cordelia. She had chestnut hair and a plum in her voice so fulsome it was thought to have been stolen from Jack Horner. Her husband was a hugely wealthy merchant, elevated to the peerage as a wedding present from the king.

He now basked in the title of Baron Richardson. In acknowledgement of which honour he had grown a van Dyke beard. Which he now stroked as wisely as he did often.

Nancy celebrated by, about a year after the wedding, producing a son, Horatio.

Horatio was some six months older than the Crown Prince and Philomena. Of all possible playmates for the future king he was considered the most appropriate. The trio became one: almost a group of musicians who harmonised with and complemented each other.

The young prince and Horatio were about five. They were playing in the football-stadium sized nursery. Gretel was close by.

"Want to hear a great joke?" asked the prince. "Philly told it me."

"Go on," said Horatio.

"What's green," the prince asked, "and travels backwards at eighty miles an hour?"

"Dunno," Horatio replied.

The prince sniffed delicately and smiled. Horatio looked perplexed. Gretel looked askance.

"Well?" Horatio asked as bad-temperedly as royal protocol would allow him to be.

"That's it," the prince replied and sniffed delicately again.

"*What's* it?" Horatio asked again.

"What's green and travels backwards at eighty miles an hour?"

"*What*?" Horatio exasperated.

The prince filled his lungs with breath and blew out every last ounce of it. And then he SNIFFED. A tidal wave of snot cascaded backwards through his nostrils.

Horatio understood!

The two boys started shrieking with laughter.

"Charming!" snootied Gretel starchly, trying to suppress a giggle. "And for one, furthermore, of lineage royal. Truly charming. Yes, young 'prince charming', that's what we shall call you henceforward."

The prince was wrapped in cotton-wool. The princess Philomena, though – as the succession was not thereby endangered –, was allowed to run wild.

And wild she certainly ran. She was almost the son her father otherwise would never have had.

The prince was allowed to play with Philomena. But her wildness would occasionally alarm him. Cotton-wooled as he had been, the prince had become somewhat solitary, and a bit studious – even, it must be said, a trifle nerdy.

Most of all, the prince hated making a fuss.

Philomena loved making a fuss.

As members of the royal family, if the children passed a uniformed soldier, that soldier had to 'scabbard swords', as it was called. This was a laborious manoeuvre which involved the soldier flashing his sword in a series of complex movements before lining the blade up directly in line with his nose, and then reversing the entire procedure, finally re-sheathing the blade.

The palace was surrounded by sentry posts. These, of course, were manned by soldiers. The prince would go to the most extraordinary lengths, when travelling round the palace, to avoid passing these sentries, to save them from this tiresome and tir*ing* rigmarole.

Philomena, though, derived great glee from doing exactly the opposite. She would run backwards and forwards in front of the unfortunate men. So fast indeed that they would not have had time to finish the first manoeuvre before she returned, and it was time for the second. Many a rookie sentry had found himself doing extra duty because he had become so confounded by the princess's antics that he had completely lost the sequence.

Philomena was considered by the sentries a menace. That's putting it politely. And what they mouthed under their breaths at her approach was certainly not polite. It is thought indeed that it may well have been the derivation of the simile to 'swear like a trooper'.

Philomena was able to lip-read before she could read writing. And she revelled both in such reading, and the later repetition of these forbidden words. Far from dissuading her from her antics, therefore, these military expletives served merely to intensify her amusement.

Oh, how the prince yearned to copy her, yearned for her naughtiness and self-assurance and sense of mischief. But if protocol debarred him from following her example, this (it must be said) was abetted by his personality. He was a thinker, the prince, rather more than a doer.

He yearned for normality, for unprinceness. He would ponder for hours how he might achieve this. He would listen hungrily as Horatio described to him in scrumptious detail his last night's supper of spaghetti bolognaise, or of egg and chips. He would drool the following day in the imagination of such sumptuous fare as he sat through yet another interminable banquetting lesson – learning which of the seven different forks to use for sturgeon soufflé, how to eat asparagus without splattering butter all over the royal chin, which shaped wine-glass to use for champagne and which for Chablis. This was not the life he would have chosen for himself.

Horatio knew the prince; he liked him. Liked him a lot, as a matter of fact. He was one of the very few who understood the prince's yearnings. But there was little he could do to satisfy them. Until one day – oh, they were a few years older then – he, for no reason whatsoever, burped.

Charming, of course, knew about burping. It is an activity natural to the human species. And he'd been told, frequently – fervently! – how to suppress it. *Never* had he been told that burps could be *manufactured* – that, as it were, hot air could be conjured up out of thin air.

Charming was charmed by the idea. This, Horatio saw, was something he *could* do for his friend: He could teach him how to burp.

Never in the history of the world has a burp resonated through a nation as the prince's was about to do.

Chapter 6

It all started inconsequentially enough. Obviously it wasn't possible for Horatio to smuggle in for the prince an unprincely meal of pizza or burger: That would have made a terrible mess of his coat. But he knew that the prince's drinks were limited to freshly squeezed juices, usually of Azrian mango or Mercian guava. So what Horatio did as second best, he smuggled in for him two flagons of what was then called 'lemon fizzy'.

Prior to this, the prince had never even heard of lemon fizzy. To begin with, therefore, he drank tentatively. Then he drank thirstily. And then gluttonously. No nectar had tasted to any Olympian god quite as delicious as that lemon fizzy tasted to Charming. When thereafter Horatio had demonstrated – volubly and voluminously – the eruptive side-effects of the fizzy's consumption the prince thought he had arrived in Valhalla.

Gretel, it is needless to say, was elsewhere during this burping seminar. (Not even Gretels can be in all places at all times.) She would have been obliged to stop it, however much (secretly) she may have sniggered at it.

At the start of the prince's schooling, Horatio found himself in some frustration. The prince was no burping natural. His first attempts found him trapping more wind than he was releasing, thus causing him quite some discomfort. But Horatio's tutelage was excellent, the prince was an avid pupil and he practised as diligently as the two flagons would allow him. Within that space of time he considered himself proficient enough to perform before an audience.

Horatio was despatched to summon Philomena.

Whose arrival was fanfared with a rip-roarer of a belch, one of such thunderous proportions that the crystal of the chandeliers tinkled and the glass in the windows rattled.

Horatio was almost as loud in his applause as the prince's belch had been. And Philomena ... Well, she was as entranced by this party-trick as her twin had been. Maybe even more so. It was a skill she had to acquire. Immediately.

Sadly, though, the prince had already drunk the flagons dry. Ingenuity was required to get more of the priceless liquid.

Gretel loved chocolate marshmallows. Chocolate marshmallows were too expensive for nannies to buy. Even to royal children they were given only on special occasions.

"Gretel?" Philomena asked her, butter-wouldn't-melt-in-her-mouthly.

Gretel had returned to the nursery. She was involved in her embroidery. "Yup?" she replied.

"What's lemon fizzy?" the princess asked innocently.

"It's gunk that stupid people drink," Gretel replied. "It mucks around with your concentration and rots your teeth. It'd be banned but for Fredvie. He insists on it. Mercian merchants, so he says, otherwise would starve." She bit off the length of crimson thread she'd just finished with.

"That's what *I* said. Well, sort of what I said. And I said too, that's the reason there's none in the palace. Not anywhere. But Charming, he's such a know-all, he always thinks he knows better. 'There's gallons,' he says, 'gallons and gallons.' So I bet him. If I lose I have to give you one of my chocolate marshmallows. But he's wrong, isn't he, Gretel? As wrong, I mean, as wrong can be?"

"Sorry, Philomena, *you're* wrong – maybe not quite as wrong as wrong can be, though." Philomena was nearly always wrong. Not because she was stupid. But because she enjoyed exasperating those seeking to instruct her. "There's plenty of fizzy in the kitchens. Enough for an army, I should think. Fredvie insists on it."

"'Kitchens'?" asked Philomena with genuine curiosity. "What's 'kitchens'? Young catches?"

"Oh, amusing, highly," laughed Gretel. "Kitchens are where they prepare the food. You just think yourself lucky – very lucky indeed, young lady – that you don't need to know about them."

Philomena started to triumph her way away from her. Gretel had chosen another needle, threaded with a dark blue strand. She started 'colouring' in a kingfisher. "It's all right, Philomena. You keep your chocolate marshmallow."

So Philomena did.

After two days of hunting, the children found the kitchens.

They also found the time in the afternoon when those kitchens were all but deserted. Within the kitchens the children found a treasure trove of fizzies: lemon, orange, raspberry, blackcurrant – a whole orchard of them. The palace's 'fizzy' bill rose dramatically.

The trio became not only expert burpers, but virtuoso ones. They thought about turning professional.

A week after they discovered the kitchens, Cordelia told the prince and Philomena about her wedding to the Azrian duke, Antonio. It was going to take place exactly one month before the prince's eighth birthday.

At one level, she told the children, she thought she ought to apologise to them. Probably it would be an occasion of ghastly pomp and grotesque circumstance. But they'd manage, wouldn't they, to have a few laughs? Despite, or maybe even because of, all the ceremony … well, of the ceremony?

And the two children agreed, that *of course* they'd have some fun, and wasn't it just fantastic news and they really hoped Cordelia would be happy with Antonio and they were sure she would be and that it was *so* kind of their sister to ask them to be bridesmaid and a page.

But inside Charming was groaning. Inside, Charming held his head in his hands.

Inside, he knew that for him the whole thing would simply be a nightmare.

Chapter 7

Cordelia had, in fact, had to coquette down considerably more palatial paths than she would have hoped before Antonio had indeed tried to kiss her. When he had done so she had made her second mistake. Her reaction had contained so much shock-horror that she had had to allure for some time, and with some purpose and persistence, before he had tried again. This time she demurred so shock-horrorlessly – and so prettily – that it was a mere three months before the ardent suitor chanced his arm – and his lips – again.

In a fullness of time Cordelia considered obese, Antonio proposed to her. And, after a suitable period of dithering, she accepted.

Belgiss was preparing again for a royal occasion. It loved its royal occasions, loved all the pageantry and tradition with which such bonanzas were stuffed, loved the parades and the parading, loved all the preparation that went into the pageantry. Indeed almost loved the preparation more than the event itself. Philomena was to be the bridesmaid; Horatio and the prince, the pages.

Cross-Bones were working themselves up daily into an ever foamier lather, wondering how, surrounded by such hordes as would be lining the streets, they could possibly 'protect' their charge.

From a practical point-of-view it was, indeed, the perfect time for them to don their alternative, their *assassins'* mantle, and kill the prince. Even Goneril, though, had told them to forbear: A slaying so public would demand an inquiry equally so.

Which had further whipped up their lather. Only for it to be whisked yet further by the king's pledge that, should one hair of the prince's head be so much as ruffled, Cross-Bones would pay by losing not only their own hair, but the head too to which that hair was attached.

***

Gretel's tizzy was equally intense, if channelled into a different direction. She had to groom the prince – physically (which was challenging enough) and, even more importantly and challengingly, in matters of etiquette.

Shoes and teeth were polished until they glistened like glass. Hair was trimmed until not one single strand was not bristling to uniform attention. And Charming was instructed – over and over again – how to walk down the aisle *slowly*, what to do with the gargantuan train which would be trailing behind his half-sister, when to sit and when to stand. NOT EVER to fidget or scratch his bottom or – perish even the thought – pick his nose!

And just as soon as the young prince had mastered all these procedures so Gretel would set him through his paces all over again.

***

Naitly and Goneril were also preparing for the wedding.

So important was the celebration that Fredvie himself would be attending it.

Fredvie was the nickname given to Frederick V, Emperor of Mercia, the biggest and most powerful nation on the whole planet. But it was also the greediest empire on the entire planet: maybe that the planet had ever known – even greedier than Belgiss had been when it too had been a world power. But that was even *before* the time that was 'once upon a'.

Fredvie had an almost religious belief that it was Mercia's imperial duty to bring the rest of the planet within its embrace. And he used an entire farm of different carrots and an entire forest of different sticks in order to further this aim.

Fredvie had promised Naitly treasure beyond counting and the lifetime's Protectorship of the state if only Belgiss would annexe to Mercia and become the seventy-third dominion of Mercia's domain. Naitly had always believed such annexation would be strongly in Belgiss's interest. The attendant treasure merely added passion to his conviction. He had done all in his not inconsiderable power to persuade the king of the efficacy of such a policy. But – mostly at HM's 'suggestion' – Cole had remained stubbornly adamant in his refusal even to discuss the idea.

Naitly, who – if nothing else – was a consummate politician, was prepared to bide his time. Everything, Naitly continued to believe, came to those prepared to wait – but who also knew when to pounce.

Fredvie, though, was not a consummate politician. In fact, the only consummate Fredvie was in anything was a consummate idiot. Fredvie made Cross-Bones look like Archimedes. Fredvie was such an idiot that no-one could quite believe his idiocy and preferred to believe his political antics were ploys of such subtlety that their depth could not be grasped by mere men-in-the-Mercian-street.

Fredvie was convinced everything came to those who *grabbed*. Waiting was what waiters did. Fredvie was not a waiter, but a diner. Not even a diner but a banquetter. Fredvie, indeed, was *the* banquetter.

There are those in the world who guarantee their own downfall. And they usually do so by one remarkably simple oversight: They believe the whole of humanity is motivated by that which motivates them. Which was exactly what Naitly did: He judged Goneril by himself.

In the final analysis, Naitly had one only love, his ambition.

"There are those who call such ego-mania 'self-love'," King Sebastian told me. "They try thus to denigrate self-love. Such denigrators propagate an untruth. Self-love is not a love which excludes the love of others; it is one, rather, which is a pre-condition of loving them – of *truly* loving them. Ego mania, on the other hand, is, like all mania, an illness. One of whose most obvious symptoms is uncontrolled ambition. And it is about as effective a way of looking after yourself as it is to protect a fireworks factory by handing its keys to a pyromaniac."

"The story, sire?" I asked. The king paused for a moment. Looked at me, studied me. And then he continued.

Naitly's ambition entirely controlled him. He thought that ambition enveloped *everyone*. He thought therefore that a similar ambition must also envelop Goneril.

She, on the other hand, over-ambitious though she unquestionably was, did too love Belgiss. And loved it truly. Once enthroned, she had no intention whatsoever of keeping her promise ... either one of her promises, in fact: either to unite herself with Naitly or her country with Mercia. Indeed she considered neither to *be* actual promises. They were merely words whose loyalty (if any) was exclusively to political convenience.

Goneril and Naitly knew the Mercian ambassador had been waiting about five minutes.

"He'll be seething," she said to her betrothed. There was building work going on elsewhere in the Decadence. It was beginning to grate.

"I *want* him seething," her betrothed replied.

"Of course you do," she said humourlessly, and sat down at the huge oak table.

"An angry man is a deaf man," Naitly pronounced sententiously.

"As you cannot stress too much?" said Goneril, mocking him. He failed to notice the provocation.

"A deaf man, pumpkin, is one who can be controlled," he said.

There was a scratch at the huge double-doors, and one of them peeped open. A dormouse of a man slinked through the crack. This, appropriately enough for a minor official, was Minor

Minor, Naitly's private secretary.

"I'm so ever so sorry, Lord Chancellor, to disturb you," squeaked Minor Minor, blinking largely through large spectacles, "but the Mercian ambassador, Lord Cha- ..."

"Somewhat, is he, hot under the collar?" asked the Lord Chancellor.

"So ever so, *so* ever so."

"It's the best way, Minor Minor, to enjoy ambassadors: toasted."

"Oh yes, Lord Chancellor, so ever so the best way. Thing is, though, Lord Cha- ..."

"Send him in, Minor Minor. Tell those builders to give us five minutes."

Minor Minor scurried from the room, and then swung the door wide open in order to allow ingress to the extremely wide ambassador.

"Your Excellency," said Naitly straightening his official grin. "As ever, a great pleasure." The noise of construction increased. Naitly's grin did not even flicker.

"I am Mercia, Lord Chancellor," the ambassador stomped, ignoring Naitly's outstretched hand and heading for the office's solitary couch – the only seat of sufficient breadth to be able to accommodate the diplomatic paunch. "Mercia has been kept waiting."

"Your Excellency must understand," said Goneril evenly, "that Belgiss too has matters which are urgent."

"Mercia, your Highness, has been kept waiting." The ambassador's tone of moral indignation had risen by a note or two. It tried to imply, that rise, that the problem with the Belges was that they understood ... nothing. The sofa creaked torturedly as it received the ambassador's weight.

"Do take a seat," said Naitly, knowing that the irony would be lost. Irony was lost on most of Fredvie's staff.

"Cutting to the chase," said the ambassador, "I have been

asked by His Imperial Majesty to inform you that he is coming to this tinpot ceremony only so that he might meet up with you. His Imperial Majesty will be prepared to grant you an audience between 16.43 and 16.48 on the day of said royal wedding. After the breakfast, in other words, before the tea. He wants grits for the breakfast. For the tea he wants muffins. Graciously, His Imperial Majesty has allowed that you wear the same clothes as you will be wearing to the ceremony. In recognition of which you are to bring His Imperial Majesty a surprise present. His Imperial Majesty gets a big kick out of surprises. This time you are to surprise him with a musical box which plays the Mercian national anthem."

"And I should, of course, be delighted so to do," said Naitly, adjusting his official grin. "Sadly, though, such are unavailable in Belgiss."

"Not any more." The ambassador waved a piece of paper at him.

"And that would be?" asked the Lord Chancellor.

"Import license for ten thousand musical boxes."

"Which play the Mercian national anthem?"

"You got it. It's what's known," said the ambassador, "as plugging a hole in the market." Naitly signed, returned the paper to the fat Mercian. "How can a country claim to be civilised that don't stock musical boxes?"

"There are plenty of musical boxes available," Goneril corrected him.

"Not," the ambassador corrected her, "*Mercian* musical boxes. And musical boxes that aren't Mercian musical boxes, Jeez, that's kinda like birdless cuckoo clocks."

"Yes," muttered Goneril, "cuckoo was a word which also came to *my* mind."

"This interview ends here," sighed the ambassador. It was a sigh signifying that he was carrying the world's weight along with his own. "Go get someone to get me out of here."

"Minor Minor!" roared Naitly. The dormouse crept back into the room. "Ambassador."

Minor Minor whitened visibly. "Me?" he asked.

"Those workmen, Minor Minor, working in the East Wing ...," Goneril suggested. "If I were you, I'd ask to borrow their crane." And she swept from the room.

It was a throwaway remark. And with it she threw away a future she might otherwise have enjoyed.

Chapter 8

Cole loathed Fredvie. And it riled him not a little that he should have to travel the considerable way to Blefton, Belgiss's biggest port, to meet the emperor off his private ship which had sailed from Biga-buga, Mercia's biggest port. But protocol demanded the emperor be met. And Old King Cole (as he was fond of saying) was a slave to protocol. So meet the emperor the king did.

Both Naitly and King Cole had pondered hard on the problem of whether or not the Crown Prince should accompany his father to Blefton. Even Gretel was brought in for consultation.

For a seven-year-old the degree of protocol involved would be taxing, and the following day would be a huge one for him. At the wedding he'd be subjected to the intimate and intricate scrutiny of the world's media. Maybe prudence dictated not expecting too much from a seven-year-old, however precocious or accomplished.

After a deal of anguish it was decided that he should stay in Wodinton and that the king would drive to Blefton with HM. She had a brother who was the captain of a privateer moored there, the *Silver Hart*. Cole would be glad of the company, and HM of the opportunity to meet with her brother again. She had a lot to talk with him about. She would make her own way back.

Together king and emperor rode to Wodinton Castle in an open carriage. Well, an open carriage, that was, closed in by weapon-proof glass. Fredvie had been persuaded he was the target for an entire army of would-be assassins. Everywhere he travelled he went with a hundred Cross-Bones-alikes. Each one of who had different, and more extravagant, ideas for the protection of the imperial person.

Contrary to both his own conception and popular myth, Cole was not universally loved in Belgiss. But even those whose fondness for the monarch was, let's say, tepid had a certain, albeit reluctant, respect for the old boy. For the Mercian emperor, however, the Belges had a contempt so absolute that even their natural courtesy could not disguise it. There would therefore have been but threadbare crowds along the route to greet the emperor. And that would have been embarrassing.

Consequently, Naitly unburied the idea of foreign insurgents. Because of the 'danger' these 'insurgents' posed to the emperor's life, he prohibited the gathering of crowds.

This was Naitly's forte. With a bit of imagination, he turned what otherwise would have been a non-event, distinguished only by a grumbling indifference, into one of substance, the attendant non-attendance at which the daily gazetteers could (at Naitly's suggestion) interpret as 'laudable vigilance in security'.

None of the gazetteers, of course, was directly in Naitly's employ. But they *were* in the employ of the gazette owners. The gazette owners without exception had either received favours from Naitly, or had been promised them. The favours were, of course, conditional. And – shhh! – they were kept utterly secret from the gazettes' readers. (Or, in the case of Teddy Dawes's publications, *gutterly* secret from their readers.)

Teddy Dawes was the most powerful of the gazette owners. There were indeed rumours (completely unfounded ones) that his friendship with Naitly was *so* strong that he could dictate government policy. The fact of the matter, though, was that Dawes now lived in Mercia. He had immigrated there from San Pedito, a place (like Yorkshire in England) where arrant rudeness was allowed to call itself plain-speaking. Dawes prided himself that he was the 'plainest' speaker of them all. And Dawes's opinion was that Belgiss was too puny, too insignificant for him to have that much interest in it. Why would an eagle waste time dictating the policy of a chicken roost? Dawes had *big* fish to fry. Belgiss was no longer a fish. It was barely a sprat.

As the king drove wordlessly with Fredvie through the deserted streets from Blefton and HM chattered at length with her sibling, Charming – for the umpteenth time and to his bored dismay – rehearsed the pageant that would be enacted the following day.

***

Which, when it came, found him wearing his page's outfit, gazing at himself forlornly in a full-length mirror. Horatio, wearing identical outfit and demeanour, was doing likewise.

They were dressed in knickerbockers of purple satin with pink cotton stockings beneath them, and red patent leather shoes with silver buckles; above the waist ruffed a shirt of sky blue, shrouded by a plum waistcoat bearing the royal coat-of-arms on its back; atop of all of which was a periwig askew with curls and a tricorn hat which kept slipping over their eyes.

"I look stupid," said the prince.

"Me too," said Horatio.

"No, Horatio. Really, *really* stupid."

"Yes, me too."

"*You* look stupid?" protested Philomena, bursting into the room. She was wearing a dress whose green was so limey the tongue coated just looking at it.

"We'll be a laughing stock," said the prince.

"We look ridicerlous," said Philomena.

"We'll be a laughing stock," agreed Horatio glumly.

"It's not fair," whined Charming.

"It's always us," whined Philomena.

"It's not fair," agreed Horatio glumly. "And it's not fair neither that we can't do nothing about it," he added, doubling his negatives with the abandon of a gambler on a hopeless bet.

The children stood morosely before their reflections, reflecting on the absurdity of their dress, the forthcoming derision, the injustice of life. Suddenly a thought hit Horatio. Almost physically. His eyes shone, his face brightened visibly.

"Burping," he announced.

"What?" asked the other two together.

"Burping," Horatio euraka'd. "It'll need careful planning, 'course. But if we time it right, if we drink enough fizzies, just as they're doing that, you know, 'I do' bit, in the pause just before they say it, we can burp. All of us together."

"They'd kill us, Horatio," said Charming, ever the realist.

"Burping's nat'ral, i'n't it?" insisted Horatio. "I mean, everyone burps, don't they, once in a while? You can't always help yourself, can you? They can't kill us, can they, for doing something nat'ral?"

The other two considered this for a moment or two.

"I suppose," Philomena eventually decided, "it *is* natural."

"We couldn't help it, could we?" Horatio was already preparing the case for the defence. "I mean, it must have been all that jiggling in the coach, mustn't it? Made us burp like that? We're terribly sorry. Really. Terribly, *terribly* sorry. They can't kill us, can they, for doing something nat'ral?"

They looked from one to the other. The adrenalin started to surge through them. And then a grin started to spread across them. It was almost a communal grin. It was one of the few real grins Charming had experienced in his life.

It was the cause of so much pain.

Chapter 9

Of course they had to get to the kitchens unseen. An entirely different complexion might be cast on their action if their prosecutors were to learn that the 'nat'ral' had been encouraged by their own wilfulness.

The prince's circumspection helped. Because of his unwillingness to disturb the sentries he knew of practically every corridor in the palace and every staircase – even those that were, you'd have thought impossibly, *below* stairs. 'Below stairs' meant the servants' quarters.

They skirted this way, the children, they skirted that. They heard footsteps and would hide themselves behind the closest door available, whether of a room, a chamber or a cupboard. They found themselves in all three.

And then they found themselves, breathlessly, in the kitchens. To be precise, behind several enormous barrels in the kitchens.

Which were abuzz with activity. So abuzz that a normal beehive would by comparison have seemed like a library. To steal the coveted fizzies would have been as possible as stealing the Crown jewels from a Coronation.

"Oh, brilliant!" exclaimed Philomena sarcastically.

"I should've thought," said the prince, angry at himself.

"Yes, you should," his sister snapped back, glad thus to shed any need to blame herself.

"Prob'ly, it was a bad idea anyway," said Horatio diplomatically.

"It was a *great* idea," Charming told him, maybe even with a vestige of truth. "Really, Horatio, a *great* idea. It's just ..." He indicated the throng before them.

"Yeah," said Philomena or Horatio, maybe both. There was resignation in the voice, a tacit 'it's-not-fair'ness. They had climbed most of the Eiger, only to be stopped, a hundred yards from the summit, by an unpassable storm. Dejected as only the thus thwarted can be, the trio started to retrace their steps.

In the quiet that accompanied these steps each was trying to devise some prank to replace the one so recently abandoned – some sign to the outside world that they were not the sad, sad … saddies their dress announced them to be. But nothing came to their minds.

Footsteps.

"Quick," said Philomena, and pushed open the nearest door. It was a heavy one, studded with cast-iron rivets – apparently made for dwarves as even the children had to stoop to get through it. Quickly they closed this door behind them. They put their ears to it. The footsteps passed by. They breathed again.

And it was that breath that caused Horatio to turn around. He had never smelled anything quite so beautiful. "Wow!" he said, as he did so.

The children found themselves in the minstrels' gallery, not of the banqueting hall itself, but of its anteroom. Half-a-dozen enormously long tables were draped in tablecloths of the most delicate white lace.

And the smell? Well, obviously several botanical gardens had been utterly denuded. Flowers seemed to be absolutely everywhere, and – as this was in the days before mass-production – their combined bouquet was so redolent as almost to be overpowering: rose mixed with sweet pea with jasmine – and with a hundred others. The palette of their colours would have shamed even van Gogh. They were as solid, those colours, and as obvious as elephants' legs, and yet as delicate as butterfly wings.

It was a sight fit for the sorest of eyes. Despite the trio's familiarity with luxuriant trappings this was so utterly magnificent it totally spellbound them. Almost as if entering Aladdin's cave, they walked open-mouthed down the staircase which led from the minstrels' gallery to the hall beneath.

"Wow!" said Horatio again.

"Wow!" echoed Philomena and the prince.

"Wow!" Horatio said for the third time.

The tables were bedecked with about a thousand cut-glass wine-flutes. They had already been filled, presumably to avoid the traffic jam that would otherwise ensue. These glasses glinted back the brilliance of the ten thousand candles which flickered onto them.

"Aha!" said Horatio, clearly "wow"ed out.

"Aha?" asked the prince.

"Aha!" Philomena confirmed. She was quicker on Horatio's uptake than her brother. "Fizzy!" they both said together.

"That's not fizzy," the prince corrected them, trying not to be too know-all about it. "It's what they call 'bubbly'. It's what grown-ups drink."

"Bubbly's fizzy, i'n't it?" asked Horatio. "And if it's fizzy it's going to make you burp. That's what fizzy does."

"It's bubbly," the prince said sagely. "Bubbly's not the same."

Horatio grabbed the nearest glass. "You're meant to hold it by the stem," the prince told him, almost apologetically.

"Why?"

"'Cos you're supposed to," said the prince. "They don't tell you why in protocol, only tell you don't."

Horatio held the glass by the stem. And was about to drink it. "You're supposed to sniff it first. Don't ask me why, Horatio. Because you are, that's why."

"It's just stupid, protocol, sometimes," said Horatio with perhaps a greater wisdom than he would have imagined. "Just downright stupid, ask me." He sniffed and drank. He pulled a face. "I tell you what," he said to the other two still grimacing in disgust, "p'culiar things must happen to your taste-buds when you grow up. How could anyone drink this?"

"We'd best be going, then," said the prince, who had now twigged what Horatio was suggesting. It had a smell, that suggestion, quite as redolent as that from the flowers, but diametrically opposite: It was a stink as nasty as the blooms' perfume was fragrant. "Maybe we could hide the glass somewh-…"

"It is fizzy, though," said Horatio. "It will make us burp."

"It tastes horrid, you said," protested the prince, whose feet had now turned not only cold but to blocks of ice.

"Just drink it quickly," Philomena said. "Like when you have to eat artichokes. Just eat them quickly you don't notice the taste."

"What do you think?" Horatio asked. "Three glasses? Better, four. Bigger burp with four."

"What'll we do with all the empty glasses?" wailed the prince.

"D'you know how many empty glasses there's going to be? More than zillions." Horatio was fond of answering his own questions. "Whoever's going to notice a few more?"

"Aah!" sighed Philomena, as she finished her first glass. She had drunk it in one. "Like I say," she said, "drink it in one and it doesn't taste too bad."

"Three glasses?" asked Horatio.

"It's got to be a *BIG* burp," Philomena winked conspiratorially. "Don't be such a wimp: four!"

"Aah!" sighed the prince. He had finished his first glass. He too had drunk it in one. He knew that would be the only way he would do it.

He felt a trifle wobbly.

Chapter 10

The cathedral was stuffed with the sage and escutcheoned. It was an impressive edifice. Two Gothic towers spiralled towards the Heaven they sought to venerate; an army of gargoyles adorned its walls to protect it from the sacrilegious or satanic. Within it, its huge vaulted ceilings resonated with the care of all the thousands of artisans who had so lovingly sculpted and tended it.

Almost the first there were the nervous bridegroom, Antonio, and his best man, an Azrian businessman, Squire Squeers. The squire was an enormous man, with a shock of carrot-red hair. It was a shock of a colour so electric that it also caused a shock to those seeing it for the first time.

Cole had decreed that it should be a sunny day. The night before, however – and just to be on the safe side! –, he had prepared his wrath in case the sun should have had the temerity not to heed him. Such preparation proved not to be necessary. The sun shone obediently and glowingly. And had invited along a gentle breeze to escort it, just enough lightly to fan the assembled throng which lined the route.

Since dawn a number of Fredvie's Cross-Bones-alikes had been handing out Mercian flags by the cartonful to these throngs. They were to wave those flags when the emperor passed.

Fredvie's wedding present was his concession that he would arrive before the bride at the cathedral.

Bar those of the bride's entourage his carriage was, of course, the last to leave the palace. He made a mental note to fire his bodyguards for having neglected to pass out Mercian flags. He saw not one throughout his entire ride. Which was ridiculous, His Imperial Majesty told himself, given the size of the enormous crowd which had turned out just to catch a glimpse of him.

He waved to them all, a master at work. He was, and he knew it, "one rootin'-tootin' waver". He never stopped glorying at the great waver he was. He had even tried to show Cole how to wave. Cole, of course, hadn't listened. Which was, Fredvie never tired of saying, just yet one more example of the way rootin' Belgiss carried on tootin' living in rootin'-tootin' yesterday. Yester*day*? In rootin'-tootin' yester*year*.

He found himself in the cathedral a good minute or two before the bride. With absolutely nothing to do. When would he ever learn to stop being so ext- ... so extra- ... he knew the word started 'extra-' ... he knew it wasn't 'extract' ... so *generous* with his wedding gifts? He should *never* listen to his tootin' advisers. He shuffled from one foot to the other and tried to twist his face to mimic the expressions of the more scary gargoyles glowering at him.

Cordelia and Cole travelled in the Wenceslas' coach. This was a landau the gondola of which, like the Cabinet table, was sculpted from one trunk. In panels around it were chiselled the Seven Labours of Hercules, three on each side, one on the back. The whole coach had then been plated in gold. The coach was so heavy it took eight white oxen to pull it – and three expert coachmen to control those beasts.

Before this coach marched the whistles and drums of the Light Cavalry's mounteband (as it was called), horses and men alike splendid in their tasselled berets and gleaming breastplates. Immediately behind the Wenceslas' landau was the carriage containing the three children. And behind them, the massed bands of the King's Foot, with their royal blue tunics and glistening trombones and white kepis, whose black patent leather peaks glittered in the sun as dazzlingly as the crashing cymbals.

Barely could the music be heard, though, so tumultuous was the roar of the crowd. Which bellowed itself as hoarse as it did, because sometimes it is a need we humans have to roar our approval. What we are seeking with such roars (though almost never do we admit this) is our own approval of ourselves. Sometimes the roaring helps us to find it.

Cordelia was aware of this. She wanted those who cheered for her to be aware that it was for themselves much more than for her that they both cheered and had a need to. Without being so specific, this feeling of Cordelia's was by some mystical process transmitted to the crowd.

And the crowd loved her for it. Oh, they knew Cordelia had her problems: Rumour had it she could be neurotically insecure. But in a world where people were made to feel only like the muck the simile had it they were 'as common as', and in which they found themselves more and more distanced from the decision-making processes, Cordelia stood almost alone in radiating a real concern for *their* concerns.

That concern was, to all intents and purposes, extinct amongst the other great and fêted. Hers endeared her to them.

She tried not to notice the whiff of her father. It was unmistakable, the smell of booze. But she knew better than to challenge him. He would not have been pleased by such a challenge. He had been scrupulous about how much of the 'bowl' he'd allowed himself: just a stirrup-goblet; enough – no more – to imbue his cheeks and spirits with the rosiness of glow required of such a festive occasion.

Through that glow he saw his adoring subjects roar their loyalty to him. And in that glow he knew that those subjects were right to be loyal and to adore him. He was a monarch worthy of adoration. He was no upstart, no 'nouveau royale' like Fredvie.

In the coach behind, the three children had succumbed to hiccups. Given the amount of champagne they had drunk, given the amazing heat of the January day, it was not surprising that all three were a wee bit weary and a soupçon emotional – as tired-and-emotional as lords, in fact. And because of their drun- … because, I should say, of their *tired-and-emotionalness* the hiccups became hilarious.

They did try to keep straight faces. They did their absolute best to do so. But a tired-and-emotional best is not … well, the bestest of bests.

They managed for a minute or two. But then one would hiccup again, and that would send them into another frenzy of giggles, further fuelled by the giggles of the others.

Cordelia stepped princessly from her carriage, helped by two uniformed stepping-down-from-carriage-helpers, whatever they are called. Another two such assisted the king to decoach from the other side. Protocol would not allow the king to wait for anyone, bar an emperor – not even his daughter on her wedding day. Timing was thus critical. The train of the princess's dress was still coiled within the landau.

Part of the task of the bride's entourage – the children, in other words – was to help unwrap this train in a way that let it slide elegantly behind the princess as she mounted the cathedral's steps. But ...

Well, the bride's entourage was tired-and-emotional. The children kept trying to approach the bride's carriage, but some invisible hand kept yanking them back. Not only that, but tripping them up as it did so.

Cordelia was scared to begin with, scared lest something serious had befallen the children. Then Philomena hiccupped. Cordelia caught the whiff of champagne. She had enough experience of the problem to diagnose it fairly quickly. Relieved that it was nothing more serious, she found the children's inebriation ... well, both irritating and amusing.

The king found nothing amusing about it at all.

Within seconds of the children's reel the royal frown had summoned a squad of flunkeys. Half of whom replaced the children in the latters' official capacity, and the other half of whom removed them from the public gaze.

The official announcement from the palace was that the children had that morning breakfasted on flakes of contaminated corn to which they had had the most drastic allergic reaction.

Waiting in the anteroom before they were due to meet the

king, the three children knew that that announcement would not save them.

They knew the punishment would be as severe as it would be terrible.

The anteroom itself didn't help. It was very dentists' waiting-roomy – a room where your presence betokened no good. A functional and a sterile room. Comfortable only in a joyless way: armchairs, yes, but with lumpy cushions; a fire, yes, but with lacklustre flames.

The children sat in the glummest of silences.

Except that, somewhere in his deepest of hearts, Charming was glad. He'd done something wrong and he was going to be punished.

That's what happened to normal boys when they did wrong things.

He was going to be treated like a normal boy.

Chapter 11

Naitly was in far from good humour. His audience with Fredvie was proving to be even more trying than he'd expected.

"Read my lips," Fredvie had told him. And then, when the Lord Chancellor's attention was concentrated there, had drummed on his lips as they thereby emitted a babyish burbling sound. Naitly had forced a laugh out of himself. He looked to Minor Minor. Minor Minor also forced a laugh – minorly.

"There's nothing rootin' funny about this, mister," shouted Fredvie. To emphasise which point, he banged his fist down on the nearest table. "Owwww!," he wailed clutching his bruised fist, "look what you made me go and tootin' do. Why is there *never no-one* around to kiss it better?"

Naitly was puckering up, but the ambassador got there just before him. "That's not a proper kiss-it-better kiss," complained Fredvie. "Not a mummy's rootin' kiss." He sucked at his bruised fist, and massaged his bruised mummylessness. "Why are you always so slow?" he asked Naitly. "Why is everyone in *Eastlantic* so slow? Who are you anyway?"

"Baron Naitly, Mr Imperial Majesty, Lord Chancellor of Belgiss."

"Of *where*?"

"Your closest ally, Mr Imperial Majesty," said Naitly. "I am a great admirer of Your Imperial Majesty's impatience, Mr Imperial Majesty. Aren't I, Minor Minor?"

"Oh so ever so, Lord Chancellor, *so* so ever so," Minor Minor added proudly. Minor Minor was still disorientated by an earlier shock: Fredvie had decided the Mercian musical box was finally *not* to his taste. Instead, as a present, he wanted ... Minor Minor.

"Despite, Mr Imperial Majesty, my esteem of your impatience, I cannot stress too much (particularly in this case) the need for circumspection."

"You Jewish?" asked Fredvie. The Mercian ambassador

whispered to him the correct meaning of 'circumspection'. "*That's* what it means?" asked Fredvie incredulously. "Now, why would there be a need for a word that means that?"

"His Imperial Majesty has studied history I know," said Minor Minor timorously. "His Imperial Majesty will have heard of England's Richard III."

"I heard of Tricky Dicky," Fredvie boasted.

"So ever so ever so not *quite* the same thing, Mr Imperial Majesty."

"It behoves us to learn from history, Mr Imperial Majesty," said Naitly. "We can learn much, in this instance, from Richard III. For one thing, Mr Imperial Majesty, that a nation's citizens do not exactly go a bundle on their leaders executing their children."

"Herod's press is still, Mr Imperial Majesty, so ever so ever so not good," Minor Minor ventured to suggest.

"Why does everyone in Eastlantic speak tootin' Complicated? Why don't no-one speak rootin' Normal?" complained the emperor. "We are in Eastlantic, right?" he asked his ambassador. This last nodded. Fredvie watched fascinated as the nod wobbled through His Excellency's hundred chins. "So? What you gonna do about ...?" He waved his hand around in the vague hope that he would be reminded of what it was he wanted something doing about.

"Three words need to dictate our progress, Mr Imperial Majesty," said Naitly: "caution, caution, caution."

"And I've rootin' three for tootin' you: Action, mister," Fredvie growled back at him, "action, action." And then he counted the words on his fingers and found out he'd said four.

"I cannot stress too much, Mr Imp- ..."

Fredvie interrupted his counting. "That's what you rootin'-tootin' *cause* me, mister: too much stress." The emperor smiled expansively. He always smiled expansively when he won debating points. And he'd just done that. "The kid, do he rootin' live? Or does my tootin' eyes deceive me?"

"With the greatest of respect, Mr Imperial Majesty …" started Naitly.

"With so ever so great a respect, sire," said Minor Minor.

"… Belgiss is not Zanoria. We can't merely kill willy-nilly, sire, those who offend or inconvenience us."

"Who's Willy Nilly?" asked Fredvie. "And why is he rootin' offending us?" Again the ambassadorial aside. "I don't want to kill rootin'-tootin' Willy Nilly. He's done nothing to upset *me*," Fredvie then told his envoy. Who explained a little more.

"And what's wrong with tootin' Zanoria?" he then asked Naitly. Zanoria was on the fringes of Mercia's New Territories, on the border of the aboriginal lands – those designated by Fredvie as belonging to "the savages". The mistake over Willy Nilly had embarrassed him. Embarrassed, the emperor was even more dangerous than he was normally. "If more rootin' countries acted decisively like tootin' Zanoria and not lily-liveredly like rootin'-tootin' France the better place the whole rootin'-tootin' planet'd be." Fredvie looked around for a softer place to bang his other fist. No-one could ever accuse *him* of not learning from his mistakes. He opted for the ambassador's pillow-like gut. "Never, never will you get civilised in Eastlantic till you understand that." And watched transfixed as the paunch wobbled, jelly-like, in its receipt of the imperial blow.

"Zanoria is a paradigm, obviously," Naitly sought to concede.

"It's the workless who are rootin' paradigms, mister. Paradigms on the tootin' rest of us working Joes." The ambassador, in whispers, explained to His Imperial Majesty the difference between para*digm* and para*site* – and between both of those and para*graph*. Para*dise* he thought prudent to leave alone.

After which, the pain finally penetrated the last layer of lard and reached the diplomatic brain. "Oww!" the ambassador yelled quite loudly, before checking himself. He smiled at the emperor through pained teeth.

In this interlude, Fredvie conceived of an ingenious solution. "Ain't there nothing in the rootin'-tootin' Constitootion here which allows you to execute someone for being drunk?" he asked.

"We couldn't train that many axemen," Naitly confessed ruefully. "Come to think of it, I doubt we could manufacture that many axes. Besides," he added, "how could we ever form a Cabinet?"

"So ever so hard it would be," agreed Minor Minor.

"You got some mighty big rootin' problems for a mighty small tootin' country," Fredvie told him with an almost malevolent glee. "For a tiny *tinpot* country," he added. "The sooner you let us handle them the happier you'll rootin'-tootin' be." His gaze alighted on Minor Minor.

"Oh so ever so, so ever so," said the official.

Fredvie knew he'd seen this creature somewhere before but he couldn't quite put his finger on where. "Nine months, mister." He returned his gaze to the big guy, the one who did something quite important in ... now, where in the heck was it that he was? "You got nine tootin' months. Kill the prince in nine months or the rootin' deal's off. If the deal's off, Mercia may consider it has no rootin'-tootin' alternative other than to in- ... in- ... interrupt ... *-cede*, I mean – it's okay, Mr ambassador, I know – inter-, as I said before, *-cede*."

"I cannot stress, Your ..."

"'And down ...'" sang Fredvie, "' ... would come baby, rootin' cradle and rootin'-tootin' all.'"

***

At the same time as Naitly was meeting with Fredvie in the Decadence's Cabinet room, so in a smaller room of the same building another group of people was also doing business.

"There are those," King Sebastian broke off to tell me, "who consider themselves so important, their time so valuable, that any occasion exists only as an opportunity. For such people no event simply is. Always it is a pretext.

"It has always struck me as curious, though," he continued, "that those who have a need to feel important rarely are. The truly important require no heralds or symbols, none of the trappings of reassurance. The importance of the truly important exudes from within them; it enfolds them effortlessly. And the truly important shun the limelight, cede it as often as they can, because they see the limelight for what it is – an instrument of blindness: one, moreover, which blinds both audience *and* actor. Some tea, perhaps?" he asked. I nodded that such would be welcome. The king inclined his head towards Elton, who scurried from the room.

"For the self-important and synthetically important," the king said sadly, using his stick to help him shift his position in the chair, "weddings are not reasons to celebrate the joy of two people in love. They're not even to venerate the abstract of love itself. Weddings are merely convenient surroundings within which to do business.

"'Doing business' for the self-important and synthetically important is a euphemism for making money. Doing business is a less grubby activity than making money. Which is why you do not find busy and important people making money; they are only ever doing business."

This meeting of important people was being 'chaired' by Belgiss's Finance Minister, Luke Garrie – mostly because it was taking place in his office. Luke Garrie was nicknamed 'Garibaldi'. It's certainly true that he was balding, but his nickname had nothing to do with hair loss. It was first coined by HM because she felt the Finance Minister, as she had quipped, 'took the biscuit'! (Along, she had then added, with anything else he could lay his greedy hands on.)

Garibaldi's office was painted in the same lemon yellow as the

Cabinet office. He loathed the yellow, but was too mean (even with himself) to change its colour. The furnishings in the room were as sparse as the hair on his head, and designed to dissuade their occupiers from a long stay.

Also there was Princess Nancy's husband, Baron Richardson. And Antonio's best man, Squire Squeers – he of the red, red hair.

Squeers was desperate to be more involved in the meeting than he was. He was being allowed to 'play with the big boys' only out of sufferance and he was made to feel as much. This further strengthened the resolve Squeers had one day to be a *real someone*, a someone of *real* consequence. Throughout the meeting he sat pondering that day.

The meeting's three *main* protagonists were people who had a *real* need to think themselves busy and important: Teddy Dawes, the hugely wealthy gazette-owner from San Pedito; Norman Leamore, mayor of Biga-Buga; and the sultan of Orismine.

Dawes was a small man with a big temper. His chin was fetchingly dimpled, but sported on its right a pronounced mole, which he would stroke when angered. It was effectively a warning of an eruption about to happen. His Adam's apple (almost alarmingly) would wattle apparently out of synch with his words.

Norman Leamore was even more hugely wealthy than Dawes. His wealth had come from inventing the 'autabac' – or automatic abacus, to give it its full name. This had been so skilfully marketed as to become a 'must' amongst anyone with the slightest cool in the entire universe.

Which was probably the coolest thing about the man. Leamore himself ... Well, there is no street in the world so undistinguished that he could pass for a man in it. There are amoebas with more presence and personality than Leamore. He was of average height, average weight, average age. He was balding even more severely than Garibaldi, and he was acutely self-conscious about it. He tended, therefore, to rub his pate – as if trying to stimulate the follicles into re-growing. Almost his most distinguishing characteristic, sadly, was the foulness of his breath. This smelt almost as badly as Cross's. Maybe it was for that reason HM called him "*literally* stinking rich".

The sultan had eyes so deeply brown the black of the iris was barely distinguishable. They were as cold, though, and expressionless as a dead man's: The dot of light which signifies life was so tiny as to be almost invisible. "Is Orisminian gold," he was telling the two magnates. "Is only ... how you say? ... correct, Orisminian gold is for benefice of Orisminian people."

Dawes was purple with rage. The mole on his chin was almost standing to attention. "I don't respond to threats, Sultan. You should know I don't respond to threats," he ranted. "We had a *deal*. Either you let us have our gold – gold that is at any rate *morally* ours – ..."

"Or?" asked the sultan.

"Not difficult, dude," Leamore returned evenly. "'Or' we tell Fredvie to invade." Unlike Cross, Leamore was aware of his breath. He had thus adopted the habit of talking sideways on to the person he was addressing.

"You bluff badly, my friend," the sultan replied. "Fredvie, he not invade. World would be against him."

"Oh, and like he really cares about *that*," sniggered Dawes, as Leamore smirked his agreement. "This is Mercia we're talking about, Sultan. Not some tinpot sultanate."

"Is *Orisminian* gold," the sultan replied. "My people starve. You want my people starving in order that you buy more peacocks for your garden."

"Claptrap!" screamed Dawes, the Adam's apple now wattling like a berserk yo-yo. "Sentimental claptrap!"

"'Case you hadn't noticed, dude, the gold is not yours," Leamore told the sultan, still sideways, still with an even timbre to his voice. "It don't belong either to Orismine or to your people. It is ours. The choice is not difficult, dude: you give us gold or we give you war."

"Gentlemen, gentlemen, gentlemen," said Richardson, eager to placate. "Today is not a day for talk of war. Today we celebrate a wedding. Today is a day of love. I urge you all – all three of you: concentrate on the wider picture."

"My picture, she is very wide," said the sultan. Despite the half-smile, his moustache was bristling with indignation. "And it is full of people with not enough food in their bellies. My people starve."

"Duh! In war, your people will not only starve, dude, they will also be butchered," Leamore told him, with more relish maybe than decorum would have recommended.

"Gold, Sultan, or war," Dawes said and marched from the room.

"Gold or war, dude," Leamore repeated with a sigh. He followed on behind Dawes. Squeers glared at the sultan in silent accord with the sentiment of the other two, before following them.

"Well," said Garibaldi, shuffling together the various pieces of paper with which he'd strewn his desk, "that went a lot better than we might have expected. Oh, Mr Dawes ..." he shouted, and rushed to join them.

"They're bluffing, sire," Richardson told the sultan. "I'm sure, once the wider picture has been appreciated, an accommodation will be found."

"Maybe," the sultan said.

"But just in case I'm wrong," Richardson continued, "I wonder whether I might interest you in some lightweight sabres which I've just taken delivery of. I've also got some rather splendid and efficient new cannons ..."

Chapter 12

In common with many with a fondness for their 'bowl' there was about Cole's usual complexion a floridness of hue. At that moment this combined with apoplexy. Cole's face was thus livid in the intensity of its redness: the blood vessels were swollen and were throbbing visibly.

The three children stood in one line, heads bowed, gazing forlornly at a floor they prayed would simply swallow them. Gretel stood in that same line, a few feet from them.

They were surrounded by a large part of the Court: the three fiddlers, Nancy and her husband, Cordelia and hers, Garibaldi and Cross-Bones. Squire Squeers was not considered of sufficient importance to be invited. All, of course, were still in their nuptial finery. Not a hem was out of place, nor a 'hm' voiced. There wasn't a fidget or a cough between them, barely a breath.

"Drunk? *Drunk*?" the king ranted at them. "The heir to the throne drunk?!" The king lurched towards the nearest table and took a steadying draught from the goblet he found there.

"We thought it was a fizzy," said Philomena who, somewhere in her boots, had found the merest drop of feist.

"What in God's name is a fizzy?" asked the king. "No, it doesn't matter. One does not wish to know. You made an exhibition of yourselves, an exhibition – which is considerably worse – of the Crown. By some, you know, that could be considered high treason."

"Execute us, then, why don't you?" said Philomena defiantly.

"Do not think, young lady," the king told her, "that one has not considered the possibility."

"For God's sake, dad," said Cordelia, a twitch of anger rippling through her left cheek. "It was high spirits. Kids-will-be-kids stuff. You're making a mountain, dad, out of a molehill."

"Remove your wife, sirrah," the king told Antonio. "She incurs one's displeasure."

"If drunkenness is a crime, you old ..." Cordelia started. Prudently Antonio clapped a hand over his wife's mouth.

"*Now,* sirrah," the king said. Antonio needed the help of a couple of sentries to drag his wife from the royal presence. The king turned his attention to Gretel. "Why should one not simply have you beheaded, madam?"

Gretel looked to the prince. He could sense her looking at him. But he was too frightened ...

"I was just too frightened," King Sebastian told me in quiet despair. He passed me my tea. "I said nothing. *Nothing.* That dumbness was to haunt me for the rest of my life."

Gretel replied quietly "No reason."

HM sidled closer to her monarch. "Wisdom, sire, urges clemency."

"Keep out of this, HM. This is family business."

"The children, sire, they've learnt their lesson, trust me. I mean, look at them."

"Not one word more, HM. Not one single word more."

HM had no choice but to play her trump card. "To execute her, sire, would be to emulate the action of Fredvie."

The king cogitated. He drank a little more from his thinking cordial. He remembered he *enjoyed* wisdom and clemency. "One chooses," he said after a suitable pause, "to mix wisdom with clemency." Again HM whispered in his ear. "One has had a good idea."

"Your modesty, sire, does you the most enormous credit," HM simpered. "An idea, trust me, of inspiration."

"You, Gretel, will be fined three months' wages," the king told her. "And it shall be for you to determine the punishment for the princess."

Three months' wages was an enormous loss to Gretel. But she was, for the moment, too relieved not to have lost her job – or her head – for its enormity to have penetrated. "I think Philomena should also be fined," she said: "maybe, three chocolate marshmallows."

"One month's wages per chocolate. Seems a trifle dear to me. Still ..." the king left the thought unexpressed. "So be it. Take them away."

"You're a beast," Philomena told her father. "I hate you."

"You will be confined, furthermore, Philomena, to your own quarters for the next month, and to your own company."

"You're a pig," said his daughter. "A big, fat pig."

"For the next, young lady, *three* months," roared the king. *Never* had he been spoken to in such a way.

Gretel was quick to whisk her away before she incurred any more of His Majesty's displeasure.

"As for you two," the king told the boys once Philomena had been taken from the room.

"It was all my fault, Daddy," the prince told him, finally finding the tongue which terror had for so long confiscated from him.

"Not interested," his father replied. "Fault is no longer an issue. It's only punishment that is. These two gentlemen ..." He meant Cross-Bones. They too were considered to have been derelict in their duty. " ... will be fined ... How much, HM?"

HM whispered into the king's ear. But her eyes were clamped on Naitly.

"You will be fined two years' wages," the king told the men.

It felt as if they'd been hit with an axe-handle. "Two yearth!" groaned Cross.

"This is not fair, sire," Naitly started to say. But the king merely looked in his direction, and that was enough to silence him. Naitly then tried to mime to Cross-Bones that they would be all right, that they should – please – remain calm. But they were reeling too much from the 'sentence' to be able to see anything.

"And you," he further told Cross-Bones, "shall determine the punishment of these two young hooligans."

In which instant the colour drained from HM's face.

"Please don't do this, sire," she begged.

"If you want to keep your head, HM, keep your tongue," the king told her. "One has spoken. Take the boys away, sirrahs," the king ordered Cross-Bones.

"Please not," pleaded Nancy. "Oh, papa, please, *please* not. I beg of you." She threw herself at his feet.

"Control your wife, sir," the king told Richardson. "She does you no favours." He scowled before adding, pointedly, "Her son neither."

"He's a child, papa," wept the distraught mother. "They're children. Good God, the prince, he's your son. Your own flesh and blood. It was a prank. A joke that got out of hand. A stupid, stupid, but childish *prank*."

The baron stroked his beard wisely. "What must be must be, my dear." Gently he helped the wailing Nancy to her feet. The baron smiled at Naitly. "We have to try to see the wider picture," he told his wife.

"Take the boys from one," the king told no-one in particular. He stooped against the mantelpiece, desolate. HM passed him his goblet. He managed to find the energy to sup from it. "They have distressed one more than one can say."

It wasn't that Cross-Bones *wore* leers, it was that they bathed in them. And it was from sight of these leers, more than the king's desolation, that the boys understood they were in deep trouble.

In very deep trouble indeed.

Chapter 13

Cross led the way. The boys followed. Behind them they could hear Bones bringing up a lame rear.

They were walking along a wooden corridor which not even the prince had previously visited. It was way up somewhere in the palace's gables. The floorboards creaked alarmingly and the prince was not sure that the entire structure might not at any moment give way entirely. That, though, was the least of his worries.

"I hateth thmall boyth, I do," thaid Croth ... said Cross ... without even bothering to turn around.

"'E 'ates 'em," confirmed Bones. "And 'e 'ates 'em double when 'is money's been took off of 'im."

"'ateth them much *more* than double, Mithter Thtern."

"More'n double 'e 'ates 'em."

"Know the only thing I liketh about thmall boyth, Mithter Thtern?" Again Cross did not bother to look round.

"You likes 'urting 'em, Mr Krantz." Bones turned to the boys, started to confide in them. "Me, I'm not too bothered one way or the other. But 'im: 'E *really* likes 'urting 'em."

"I *really* liketh hurting them," Cross confirmed.

The thought of being hurt terrified Charming. His heart was beating so fast that he could scarcely breathe. Certainly he could not speak. Nor could he look at Horatio – as Horatio could not look at him.

They came to a door. It was as small and heavy as that which had taken the children to the minstrels' gallery. Cross and Bones had to bend almost double to get in.

The door gave onto a long, low-beamed rectangular room. Two small round windows let in a surprising amount of light, the pools of which were aglitter with a million dust flakes. It smelled of sweat and seasoned timber, and had the feel of a rather rundown gymnasium. Except that its only 'equipment' was an upright chair placed directly in the room's centre. The image was so strange that in other circumstances it would have appeared unreal, even surreal. But in these, both boys knew that its reality would all too soon be all too painfully apparent.

"Thtand there," Cross told the two boys, pointing to the wall adjacent to the door. "Your 'ighneth," he added sneeringly. He and Bones went over to the only other piece of furniture in the room – an umbrella stand made from an elephant's lower leg. This housed a variety of canes and birches.

"Now, which o' these little beauties, Mr Krantz," asked Bones, "do you think would be the best to stripe the royal bum?"

"Wouldn't it be only proper, Mithter Thtern, to athk Hith Highneth himthelf?" suggested Cross.

"Like a menu, Mr Krantz, sort of thing?"

"Ath you thay, Mithter Thtern, ath you thay."

They turned to face the two boys. They brought the umbrella stand over to where they were standing, a couple of Fagins trying to sell nicked handkerchiefs to toffs. Cross felt along the length of one of the sticks; Bones bowed another almost in half.

"Just get on with it, can't you?" said Horatio.

"Oh, congratulations," said Bones. He brought his stubbly face close to the young man's. "No, really: well done. That little remark of yours, it's won you today's special prize, ain't that right, Mr Krantz?"

"Today'th *thtar* prithe, Mithter Thtern."

"Know what today's star prize is, lad?" asked Bones, whose face had not moved from Horatio's, and whose foul breath was curdling Horatio's nostrils. "Tell 'im, Mr Krantz."

"A whole ecthtra thtroke of the cane. All for you. Ain't you lucky, lad?"

"Really, really lucky."

"Thay 'thank you' to the nithe man for being tho lucky."

Horatio said nothing.

"Oh, goody," said Cross. "*Two* thtroketh more." Still Horatio said nothing.

"Three," said Bones, his face still glued to Horatio's, his eyes glinting with menace.

"For God's sake, Horatio," pleaded the prince, "say 'thank you'. Thank you, Mr Krantz. Mr Stern, thank you. Thank you very much. Very, very much. Both of you. Thank you. Thank you."

Begrudgingly the two men accepted the prince's 'thank you' on behalf of his friend.

"Bend over that chair," Bones told Horatio. The young man broke from Bones's stare and marched defiantly to the chair in the room's centre. Where, defiantly, he did bend over it.

"*You're* good at maththth," Cross told the prince. "On behalf of the king, we wath going to give 'im sicth sthroketh. Then he won hiththelf three more. How many thtroketh do you reckon that maketh it, your 'ighneth?"

"Please, Mr Krantz. We've said 'thank you'. Please, no more than the six."

"Theemth, Mithter Thtern, we've got a lad here somewhat lathy about hith maththth. What do you think the penalty should be for that?"

"Nine," whispered the prince.

"What wath that?" asked Cross.

"Nine," the prince all but shouted. "Nine. Nine. What bloody more do you want from us?"

"Temper, temper," tutted Bones.

Horatio was still bent over the chair. "Get on with it," he ordered them.

"Which brings it up to a round ten. I do like to keep my figures round. Will you do the 'onours, Mr Krantz?"

"Jutht, ath it were, got to get my eye in, Mithter Thtern."

And he swished the cane. As it whipped through the air, it whined. Both boys winced noticeably. It fell against the wall. Where it cracked like wood splitting in a fire. Both boys winced again. Cross picked another. Went through the same process. And a third. For the third time he repeated the exercise. Visibly now the boys were trembling.

"Yeth," said Cross of the third one, "thith one should do. Just about whippy enough. Dethigned to cauthe the macthimum agony."

Swish! It whistled through the air. Again the boys winced. Swish!, once again. And several further times.

"Right," Cross said eventually. "I would appear to be ready."

Horatio had steeled himself. He was determined he was not going to cry. *Determined.*

"Would you count the thtroketh, Mithter Thtern?"

"Delighted," Bones confirmed.

Cross positioned himself behind Horatio. Raised the cane. "No," he said. "Now that I'm here, I'm not too happy with thith pothition. Maybe we should move the chair."

Horatio stood. Moved the chair. Unbidden, he bent over it again. He was not determined he would not cry. *Determined.*

The cane whined. And came crashing down on Horatio's bottom.

"One," Bones said gleefully.

The prince shrank within himself. He felt the cane's sting almost as badly ... "Two." ... as if it had struck *him.*

"Three. ... Four. ..." Horatio was by now grimacing badly. The prince could see this, could see how the pain was searing through his friend. "... Five. ... Six. ..."

"Aah!" screamed Horatio.

"Seven," said Bones cheerfully.

"Oh, I don't think tho, Mithter Thtern," said Cross, resting for a moment from his labours, making a few casual passes with the switch just above Horatio's bottom. "I think you mithed out sicth."

"I think you are mistook, Mr Krantz."

Horatio's face was now bathed in sweat. The prince could also see that, dribbling from his left eye, was a lone, but desolate, tear. He was grimacing in so much agony that he couldn't open his eyes, and clenched them – and his teeth – together.

"Happen you're right, Mithter Thtern," said Cross. "Thtill better one too many, no, than one too few? Don't want our little ladth here thinking ath how we're short-changing them nor nothing."

"As you say, Mr Krantz," agreed Bones. "Seven," he said as for the eighth time the cane left its vile sting.

At this stroke Horatio could no longer control himself. He started howling. His screams as the 'ninth' and 'tenth' strokes fell (which were, of course, the tenth and eleventh) were hideous, and tore through the prince as though they were the claws of a tiger.

Finally, though, his ordeal was over. Cross handed the cane to Bones. Horatio started to stand.

"Where d'you think you're going?" Bones asked of him.

"He's had his ten strokes, Mr Stern. He's even had eleven. It's my turn now."

"For which little speech of cheek, your 'Ighness, you will get another stroke. Bend over," he told Horatio.

"No," said the prince. "It's me. It's *my* turn."

"Six strokes on the king's orders are to be administered ..."

"It's me you have to flog," insisted the prince. "*Me.*"

"Pluth one," Cross reminded him.

"As you say, Mr Krantz. Administered to the posterior of the Crown Prince? I think not, Mr Krantz. Could be found guilty or something of battering a member of the royal family. Could find myself done, Mr Krantz, for 'igh treason or some such."

Horatio's face was already streaked with tears. His sky blue eyes pleaded with his friend, pleaded with the two torturers.

"*Noooooooooooooooo!*" screamed the prince. "No, please. Beat me. Beat me double the amount. Only beat *me*. Please." He dropped to his knees, grabbed hold of Bones's thighs. He started to wail.

"Get 'im off of me, Mr Krantz, if you would be so good." Cross manhandled the prince away. "You, worm," he told Horatio. "I thought I told you to bend over."

They were in a room which had hitherto been thought soundproof. The screams, though, were heard throughout the whole palace. And it broke the hearts of all those who heard them. Not those of Horatio which were those merely of pain, but those of the prince.

His were the screams of torture.

Chapter 14

Nancy never quite forgave her father for the punishment inflicted on her son. Nor did she forgive Naitly – who had, after all, employed Cross-Bones. And who, despite considerable misgivings within the palace, continued to do so. This lack of forgiveness was to have political repercussions far beyond the compass of a bruised bottom – even a severely bruised bottom.

Nancy's husband, though, was less incensed. He was spending a lot of his time in those days training a grin in the hope that it would rival Naitly's; and he was, as he always was, able to see the 'wider picture'. Richardson told his distraught wife that the punishment, whilst harsh, was a good lesson for his son to learn in life – indeed the *more* so for being so palpably unfair: That's what life was, it would make him aware of life's reality, it would toughen him up.

What he neglected to tell his wife was that he was presently negotiating a deal with the government. This was at its delicate stage. He could not therefore afford, as he saw it, to antagonise the Lord Chancellor. Not at this juncture. And not for the sake of a bruise which would anyway disappear in a week or so.

Horatio was bruised until the day he died.

The prince likewise.

But their real bruises could not be seen.

***

Cordelia also found the punishment hard to forgive.

There'd been some making up necessary between her and her recent husband: She had not been exactly enamoured of the way he had 'supported' her before the king.

They'd talked, though, and at the time she'd heard the screams they'd been making up in her boudoir. Before she could trace their source, however, the ordeal was over.

The sound of those screams was one whose echo she could never fully remove from her ears.

In a month's time it was the twins' birthday. She decided to prepare a party for them and Horatio. The birthday was a pretext. Protocol forbade her absolutely from apologising directly for the actions of her father – who was, more importantly, also her monarch. The party was designed to deliver that apology without directly saying "sorry".

The time between Cordelia's wedding and the 'birthday' party was not a happy one for any of the children. Although the king had lessened the time of the solitary confinement (meted out first to Philomena, but then repeated for the boys), for this month they were forbidden from seeing each other.

And, if truth be known, they really didn't *want* to see each other. They would in time. But they needed time to heal; and – just at the moment – the others' presence would only return them to that day of misery.

The prince was not, in his younger years, a sportsman. He had then only one area of athletic expertise: He was a superb horseman. From the first time he sat astride a pony, he and his steed became one. The prince could empathise with his mount to the point of apparent fusion; and for their parts, the mounts that bore him seemed able to intuit what he wanted before even a tug had been applied to the rein.

The prince never used a whip or a crop; he always saddled his steeds himself, always checking and re-checking the girths were tight enough but not too tight. He knew to within millimetres the capability of his horses and, whilst he would push them absolutely *to* that point, he never sought to push them beyond it.

During that bleak month, riding was the prince's only comfort.

No, more than riding it was the *being with* horses which was his comfort. Escorted by Cross-Bones, the prince would sometimes spend all day in the surrounding forest, just him and his mount.

It was the same forest with which Parisfal palace continues to be surrounded. In those days it was huge. It stretched uninterruptedly thence to Wodinton Castle, and as far in the other directions. So lush was (and is) its vegetation that, even in summer daylight, within the forest it was dark. Many found it spooky.

Cross-Bones found it spooky.

Prince Charming found it reassuring.

Often within the forest he would dismount and walk alongside the horse or pony he'd chosen from the royal stable. He never held the reins. He had no need to. Horse or pony would escort him of its own volition.

There were badgers in this forest, foxes, otters. Some claimed to have seen bears. One day they heard the howl of wolves. The prince would glory in those sights and sounds. Cross-Bones would merely squirm, and get scared and wish themselves back at the castle.

It was during one such sortie, however, that the idea came to them that a riding 'accident' would be a really good way 'innocently' to rid the country of a Crown Prince.

Having had which thought, on days when the prince was at his schooling, they would steel themselves to re-enter the forest, princelessly, to engineer the most devilish of traps – only for the prince, on his next ride, (such was the cussedness of their fate) to go off in another direction altogether.

So many innocent riders got so badly hurt by these traps that the forest started to germinate its own folklore: about wolves who dress up as grandmothers, for instance, and witches who live in marzipan houses. To this day there are some of the local citizenry, usually the more elderly, who continue to believe the fables.

***

Naitly and Goneril were not impressed by Cross-Bones's craftsmanship. They didn't care about the amount of attempts there had been on the prince's life, the amount of traps set which had killed others. All that concerned them, as they kept telling Cross-Bones, was results. They were (as they kept telling Cross-Bones) 'happening' people. Botched attempts were no attempts at all. As such they were non-events. It was (as they kept telling Cross-Bones) a contradiction in terms for non-events to happen to happening people.

Fredvie was also a happening person. His ambassador was at the Decadence weekly inquiring – diplomatically – when the heck – *finally* – the "rootin' happening" would be "tootin' happening". Did they know almost a whole "rootin'-tootin' *month*" had gone by?

Shortly before Cordelia's party Cross-Bones were therefore summoned back to the Decadence. Cross-Bones were two of the very few people allowed to see Naitly's smileless face. "Well?" he asked them.

"Ecthtremely, Lord Chanthellor," Cross replied. "How kind of you to athk."

"Not what I meant," Naitly told him.

"If I might ..." Goneril lay a condescending hand on his forearm, as if to quieten him. "Your brief, gentlemen, was, like Androcles, to remove a thorn from the paw of Belgiss. And yet still Belgiss continues to be thorned -- and continues to mew horribly in its pain. You are feckless, gentlemen."

"Thank you, your Highneth. We doeth do our betht."

"You are such a dolt sometimes, Mr Krantz. 'Feckless,' 'er 'Ighness said. Don't you know what that means? Soon as we leave 'ere, Your 'Ighness," said Bones, "don't you fret, we'll go and find us some feck. And that's a promise." Goneril did not look impressed.

Cross noticed this. "We've got a plan," he said.

"Very well," said Goneril in a way that signified "Let's hear it".

"It's a plan which ..." repeated Bones, excavating around in his brain and finding only the selfsame nothing he always did on such digs. "... a plan which ... which ... which ..." Inspiration had struck! " ... Mr Krantz can explain a lot better 'n me."

"Mr Krantz?" Goneril turned her light blue eyes to him. The look was one designed to intimidate – and which usually did.

"Birthday," exclaimed Cross. "The printhe hath got a birthday coming up."

"Scarcely news," said Naitly who was stopped from saying more by the withering glance aimed at him by his 'fiancée'.

"Your sister's giving him a party," said Bones, who had intuited that Cross had passed him the baton.

"Half-sister," Goneril corrected him.

"Half-thithter, right."

"Parties 'as cakes," said Bones, running with the baton.

"Caketh. Alwayth."

Inspiration again struck. "We'll get Gretel to bake a cake," said Bones.

"Poithon the cake."

"The prince'll die."

"Gretel'll get the blame for it," said Cross.

There was a moment's pause. Cross-Bones felt their necks.

"Brilliant!" chorused Goneril and Naitly.

"'Courthe some of the other children will altho die."

"There is no war," smiled Naitly, trying to imbue the smirk with sadness, "without casualties."

"We cannot be diverted from our glorious goals by mere sentiment," said Goneril.

"Right," agreed Cross-Bones.

"And you are still here why?" asked Goneril.

"Lord Chanthellor," said Cross as a good-bye.

"Your 'Ighness," said Bones likewise.

They closed the door to the Cabinet office. Minor Minor was

working at his desk – minorly. He knew he was on his way to Mercia, but Fredvie had not yet sent for him.

"'Scuse me, mate," Bones asked him, "only you got any idea where we might find ourselves a feck?"

Chapter 15

The best laid plans, though, of mice, men ... and murderers: Gretel was not a cook.

Even if she had been, in fact, it would have availed them nothing. Cordelia had already decided it would be she who would be cooking the cake: a further act, on her part, of apology and/or atonement.

Which was not quite the way Cross-Bones saw it! *They* ascribed it, again, to the cussedness of their fate. A diagnosis reinforced by the fact that Cordelia would be cooking said cake in her own kitchen. Which Cross-Bones had as much reason to be in as a penguin in equatorial Africa. And which would have been about as inconspicuous.

With greater sheepishness than Australia Cross-Bones returned to the Decadence. On this occasion Minor Minor was also in the Cabinet office. So was another man, even smaller than Minor Minor, a weasely but weedy sort of a man, gnarled like a diseased tree trunk.

"Wimps!" sneered Goneril. "Feckless ... wimps!"

"This, gentlemen, is Eustace," said Naitly, his smile somehow even more sinister than usual. "Step forward, Eustace."

Eustace did so, shook hands with the two men. "'*Useless* Eustace,' they call me," he said, effervescing in the accolade.

"Useless Eustace, gentleman, is the worst axeman in the entire of Belgiss," Naitly continued, his smile preceding him.

"Useless," confirmed Eustace cheerfully. "Completely hopeless. Can hardly lift the axe. Make a terrible hash of it. Frightful. I've never done it well. Never."

"I do so hope you don't need to meet Eustace again," said Naitly.

"A pleasure, gents," said Useless Eustace, and withdrew to the corner of the room.

"There'th alwayth plan 'b'."

"And what," asked Goneril, "might plan 'b' be?"

"Tell Her Highneth about plan 'b', Mithter Thtern."

"There ain't no plan 'b'," snapped Bones. And then he saw Goneril's face. She seemed about to summon Useless back. "There ain't, Mr Krantz, no plan 'b' *better*, that's what I were trying to say, than the one ... Mr Krantz 'as got 'idden away in 'is brain somewhere."

"But, Mithter Thtern, it'th *your* plan," insisted Cross, involuntarily wagging his neck, realising suddenly how (in both senses) attached he was to it. "Fair do'th and all that. You detherve the credit."

"You're too modest, Mr Krantz. 'E's too modest, 'e is. ..."

"I'm so ever so sorry to barge in," said Minor Minor.

"Is this important, Minor Minor?" asked Naitly. Goneril had adjourned to the couch where she sat, stroking a pout, brooding ... hatching ...

"*So* so ever so sorry," said Minor Minor. "But there's this dog ... these dogs, I should say ..."

"Dogs?" asked Goneril. "We've got two curs here already. What would we want with any *more* dogs?"

"Oh, droll, Your Highness, so ever so droll. These dogs, Your Highness – well, not *these* curs, but the dogs to which I am alluding – they're ... savage ... so ever so savage, in fact."

Naitly's ears pricked up, as did Goneril's – almost, in fact, *like* a dog's. "Go on, Minor Minor," said Naitly.

Minor Minor was not used to being the centre of attention. He stammered lightly, his eyes found it hard to settle. "Well, these dogs, sir ... they're to protect the castle grounds at night ... so, as I said, ever so savage, they are ... they're trained to kill, sir, on command. On the hearing of one word. They're not even really dogs. Half wolf."

"The prince has a sentimental attachment to animals," said Goneril, following Minor Minor's train of thought.

"If he was to be given one of the dogs for his birthday ..."

Goneril heard LC's grammatical slip, but was too busy hatching to bother to correct it. "Even if the dog *didn't* savage him," she said, "no-one would be surprised if it did."

"We could lie about it, you mean?" asked Bones excitedly – as if the lying would add a frisson of naughtiness absent in a lieless murder.

"Dogs do unpredictable things," Goneril continued: "They bite horses' shins, terrify a young man so he falls over a cliff. ..."

"One tiny thing, Your 'Ighness," said Bones: "'oever gives the prince that dog, that 'oever's going to have, like, a tête-à-tête with old Useless Eustace there. Or maybe I should say a tête-à-*lack-of*-tête. I mean, talking frankly, I can't see queues of volunteers stretching round the block – yeah, and maybe I should have thought of another word for *block*, an' all."

"Gretel!" Cross trumpeted loudly.

***

Unlike the idea of baking a cake, Gretel was immediately enchanted with that of presenting the prince with a puppy. He needed something to love – something that would love him back, and without any protocol attached. There is no class-consciousness in dogs.

Before being shown to Gretel, the puppy was separated from the rest of the pack. Even so, the first sight of it alarmed her a little. It was so ... *big*. But the puppy was on its best behaviour. Alone, it looked fairly defenceless and a bit soppy. It nipped Gretel's finger and rolled over on its back that she might scratch its tummy. Gretel started to think the puppy delightful. Just what the doctor ordered. It'd make, she felt sure, a wonderful companion for the prince.

Indeed so frolicsome and unthreatening was the mutt that, when Gretel had left, Cross-Bones wondered of its handler whether the dog were up to its savaging duties.

The handler was a rather county, twinset-and-pearly sort of woman with a stout stick in her hand, and a steely eye that would have won the silver medal to Goneril's gold. "Peppermint!" she said, in the voice of a command.

The transformation was of Dr Jekyll to Mr Hyde: The innocent lolloping bundle became a snarling mass of angry fangs, the yellow of its eyes turned from soppiness to malevolence, the softness of its downy coat turned to the hackled quills of a porcupine. It was no longer a puppy, it was a delinquent cub. And that cub tore at the stick and had, within a second, crunched it into splinters.

"Spearmint!" the handler then 'commanded'. And the cub again became a puppy. It picked up one of the splinters and, with wagging tail, glinted at the handler that she should throw this for it.

"Very imprethive," said Cross softly and with admiration.

"Very," said Bones.

***

By a million miles the gift of the dog was the prince's best birthday present. His heart ached in his gratitude to Gretel for it. The smile he bore as a consequence stretched his dimples into bows.

And Gretel smiled to see the prince smile so broadly. The whole palace smiled.

Only HM did not smile. Minor Minor was not the only person to know of the existence of these dogs. HM knew them to be killing machines.

She tried to persuade the king somehow to confiscate the dog. But – his harsh treatment of his son notwithstanding – the king did have feelings for the lad. He liked seeing his son happy. It stopped him having to wonder whether there might be something he should be doing for him. He borrowed a phrase from Cordelia and told HM she was making a mountain out of a molehill, and to stop making such a fuss.

Then he smiled, watching boy and dog together.

***

And Cross-Bones smiled hugely as well.

Little did they know that smile was about to be relocated to the *other* side of their faces!

Chapter 16

Cordelia was not *surprised* that Goneril should have come to visit her in her kitchen, she was *astounded*. As astounded as if she *had* come across a penguin in equatorial Africa.

It was a big kitchen, as welcoming as it was warm, used socially as much as it was as a workplace. It was ramshackly and messy, strewn with gazettes and cushions and pots of jam and cooking pots. Bread was baked there, and coffee ground – whose smells were joined, at various points, by cinnamon and nutmeg and thyme.

Goneril had secreted about her a tiny phial of lethal venom.

Oh, sure, savage dogs were all fine and dandy, but her experience of all animals (including the human ones) was that they could not be relied on for *anything*: Man-eating tigers would suddenly become vegetarian, emus would start flying, snails would become claustrophobic. The only person – the only *thing* – that could be relied on to do a job properly was you yourself.

Even then you had to be careful. Even Goneril had been known to let Goneril down. Not too often, that was true. Mostly because, at one level, she was as frightened of Goneril as everyone else. Goneril gave herself just as hard a time as she gave the rest of the world, perhaps even harder. Therefore, if only to avoid her own displeasure, she tended to excel. Positive pleasure in herself was a sensation she had never experienced; she would have sneered even at the idea.

Cordelia was baking a cake. Goneril scooped some of the mixture from the bowl with her finger, and then licked it, priding herself on her knowledge of practices domestic. "Needs vanilla," she said. Her knowledge of cake-baking was roughly that Fredvie had of rocket-building. She simply needed Cordelia to disappear … just for a moment or two … just for long enough …

"It does not need vanilla, Goneril."

"It needs *something*." Goneril tried the mix again. "More sugar maybe?"

Cordelia dipped her finger in, tasted it. "Maybe." She sprinkled a bit more sugar into the mix from the shaker alongside the bowl on the unvarnished kitchen table.

What, Goneril wondered in some despair, was kept in a larder?

She again dipped her finger into the mix.

"I still think it needs vanilla," she said.

"No vanilla, Goneril."

"Pepper, then?" she suggested, such being one of the few other flavourings she'd heard of.

"In a cake?"

"Might be novel."

"Mint."

"As in the 'mint', I suppose, your husband's making?"

"Is he?" Cordelia had no idea how her husband's business was doing – such interests were of no interest to her!

"Oh, a mint and a half," said her half-sister.

"Not that kind of mint, Goneril, mint as in … mint. You know, the herb, from the garden. Would you be kind enough …?"

"I would. Of course I *would*. But my allergy, you know," said Goneril, seizing what she thought was her opportunity.

"Allergy?"

"To mint."

"I didn't know you had an allergy to mint."

"I try not to make a fuss about it," Goneril martyred.

"Well, best not add any mint then. We don't want you not being able to have a piece yourself."

"NO," she said. Goneril needed Cordelia to go into the garden. "No, don't you worry about me, dear Cordelia. Do add mint. Yes, it could do with some mint. Mint, certainly," Goneril insisted. "Birthday cakes, they're only for the children, aren't they? Not anyway a big eater of cakes, me. What with my allergy to cakes, and all." She also needed to establish that up-front.

"You seem to have developed a lot of allergies recently," said Cordelia.

"The price, dear Cordelia, of responsibility," martyred Goneril for the second time.

"Allergic to cakes, but not cake *mix*?"

"Whimsical things, allergies," said Goneril and laughed Naitlily.

"I'll just go and get some mint, then," said Cordelia.

"It'll taste superb," said Goneril, and kissed her extended fingers in the international sign for 'delicious'.

Cordelia slipped into the garden.

And Goneril?

Goneril slipped the poison into the mix. Her eyes glassed over as she did so, as if they were too ashamed of their owner's action to be able to witness it.

***

Most children have clothes which are their party 'best'. In the prince's case they were his party 'worst'. Jeans had, of course, yet to be invented. But it was when going to parties – and only then – that the young man was allowed to wear their equivalent. For the brief two hours of such events he was allowed to let his hair down.

Thanks to a massive advertising campaign, the rage that February was for Mercian musical boxes. Baron Richardson was selling them throughout his chain of emporia. (Em-*poor*-ia, HM 'joked', which en-*rich*-ed the baron considerably!) From one of those emporia he'd taken two and given them to Horatio, for him to present to his royal cousins.

There was a stiffness in the air when the three children met again. "Contrary to myth," the king told me, holding up his cup to Elton that it might be refilled, "there is rarely a community of suffering. Pain inclines us to isolate ourselves from our fellows.

And pain often introduces us to our selfishness: As long as it is removed from *us* we tend not to care on whom else that pain might be inflicted. For many of us it is a sobering introduction.

"I think there was a part of Horatio which knew it wasn't my fault that he should have been beaten in my place. But another part of him didn't care. And a third part found my company simply too dangerous: What would be the next punishment he'd have to suffer on my behalf?

"Philly was aware that an openness and innocence that had hitherto been the hallmark of our relationship had been shattered. And that thus it would remain. You cannot reglue a shattered innocence.

"And me myself? I was full of so much shame and guilt that I found anyone's company difficult – particularly that of anyone who reminded me of how shameful and guilty I felt.

"It didn't matter to me that Horatio's beating was not my fault. Its reality overwhelmed considerations of fault. Huge surges of hatred welled up inside me for Father and for Cross-Bones. These, though, were dwarfed by the tidal wave of *self*-loathing which crashed over me several times a day: *self*-loathing and loathing of *what* I was. Probably, at some point, every Crown Prince in the world has become an avowed republican. None in history has been more energetically so than I was at this time."

***

The cake arrived agleam with sixteen candles – eight each for the two twins. Between them they blew out the candles.

They made their wishes.

Goneril watched from, as it were, the side-lines. The fruition of so much hatching was only moments away. She'd show Naitly, show those idiots he'd employed – even show Fredvie! Her heart was beating so hard it felt as if it were trying to escape.

The prince, however, point-blank refused to eat any cake. He didn't *deserve* any cake. Instead, as a token of appreciation for all his hostess's hard work and as an act of penance, he ate four of the candles.

Protocol determined that the prince's refusal to eat cake meant that none of the other, non-royal, guests could. This peeved the assembled non-royal children.

Goneril it incensed. She had to fight an instinct not simply to shove the cake down the prince's reluctant throat. And then she was aghast:

Horatio was damned if he were going to let the prince's precious conscience stop *him* from eating cake. Especially *chocolate* cake. Especially *Cordelia's* chocolate cake.

Goneril took half a step forward to stop him, and then realised she could do nothing without implicating herself.

In an act every twitch of which was supposed to embody defiance, Horatio looked the young prince in the eye and picked up the cake. Charming was trying to tell him, *please,* he'd be *happy* for Horatio to eat the cake – all the other children likewise. The cakelessness, that was *his* punishment, not anyone else's. He didn't *want* this stupid protocol; Horatio, *please,* had no need to 'defy' him in this way.

But Horatio couldn't see what lay behind the prince's eyes. And therefore it *was* in defiance, not just of protocol but of what he also perceived to be the prince, that he crammed the squidgy substance into his mouth.

Philomena watched every nuance of this exchange.

She knew what loyalty meant!

If Horatio were going to be punished for defying protocol, then she would be punished right alongside him. Mimicking her cousin's defiant stance, she too started cramming cake into her mouth.

Suddenly, and almost simultaneously, both stopped their cramming.

They grabbed their throats.

From which a hideous gurgling rattle emerged.
Their eyes sheened over.
The prince looked terrified. Goneril looked appalled.
Cordelia screamed. She ran to the children.
And then she *screamed.*

Chapter 17

The more gutter of the gazettes goried, in rank detail, on the agony of the children's deaths. We don't have to so sully ourselves here. It was horrible that the children died. More horrible yet that they died horribly. The taking of a healthy human life is always murder. Murder is always violent. Violence is always ugly.

Neither Philomena nor Horatio was of a status sufficient to the declaration of official mourning. But Belgiss grieved. It grieved intensely. Even the sentries grieved. And the Court grieved alongside the nation and the sentries. And mourned as well for itself.

Cole grabbed HM and retired for several weeks into his inner sanctum. From which he would sometimes call for his pipe, and often call for his bowl, but *never* for the other two fiddlers.

Goneril, for the rest of 'the' evening, felt somewhat morose. It was sad, losing her nephew and niece like that. Naitly, though, felt no such qualms. He chided her for her sentimentality and sermonised again about being involved in a war, and about no war being casualty-free. Goneril immediately saw the sense in that, and with one mighty bound her conscience was absolved.

Fredvie showed his usual impeccable courtesy by being rootin' quick to despatch his ambassador with His Imperial condolences to figures as insignificant to him as King Cole and Princess Nancy. And he showed his equally impeccable *determination* by being even quicker to convey His Imperial 'I'm-*real*-unhappy'nesses to Goneril and Naitly. Couldn't the tootin' two of them *ever* get *anything* rootin' right?

Via the Belgic ambassador in Biga-buga, Naitly replied to the emperor that, if circumspection had been needed before, it was quadruply so needed now. If he and Goneril were implicated in the children's murder then so would Mercia. Such an implication would effectively block annexation for at least a generation. They needed His Imperial Majesty's co-operation not his censure.

To the surprise of the ambassador, Fredvie understood – well, the words, anyway. What Fredvie did not, what he *could* not understand was the attitude. He wasn't prepared to wait forever. This kind of lily-livered chickenness was not what had made Mercia great. He'd give them an extension of two years. If nothing had happened by then ...

Two years, as far as Naitly and Goneril were concerned, was two years away. They had more pressing problems. They had to expunge any idea that might be circulating that they were somehow implicated in the infanticide. Naitly immediately announced that, alongside the police investigation, Lord Nelris would hold a detailed enquiry.

Even before that, Gretel was summoned to the Decadence. She was given a choice: Either she could withdraw immediately into the outer reaches of Belgiss or she could risk a public trial. She would in that case be charged with a dereliction of duty so gross as to constitute an act of treason. Lord Nelris would preside over the trial. The 'if' of '*if* found guilty' was therefore, and Gretel knew it, entirely academic. And 'if' found guilty she would suffer the only penalty available for such a crime. Gretel knew that the choice she had was none.

She was forbidden absolutely – on pain also of death – from any further contact with the prince. But at that time the prince was, almost literally, shattered by grief. He had reached a point of what might be described as terminal sadness. Even if she had said good-bye, it's doubtful he would have reacted heart-brokenly – if at all.

Gretel, though, was not to know that.

Lord Nelris's enquiry found her negligence to be the most significant contributory factor in the deaths of Philomena and Horatio – that which had escalated the event from an accident to a tragedy.

Her exile was made more miserable yet by the thought that

Charming also blamed her; that therefore he no longer loved her. She tried to mitigate that misery by plotting revenge. Only when the prince was a grown man, and married, was she able to exact it.

In fact, the prince did not blame Gretel, nor did he ever do anything other than love her. He knew (as, it must be added, did most of the country) the enquiry was a nonsense (as were most of the 'enquiries' chaired by Lord Nelris), knew her to be incapable of having anything to do with such a heinous deed, even by default. Much of the Court, much of the nation, even the world likewise.

***

Far from the tragedy pulling them closer together, there was a time when Nancy and Richardson found themselves hating each other: If they hadn't met they wouldn't have married. And if they hadn't married they'd never have had Horatio. And without Horatio they wouldn't be suffering the indescribable anguish now of his death. Both attributed their suffering to the other. Therefore even the sight of that other was enough to rub a very caustic salt into an already open and festering wound.

***

As for the police investigation ...

The world's greatest detectives (Sherlock Holmes and Miss Marple amongst many others) have implied that Scotland Yard is staffed by clod-hopping nincompoops. By comparison with the Belgic police, however, even Scotland Yard's dimmest is a sleuthing genius.

But not even the Belgic police, particularly after a tip-off from the Decadence, could fail to make a connection between the cake and the death of the children. The toxicology report, after a tip-off from the Decadence, confirmed that the cake contained poison – one made from the pestled pulp of a toadstool prevalent in the castle's grounds.

The Belgic police discovered that Cordelia walked in the grounds. She'd also made the cake. There could be no question about it (particularly after a tip-off from the Decadence): Cordelia was guilty of murder. She was arrested.

The Belgic police congratulated themselves effusively on a case well solved. And they looked forward to a rare moment of public approval, if not approbation.

But Naitly immediately slapped a 'C' Notice on the news.

'C' stood, not for Cordelia, but for Confidential. If news were considered such that its broadcast would be 'a danger to national security', a 'C' Notice could be put on it. This forbade the gazettes from publishing the story, even from mentioning it.

What constituted 'a danger to national security' was something decided entirely by the whim of the Lord Chancellor. There was no appeal against his decision. And even news that a 'C' Notice had been imposed was a breach of it. Very many more were imposed than the public was ever aware of.

Anything that wasn't flattering to Naitly, for instance, he considered 'a danger to national security'. A Lord Chancellor who was criticised, he would rationalise, was a weak Lord Chancellor. And weak Lord Chancellors would invite foreign invasion. So, ensuring the gazettes painted him only in glowing colours was in the national interest; and for them *not* to was clearly detrimental to it, thus 'a danger to national security'.

In times of what Naitly liked to call 'crisis', the Lord Chancellor also invoked 'C' Notices on matters relating to Cole and his family.

He wasn't a fool, Naitly. He, of course, wanted the royal family to become unpopular. That would make the annexation to Mercia an altogether easier task. But he couldn't be *seen* to be making the royal family unpopular. Such shenanigans, in Belgiss, had a habit of back-firing. So he would impose a 'C' Notice, and then – very slowly, very gently – he would start himself to leak the forbidden story. This was followed by another leak that the 'C' Notice had been imposed, not by him at all, but by the king.

As far as this specific case was concerned, Naitly was caught on the very sharp horns of an ill-tempered dilemma. The would-be Protector of Belgiss (such he would be after annexation) was thrilled with the idea of trying a member of the royal family, of having her publicly shamed and denounced as being a murderess of children. But Naitly the pragmatist could not afford for Cordelia to face public trial: too many uncomfortable facts could have been presented by her defence.

There was therefore no trial of Cordelia.

Finally, because there was no need of one.

Chapter 18

HM had to move fast. There was the prince's welfare to consider. Naitly would see Gretel's exile as an ideal opportunity to nominate his own candidate for the job of nursemaid. What price then the prince's life? She wanted Cole to have appointed Gretel's successor even before Gretel had been discharged, and certainly before Naitly had a chance to present his nominee – or Goneril hers.

The young woman before her was not perfect, but she was available. Her name was Edwina Cormer, and she was scarcely more than a child herself. No bad thing, in the prince's friendless state. She was squat, Edwina, not quite dumpy, and with short dark hair which sprouted considerably more curls than she would have wished. The unkind called her nose 'hooked', the diplomatic 'aquiline'; as the diplomatic called 'beauty spots' what the unkind called 'moles' – or even 'warts'. Her face was freckled with them. She was, frankly, ugly. Also no bad thing: unlikely therefore to be distracted by moustachioed hists or flutters of the heart. She was clearly the person for the job.

On top of all other considerations, appointing Edwina would net HM a million brownie points from her, HM's, father.

HM's mother had died a couple of years before Charming had been born. For the last two years her father had been 'walking out' with the widow Cormer, albeit with a growing reluctance.

The widow Cormer's late husband had died in circumstances the police remained unconvinced were purely accidental. But they lacked sufficient evidence or (if truth be told) interest to want to extend the case's solve-by date and so it melted into a sort of begrudged no-further-actionness. The widow's first name was Primrose. She was known as Prim. It suited her.

Had the late Mr Cormer left Prim with more money, she might have become a widow merry enough to rival her of operatic fame. But merriness in poverty is not possible. Not that Prim was poor to the point of penury; her poverty meant rather that she could only afford those 'good things in life' which were shop-soiled. Such to Prim was quite enough to tarnish life's gloss.

She had two daughters – Virginia, the elder, and Edwina. And she was prepared to dote on them. But they, in turn, had to do *their* bit. This bit consisted of magic-carpeting her to a land of plenty. She wasn't particular about which land, nor which daughter should do this for her; but she was supremely convinced that such a voyage should be in the forefront of both their duties. Prim considered her daughters' dereliction to date of their duty a breach of whichever Commandment it was demanded, dearie, thou shalt honour thy mother – especially, as she proclaimed herself to be, thy as-near-as-dammit *starving* mother.

Since her husband's demise Prim had entertained the odd suitor. HM's father was the latest. But this suitor (as, to the chagrin of her father, HM had 'joked') was a very odd suitor indeed – a suitor that definitely did not "suit 'er"!

Or that, even more definitely, did not suit 'im!

If HM could get Edwina the job of royal nanny her father could, with clear conscience and considerable relief, dissociate himself from the widow.

The king at this time was permanently extremely tired and, understandably, highly emotional. When HM had proposed Edwina as nanny, consent was given by the merest nod of royal consent.

HM introduced Edwina to the prince only moments before Cordelia was due before the king. Charming barely acknowledged, or even noticed, her arrival.

***

Cordelia was in big trouble.

The leave of all Belgiss's axemen had been cancelled.

The princess was in chains, guarded by two sentries. With her, unchained but with the countenance of the condemned, was her husband. His face was grey with worry, hers white with terror and sleeplessness. But its alabaster was sheened with determination. The twitch that betrayed her anger rippled through her left cheek.

Cordelia knew she was going to die. She was determined she would do so with dignity. She also wanted to do so in a way in which both she and her innocence would be remembered.

They were waiting in the anteroom to the throne room. Naitly and Goneril were also waiting there. He had donned his 'black cap' smile; she was boa'd in smugness and self-congratulation. Ever since the birth of Nancy, Goneril had always considered half-sisters bothersome. She didn't know about common-or-garden sisters, of course, but *royal* and *half*-sisters were dangerous. Should something 'unfortunate' happen to their elder, they would (once the amendment had been made to the Constitution) have a claim to the throne. Therefore, for as long as there were royal half-sisters around, Goneril could not be at all sure that they weren't plotting against *her*. Goneril knew the best way to demolish plots was to demolish the plotters. Two down, one to go.

HM bounced in. Apparently without a care in the world, certainly without a care about Cordelia. This was HM's way. She was relieved that, at least, Edwina was now in place.

Cordelia didn't blink, Antonio didn't baulk. Both Naitly and Goneril looked as if they'd eaten an extremely sour plum.

"His Majesty has been whining for you," Naitly told the jester, with all the sourness of that taste.

"I'll be with him only for a trice," HM replied. "We need words."

Naitly snorted contemptuously. "I think not. I cannot stre- ..."

"We *need* words, Baron, trust me," said HM. "The *three* of us need words." She opened the door to the throne room. "Your

Majesty," she said within it, and curtseyed deeply.

"One is glum," the king could be heard saying. "Make one laugh, HM." Simultaneously HM allowed herself to splat from the curtsey onto the floor and to kick the door shut. The king's laugh could be heard even as the door was slamming closed.

A few moments only passed before it was again opened. This time to the accompaniment of the king's raucous guffaws. "Be right back, sire," HM said, closing the door. "Shall we?" she asked of Naitly and Goneril, extending an 'after you' arm.

Naitly and Goneril swept from the anteroom. As she passed them, HM tried to inject reassurance into the smile she pointed at Cordelia and Antonio. In their turn they tried to convince themselves of the reassurance's potency.

Even as HM arrived Naitly had started pacing the corridor.

"Well?" he asked of the jester. "Don't say, 'Fine, thank you'."

HM withered him with a look. "I know what you've done," she said, without even a hint of frivolity. "Oh, I can't prove it. But I do know."

"I have not the slightest idea," said Goneril with a petulant iciness, "to what you are alluding."

HM ignored this plea of innocence. "I've appointed the royal nursemaid," she told them. "I've also persuaded the king to spare Cordelia's life. We all know she didn't kill anyone."

"Are you threatening me, jester? I cannot stress ..."

"No threat, Lord Chancellor, trust me. Just a clear understanding of where we all are. Miss Cormer (she's the new nanny) will stay, so will Cordelia's head. In which case my tongue too will stay stayed. If either is forfeit, however ..." She felt no need to finish the sentence, other than to repeat, "Trust me."

Naitly was about to erupt. As was her wont, Goneril laid a steadying hand on his forearm. "At this time of national grief," she said, "it is important that we should set aside anything which compromises unity."

"One day, jester," Naitly said, "you will push us too far."

"I wonder, will that day be before or after you overreach yourselves? For overreach yourselves you certainly will. Trust me. If you will excuse me ..."

***

Cordelia had been summoned into the throne room.

This was smaller, and more Spartan, than might be imagined. There were two thrones, in fact – that for the queen was, obviously, unoccupied. These two pieces were the chamber's only furniture. From the wall hung a few tapestries – mostly of hunting scenes. But these were embroidered predominantly with earthen colours and served thus only to accentuate a gloom which seemed anyway inherent to the place.

With Cordelia was Antonio. Naitly and Goneril were in attendance, and HM, of course, along with assorted soldiers, sentries and guards.

Nancy had threatened to kill Cordelia – if necessary with her bare hands. It was therefore thought politic to keep these proceedings secret from her. Richardson had been quick to acquiesce. Beard-stroking had persuaded him to view the wider picture. It had also enjoined him to remind Naitly about the importance of trade between Belgiss and Azrac. Naitly needed no such reminder.

"I did not do it," Cordelia insisted.

"The police, though, are convinced that you did," said the king.

"Them! They only catch a cold when they're told to!"

"Lord Nelris would preside at your trial," said Naitly, the edge of his smile threatening to lacerate his right nostril.

"Just so long as it's public," Cordelia retorted stubbornly.

"It's not going to happen, Cordelia," said Goneril.

"It was her, Daddy. Goneril. It's so obvious. *Goneril* killed them ..."

"This," gasped Goneril, "is an outrage."

"She was in my kitchen. She put the poison in the mix."

"Your words are slanderous. I give you fair warning, Cordelia."

"Warning? What'll you do to me, Goneril? Sue me? I went out to the garden for some mint. What were you doing then?"

"How dare you?" spluttered Goneril, so livid she could barely form her words.

"Come to think of it ..." Cordelia's words were cascading from her. Her splutter was caused by the desperation to get them voiced. "... there was that flash of black flitting around a bush, that too. When I found the prince suffocating in his pram."

"This is calumny," said Goneril, some decorum having returned to her. "Slander. Stop her, father. I demand a retraction. Immediately. Demand an apology."

"It wasn't me who killed the poor things, it was you, Goneril. Think about it, Daddy. Think 'why'. 'Why' would *I* have?"

"You poison words, Cordelia," her half-sister spat at her, "as you poison children. If we lived in a civilised society such a tongue would be treated as the rabid dog it is. It would be ripped out of you, madam. And, believe me, when I am ..." She stopped herself abruptly.

"What were you going to say, Goneril? 'When I am *queen*' – was that it? Can't you see, Daddy? Are you *really* so blind? They say that, don't they, of those who drink too much? That they're *blind* drunk!"

"You kill two innocent children, madam, and then you slander *me*?" fumed the king.

"And me, Father," fumed Goneril.

"And your half-sister," fumed the king once again. "One has always tried to be a good father," he continued, toppling into an abyss of ruefulness. HM passed him some more of his thinking cordial – such a solace when trapped in that abyss. "One had always hoped that one's children would take a leaf out of one's own book and love each other and support each other. Oh well … One has, one feels, done one's best."

"Best?" sneered Cordelia. HM fired a warning shot across her bows. Sixth sense told her to heed the jester.

"Inadequate, no doubt," the king continued. He loved being so reasonable and humble. It was good for his merry old soul. "Nevertheless, one's best."

"How sharper than a serpent's tooth it is, sire, to have a thankless child."

"Original, HM?"

"Almost, sire."

"Rather good," condescended the king. "One almost wishes one had said that oneself."

"Doubtless, sire," said the jester, "you will."

"One has a great love for you, Cordelia – thankless child though you are. And one will miss you." Goneril couldn't stop the smugness from swamping her face. "You will keep your head!"

"Father!" stormed Goneril. "She has slandered me!" She saw HM incline her head towards that of her father. "But, then, of course, you know what a wet, sentimental thing I am at heart."

"However," the king continued, "on pain of instant imprisonment you and your husband are to be banished from Belgic territory and are to be returned to Azrac. Take them away," he told the guards, and absent-mindedly extended his arm towards his goblet.

***

The exiled had twenty-four hours to leave Belgic soil. Not enough time for Cordelia even to make a start on packing up her belongings. Naitly promised her that this would be done for her.

In a private conversation with Antonio, he voiced his hope that this 'little', this 'domestic' …'difficulty' would not affect the 'favoured nations' treaty between Belgiss and Azrac as far as trade was concerned.

The Belgics were, Naitly reminded Antonio, a somewhat sentimental bunch. They worked themselves up into a state about certain things – the killing of children, for instance, or cruelty to foxes. But their memory was short. Give it time. Let the incident blow over. Naitly couldn't imagine it would be, oh, more than a few years before the exiled couple were allowed to return.

For his part, Antonio assured Naitly that, whilst politics was politics, trade was sacred.

***

The prince had already nicknamed Edwina "Winny".

Winny watched carefully as HM broke the news to Charming of Cordelia's banishment. This HM did as gently as she could. She knew it would be another devastating blow. With Cordelia and Gretel gone, the young man would, at Court, only have HM looking out for his interests.

Charming listened, as he did everything, unemotionally. He was the cause of considerable worry to HM. Oh, he did everything required of him: He ate, slept, took his exercise, applied himself to his schooling. But he did them all as an automaton might, with an apparent absence of *any* emotion. He had always tended towards introversion. Now this tendency was aggravated to the point where he had become almost hermit-like.

HM had often found herself thanking God for the dog she had tried so hard to persuade Cole to confiscate. This had become the prince's constant, and only, companion. He called him 'Nose'. He had started to train Nose using a set of whistles known only to himself.

The prince was stroking Nose when HM told him about Cordelia. He had the dog's ears in his hands, almost as if he were giving him a good talking-to. "Do you hear that, Nose?" he asked. "Aunt Cordelia's going a long way away. Isn't that sad? Isn't that sad, Nose?" he repeated, slightly shaking the dog's head. "*Very* sad, yes. 'Specially as we know she didn't do it, don't we, Nose? Oh yes, we know she didn't do it."

Nose licked him and he laughed.

HM shook her head very, very slowly. It was probably the saddest thing she'd ever seen in her life.

Chapter 19

Alongside Cordelia, *smiles* seemed to have been banished from the Belgic Court. Even Naitly's grins spent much of their time in a black armband.

His twice-weekly meetings with the king became, weekly, more difficult. Cole appeared to sink deeper and deeper within his bowl, and the reins of government passed increasingly from His Majesty to HM. Whose only concern, apparently, was – at every turn – to thwart the Lord Chancellor.

The king would be sprawled across three large downy cushions, the central one of which was a present from the Sultan of Orismine from the days when he had still been an ally. It was of green silk embroidered in satin threads with the motif of a one-tusked elephant – the national symbol of the sultanate. The king would be smoking his hookah, his goblet within easy reach. He would blear at his Lord Chancellor through watery eyes.

"It pains me, sire, to talk of difficult matters," Naitly would say. "Particularly in such difficult times."

"Then don't talk about them," quipped HM. But there was bite in the quip; it was seasoned with threat.

"Would that I *could* forbear, jester. The matter, though, brooks of no delay. We are, sire, only a single heart-beat away from a crisis."

"You thinking of having a heart-attack, Lord Chancellor?" jested the jester. Cole snorted – albeit sadly – and took the merest drop more of his thinking cordial.

"His Majesty is well aware whereof I speak. We pray to God that nothing does befall the young prince – or His Majesty himself, self-evidently. But if the recent tragedy serves any purpose it is to remind us all of our own mortality. His Majesty's eldest daughter is a woman of the greatest ability and integrity. I cannot believe His Majesty would prefer his throne to pass to that barbaric cousin of his from …" and here the baron paused to inject the forthcoming word with the sort of distaste usually reserved for the more indelicate of bodily functions, "England."

"Some fine things have come from England," HM reminded him.

"Certainly they have," Naitly agreed. "Fine, *fine* things! Like hooliganism, illiteracy, drunkenness. Not," he added quickly with a furtive glance at the king, "that drunkenness is not a fine thing per se, sire, just not the English version of it. There's little wrong either with musical boxes. Mercian musical boxes, though ..."

" ... play the Mercian national anthem," the king griped.

"Quite," Naitly confirmed. "We need a referendum, sire. I fear for the consequences of this ..." Again, that heavy distaste: "... Englishman taking the throne. I fear it might provoke revolution."

"The king is in mourning. This is not the time, Lord Chancellor," HM told him.

"I cannot stress too much, sire ..."

"Not, Lord Chancellor, the time," HM announced. There was no quipping now, and no equivocation.

"My boy's unhappy, Naitly," blubbed the king. "What are we going to do, Naitly, about my boy being so unhappy?"

"Youthful unhappiness, sire, is good for future leaders," Naitly told him. "It trains them for disappointment. It gives them stamina and spine. My own childhood was not devoid of unhappiness. Today I see that as a gift. It honed steel for my armour. That armour, sire, deflects many of fortune's slings and arrows. If Your Majesty will excuse me ..."

The same meeting, twice a week, was replayed week after week. Goneril started to blame Naitly for the king's inertia; and Fredvie continued to blame them both for the king's in- ... in- ... oh, for the king's – ah! – inactionlessness.

And Naitly blamed HM ... and blamed Cross-Bones ... and blamed kismet and the weather and all those idiot Belgics who stubbornly refused to understand what a good man he was, and how much good he was doing for them.

Eventually he had no choice. He had to go to war.

***

The prince continued to robot his way through the day. And then to robot his way through the next one.

The tradition of official birthdays dates from that time. The prince could not, *would* not 'celebrate' his birthday again. The reminder would simply be too painful. But the prince had to be allowed to receive gifts. Visiting emirs and legates had a need to bestow, as it were, their frankincense and myrrh.

The prince's official birthday became the 5th May. "Later Karl Marx was born on the same day," the king said in an aside to me. "When, as King Sebastian, I heard about it it was an irony which was not lost on me. Though it was apparently on Mr Marx. Nowhere in the vastness of his omnibus does Mr Marx make mention of this coincidence." I could not decide whether or not King Sebastian were joking. (May 5th is also remembered as the date on which both Napoleon and Walter Sisulu died. Sisulu was one of the very few true heroes of the twentieth century. May 5th, it turns out, is an awe-inspiring day on which to celebrate a birthday.)

At HM's suggestion, Cole started worrying in February what to give the prince for this official birthday, officially his 'ninth'. A week later, and now desperate, Cole asked HM what he should give his son. HM asked Winny. Who suggested that, maybe, ... well, his own horse.

The king summoned the Master of the Royal Horse. He'd formed the idea, he told the Master, of buying the prince his own horse. The Master of the Royal Horse was to scour Belgiss for a steed majestic enough to carry such a royal rider.

Just in time for the prince's birthday the Master of the Royal

Horse returned to Wodinton. The Master watched tearfully as the king explained to his son how he, Cole, had scoured Belgiss in order to find this magnificent beast.

It was a young mare, just over two. Her coat was chestnut, almost the same colour as Nancy's hair, her mane and tail likewise. The colouring looked almost too perfect to be natural. But natural it was. She was a touch on the small side, maybe twelve hands.

For both boy and horse it was love at first sight. The prince's eyes demisted in a single wink. He gazed with adoration on the splendid creature. And the horse understood – as horses do – that she was being gazed on adoringly, and that she would be looked after by the person so adoring her.

Charming didn't need to think about it. He called the horse 'Filly', and thus it was spelt by her grooms. In his head the prince had spelt that 'P-h-illy', but ... the prince hated making a fuss.

In later years, both as prince and king, Charming was accused of lacking imagination. It was from this misunderstanding of the spelling of his horse's name that that accusation first stemmed. Once such digs have been voiced, however, they cannot be unvoiced. They start to proliferate. And to grow roots. Soon they have become embedded. Like weeds. They are as unsightly as weeds, they mushroom as weeds do, and, like weeds, they strangle the blooms of truth.

So rapturously did Charming receive this gift that Cole, the next year, again summoned the Master of the Horse. To similar effect. That year the horse found for the prince was a piebald stallion. His *eleventh* birthday present was of a white gelding – which, for reasons known by no-one, accurately should be called a 'grey' gelding.

The king was grateful to HM. She'd solved his birthday present problem till his son reached adulthood: He'd receive one horse a year.

The prince, though, was not complaining. He called the

stallion 'Horsatio'. The gelding Winny had high hopes he would name after her. Didn't the gelding, after all, whinny? But instead he chose the name 'Peggy', short for 'Pegasus', because the horse was 'magic', because it ran so fast effectively it 'flew'.

And it flew so fast one day it threw him. This cost the prince a badly sprained ankle. It was when strapping this that Winny saw the bandaged toe. The bandage, she felt, was in urgent need of being replaced. It was thus she saw the tattoo. This sighting would entail an entire chain of consequences – not, by any means, all of them bad.

In a way similar to that he'd used on Nose, the prince trained his horses with a series of whistles, so they would do his bidding even if running free.

Far from resenting this (or him), his horses all loved the prince. Even within their stalls they could recognise his tread. And as soon as they heard it, they would hold themselves upright, they would paw the straw of the stable floor, their eyes would apparently stop blinking, their ears would point, ready to hear the slightest sound. They would neigh, all three of them. "Please choose me," each seemed to be saying. "Please, prince, choose me."

***

The year of his eleventh official birthday was to be a noteworthy one for the prince. All previous biographies claim it was at this time the prince was sent for schooling to San Pedito. (But, then, an amazing amount of his biographies make scant mention of Philomena, and none at all of Horatio.)

For far too long these years were, like Cordelia's indictment, the subject of a 'C' Notice. This 'C' Notice was lifted only a short time ago. And then only at the express command of the king. By that time myth had become history.

Much of what is taught us as 'history' is exactly this kind of myth.

Of which myth war is a great generator. It is one further reason why, despite its inevitable protests to the contrary, government has a deep-seated fondness for war. The first casualty of any war is truth. And truth is the sworn enemy of almost any government.

***

Mercia was almost never not at war. It was involved in one at this time. (Though, by comparison with what it was later to become, the 'war' Mercia was then waging could almost have been described as a skirmish.) It was pitched against the Waifu and Tay nations, whose territory shared a border with Zanoria – Mercia's Westernmost boundary and one it was eager to extend.

Dawes's gazettes at that time made scant mention of this conflict. Neither the Mercians as a whole nor the world at large therefore attached much importance to it.

The same could not be said of the situation in Orismine.

Having equipped his army liberally from Baron Richardson's stock, the sultan had made good his threats and had indeed nationalised the sultanate's gold mines.

Publicly, Dawes's gazettes had denounced in outraged fury this crime against free trade, this anti-democratic act of financial terrorism.

Privately, he and Leamore (both of whom had large shareholdings in these gold-mines) had demanded a meeting with Fredvie. At which they had instructed him, immediately, to invade Orismine. They didn't pay vast sums into the emperor's coffers merely to watch him back off from a fight – especially one demanded not only by financial responsibility but also ... well, by morality itself, for God's sake.

Fredvie had immediately seen the sense in this. These were two rootin' good friends of his, for heck's sake. And good tootin' businessmen as well. The backbone of Mercia. As well as two major rootin'-tootin' contributors to the emperor's coffers. Added to which, boy!, they could turn mean, these two guys, if they didn't get what they wanted.

To the cheers of Dawes's gazettes, Fredvie indignantly deplored the "criminal" actions of the sultan and announced the departure of an expeditionary force to oust the sultan and to liberate Orismine – 'liberate' in Fredviespeak meant 'annexe to Mercia'.

This 'liberation' was not an action approved of by a lot of the unMercian world. Fredvie therefore needed other 'independent' nations to support him. He decided Belgiss would fill such a role nicely.

Naitly was under pressure. He'd been given two years to get rid of the prince. Those two years were all but up. Naitly needed to buy some more time. Which is the actual reason why (whatever else the history books might seek to say) Naitly sent Belgic bluecoats to Orismine in support of the Mercian expeditionary force.

At that time the young prince wouldn't have cared. He cared about his animals – about Nose, Philly, Horsatio and Peggy. He cared about nothing else. Not people or places – not even ideas.

He *couldn't* care about such things. He simply couldn't. Broken hearts take time to mend. And broken hearts cannot contain care.

It was only later, only *much* later, that he would come to weep for all those Belgics killed in Orismine. Killed only so that Naitly would have more time to kill *him*.

It was only later that he would come to understand that every single name on every single war memorial is chiselled there by a million tears.

Chapter 20

No-one had known a fog like it. Oh, mists were frequent enough. But not fog. Not like this. Particularly not at the end of May. What was happening to the weather?

Most of the castle arose thus ... well, mistified.

Goneril didn't. Goneril awoke only a little after the servants. She saw the fog and she knew, this was it: the perfect day. Murder would be committed that day.

Naitly had spent the night at the castle. That wasn't unusual. He often did. Particularly if he had a meeting with the king. It saved him the time he'd otherwise need to 'travel'. Naitly was a busy man. Time was a precious commodity for him. And for Goneril. It took her no time to locate the Lord Chancellor. And she wasted no time in rousing him.

"Today, LC," she rejoiced, gleaming at her betrothed. "Look out of the window."

Naitly didn't need to stir in order to be able to do so. "It's foggy," he said. He had a penchant for stating the obvious, but this was particularly prevalent before breakfast.

"Perfect," said Goneril. She could see that the Lord Chancellor still had not ... if you will forgive the pun ... the foggiest. "Fog," she said. "Men get lost in fogs. They have accidents. Crown Princes, for instance."

In that instant the Naitly grin was back on parade, boots and buttons gleaming. It was his real grin, his Sunday best one. Three seconds after his smile, Naitly was also on parade.

Usually he scoured every tooth until it glistened like a subaltern's sabre. Today he didn't have time. The Lord Chancellor was a busy man, for goodness' sake. He hadn't time for mere fripperies and indulgences. He buffed his smile for no more than fifteen minutes, and slicked his hair for no more than twenty. He had people to see, things to do.

He found Cross-Bones still abed. And was displeased that he

should have done so. Cross-Bones belonged to that sector of society which was supposed to wait for him.

Cross-Bones shared a room in the castle's basement, only one storey above the dungeons. It was the size of a monk's cell and as cheerless as a prisoner's. There was no decoration on the stone of the walls, nothing warm or soft to mollify the cold of the floor. It was gloomy and dank. A stub of a candle perched sadly in the neck of a flagon. Nowhere was there a picture or a book. Their clothes lay in a ragged heap in one corner. In the other there was an upright chair of similar design to that on which they had beaten Horatio. The room reeked of a fetid airlessness. It exuded a lack of cheer that only compounded its natural chill. Naitly shivered as soon as he entered it.

"Today," he told them.

"Today?" asked Bones, unenthusiastically rubbing the sleep out of his eyes.

"Today's the day," Naitly explained, an impatient teacher with the class dunce.

"Today'th the day?" asked Cross.

"*The* day," said Naitly.

"Right," said Bones. With which he pulled the woollen fleece over his shoulder again, and prepared to drift back to sleep. "Oh," he said, the truth dawning a lot more slowly than the dawn itself. "*The* day."

"*The* day," Naitly confirmed and smiled. The return of his Sunday best one.

"Right," said Bones, and pulled his lame leg onto the stone floor. The good one followed. "*The* day, Mr Krantz," he told the still supine lump in the other bed.

"And what day would that be, Mithter Thtern: May Riddle day?"

There was a fragile knock at the door.

"We having a convention here, Mithter Thtern, and no-one thought fit to tell me?"

"Come in," said Naitly.

"Do make yourself at 'ome, why don't you?" Bones told him. Before Naitly could respond the door swung open, and the prince came in. He had started to become a bit gangly, his limbs weren't too sure how to operate in their new size. His voice was threatening, almost daily, to break.

It is the tradition of Western art to portray saints with haloes above their heads. That is probably because the aura around such holy people is brighter than around most of us. In a way similar to that of writers abbreviating Mister to Mr, painters have abbreviated that aura to one around the head. But it is not only saints who are surrounded with an aura. All of us are. And, whilst it is given to very few to actually *see* that aura, most of us can feel it. Animals can nearly always feel it. And so can children. That children are not embarrassed by this is one of the (many) reasons why a child's intuition appears to be so much sharper than an adult's.

The aura that surrounded the young prince, and that which also exuded from him, continued to be one of the greatest sadness. But just beginning to encroach gently on its fringes was a certain preparedness to live in the moment: to experience that moment for what it was without allowing either past or future to impinge on it too far.

There was about the prince that morning a resonance of excitement as close to happiness as, at that time, the prince was going to arrive at. Nose, of course, was with him. But the dog didn't enter the room. He growled softly from its threshold.

"I'm going riding," he announced. "I'll be waiting for you both in the stables. Good morning, Lord Chancellor," he added, surprised to find so eminent a figure in so lowly a dormitory.

"Your Royal Highness," said Naitly, allowing his grin to bow even more deeply than he did. He tried not to be alarmed by the continuing low growl which continued to emanate from Nose. Naitly knew what the hound was. The sound of his growl was like the noise of an arrow being bolted into a crossbow.

"You're very welcome to join us," the prince told him.

"If only, Your Highness. Alas, sir, the ship of state does not steer itself."

"No. Of course it doesn't," said the prince. "I'll see you in the stables," he repeated to Cross-Bones. And withdrew.

"*The* day, right," said Cross. As he had only two teeth left to clean he rarely bothered. It seemed an extravagance of toothpaste. However, neither he nor Bones wanted to get to the stables too soon. Grooming horses was not the preferred pastime of either one of them.

Nor was grooming themselves. The closest either got to spruce was less dishevelled than usual. Today was clearly a day when 'spruceness' was needed. They would need their wits about them that day. A good wash encouraged wits to hang around.

A 'good wash' was to flick a few drops of water at each palm, at their foreheads and armpits. Anything more than that was considered to be water profligacy. Their stubble remained unshaven, their hair matted both by grime and uncombedness.

In the last year or so – probably nearer to eighteen months – Bones had started 'walking out' with Winny.

Coincidentally, Cross had also started seeing Virginia – 'Ginny' as she was more commonly known.

The liaison with Cross-Bones was not one that Prim had exactly dreamed of for her daughters. Not even close, as a matter of fact. Clearly neither Cross nor Bones had incomes or prospects sufficient to winging her to the land of plenty. Thus these suits of her daughters were received by Prim ... well, primly.

Winny, for goodness' sake, was in daily contact with Baron Richardson. Didn't she have any initiative? Didn't the baron have any millionaire friends that Winny might entertain? Or who might entertain Ginny?

In her heart of hearts, Winny also knew that Stern was not her ideal man. But then, in her heart of hearts, Winny also knew that *she* was not her ideal woman. And that knowledge was agonising to her. She therefore very rarely delved that deeply. At the level above it, Winny saw herself as a beautiful and accomplished young lady. She continued to be both enraged and bewildered by the fact that mirrors seemed so avidly to disagree with that opinion. She tried to blame the mirrors. Sometimes she even succeeded.

Mirrors told her she was ugly. And ugly people, Winny knew, were lonely people. Winny was already too lonely not to accept that, bedraggled starling though he was, the Stern in her hand was a considerably better bet than whichever brace of howsoever magnificent peacocks in howsoever accessible a bush.

Likewise her job.

Looking after the Crown Prince was by far the best job Winny was ever going to get. She knew that neither it, nor indeed her head, would survive the most trivial of hiccups. She therefore applied herself to it with a diligence that was as near obsessive as made no difference.

***

Cross-Bones's worry about getting involved in the grooming was not a real one. The prince insisted on himself grooming all three of his horses. No horse ever had a better stable-lad. In horse terms, they daily had treatment from a hairdresser, a manicurist, a masseur and an aromatherapist. They had a horsy sauna, Turkish bath and make-over.

The air was energising; it smelled slightly of carbon but there was a kick of oomph in it. By the time Cross-Bones joined the prince in the royal stable, the horses were saddled and enlivened. All ready for the off, in fact. In fact, chomping at the bit. They were getting impatient. As were Nose and the prince.

Who would have been quite happy to have ventured forth

unescorted. But the sentries were under the strictest orders not raise the portcullis for the prince without his bodyguards in attendance. When these arrived, though, suddenly Nose appeared not to want to go. This was almost unprecedented. Nose loved these walks in the forest. But today he kept barking at the prince, kept trying to go back indoors.

So much so, indeed, that the prince got quite sharp with him. "Any more out of you, Nose," he told the dog, "and I'll leave you here." Nose whimpered into a sulky grizzling.

The prince had decided he would ride Philly. Cross mounted Horsatio, and Bones Peggy.

The portcullis was raised and the bridge lowered. Across which the trio galloped. Thence to the forest.

To the sentries, again lowering the portcullis, it looked like the forest had eaten the young prince.

Such was the strength of local superstition that for some time there were those who believed it had.

Chapter 21

The fog was thick, a blanket – albeit a blanket with holes in it. Totally impenetrable one minute, suddenly it would clear – just for a bit, just enough to lull the unwary into believing the danger was past; only (equally suddenly) to regather even more thickly than before.

As has already been mentioned, mists were common in Belgiss, particularly (for some reason) around Wodinton. And mists in and around the forest could be beautiful: Wisps of cloud would hang off the branches like Christmas tinsel, strands of it would be caught on needles as if they were goats' hair, plumes would lattice the bracken like feathers. This, though, was not that kind of mist.

This wasn't any kind of a mist, in fact, but a fog. A fog that was cold and forbidding. The ancient Greeks believed, in order to get to the after-life, the dead had to cross a river, the Styx. This was the fog you'd imagine hung over the Styx. There was something infernal about it, something sinister and forbidding.

In this fog the forest, eerie at the best of times, became daunting. "Abandon hope," it seemed to wail, "all ye who enter here." To ride in it was preposterously dangerous. Fallen branches, a hazard even on the brightest days, in this pea-soup were invisible; each pace could be one into a quicksand. Unseen hazards shadowed every move. On horseback even to have *walked* through the forest in such conditions would have been perilous to the point of lunacy. The prince, though, wanted to *gallop* through it.

He couldn't, of course, see the faces of Cross-Bones. But in his mind's eye he could picture them: So hard would they be frowning that their wrinkles would seem to be chiselled into their faces. Bones would be biting his lower lip and Cross would be stabbing at his with his solitary upper tooth. Their eyes would be riveted in both concentration and terror. Sweat would be coursing through the furrowed gulches.

The prince laughed aloud. It was a harsh laugh, even a cruel one. It had about it not the slightest shred of charm, not even of humanity. It knelled, indeed, like a laugh from the grave: Because, on the day that Philly and Horatio had been killed, the prince too had died.

Not literally, of course; and not, of course, that the prince realised it. Not as such. It was inside of himself that he knew – in that part deep within himself where language never ventures. His continuing presence on Earth was a parenthesis, no more, a brief breathing space whilst his body twigged on to what his soul already knew ... no, what his soul had sensed: that he had passed on, or passed away ... that he had ... died.

You cannot die twice. And that consciously the prince knew. Having already claimed him, death therefore no longer posed any threat to him. The prince could treat it with a disdain – with almost a contempt – denied those of us still living.

And so he galloped fearlessly, the prince. He galloped with disdain, and with a contempt for those who were frightened to gallop. He enjoyed their fear. And he enjoyed his contempt for it. He galloped deep into the forest, the prince. Galloped as if his life depended on it.

Nose galloped beside him, less disdainful than his master. He seemed anxious, constantly looking behind him, apparently checking the whereabouts of the other two riders.

Boof! The dog ran straight into a tree.

As he reeled from the shock he yelped appallingly. The prince tugged gently on Philly's reins. But the horse had already sensed the prince's wishes. She thundered to a skidded halt.

The prince leapt from her back to tend to the wounded dog.

Nose was concussed, and was weaving about, as it were, drunkenly. The prince was horror-struck. He suddenly realised how reckless it had been, his riding. He had endangered Nose. How could he have been so stupid? So irresponsible? He'd endangered his horses as well, and Cross-Bones.

He felt around Nose's body for broken bones. Nothing. If dogs got headaches, Nose would have one for a day or two. But nothing more serious appeared to be wrong with him.

Just as the prince was finishing this examination, so Cross-Bones bedraggledly arrived. They took a moment or two to catch their breath. Still the fog was too dense to make out anything but the haziest of detail.

The prince was shaking. He realised he could have killed one of these creatures. He was experiencing the terror of that. In that terror he realised that even the dead have a responsibility to life, to cherish it, to allow those alive to live it. Being dead does not entitle you to confiscate the life of others.

"Sorry," the prince murmured to his bodyguards. And then more loudly he repeated, "Sorry. I wasn't thinking. Sorry." He patted Philly, who was standing nearby. He went over to stroke Horsatio's head and to scratch Peggy's nose. The apology was also directed at them – maybe, even, *especially* directed at them.

Cross-Bones had dismounted. They were trying to shake their legs free of the jelly which had overrun them.

"God knowth where we are," said Cross.

"We'll never find our way back," said Bones. He was still panting deeply, plumes of frozen breath hiccupping from his nose and mouth. The horses were panting too, their breath also frozen, steam rising from their bodies as if they were standing guard before a bonfire.

"Horses can always find their way home," the prince reassured them.

"That a fact?" asked Cross, with a knowing leer at Bones.

"Well known," said the prince.

For a moment the fog retreated. They could see that they were in some sort of clearing. Bluebells seemed to carpet the whole area. A way down the path, Bones also noticed, lay the trunk of a silver birch.

Bones knew the moment had come. *The* moment had come. He looked to Cross – who also knew this was it, the moment.

Nose was still woozy, but he was regaining sobriety by the minute.

Never, and Cross-Bones knew it, would fate present them with a better opportunity. They knew what they had to do. This was the moment of their destiny.

Their throats were dry, their tongues were cemented to the roof of their mouths, their hearts were beating like tom-toms played by dervishes.

They were watching Nose with eagle eyes, waiting for the moment that the concussion passed and he could again be relied on to do their bidding.

Discreetly Bones tied the reins of both Horsatio and Peggy to a fallen trunk. This alarmed the horses. Still shaken by his recent conduct, the prince failed to notice this.

Equally discreetly, Cross picked up a sturdy, truncheon-thick stick.

The prince continued to be abject. "I had no right," he said. "No *right*. Not to risk your lives like that, Nose's, the horses'. You all right, boy?" he asked Nose. "You okay? I'm so sorry, Nose. So very sorry." His face and the dog's were millimetres apart. Nose returned the prince's rueful gaze with one not only of forgiveness, but of adoration.

The prince's neck was exposed. It would offer no resistance at all to a set of frenzied fangs: a knife through melted butter.

The prince would die instantly.

And if he didn't ... well ... to put him out of any misery, Cross had the stick ready to deliver a coup-de-grâce.

"Peppermint!" commanded Cross.

Nose stopped his playfulness and adoration. Dr Jekyll kerpowed into Mr Hyde. His yellow eyes steeled into malevolence. His fur bristled into porcupine quills. He snarled viciously.

He looked at Cross.

And then he glowered at the prince.

Who had no idea at all what was happening. "Nose?" he asked, perplexed.

The dog looked back at Cross, then back at the prince.

At Cross. At the prince.

At Cross.

And he lunged.

And he savaged the stick Cross was holding, reducing it to splinters!

Chapter 22

The prince whistled at Nose. But the dog kept on savaging. He whistled again, more frantically. Never had he known his dog to behave in this extraordinary way. Was it the fog? The concussion? What?

For *his* part, though, Nose seemed not about to obey anything other than his bloodlust – or, apparently more accurately, his timberlust!

Once finished with Bones's stick, therefore, he went off in search of a similar one. Which in seconds he found, and in even less seconds had also reduced to kindling. This seemed momentarily to appease him.

He turned his vicious eyes on Cross. And started menacing towards him, snarling, threatening. Cross soon found himself backed up against an ancient and unyielding oak. Too terrified to speak, he looked to Bones for help. Bones looked back: Include him out. There was *no way* he was going to intervene. There was even a part of him quite enjoying the spectacle.

"Thpearmint," Cross commanded. Still the dog advanced, snarling, threatening. "Thpearmint – there'th a good doggy – thpearmint, thpear-bloody-mint." He added a final, desperate "*Thpear*MINT."

The edge of panic in his voice was serrated. Still Nose's hackles were raised.

Still the prince kept on whistling at him.

The dog turned his attention from Cross to Bones. Now that it was he the object of canine attention, Bones suddenly found the scene a lot less entertaining.

"Spearmint!" Bones commanded. And instantly Nose reverted to the lolloping hound that the prince had only ever known him as. "*Th*pearmint!" Bones sneered at Cross, mimicking his lisp.

"Spearmint?" the prince asked, as he started stroking the dog which had now returned to him.

"No, thankth all the thame, Your 'ighneth," said Bones, trying again to find paniclessness and equilibrium.

"No, that's not what I meant. You just said … oh, skip it," said the prince. "It's not important." He turned his attention to the dog. "You okay now, boy? What was it? See a snake or something, did you? All right, boy? All right?"

"I think, sir, beggin' your pardon an' that, we should be, like, 'eading back," said Bones. "Fog gets much thicker, not even the 'orses is going to find their way 'ome."

"I'm afraid Nose isn't yet quite himself," replied the prince. "Just give me five minutes, let me walk him round for a bit."

"Five minuteth, your Highneth, not going to make any differenthe, ith it, one way or the other!" jollied Cross, before whispering crossly to Bones, "You mad? What? Go back to the cathtle?! We've got to … you know … him."

Bones had unknotted the reins he had secured to the trunk. Horsatio's he gave to Cross. "When the fog lifted, did you see that silver birch?"

"What thilver birch?"

"It's the silver birch we used to mark the quicksand." He mounted Peggy.

"Ah!"

"'Is 'Ighness really oughtn't to be galloping in these conditions, Mr Krantz."

"We kept trying to tell him, thire," said Bones, now astride Horsatio.

"But would 'e listen? Would 'e, pardonin' my French, 'ell!"

"Your Majethty," Cross mimicked his address to the king.

And Bones echoed, "Your Majesty." They laughed cutthroatly. There was no fun in that laughter, only maliciousness.

"Okay, gentlemen," said the prince. "Nose seems to be all right. I'll get him checked out back at the castle by the vet. I think you're right, Mr Stern, the fog seems to be coming down even more thickly."

"Fanthy, your Highneth, making a rathe of it?"

"You know I'll win," snorted the prince.

"I am riding Peggy," Bones reminded him.

"Even so, Mr Stern. Still, if it would give you pleasure. I'll give you a start. Two minutes, say."

"Your Highneth joketh with uth. He knowth we can't do that; knowth we cannot let him – you, thir – out of our thight."

"Ready, then?" asked the prince, and without awaiting their reply, continued, "Steady … Go." With which he and Philly galloped off.

Cross-Bones had thought to stay a prudent distance behind. Peggy and Horsatio, however, had other ideas. They thundered behind their stable-mate, almost in her dust. It was only by using all their weight to haul back on the reins that Cross-Bones were able even to check their horses' gallop.

Philly was galloping hell for leather towards the fallen birch.

For Philly the obstacle was nothing, a mere toothpick that could easily be skipped over.

She would jump the hurdle breezily and land, plop, straight into the lethal mire beyond.

Out of which, for neither horse nor rider, would escape be possible.

Cross-Bones allowed a broad smirk to pass between them. No more cell-like bedrooms, or ugly girlfriends, no more second-hand clothes and hand-me-downs; riches would be theirs, prestige, status. And the fall which they'd been told since infancy was the consequence of pride? That fall would only be the prince's – his and Philly's.

Closer the silver birch was getting. Closer, closer.

They could see detail on the trunk now, a gnarled knot, a natural sack of sap. And they could see too how confidently, even scornfully, Philly was approaching the jump. This, her determined flanks were proclaiming, was a hurdle even a colt could jump, even a pony.

What no-one had told them, though, is that most horses can smell quicksand – and it spooks them. It may only have been at the last minute, but Philly was true to her species.

Suddenly her head shot up in the air, she whinnied loudly and just as she was preparing to launch she swerved violently to her left.

Horsatio and Peggy were immediately behind her.

Peggy also smelled the quicksand and swerved to its right. Horsatio, though, had nowhere to go. To the, almost, squeal of hooves, he just slammed on the anchors.

And Cross went sailing straight through his ears.

Plop into the quicksand.

Horsatio didn't hang around. Without a moment's hesitation, he turned tail and started to gallop back the way he had just come. The prince whistled – but to no effect at all.

Before even he had started to do so, Peggy reared. It threw Bones off its back and onto the mossy ground beneath. It also wasted not a second in galloping back the way it had just come. Again the prince's whistles seemed not to be heard.

Nose was barking at the prince. He started running after the horses. Then returned to see why it was his master had not followed.

The prince himself was caught on the horns of a huge dilemma. He loved his horses. He did not love Cross. He had never loved him, but since the beating ... Well, frankly, he had wished more than a few times for just such an occurrence, prayed indeed for the man to die.

But now that he was dying ... there ... in front of him ... it was different. He was floundering in the mire. His eyes streamed terror and panic and supplication. "Help," he screamed. "For God'th thake, help."

He couldn't simply leave the man to die. He couldn't. Not like this.

Still Nose was barking at him.

In the distance he could see that Horsatio and Peggy had ceased their bolting. It was almost as if they were waiting for the prince to catch them up.

The prince had dismounted, and was looking around for some sort of pole to haul Cross from the bog.

A winded Bones, however, got there first. He dragged a bushy spruce branch with him. Using all his might he managed to upend this so that it lay within Cross's grasp. Cross started hauling himself in.

"You couldn't, I thuppothe, Mithter Thtern," he panted at his colleague, "have found a pricklier branch? What'th the matter," he spluttered as he spat out the quicksand's gunk, "no holly anywhere?"

The prince saw that the man was safe. He therefore knew his next obligation was to go and tend to his frightened horses.

As he was remounting Philly he heard Bones reply, "I could jus' leave you to die, Mister Krantz."

"Horses," he told both men, as he prepared to gallop away. "I've got to go and get the horses." He could hold Philly no longer. Almost imitating the drive of a greyhound she shot out of 'the slips' and charged after her two missing stable-mates.

Nose loped alongside. His tongue bounced freely. He gazed adoringly at his young master. The dog looked more relaxed than he had done at any stage in the ride.

Chapter 23

Only later did the prince understand that Nose and the horses were trying to save his life. Maybe in the same way that they could smell quicksand they could also smell skulduggery. At the time it just seemed to him that the horses – the, even, "bloody horses" – were … well, almost teasing him.

They would gallop off into the distance, wait for the prince to get to within grabbing distance, and then gallop off again. The prince was far from amused with the 'game'. The more so, as it seemed to him, fog and dusk were both getting thicker. But no amount of secret whistling, no amount of ranting or pleading seemed to have the slightest effect on the recalcitrant beasts.

With each little teasing caper, they got deeper into the forest, further away from the castle – further away from *anything*, in fact, which was familiar to the prince.

The prince started to become anxious. So anxious indeed that at one stage he feigned abandoning the two loose horses, and steered Philly in the direction of home – or steered her, rather, in the direction he *thought* was home, that *Nose* told him was home.

Apparently, though, both Nose and Philly were also in on the conspiracy. Because after an hour of what the prince was sure was setting Philly on homebound tracks he found himself back at the same place from which he'd started.

The tepid sun continued to be masked by the fog. The prince therefore had only one timepiece left to tell him the time of day: the rumbling of his tummy. This was a watch which tended to run fast.

Lunch had been and gone. So had afternoon tea. The prince was sure of it. When his tummy growled at him that it had to be night it was actually no later than early evening. But the prince decided, if it were already night, they'd be better off resting up, hoping that in their sleep the fog would lift, and making an early start the following morning.

Meantime, his timepiece was also telling him he was ravenous. What to eat? He knew the forest well as a sports ground, but not at all as a larder. What on earth *could* you eat?

He noticed the horses were grazing on a bush. Maybe he too should try that bush. Then he remembered, horses also ate yew, and yew can kill them. Horses, he therefore deduced, were not the safest food-tasters in the world. He opted for hunger and safety. He found a few nuts he knew were okay, and drank from a brook which appeared to be clean.

He also found a fallen elm, hollowed out by the forest's termites.

He unsaddled Philly. He scratched her nose. She tossed her head in appreciation, then continued to graze. Having seen this happen, Horsatio and Peggy approached so that they might also be so disencumbered.

Off all of their backs the prince pulled the caparisons. These would serve as a blanket. He would need something substantial to ward off the night's chill. Still desperately hungry, but even more tired, he crawled into his canoe-like bed and pulled the caparisons right over his head. Nose curled up on top of those blankets and nestled into the crook of his legs. The prince felt entirely safe. There was nothing in the forest foolhardy enough to challenge Nose.

He suddenly realised that never indeed had he felt *safer*. Nor, despite his hunger, had he ever felt more at peace.

***

Elsewhere in the forest Cross-Bones were making their way blindly back towards the castle.

Bones's gammy leg was hurting him badly. Cross was still coated in the quicksand's slime. They'd made a half-hearted attempt to clean off the worst. But they didn't want to clean it too well: they needed the gunk to substantiate their story.

"You could've crowned 'im one, Mr Krantz."

"You don't have a dog, Mithter Thtern, and bark yourthelf."

"No, Mr Krantz, *you* 'as a dog, s'pposed to savage princes, 'stead savages twigs!"

"And jutht how ecthactly ith that *my* fault?" Cross sniped back.

"We're going to die out here. You do know that?"

Had they done so, the future history of Belgiss would have been entirely different. It is not only kings and generals who dictate the course of history. Indeed (again despite what our school history books tell us) it is *rarely* by such luminaries that history is dictated.

Cross-Bones plodded on. Weary, despondent. Dead in the water. Dead if they stayed in the forest, dead if they returned to the castle. Strategy was called for. They started to devise one.

If the prince were still alive, – "sure as eggs is eggs" – he'd report them for attempted murder. It'd be his word against theirs. And he was a Crown Prince. That served in a Court of Belgic law much better than any evidence. Their goose would be cooked. Roasted, stuffed and basted.

But ... Alone in the forest, the chances were extremely good that he *would* fall into another quicksand, or be savaged by wolves or bears or something. If the prince were *dead*, there was still a chance they could make this situation work for them.

Still embroiled in their strategying, Cross-Bones almost missed the sound nearby of conversation. Indeed it was only because that conversation was so loud that they did hear it. They "hello"ed loudly.

A small detachment of cavalry came bounding towards them. Winny was within them. And at its head was the seriously unjokering figure of HM.

Like most jesters, HM was at heart deeply serious. Nothing did she take more seriously than tracking. She was certainly the best tracker at Court, probably in the whole country. And tracking the heir to the throne ... Well, there was no levity allowed for in that. None at all.

"Where's the prince?" she demanded. "The king is frantic."

Cross-Bones elongated their long faces still longer.

Winny caught the look. "Oooooh," she wailed, "my job. My *baby*, I mean, for pity's sake. My poor, poor royal baby. Dead?"

"Quickthand, HM. There wath no thaving him."

"Mr Krantz ... well, you can see it, 'e dived in after 'im. You can tell, can't you, just by the state of 'im?"

"We did try to rethcue him. We did all that wath humanly pothible."

Winny, still mounted, was sat with her arms wide open, waiting for Bones to come and comfort her. Bones, though, was rather more concerned with HM and her attitude: His entire future hung on them.

"And where are his horses?" HM asked.

"Bolted, HM. We tried to catch 'em. But, well, 'orses are 'orses, ain't they?"

"You're going to die, gentlemen," HM told them.

"'Scuthe me, your high-and-mightineth, '*scuthe* me, but we're something like heroeth, uth – me, at any rate – diving into the mire like that, rithking life and limb ..."

"*Slowly* you will die, gentlemen, trust me," HM continued as if Cross had said nothing, "and painfully. Useless Eustace will do his worst." Bones tried to gulp, found he couldn't. "I know what your little game is. You've got one chance, gentlemen, and only one: You do exactly what I say. You follow my orders to the letter – to the curlicue, gentlemen, of that letter.

"You say nothing to the king. You understand? Not one word. As far as the king's concerned the prince is missing, no more. You know only that the prince is lost, and that I have gone on alone to find him."

"There'th no point." Cross tried to camouflage despair for his life with that for the prince's.

"Where there's no evidence of death, Mr Krantz, it has to be supposed there is life. And where there is life … there is *every* point, Mr Krantz."

"I'll come with you," Winny volunteered.

"I need to move fast," HM told her, not unkindly. "I can move faster alone. That his horses aren't already back at the castle means, in my opinion, the prince is still alive. Though in what state, who can say? I suspect he might just have made a 'miraculous' return from the quicksand. On my return, gentlemen, you and I will have a little chat. I represent your only hope, gentlemen, of salvation."

"Yes, ma'am. Thank you, ma'am."

But HM didn't hear them. She had already galloped off.

Winny wasn't too sure about letting Bones share her saddle. He hadn't come to cuddle her in her hour of want – and appearances certainly seemed to indicate that very shortly he would, at best, be minus a job, if not minus a head. Dating an ugly man was one thing. A jobless or a headless one was quite another.

But her renowned pragmatism soon returned to her. He wasn't headless *yet*, was he? And at least sight of Bones in her saddle would confirm to her doubting girlfriends that she did indeed have a beau. Cross rode pillion with one of the soldiers.

***

HM hunted Charming like a thing possessed. To find the prince she knew she'd need every ounce of her tracking skill. Fog didn't annihilate tracks, in the way, for instance, snow did, or rain. But it did make them harder to find. Snapped twigs were less easy to spot, crushed toadstools and animal droppings had to be looked for.

But, freed from the irksomeness of being the Court jester, allowed for a moment to be her own serious self, Mandy not only knew she had the skill that would be required, but she had the ambition too with which to complement it. She *would* find the prince. She would.

She owed it to herself. And to the country.

***

"What do you mean," asked Goneril of Cross-Bones, "you *think* he's dead?"

"The evidenth, your Highneth, would theem to indicate ath much."

The king had been too distraught even to see the two minders. A lackey had entered the king's study to announce them. They had heard a goblet crashing against a studded door. The lackey emerged to tell them that their presence was not desired.

It *was* desired, however, at the Decadence. From the king's office they had been marched straight thither. Cross still hadn't had time to change his mired clothes.

Naitly and Goneril had been waiting for them. No sign of the Naitly smile now, neither his real nor his prosthetic one.

"Seem? *Seem*?" he ranted. "*Seem* to *indicate*?!"

"It *was* foggy, Lord Chancellor."

"Definitely," said Cross. "Foggy, definitely. Very."

"HM's gone looking?" Goneril asked.

"Quickthand'th quickthand, your Highneth. Not even HM can find someone buried by quickthand."

"You'll be lucky, the pair of you," Naitly threatened, "to escape with your lives."

"Oh God!" exclaimed Goneril.

"What's the matter, pumpkin?" Naitly asked meekly.

"How you got to be Lord Chancellor ... well, frankly, 'my dear', sometimes it just amazes me."

"What, pumpkin, have I done now?"

"You've got Fredvieitis, LC. Clearly it's contagious. The only possible way that we're going to extricate ourselves from this with any credit, 'my dear'," she said icily, "is to acknowledge these two men as heroes."

Cross-Bones looked at her, gob-smacked. Then at each other. And then they wagged their heads philosophically. Well, fair do's, really. I mean, when you thought about it, they *were* heroes really, weren't they? Yeah, *real* heroes.

***

HM continued her tracking throughout the night.

The prince was awakened the next dawn by the smell and crackle of a camp fire. Even more enticing than *that* smell, though, was that of bacon sizzling on an open flame.

He bleared into the early morning sunlight.

HM was cooking breakfast for him.

Chapter 24

Al fresco ablution was a new experience for the prince. The brook water was icy to the touch, and it caused his teeth to hurt. But, once it was over, it was an experience which invigorated him. Once HM's bacon had been ravenously devoured he felt ready for any rigour the day may hold.

"You want the bad news first, sir, or the good news?" HM asked.

"Always the bad news first, HM. *Always.*"

"The bad news, sir, is that there is no good news."

The prince gave a doleful chuckle. "Okay. The way back's going to be tough, is that what you're trying to tell me?"

"No, sir, not exactly. It would be truer, sir, to say, that there is *no* way back." The prince didn't understand. "The Court is not safe for you, sir. And it can't be made safe. There are too many enemies there, in positions of too much eminence."

"Isn't it for that reason, HM, that I have Cross-Bones to protect me?"

"It's a good name for them: Like pirates they're cut-throats." HM took her time. "They're not there to protect you, sir, but to kill you."

The prince considered this for a bit. "No!" he finally responded, with an incredulity that was rapidly waning. "You're joking again, right?"

"I never joke about your welfare, sir."

Again the prince reflected for a silent while. "And Winny?" he asked eventually. "Is she too trying to kill me?"

"Winny, sir, was *my* suggestion," HM replied deliberately.

"Oh." The prince slowly absorbed the information. He let it sink. And as it sank so it also hurt. Deeply. More deeply yet. "Right."

"My brother, sir, captains a galleon ..."

"The *Silver Hart*, I know."

"It's still moored at Blefton. I've spoken to him."

"Spoken to him, HM?"

"We correspond, sir, by carrier pigeon. He's prepared to take you to Azrac."

"To *Cordelia*? Now, Cordelia, she *did* try to kill me."

"No, sir, she didn't. Think about it. What possible motive did she have? Why was she never brought to trial? You'll be safe with Cordelia. She loves you, sir, as much as I do. Trust me."

"And what does my father have to say about all this?"

"Your father is, of course, distraught. But your father is not one ever to shrink from doing the right thing just because of any pain it may cause him."

"Well, I suppose, in that case, Blefton, here we come."

"I'd like you to change into these, sir." HM produced from her saddle-bag a suit of clothes. They weren't those of an urchin – the softness of the prince's skin and manner would not long countenance that depth of disguise – but neither were they those of a prince. Normality for the prince was beginning to lose some of the sheen with which his imagination had endowed it.

***

The ride to Blefton was a long one. Made longer by the fact that HM wanted to keep within the forest for as long as possible. She didn't want anyone seeing the prince. The disguise was adequate, but *only* adequate – and that only outside the castle's vicinity.

For a similar reason she didn't want to get to Blefton before nightfall. Any witness to their flight was a potential hole in the bucket of HM's plan – any witness to HM even *being* in the Blefton area.

As so often on the day after a fog, the light that day was particularly strong. The shafts that pierced the overgrowth did so forcefully, like arrows. There was a newness to the forest, a freshness – almost a rebirth. On other occasions it would have been a joyous ride.

They stopped by a stream, to let the horses rest for a bit and drink. They dismounted.

"Talking, sir, of pain ..." There was a nervousness in HM's voice which boded the prince no well at all.

"Ye-es?"

"Nose, sir."

"Nose?"

"My brother's got a cat. Ridiculous moggy, but he's devoted to it. Keeps the rats away, he claims. But for that reason ... Well – there's no easy way of saying this, sir: – Sir, he won't allow dogs on board."

"Well, he'll have to make an exception, HM. I *am* the Crown Prince. Remind him of that."

"There are no exceptions, sir, trust me. I'm so sorry."

"Then I'm not going, HM," the prince said obdurately. "If I can't have Nose with me, then I'm not going."

"You *can* have Philly, sir, and Peggy and Horsatio. If you stay, they'll kill Nose to get at you. These are ruthless people, sir. Trust me. You wouldn't, would you, want Nose's death also on your conscience?"

"No," said the prince, too choked to say anything more. His heart was cleaving. He knew, though, if he allowed himself the tears he wanted it would upset the dog. And his upset at upsetting the dog would be several upsets too many.

"There'll be other dogs in Azrac, sir," HM sought to console him.

"None of them will be Nose," the prince snapped back. As if on cue, the dog arrived and pushed his snout into the prince's hand. The prince smiled, a smile of sadness, and stroked his head.

HM noted the sadness. "I have – trust me – plans afoot. God willing, in a month or two you'll be coming home again. I'll look after Nose till then."

"You promise?"

"Jester's honour!"

"I'm not joking, HM."

"I understand that. Trust me."

"*You*, HM, you. You have to promise me, HM, that *you'll* look after him: feed him, see he gets enough exercise, stroke him from time to time."

"It won't even be a duty, sir, but a privilege."

"Thank you, HM."

For the rest of the ride HM tried to revive the prince's spirits. She ran through an entire repertoire of jests, japes and jokes. But the prince was inconsolable. If it had only been his own life that would be endangered he would not have gone. That was still of little consequence to him. It was only the threat to Nose which persuaded him. Too many had already been killed. Already *far* too many.

Nose seemed to sense that something was about to happen. Never had he strayed far from his master. On this trip, though, until they got to Blefton, he seemed glued to him.

Each time they stopped to water and rest the horses, Nose demanded attention. And each time the prince gave him that attention it was with heavier heart. Because each stop meant they were closer to Blefton. Closer therefore to their separation.

And closer to the prince's new life.

***

Before he could see the sea, the prince could hear it. And there was, in that rhythmic crashing of waves on shingle, something both mystic and reassuring.

Despite his misery, maybe even because of it, the prince at that moment had what can only be described as a Canute moment: A moment when he realised just how feeble was the power of the so-called powerful.

Throughout his young life, the prince had been surrounded by those powerful people – both those with genuine power, and those who imagined they had it. He had been surrounded by Belgic people of power, and by powerful people from throughout the globe. And not one of those people, not even all of those people together, could affect, not by one single drop, the way those waves crashed on the beach.

It is the vanity of mankind, the prince realised at that moment, to think of itself as 'powerful'. Like most vanities, that one too contained elements that were both toxic and pernicious.

Blefton had the reputation for being somewhat posh. True, the prince and HM arrived under the cover of darkness. But the prince could see little evidence to substantiate the poshness of its reputation.

The main thoroughfare, the King's Parade, was full of Richardson's emporia, the frontages of which were identical to those of his emporia in Wodinton or, come to that, even in the far reaches. It was also full of stray dogs who would have been interested in Nose had the latter not snarled back at them his active *dis*interest.

If the King's Parade was the river, its tributaries were narrow, ill-lit alleys. Against the corners of which leant floozies in stained and scarlet dresses, clay pipes dangling from ulcerated mouths. And from the depths of which reeled drunken matelots looking for a place, apparently, to throw up.

Again long before he could see it, the prince could smell the sea. But the musk of ozone, usually one so uplifting and wholesome, was here encrusted with the reek of stale ale and sweat and that inescapable, almost tangible, tang of grubbiness.

Nose was lagging now *behind* the horses. He followed only when otherwise he would lose sight of them. The prince sensed this was happening. But he didn't dare look around to confirm it. The outside of his face was bland, but inside, akin to caves whose walls are lined with water, his cheeks were running with tears. It was only with the greatest of effort that he was able to hold the flood within.

HM knew what was happening to the prince. She didn't want to add to his pain by telling him she was aware of it. She therefore chose to continue her jollying of him. And not because that would stop his pain, but because it would enable him to veil it.

In the relative still of the night, the clop of the horses' hooves on the cobbles sounded like the hammering of a wooden stake. It felt like that to the prince, each blow driving the stake deeper into his heart, cleaving it more and more in two. Deeper, deeper.

The *Silver Hart* was a magnificent three-master. Moored and in the moonlight it looked more magnificent yet, its rigging like silver cobwebs glistening on the ebony trunks which were its masts. The prince could hear the timber creaking and the rope stretching, he could hear the water lapping against the ship's hull. Were it not that he was so shortly to be separated from Nose he might have been entranced by these sounds. As it was, though, all the sensations seemed imbued with menace, as if they were all part of a hostile world determined to separate him from anything dear to him.

"I think, sir, we should leash Nose now."

"Couldn't you have another word with your brother, HM?"

"Trust me, sir, I did my best. He just wouldn't hear of it."

"And you're sure, HM – like a hundred per cent – that they would kill him to get at me?"

"Trust me," HM replied gently but firmly.

The prince had dismounted. Nose had disappeared. "Got any rope?" the prince asked. HM, who if born at a later time would have made an exemplary girl-guide, passed him the length she had brought for precisely that purpose. The prince received it as if it were the noose which was going to hang him.

A light breeze started to blow. Charming could hear the water lapping more energetically against the hull, could hear it rustling the canvas of the sails. He could also hear the mumble of distant talk.

Nose had disappeared. The prince whistled. Usually when the prince whistled it was bounding that Nose returned to his side. This time he sidled there, as if he'd done something wrong.

"I'll miss you, Nose," the prince told him as he put the halter around his neck. "You have no idea how much, boy, I'm going to miss you." Nose tried to wag his tail, but the effort was lacking in conviction.

HM tied Nose's leash to a capstan. The dog had never been tethered before. At this stage he was just perplexed by the experience. He didn't understand either the purport or the import of his tethering.

Dismounted already, the prince continued to walk until he got to the gangplank, around which a group of maritime Cross-Bones-alikes was chewing the cud and quids of tobacco – spitting out expertly the tanned saliva into the water between ship and jetty.

"Captain Bligh on board?" HM asked one of the sailors. He had cornflower eyes and had set his straw hat at what he thought was a jaunty angle. The sailor spat out yet another great gob of tobacco juice and, his head now at an angle to match his hat, nodded that he was.

HM had tethered her own horse next to Nose. Squeezing past the sailor who, sat at the bottom of the gangplank, clearly had no intention of moving, she led Peggy and Philly aboard. The prince led Horsatio. The clomp of the hooves on the unsupported wood of the gangplank was even more resonant, and drove the stake deeper. Deeper, deeper.

Clearly they were expected. As they arrived on the deck there was a sailor waiting to take the horses to their quarters. He had a scar which ran the length of his left cheek. The prince patted each of the horses and assured them he would come and visit them soon.

They found the captain leaning over the handrail of the ship's stern, gazing at the moon's shimmering reflection on the sea. Brother and sister embraced. "This is Squire Wodinton," HM told him. "The gentleman we talked of."

"Delighted, Squire," the captain said with a grin as broad as his Blefton accent, "as to how to make your acquaintance."

"How do you do, sir?" the prince enquired and extended his hand.

"Well, I do right well, thankee, Squire," chuckled the captain, as his huge hand effectively clammed over the more modest one of the prince. "I do, as you might say, Squire, *royally* well."

"I have to get going," HM said, in a tone which sought to hide sadness behind brusqueness.

"As do we," the captain chuckled yet again. "Time and tide, as the wise man said, waits for no man."

"I'll send you the pigeon back ..." HM added, with an emphasis to her brother denoting some kind of secret, "... just as soon as I know." She took the carrier with two pigeons in it.

"Might I just say good-bye to Nose, sir?"

"Nose?"

"His dog, brother."

"No shilly-shallying, then. Time and tide, as the wise man said, ..."

The ship was gathering in activity with the passing of each second. It was a tiger waking up from sleep, stretching, preparing itself for a hunt, about to start.

HM and the prince trotted down the gangplank, which bounced alarmingly as they did so.

Nose was sat, even tranquilly. His gaze was centred on the gangplank. He seemed not even to blink. As the prince approached so he rose, and performed as much of a gavotte as his tether would allow him.

"Good-bye, boy," Charming told the dog, scratching his head between his ears. "I'll see you soon, Nose. Just as soon as I can. I promise. You will look after him, HM?"

"Trust me, sir. Remember, show the toe to no-one. To no-one, sir. They won't know what it means but it will arouse suspicion."

"Thanks, HM. Thanks too ... well, for everything. You know."

"Yes, sir," said HM gently, "I know."

"'Bye, boy," the prince said finally. He had to run up the gangplank. No other momentum would have got him to the top. And he rushed then to the far side of the galleon. Again he *had* to. He didn't dare risk a glance back at Nose.

Who for a moment or two watched the empty gangplank. And then watched it being raised.

As it rose, so, almost in synch with it, the dog raised his snout to the moon.

And he howled.

This was not the howl of the hunt. It was a wail of loss. It was the howl of a dam who had lost her cub.

Chapter 25

Nose had started to realise what was the purport and import now of the tether. He was bucking against it like a bronco in a rodeo.

And he howled. And howled. And kept howling.

He kept howling as the hawsers were released and the sails set. He kept howling as sailors swung through the rigging and ran along the decks. And when, like some gigantic swan, the ship glided effortlessly into the open sea, he howled his abject despair.

Each of those howls Charming swallowed whole.

The captain's geniality was clearly a landlubber. From the moment the *Silver Hart* pulled away from the jetty, it was seen no more. "And just what in the name of all what's holy does you think you mights be doing?" he asked 'Squire Wodinton'.

"Nothing," the boy replied, trying not let his voice snuffle as much as it wanted to.

"Nothing?" roared the captain. "*Nothing*? No-one, Squire, does nothing on board this ship. D'you hears that? The *Silver Hart* do not take passengers."

"Sorry. I didn't know."

"Sorry, what?"

"Sorry, *sir*."

"Remember that, Squire. Sir or Captain. Never nothing."

"Yes, sir."

"*Aye-aye*, sir," Bligh corrected him unpleasantly.

"Aye-aye, sir," the prince repeated. Nose howled again. Again the howl tore through him.

"You finds the galley, Squire Wodinton, and you finds the cook. And you asks the cook, Squire Wodinton, for the captain's grog. And then, Squire Wodinton, you brings it to me. Straight away. Thinks your delicate little brain can handle all that, Squire?"

"Ye- … Aye-aye, sir."

"You'rse still here?!" bellowed the captain, apparently unable to believe such a breach in naval discipline. The prince scurried away, Nose's haunting howls lacerating the whole inside of him.

"Excuse me, sir," he asked of one of the sailors, him of the cornflower eyes, the one with his hat at a rakish angle, "could you, do you think, direct me to the galley?"

"Galley?"

"I think that's what he said."

"Oh, galley's what he said, right enough," the sailor confirmed. With a wink to his colleague – him who had been sat at the bottom of the gangplank – he pointed to the crow's nest, the look-out point at the very top of the central, and highest, mast. "There 'tis. Right there, see. At the top of that there mast there."

"And might that be where the cook is also? I have to find the cook as well."

"Oh, he be a mighty short man the cook be," the sailor told him. "Happen that's why you can't see him from here. He's up there, all right. Lurking, like as not, behind one of the sails or some such."

"And that's the galley?" the prince asked again, again uncertainly.

"You calling me a liar?" the sailor asked threateningly.

"Oh no, sir. Sorry, sir. *Very* sorry."

"Well, snap to it, lad," said the second sailor. "Don't want to keep the cook waiting."

"No, sir. Thank you, sir."

The prince started to climb the rigging.

Like many skills the accomplished make this look easy. The apprentice rigging-climber, however, finds himself constantly slipping and swinging, sliding and wobbling; he finds himself burning his palms, scraping his thighs and kicking his own shins; he finds it daunting to look up and terrifying to look down. And all these things happened to the prince whilst Nose continued to howl from the quayside.

Where HM was having the devil's own job even to approach the dog. It seemed to HM indeed that the only break in the howling came when she approached and Nose snarled – a snarl of undisguised hostility and bristling menace.

HM needed Nose. She couldn't leave Blefton without him. But there was no way she'd be able to take his leash in his present mood – not and keep both her hands.

She decided she'd go for some refreshment, see whether in that interim the dog might not have calmed down a bit.

She'd noticed on her way through the city what had looked like a half-decent tavern, the *Admiral Benbow*. She'd go and get herself a hot meal, maybe a glass of wine, return when the *Silver Hart* was sufficiently distant for Nose to have accepted his master's going.

But Nose was in no mood for acceptance. As soon as HM vanished, he started gnawing at the rope which held him. He kept flicking glances out to sea. The ship was getting further away. His master was getting further away. An increasing franticness possessed his gnawing.

Finally he tugged at the frayed hemp and the tether snapped. Without further thought Nose leapt off the jetty and started swimming – swimming as though his life depended on it – towards the ship.

"What in the name of all what's holy does you think you's doing *there*?" shouted the captain.

Charming didn't dare look down. He didn't need to, though. He knew it was he being yelled at. "Going to the galley, sir. Sir, like you said, sir."

"Stops this game right now, mister, and gets down from there this *instant*," the captain bellowed again.

The 'squire' scraped and slithered and started to scratch his way back. As he was so occupied, his glance wandered off to the sea. There, lit only by the moonlight, he could see the head of his beloved dog struggling to reach him.

Nose was clearly not in a natural element for him, clearly also rapidly running out of energy. His head almost appeared dismembered; the eyes were exuding, in equal measure, despair and exhaustion. Nose was struggling to reach him, desperate to reach him.

Struggling, struggling.

"Go back, Nose," he shouted to the dog. He was still grappling with the rigging. "You'll drown, you stupid dog. Go back, go back." The tears, so long kept in check, were now coursing down his cheeks. He didn't even notice that his body had swung round so that, if he lost his grip, he would fall straight into the sea. He tried to whistle. But the tears prevented him from forming his mouth correctly.

"What in the name of all what's holy are you playing at?" the captain bellowed yet again. "I thoughts I tolds you to get yourself back on this deck."

Under his breath the prince repeated a few of the words he'd heard the sentries use on Philomena's approach. Aloud, he yelled back, "Coming, sir. As fast, sir, as I can, sir." He'd checked the tears, but now it was the wind which stopped him puckering his mouth to form a whistle. He turned his face out of the wind's path, licked his already chapped lips and, in the absence of a signal which meant 'go back' emitted the closest equivalent he could think of: 'Leave'.

He saw Nose hear the command. He saw him stop his paddling. The poor dog actually had to. He had no energy to paddle more. He saw the desolation in his eyes as slowly, but inexorably, he allowed the ship to glide further away from him. He saw him start to turn.

He prayed to God that Nose would reach the shore again. He prayed fervently to God. He didn't care what happened to *him*, only – please, God – *please* keep Nose safe.

"I shoulds have the skin off your back," the captain ranted at him when the 'squire' was again on deck. "If you don't knows something, Squire Wodinton, you asks."

For a split second the prince thought about protesting that he *had* asked. Self-preservation, though, is an excellent supplier of instinct and he therefore said, in mock abashment, "Aye-aye, sir."

"Mr Raleigh here, he'll shows you where the galley be," he said with ill-defined menace, talking of the sailor with the cornflower eyes. To whom he said pointedly, "Won't you, Walter?"

"Happy, Cap'n, to oblige."

"And puts your bloody hat on straight!" he screamed at the rating. "This bain't be no Sunday morning promenade, Raleigh. This be a merchantman. And you, Drake, you wipes that silly smirk off of your face!"

"Aye-aye, Cap'n," said the sailor who had been sat at the bottom of the gangplank.

"Well?" screamed Bligh again.

"This way," Raleigh said to the prince.

And he led him through the hatchway below decks. It felt to Charming as though he were descending through the jaws of Hell.

He was.

Chapter 26

The prince's prayers were answered: Nose did find land again.

But he was so exhausted that he just collapsed on the beach, unable to move a millimetre more, unable to do anything except just pant. Occasionally his right hind-leg would twitch. For the rest, he was spent. He badly needed to sick up the salt water he had involuntarily drunk. But he lacked the energy even to be able to do that. For a good hour he just lay collapsed on the shingle, panting deeply, the brine just trickling of its own volition from the corner of his panting mouth.

He could hear HM calling for him. But he lacked either the strength or the inclination to go to her. Eventually *she* found *him*. And he tried to be grateful to her for that. But he couldn't be.

She guessed immediately what had happened to the dog. She pushed on his stomach, so that Nose had no choice other than to retch. The salt water started to gurgle from him.

HM took the caparison off her horse, dried the dog with it, then wrapped him in it. Slowly warmth started returning to the animal, and some sort of vigour. But not liveliness, not joy or enthusiasm. His mood was similar to the prince's in the years immediately succeeding the deaths of Philomena and Horatio: He was seized with an apathy so absolute it couldn't even be called indolent.

HM was eager to return to the Court as soon as she could. Much of the journey from Blefton was therefore taken at the gallop. And Nose kept pace with that gallop. But sinews which usually would stretch luxuriantly into this exercise did so on this trip only sulkily. Nose's tail was extended exclusively for balance; there wasn't so much as a twitch in it of fun, not so much as the flicker of a wag.

Her eagerness notwithstanding, within sight of Wodinton Castle, HM again opted to spend that night in the forest. She wanted to arrive first thing in the morning. She had things to do before the king awoke.

***

Goneril and Naitly liked their early morning conferences. First thing in the morning was therefore an extremely good time to find both of them together. HM wanted to speak to them together. The only question she had to answer was would Naitly be with Goneril or she with him. HM opted for the latter and thus headed straight for the Decadence. She'd guessed correctly.

The butler had wanted to announce her, but HM had told him not to be ridiculous, that she was far too busy to cope with nonsense like that. Goneril and Naitly were breakfasting together.

Naitly was startled by the interruption. He leapt up and marched to the window. He looked abashed. This quickly metamorphosed into indignation. Goneril was equally *un*abashed. She arched one of her carefully tweezered eyebrows. "It is our custom," she said, "to breakfast together."

"The whole palace knows that," HM told her.

"Indeed?" she asked and crunched her toast.

"Trust me," said HM.

"That the prince's dog?" asked Naitly. "Does that mean you've found him? The prince, I mean?"

"Oh yes," HM told him. And then, simply by moving her eyes, she told Goneril as well. For a second Goneril stopped crunching. Then she forced herself to eat on. She was thinking, though, ...thinking, thinking.

Naitly's chamber was a big one, even an opulent one. One end of it was dominated by a huge four-poster bed, the columns of which had all been carved with the same intricate relief: Adam and Eve at the tree of knowledge, coiled around which was the serpent. It occupied its own small platform, and was covered in expensive furs, gifts from various rulers of exotic, if cold, climes.

Below this dais was the living area: a brace of identical plum-coloured couches divided by what we would today call a coffee-table, fashioned from stout cane. These were before the large fire. To the left of this seating, by the window which gave out to the sprawling and rolling park beyond, was a round dining table which could seat four. No more than two had ever sat at it.

"I don't care for livestock in my living quarters," said Naitly, his eyes curling in distaste. He sat down again at the table.

"I wouldn't say that too loudly, Lord Chancellor," HM told him. "This dog understands more than you would imagine. He's also trained to kill. But, then, you know that, don't you? Both of you? Which is why you arranged for Gretel to buy him."

"This is slander, jester," Naitly fumed. Goneril had replaced the unfinished toast on her plate, and was brushing the shard-like crumbs from her fingertips. But her concentration was solidly on HM. She watched every dart of her iris, every nuance of her mouth.

"You have to ask yourself one question," HM told them and waited.

Naitly was about to explode. Goneril lay her usual placatory hand on his sleeve. "Go on," she said.

"Do you want the prince alive or dead?" HM asked, in very much the same manner as she might have asked, "One lump or two?"

Naitly started to erupt from his seat. "This is outra- ..." he started to splutter. Again he was checked by Goneril's hand.

"Go on," she said again.

"The prince is aboard my brother's ship."

"Clever," Goneril admitted with, apparently, genuine admiration.

"I can tell him to push the prince overboard ..."

"*Very* clever," said Goneril in the same tone.

"Or I could return him to Court. He would think I'd saved his life."

"Choice?" raged Naitly. "There *is* no choice, jester. Return him to Court, of course. The very idea. The very suggestion ..."

"Oh get real, LC, *please*," said Goneril.

"But pumpkin ... I mean ..."

"You're supposed to be a political wheeler-dealer ..."

"I think I'm a pretty straight guy," said Naitly almost soulfully.

"If we want to find the infinite in this world," HM reflected philosophically, "we have only to look at man's capacity for self-delusion."

"You're *known* as a wheeler-dealer, LC ..."

"I think most people who deal with me think I'm a pretty straight guy ..."

"*Famous*, LC, as a wheeler-dealer."

"Trust me," said HM.

"Wheeling and dealing require brain-cells. You have to have them, LC. *Start using them*."

"You've lost me," said Naitly.

Goneril sighed the sigh of "If anything needs doing you've got to do it yourself". "What do you want?" she asked HM.

"Power," HM replied. "Not pretend power or surrogate power or vicarious power. Real power. Mine. Acknowledged to be mine."

"Ministry, you mean?" asked Goneril.

"Only one of the big ones."

"Finance?"

"That'll do."

"Fire Garibaldi," Goneril told Naitly.

"Oh. Oh right," said Naitly, who had been unable to keep pace with the rat-a-tat of the exchange.

"For your part ...?" Goneril asked HM.

"I'll get word to my brother."

"And ...?"

"Trust me."

***

"That's his waistcoat," Cole said blearily.

"Alas, I found it, sire, beside a quicksand," HM told him, her entire demeanour abject. "Nose was howling next to it."

"Nose?"

"His dog."

"You think then he's …?"

"I think, sire, you should start to resign yourself to the worst. However, please be assured, sire, that whilst there is breath in my body, and for as long as the body of the prince has not been recovered, I shall not rest from my search for him."

They were in the king's bedchamber. A Vermeer-like light barged its way in through the two large and latticed windows. Cole was not long awake. He was still pale therefore, and a bit shaky. He pulled the sable blanket up to his chin. The usual mild disorientation of his levée was developing into severe confusion.

In any power struggle, HM knew, there was a winner and a loser. If you hadn't grasped that from history then you hadn't grasped anything. Lesson two of history is that the eventual winner is not always clear at the outset. The only way to *guarantee* being on the winning side at the end is to be on *both* sides. As such was clearly impossible, HM had to *seem* to both sides to be on theirs. Whilst remaining loyal in fact only to a *third* side: her own.

She would, of course, have to tell her brother to kill the prince; which – yes, of course it was – was sad, but, hey, you can't make omelettes without breaking a few eggs now and then. For as long as she could, though, she would hold out some hope to the king. Because that hope would make him even more dependant on her.

The king leant over and drank from the goblet that had rested overnight on his bedside table.

"That'll be stale, sire. I'll ring for some fresh."

"One doesn't wish to make a fuss, HM."

"Your Majesty's selflessness knows no bounds."

The king drank deeply. His face creased suddenly into deep sorrow. Almost crumpled into it, in fact. "One was not a good father, HM," he said.

"His Majesty is too hard on himself."

"No, HM. However bitter, one has always swallowed one's pills. One was not, HM, a good father."

"No, sire."

"You're agreeing with one???" Cole ranted at her, a fire having whooshed up within him from nowhere.

"Oh no, sire," the jester quickly replied.

"You're *not* agreeing with one?" the king ranted again.

"Sire, you're upset. You need rest to recover from the shock. Plenty of rest, Majesty. You need to drink deeply, sire, from your goblet."

"One supposes you are right, HM," the king agreed stoically. "One has to make things up to one's son, however. Be a good father, as 'twere, post mortem. Bring one ... what is the dog's name?"

"Nose, sire."

"Bring one Nose."

"I am, Majesty, yours to command," said HM, backing out of the door.

It might be imagined that HM's rush to be by herself would be to catch up with a bit of sleep-in-bed, as opposed to that on-moss. But not a bit of it: HM was a Minister now – *the* Minister of Finance. That meant she was entitled to an ermine smock.

She was most eager to see her tailor.

And she had a pigeon to send.

***

The very best time the prince had on board the *Silver Hart* was a neutral one, a time when he wasn't having a bad time.

Such crumbs of positive joy as the prince did get he derived from visiting his horses. He'd rise an hour before his duties started in order to spend time with them. He groomed them as he always had. As he always had, he talked to them. They were the only ones allowed to see his tears.

And there *were* tears. A lot of them.

His time on board was gruesome. He was the butt of everyone's joke, his bottom was at the end of every toe.

Consequently, however, the prince – so long numb – did start feeling again. The feelings weren't pleasant. But they were real. And they enabled the prince once again to start living.

His biggest stroke of luck came when he found himself sharing a cabin with Squire Squeers, Antonio's best man – he of the hair so red, it was less a head than a beacon.

Because of the prince's ... condition at the wedding, and his consequent absence from it, Squeers did not know the true identity of the young man. But he was clearly of good birth. Maybe even of a birth (if such a thing were possible) as good as Squeers's himself. This, to Squeers's mind, set them both apart from all the other vermin and varmints aboard the ship.

To call what existed between them a 'friendship' would be to overstate the case – and to demean friendship. But there was a jerky and uncomfortable support ... no, rather a mutual forbearance ... of each other.

The captain had told Squeers that once his, the captain's, business had been done he, Squeers, might avail himself of the boy. And the temptation to the squire was too great: his breeches needed pressing, his nightshirt washing, his shoes cleaning. But, once the chores were done, there was, on the squire's part, a lack of that unnecessary bullying or of that cavalier cruelty which was the hallmark of the *crew's* treatment of the young man.

The prince knew this cruelty, this bullying was a temporary state of affairs. Things would be different when they got to Azrac.

But he also knew he *had* to know that. If he *didn't* know that, he would open the gate to despair. He feared that the gate-crasher would be one he'd never again be able to get rid of.

In the same way, he *had* to know that, once in Azrac, things would prove never to have been better.

How long could the journey take, for God's sake? It was to Azrac he was going, not San Pedito. It couldn't be *that* long. Surely.

What the young man didn't yet know was that, by comparison with what was about to befall him, the gruesomeness of the ship was nothing.

It was nothing at all.

Chapter 27

When the pigeon returned, the prince was polishing the captain's cutlass. It coincided almost exactly with the look-out in the crow's nest (as now the prince knew was the correct term for what he had been told was the galley) shouting: "Ship ahoy!" The look-out was Raleigh, the sailor with the cornflower eyes.

The prince noticed an increased briskness in the ship's business, but nothing more than that. There was scant indication of concern, none of panic. Not yet. It was the quiet before the storm.

Charming had watched the pigeon as it circled overhead and then bore down directly to its coop. No-one had told him to take it to the captain. It just seemed to him the sensible thing to do. To how many of us does it fall, to be the porter of our own death warrant?

He grasped the bird firmly but gently. It was still panting. Scarcely surprising, the prince rationalised, after such a long flight. Let it rest awhile, he thought, before he took it to the captain. He'd go and *tell* the captain it had returned. He stroked it gently on its breast, and then under its beak. It occurred to him that the bird had seen Nose after he had. Suddenly he wanted to question it about the dog's health, his spirits, his happiness. And then, abruptly, he told himself, for God's sake, to grow up, to stop being ridiculous.

The sun glinted through the rigging. Some fifty yards off the port bow a pod of dolphins was frolicking like children in a paddling pool. The sea was calm and very blue – a deep, impenetrable blue. It looked harmless. Inviting. Almost walkable-on. And fertile.

When the prince found him, the captain was peering at the distant ship through his telescope. Drake was with him. The prince had never really looked at Drake before then. He had, the prince now saw, a flattened nose and ears that looked like walnuts.

"What d'you think, Cap'n?" Drake was asking as the prince approached. Charming had already learnt not to interrupt the captain, just to wait until told to speak.

"I thinks we'd best be on the safe side," said the captain, almost casually. "Don't sound no alarms, like, but pass the word. Don't let 'em sees we's doing anything other'n believe their French flag."

"Aye-aye, Cap'n," said Drake.

"What are you doin' of here?" the captain asked bad-temperedly of Charming.

"The bird, sir, the pige- ..."

"Bird, Squire? *Bird*? I's got more important things on my mind jus' now 'n *birds*. We could have visitors, lad. Pirates. They's flying friendly flags, but I's not so sure, lad. Not so sure. Where's my cutlass?"

"I was just cleaning it, sir, when the pige- ..."

"I di'n't asks you for its life history, boy. Bring it here. Smart about it. Run," he shouted at him.

The strange ship had run down the French flag. In its place was hoisted the skull-and-crossbones. It was about fifty yards away. Raleigh scuttled down from the crow's nest. "*Run*!" the captain shouted at Charming more urgently. Ring the alarm bell!"

There was a low whistle, a whirr, a flash of light.

A cannon ball tore into the side of the ship.

The captain fell over, as if pole-axed. Charming didn't need to investigate. He knew the captain had been killed.

Apparently so did Drake. Who immediately assumed command.

Not that there was a great deal of commanding possible. The noise became almost immediately deafening.

The hideous roar of the cannon, the teeth-souring whine of their balls were interrupted by the snapping of timber, by the ripping of canvas – and by the screaming of the wounded, and the wailing of the dying.

Charming found the captain's cutlass. It was no good to the captain, he reasoned, he might as well hold onto it.

All was now chaos.

Smoke filled the air – black smoke, white smoke, white-and-black smoke, grey smoke.

Bits of mast and rigging crashed from above, splintering both themselves and the deck.

Before him, a man's leg was blown off just below the knee – a cut apparently as clean as a surgeon's. The man screamed in such agony that for a moment it was only his screams that the prince could hear.

And then he heard the neighing.

Neighing like he'd never heard before. The neighing of panic.

And then he heard the horses kicking. Charming knew he had to get to the horses. He just had to.

"Get down there, Raleigh," shouted Drake. "Get them horses quiet. If they carries on like they are, theys'll kicks a hole in the hull."

"Go down there?! You thinks I's mad, Mr Drake? I goes down there, it'll be me theys'll kicks a hole in!"

"I'll go," the prince volunteered.

"Do it NOW," Drake said to the prince. "Give your cutlass to the squire."

"Well, obliged, I'm sure. Enormously obliged," said Squeers. "Fighting, though, not my thing precisely."

"Gives him the cutlass, boy." The prince did so. "Gets to the horses. Calms them down. Theys'll kill us faster 'n the pirates."

The deck was alight now with four or five different fires.

Sailors were tripping over their fallen, often their limbless colleagues and, as they hauled themselves to their feet, they would curse those colleagues for being in their way.

There was nothing glorious about any of this, nothing heroic or fulfilling. This was just base. Base and evil.

The prince decided that no-one should give an order for war who had not experienced battle. It was a decision that was later vital to Belgiss.

War, the prince realised at that moment, was no zenith. To the contrary: it was the *lowest* point to which Man could sink. Men could do – *did* do – heroic things within it, but to think of war as glamorous in some way or noble is to think that black is white.

The companionway from the hatch had been smashed. The prince had to swing his way below decks and jump the last few feet.

The scene below was of a carnage as brutal as it had been above, but also mostly in the dark. The roar of the cannon was even louder here, even more sickening. The smell of the cannon-fire blended with that of smoke, and that too of freshly felled timber and singed skin.

Everyone was coughing. Even the injured. Many unable to scream simply because they were coughing too much.

These men weren't bullies, any longer, or tormentors. They were just men: scared men or hurt men, angry men or men who were dying.

The prince continued to pick his way through them.

There was a man there praying to God – please – to let him die; another there, half of whose throat had been sheered away; there a man speared by a loosened shaft of timber.

Still the prince could hear the neighing. The neighing of panic. The kicking.

One of the sailors came over to the praying man and slit his throat. It was an act of charity. The gesture went unnoticed.

Another threw his tunic over a wounded colleague; a third found time to give a fallen comrade water. It is this, the prince saw, that is heroism. The phoney heroism, that which involves military feats to further the slaughter of others, that is not heroism at all but derring-do, not bravery but bravado.

Now *all* the prince could hear was the neighing.

A fallen man grabbed the prince's ankle. He nearly kicked him. The stricken man gazed with tortured eyes at the young man. He couldn't articulate, but his eyes asked him just the one word: "Why?" and then he died.

The prince shook himself free.

He had to get to the deck below. It was there that the horses were stalled.

A few small fires had started here as well. Sailors were merely beating these out as they rushed to other duties. Fire was only a side-issue now.

Still the deafening noise, still all the hideous shrieks of war, still the coughing. The coughing and the screaming.

The companionway between this deck and that below it was still in tact. Charred, but not damaged beyond that.

He knew where the horses were, of course. He knew it blindfold. And it was blindly that he found them.

Such is the power of hope that, if the fall of a pin represents it, inside a sonic boom you will hear that pin falling. Amidst all the neighing and stomping, amidst the men screaming and the horses whinnying, his horses heard the prince's approach. And immediately they heard it, they were calmed. They were still frightened, of course, but it was a controlled fright now, no longer its earlier franticness.

A hurricane lamp had smashed. This had set fire to some trails of hay on the floor. The prince quickly stamped these out.

It wasn't any longer that he thought anything about it. Man's ability to accept the unacceptable and to normalise the abnormal is one of both his greatest achievements and his most devastating failures. Certainly it is one of the reasons why Man has become the world's most powerful animal. But it could also be one of the reasons why finally Man will destroy himself.

It had been less than half-an-hour since the pirates invaded. Already the prince – and he could without being so specific somehow sense this – was becoming inured to the sight of limbs being blasted from healthy trunks, the wounded being kicked out of the way, the dying being cursed. Almost the most horrifying thing about war is the speed with which we do, all of us, become inured to it.

Although we never do.

It's one of those paradoxes. We think we do. But we don't. It's almost a rule of thumb: The more we think we are inured to it, the less we actually are. The horror festers. And then it starts feeding on itself. And then anger further distorts the picture. Finally you find yourself doing today that which yesterday horrified you: a today in whose tomorrow you start countenancing and condoning those horrors. The day after that, you start advocating them.

It is not only directly that war breeds war, but (thus) also indirectly.

If any war does *not* provoke another it is only because the soldier's children are wise and brave enough – *heroic* enough – to insist that they will *not* fight. It takes more courage to lay down arms than to pick them up. The greatest courage is never to resort to them.

The horses started calming. And because these three horses started to get calmer so did those around them.

The bucking started to wane, the snorting and the baring of teeth to ease. There was a sense amongst the horses that, whilst the situation was certainly scary, with the prince there things would work out all right.

He advanced on them. Carefully. Stealthily. Frightened animals are dangerous animals. They'll lash out, driven simply by fear. The prince knew he had to be careful. Very careful.

This stable area normally looked like a wide mine-shaft. Lengths of untreated timber supported the deck above and divided the floor-space. Any light that came in was artificial. Now, with the hurricane lamps smashed, it entered only through a few holes in the hull where the tar had been worn away – pencil-thin shafts of light, lengths of golden twine linking sky and earth.

One horse had been killed, its skull smashed by a beam which had fallen on it from above. The prince trod over it. He got to Philly. Another section of the deck's ceiling had crashed in front of her. She had been hemmed in – and into a very confined space.

Her eyes were almost at the side of their own sockets. Each creak in the timber brought more fear to the creature. Charming knew, before he could start to clear the wreckage, he had to calm her.

He'd made reassuring noises as soon as he'd arrived on the horses' deck, and throughout his approach. It didn't matter that the cacophony around him made it unlikely the horses could hear him.

Nor did it matter that in the gloom all he could make out were not the horses themselves but only their shapes.

Now those shapes had become identifiable. "Easy, girl," he was saying. "Easy, Philly: there's a good girl. Easy. Easy."

He clambered on top of the splintered wood. He cut himself on a pointed beam which stuck out from one of the timbers like a gigantic splinter. It made him aware of other hazards to the horses – outstanding nails and bolts, for instance. "Easy, girl. Easy."

Peggy whinnied and forced its way a little closer to the prince. "Okay, Peggy. It's going to be okay."

A blast from another cannonball tore through the ship's hull. This sent the animals again into a frenzy.

But then around them there was a sudden still. Almost an eerie still. A still that was even violent in its suddenness.

The prince by now had hold of both Philly and Peggy. He was stroking their noses. The hole made by the most recent cannonball had released a deal more light into the shaft.

Charming could see Horsatio backed into a corner. He left the other two horses, started clearing a path towards Horsatio, hurling timber to the far side of the deck.

The ceiling was creaking alarmingly now. It could give at any moment. He had to get the horses to safety. He had to.

The prince worked like a man possessed. The sweat was drenching him. He didn't even notice it.

He got to Horsatio.

Quickly he stroked the beast, tried to quieten him, to reassure him. He couldn't dally, though. He couldn't afford to. It was going to cave in, the ceiling. Any minute.

He had to get the horses to safety. Now.

He took Horsatio's halter, started leading him through the piles of shattered and splintered wood. Then he had to go back for the others. He slapped Horsatio on the rump. "Go, boy," he told him.

Instinct again took over. Horsatio started making for the companionway. Even as the prince was grabbing the halters of Philly and Peggy he could hear Horsatio's hooves clomping up the wooden stairs.

The others horses he "yaa"ed and "go on"ed at. They followed heavily behind Horsatio.

Philly didn't want to move. She was too frightened. He had to release Peggy. Had to hope it'd follow the other horses. He heard its clomp behind them.

"Come on, Philly," he told her. "Come on, girl." But the horse was still too frightened. Far from coming closer to the prince she backed away from him.

"Come *on*, girl," the prince urged. "You'll die, Philly, you stupid horse. You'll be killed." The despair in his voice was seized with its own electricity.

And then Charming saw the problem: There was a shard of broken glass which would have to lacerate her as she passed it.

The prince smashed the glass with a length of wood from the copious amount now littering the deck. He pulled Philly to safety.

Literally the moment afterwards the ceiling did collapse.

But by then Charming and Philly were making their way to the companionway. The crash caused a lot more dust to fly around but there was no other harm done.

They made their way *up* the companionway.

To the deck.

Where a smiling face was there to greet them.

It belonged to the pirate captain.

Chapter 28

All was not right in Prim's world. But then in Prim's world all was never right. The best that Prim's world ever got was for everything not to be dreadful. Things were not at that moment dreadful in Prim's world. Therefore all in Prim's world was as good as it was going to get.

Prim had a new what in those days was called 'gentleman caller'. Until they had called three times (according to Prim) they weren't, the gentlemen, "calling". They were popping in. Poppers-in were not encouraged. To get from 'popper-in' to 'caller' required from the designated gentleman a determination which deterred all but the most ardent suitors. Prim did not therefore often have gentlemen callers. Indeed since HM's father had stopped calling, the only gentlemen in Prim's life had been gentlemen passers-by, and one or two gentleman flitters-in.

The one 'caller' since HM's father had, like Prim, lost his spouse. He was called Squire Anderson. Like Prim too he was the parent of a daughter, albeit of only one. This daughter was several years younger than Winny. She was a rather compliant child, the spark of whose feistiness had been dampened by her mother's death. Her father, on the odd occasion when his mind left business, was beginning to wonder whether she would ever find the self-assurance to stand up for herself.

Prim united with her daughters in their common dislike of this girl. Both Winny and Ginny sought to have as little to do with her as possible. Joint outings, picnics and their like, were discouraged. It was the daughters' opinion, that, while Prim was, of course, old enough to choose her companions for herself, so far as including *them* in any social schemes she might be planning (or that she and her 'gentleman caller' might be planning together), ... well ...include them out.

For his part the widower Anderson was smitten with Prim. When his wife had died a few years previously he had liked to think he had been grief-stricken. It would be more accurate to describe him as having been inconvenience-stricken. His late wife had organised the entire of his domestic life. He had had no idea of the organisation required to run a house, let alone a home. His house had not been a home since his wife's death. It wasn't that the squire particularly yearned for a home. He thought, though, that's the sort of things good fathers were supposed to supply for their daughters. Most of all, a home would allow him to devote his time to his chief love: business.

The squire was not looking for a Juliet to his Romeo, more a housekeeper to his house-owner. In his dreams, even a shrew to his tamer.

And Prim had decided, if he wanted to be a tamer, then she'd show him what a *real* shrew was made of.

***

Love had never featured largely in HM's life. Oh, she'd been kissed occasionally in her infancy, on odd occasions told a bedtime story. Her adolescence had been sprinkled with flirtations. There had been one serious romance (on her side), the ending of which occasionally would return to smack her in the face.

Never though had she felt love as she did now. This was a true love and a deep love. A glorious, a noble love, an all-embracing love: the love she had for her ermine smock.

She loved everything about it. She loved the feel of it, the scratchy tweed and the soft, soft ermine; she loved the smell of it, the cardboardy tincture of the fabric, and the sour musk of the fur; she loved the way it made her feel: important, accomplished, successful.

And she loved, loved, *loved* the way that other people looked at her when she was wearing it: *as* someone important, accomplished, successful.

She'd never previously been one to want a city life. She preferred the isolation of palace life or the seclusion of forest hunts. But now she wandered down Wodinton streets, basking in the stares, even the glares, of the non-ermined. It didn't matter to HM that there were those in the street who resented her. It mattered only that they *noticed* her.

Greatness may be thrust on the unwilling. *Fame*, though, is (except in the most extraordinary of cases) seized. And those who seek to seize fame (like those who seek power) are, dint of their seeking it, not worthy of it. Admiration for the famous is therefore (in any but the most extraordinary of cases) misplaced. Most of the famous are not the most accomplished but the most needy.

HM kept her word to the prince and did give Nose the 'occasional' stroke – roughly, once a fortnight. Most of Nose's affection, though, came from the king.

Deprived now of so much of HM's company, Cole grew increasingly morose. Nose couldn't demorose him. The dog didn't make him laugh in the way that, pre-Ministerially, HM had done. All he did, he provided *some* relief to the never-ending tedium of being king.

Cole decided he had to marry. He had to get another son. Then he could abdicate in his son's favour. And then, relieved of the duties of state, he could indeed start enjoying himself. He felt that he had done his bit, more than his fair share, that he was owed a break, that it was time he should start enjoying himself.

He was entitled to, wasn't he?

Well, wasn't he?

***

Cross-Bones had pointed shoes. This set them several points above even the polloiest of the hoi.

And this improvement in their status, if not salary, rendered their suit more ... suitable to Prim.

It wasn't that they were yet grata as personas, but their non-grataness had without question lost some of its acidity. And whilst their mother's approval was by no means a condition of her daughters' choice of escort, it did make life for them a little smoother.

Winny was still retained at the palace. In case the prince turned up. Or in case the king sired another son. It was the happiest time of her life. Her days were filled with idleness and her evenings with dalliance. Time passed. And she could wallow in it, the passing of such balmy time.

The more so as Ginny was working for a mere earl and his wife. Their four children were as healthy as they were impish as they were impudent. Ginny's working day was therefore extremely tiring. The one-upwomanship Winny thus enjoyed over her elder sister added further zest to the already scrummy.

Life, Winny thought, was not going to get better than this.

***

There was one problem with HM's new appointment to the Ministry of Finance: She was lousy at maths. Not that Garibaldi had seen that as much of a handicap. But HM was not the quintessential politician. There was that within her which still cared. Cared – on occasion – even deeply.

It wasn't that she'd been raised exactly in poverty. Indeed by the genuinely poor she would have been considered wealthy. And even she didn't consider she had been hard-up or hard done by. But she did have an understanding of poverty, and she had experience of want. And at the very least she lived in greater contact with the real world than did the rest of the Court's circle, or the Decadence's.

She knew there were problems in that real world, and she knew how painful problems were. It pained her that the real problems faced by the real people of that world were treated by most of those whose work was to help solve those problems as intellectual exercises; that they were considered by them as crossword puzzles: enormously satisfying if solved, but no big deal if not.

The more HM grew to know of government the more disenchanted she became with the process.

Everywhere she looked she could see mammoth problems growing mammothly. And everywhere she looked she could see nothing being done about them. Indeed the only doing she *could* see was of people looking the other way, pretending that there were *no* problems.

And everywhere she looked she saw Mercian inroads.

Mercia was organising it such that the Belgic economy would be *dependent* on Mercia. And Mercia was pushing Belgiss further and further into a cul-de-sac. As if *it* were a bear, and Belgiss were a cat. For the moment, HM could see no way that her cat could sidle past the bear and escape. It seemed to her the cat's room for manoeuvre was getting smaller and smaller.

However, HM also feared the Belgic love of its independence. She feared that if Belgiss were to become inextricable from Mercia there would be a gigantic and bloody backlash. If such happened, the backlash would rally around the king. HM had therefore to continue to keep close to the king.

She went to see him. He was, as usual, stroking Nose. And he was grumpy. "Oh," he snootied, "nice," he snootied, "of you to drop in, Miss terribly important Minister of Finance," he snootied.

"Your jester first, sire."

"It doesn't feel like it. One is severely not as amused as one was, HM, when one had as a jester an *Un*minister of Finance."

"If I disappoint Your Majesty ..." She made to go.

"You *do* disappoint one, frankly, HM. These days you're by *dis*appointment to His Majesty the King. However, one doesn't wish you to go. There's too much change, HM. One doesn't like change."

"Water, sire, that doesn't move become stagnant."

"See? Not a barrel of laughs, was it, honestly, that answer?"

"My wit, sire, needs honing."

"And what about one's wife?"

"Sire?"

"One needs a wife, HM. Have you yet found her?"

And then the most devilish idea suddenly occurred to HM. "Maybe," she said.

"Maybe? What's a 'maybe' wife?"

"I'm a bit shy about mentioning it."

"You?"

"Yes."

"Shy?"

"Yes."

"Another change."

"Maybe."

"Well?"

"Well?"

"One's wife?"

"Yes."

"Well?"

"Me."

"You?"

"Me, sire."

"You, what? One doesn't understand."

"Me, sire. As your wife."

"You?"

"Yes."

"*You*?"

"Yes, sire."

"You, HM?"

"Yes."

"You're not being serious?"

"When am I ever?"

The king looked at her quizzically. He didn't know how to take her suggestion. He started with a gentle, almost apologetic chuckle. HM returned his look, blandly – the pierrot who cannot laugh. The king laughed briefly loudly. Still blandness in HM. And then the king, he started to roar. To bellow his laughter. Nothing registered on HM's face, not a twitch or a glimmer. But inside her heart was breaking. It wasn't breaking as a jester, and certainly not as a Minister of State. It was breaking as a woman.

The Minister never had anything to forgive the king for, and the jester was just doing her job.

It was only the woman who had trouble forgiving the king.

And the woman never did.

Chapter 29

On board the *Silver Hart* a party was in full swing. And a riotous time was being had by all. By all the *pirates*, that is. The original crew, on the other hand, was having a very *un*riotous time. Most of them had been locked in one of the cargo holds, at the very bottom of the keel. The dead and the dying, whether captor or captive, had all been thrown overboard. The screams of the maimed testified, hauntingly, to the presence in the ocean of man-eating sharks.

The pirate crew had been imbibing heavily from the *Hart's* grog. They continued to swig expansively from it. The *Silver Hart* was a good prize, perhaps even a great one, not just the sheep that you might as well as a lamb get hanged for, but the entire flock. They were going to enjoy it. If it killed them. Well, not them, of course, but all the rest!

Their captain was a notorious corsair from Flanders, Trim Foocs. Before hurling Bligh's corpse into the water he had stripped it of its clothes. He now swaggered around in them looking like a rather unkempt captain of a privateer. He considered himself very dashing.

Charming could not see this, however. Oh, he was on deck all right. But he was blindfolded. A rope had been tied around his midriff. He had become a sort of human yo-yo. One group of pie-eyed sailors would push him towards another group, sited virtually at the rope's end. Thus would the rope uncoil. The receiving group would then send the prince back, re-coiling it. To add spice to their game, sometimes the yo-yo was assisted by a well-directed boot to the prince's rear, sometimes with the tip of a cutlass.

Above him the prince could hear the seagulls cawing and around him he could hear the savage guffaws of his captors. Around him too there was a noxious cocktail of smells: brine and booze and sweat and tar; stale breath and stale gunpowder. And still the stench of singed flesh. Still too the screams lingered in the air, like unseen vultures almost, hawking for carrion.

He knew the pirates were going to kill him. And that, almost curiously, was less alarming to him than the yo-yo induced giddiness. Suddenly he could see Horatio again bent over the chair, ready to receive his beating. "You're going to kill me," he said, seeking to match his cousin's courage and dignity. "For God's sake, get on with it."

This elicited another great roar from the assembled buccaneers. "Well, well," he heard in his right ear, as yet again he was sent spinning, "got bottle, the toff." In his left ear, "'Ere, Cap'n. 'E think 'e's cap'n, Cap'n." From somewhere further in the distance a mimic: "For God's sake, get on with it." This caused yet another barrage of laughter. And then, obviously, another mimic though the prince did not know of whom. It was just that the voice was laced with a poshness so phoney it had to be mimicry. "These are severest offences. Which call for severest penalties. Off with his head." Another guffaw. The prince was sent reeling back to the first group of pirates.

"Plank," he heard from someone a little above him, presumably on one of the masts. The word started to be incanted. "Plank, plank." Shortly two or three others had joined the litany ... "plank, plank" ..., within short order the entire of the ship's new company.

"Plank, plank, plank, plank," they chorused together as their hands clapped out a steady rhythm.

"Not yet, not yet," said Trim Foocs, his Flanders accent flattening the vowels. "Too many sharks, boys. He'll not have a chance to drown."

"Plank, plank, plank, plank."

"You *want* him eaten by de sharks?" asked the captain. A great roar of approval. "You don't want to wait und watch him *drown*?" A great boo. "It seems," said Foocs not far from Charming's right ear, "dey want you to die *quickly*. Und dey say pirates are bloodthirsty?!"

"Pardon my intrusion," said a genuinely posh voice, one which the prince did recognise. It belonged to Squire Squeers. "I can't help feeling, don't you know, we're missing a trick here. Enormously missing a trick." The intrusion was greeted with a concerto of boos and catcalls and whistles.

Again the refrain was taken up: "Plank, plank ..."

"Well, I'll be. I thought," said the squire raising his voice above the hubbub, "you gentlemen were interested in gold. Enormously interested." The noise of derision stopped suddenly, almost as if cut by a knife. "I say again, I can't help feeling that we're here missing a trick."

"Go on," said Trim Foocs.

"This is a good-looking young man, personable, presentable. Enormously all three," said the squire. "He also has three quite splendid horses. Enormously splendid. Think, gentlemen, of what these might fetch at market in Biga-buga. The boy in the slave market, the horses ... well, self-evidently in the horse market. A boy like this, horses like those, you must be talking fifteen, twenty thousand."

"Doubloons?"

"Doubloons." The prince could hear a gasp and avaricious whispers from the crew.

"De only problem beink," said Foocs, "dey won't let us in."

"They'll let *me* in, dear boy," Squeers told him, and therefore the crew. "You give me my life, I give you entry into Biga-buga. And therefore fifteen, twenty thousand doubloons, don't you know. A fair exchange – an enormously fair one, no?"

"Dey'll only arrest us."

"Take me hostage, then."

"If we take you hostage dey won't let us in."

"Ah. A conundrum. Enormously so. Take one of the crew hostage then. Take two hostage, dear boy. My dear friends Drake and Raleigh, for example. They can look after my diamonds for me, don't you know." The squire withdrew from beneath his gold waistcoat a small leather pouch. He opened it sufficiently that the captain and crew could see within it the dozens of sparkling gems. "Let them go together on your ship. What's it called?"

"The *Gimmy More*."

"Right. Put all three aboard the *Gimmy More*. Unless, Captain, you and I, we've rejoined them in, say, ten days, let the hostages be killed and the diamonds forfeit. Is that not fair? Enormously fair?"

There was, the prince could hear, a murmuring lull, a sort of guttural cogitation. It was the turn now, instead of his body, for his head to spin. What was going on? What was being decided?

"Plank, plank," he heard again, "plank, plank," rising again in a crescendo of voice and clapping.

And then the squire's scream: "NO!"

"Plank, plank, plank, plank."

"There's sharks there, waiting," screamed the squire. "Please, no. Please. Anything but that. Please," he begged. "Please, please."

It was a solo voice, behind which was a Ninth Symphony orchestra and chorus, stamping out "plank, plank, plank, plank."

"No! ... NO-O-O-O!"

"Plank, plank ..."

"Please ... please ... Here's my watch ..."

" ... plank, plank ..."

"...my gold waistcoat, my clothes ..."

"... plank, plank ..."

"... please ... anything ... PLEASE ...There's sharks. PLE- ..."

SPLASH!

Splutter, splutter.

Small splash, small splash.

Aah!

Aah!

AAH!

AAAAAAAAAAAAAAAAAAAAAAAAAAAAAAAAH!

Silence.

"Plank, plank, plank, plank."

Still trussed and blindfolded, the prince felt rough hands grabbing his arms. He was frog-marched across the deck.

"Plank, plank, plank, plank."

"Wants a look, does ye, at the little fishies?"

"Plank, plank, plank, plank."

He was forced onto what he could feel was a flight of steps. He felt each one. One ... "plank, plank" ... two ... "plank, plank" ...three. "Plank, plank, plank, plank."

In the small of his back he felt a cutlass's sharp point. It urged him forward. He knew he was on the edge of the plank. Knew that each step may well be his last. "... plank, plank ..." Please God, let him die quickly. Let a shark bite straight away into a vital organ.

"Plank, plank, plank, plank."

Now beneath the plank there was only air. He could feel the additional spring in the wood.

Behind him he could hear growing excitement in the pirates' chant. He could sense beneath him the sharks circling.

"Plank, plank, plank, plank."

Please God let there be a God. Let him be on his way to seeing Philly again, Horatio again. "Plank, plank, plank, plank."

Under his left shoe he could feel the edge of the plank. He knew his next step would be his last one. This would therefore be almost the last second of his life.

He breathed in the air. It felt so good. It smelled and tasted so good. He heard – again – the cawing of gulls, felt again the sun on his cheek, the wind in his hair. That was life, he supposed: Just as he was about to leave the world, all was right with it.

"Plank, plank, plank, plank."

He took a big step forward.

Chapter 30

He fell through space, plunging towards the water, towards the sharks. His life did not pass before him. Nor did time stand still for him. He was frightened, gasping for air, sure he was going to die.

Before, though, these emotions could even properly register he was jerked short. He had remained trussed from the yo-yo game. Clearly the other end of the rope had been attached to something solid, probably the ship's hand-rail.

The jolt hurt him badly. A hurt aggravated by the fact that, dangling, he was being bounced helplessly against the side of the ship. Above him he could hear the massed guffaws of the pirates.

He started trying to loosen the stays about his wrists. If he could free his hands, then he could pull off his blindfold. With the use of his hands and his eyes ... well, he had a chance. So, okay, maybe the pirates *would* end up killing him, but he'd give them a run for their money.

The wrists were already chafed, and each tug caused a sharp pain to race through his entire body. The bruise around his midriff was sizzling into a burn. His body wanted to stop the struggle, to give his wounds time to heal. But his spirit was damned if it were going to give up without a struggle. *Damned* if it were going to – and without, as well, a damn *good* struggle.

Even as he was thinking these things, he felt a tug on the rope. He was being hauled upwards. Back towards the deck. Presumably there he would – again – be made to walk the plank. This time, presumably, *without* the rope. Well, he couldn't do much about that, but what he *could* do, he could make things a bit more difficult for them.

Another tug.

He'd show them, he'd *damn* well show them.

Another tug.

The prince passed out.

***

Nancy was furious. The plum in her mouth had turned into a prune, and this rounded the vowels until they ballooned. "How could you, Baron?" she was saying. "How *could* you?"

Richardson was not yet the smiler that Naitly was. There was no virtuosity yet to Richardson's smiling. But he had hopes. The smile Richardson opted for on this occasion was an advanced one. It was supposed to demonstrate to Nancy understanding and compassion, tempered with a sage pragmatism, honed by a general philanthropy which informed all his decisions and deliberations. What Nancy saw, however, was a sort of asinine and skewiff grin.

Richardson stroked his beard van Dykely.

"If it was for me alone," he said, dribbling wisdom, his grin settling more deeply into its asinine skewiffness, "then, of course, I wouldn't dream of it."

"You are talking, Baron – may I remind you? – of the woman who murdered our son."

"There's now a body of evidence, my dear, to suggest that, in fact, she did not ..."

"... Who, Baron, murdered our son," Nancy repeated. "Don't tell me, dear heart, to see the wider picture."

"Without the wider picture, my dear, you're seeing only part of the picture," said the baron.

"Pretty words," Nancy spat at him. "But *just*, Baron, pretty words. They mean nothing."

"Business associates aren't friends, Nancy. We don't get to choose them in the same way."

"What's the point, then? What is the point of money, Baron, if we don't use it to choose who we choose to spend our time with?" she said, unsure just how much sense she had then made.

"Those who *choose* their friends, my dear, will already have frittered away their money on precisely that luxury."

"So you're going, are you? It doesn't matter what I say. You're going? To Azrac, I mean?"

"You're eating peaches."

"Despite everything, I mean? Everything I say? Everything I may be feeling?"

"Tomorrow you'll want figs."

"Please, Baron, do not fruit at me."

"They come from Azrac, my dear." Nancy looked at her half-eaten apricot as if it had turned into a spider. "If you want peaches and figs we have to trade with Azrac. If *we* have to, it makes no sense that *I* don't. Wider – as I keep on saying, my dear – picture." He started speaking a mite more calmly and considerately. He tried a new smile too. But his face was not yet malleable enough to be able to accommodate it. "I'm not dealing with Cordelia, my dear, I'm dealing with Antonio. And if *I* don't deal with Antonio then someone else will. The consequences to Antonio will be nil."

"He's married to a murderer!"

"It would be a curious way of punishing a murderer," Richardson said: "forcing the parents of his victim into the work-house."

"Work-house?" Nancy snapped back.

"It's full of those, my dear, whose picture was too narrow."

"You won't be seeing Cordelia? Promise?"

"I'll only see her – I promise you, my dear – in the context of a wider picture."

***

Had the prince been conscious when he arrived back on deck he would have seen Squire Squeers standing there as large as life.

His 'walking of the plank' had been just a joke.

The joke now, though, was rather on the pirates. There were severe rope burns around the prince's middle and his wrists. And the lad was comatose. In the slave market this very definitely marked him out as shop-soiled, if not as seconds. An urgency, even a tenderness, entered into the care of the prince – whose true identity, it is worth remembering, was known aboard only by the late, and unlamented, Captain Bligh.

Few indeed (if any) are those born wicked. Almost always, brutal men are bruised men. Almost always, confronted with a fallen bird or a tear-stained child, even the most brutal of men will show an apparently uncharacteristic kindness. What is so rarely understood (even by the brutal themselves) is that it is not the kindness that is out of character but the brutality.

Trim Foocs would have nothing to do with Charming's care. But that was because, at a level unconscious to him – and, God!, how he would have hated to be told this –, he was frightened. He was frightened of his own kindness. He was the dairy farmer who has to employ hands to do the milking because he knows that, should he get to know his cows too well, never would he be able to send them off for slaughter. Trim therefore ordered Drake and Raleigh to look after the unconscious boy.

To begin with, their care was slapdash and casual. But then the prince started to rally. The first time he opened his eyes, Raleigh felt something move in his heart he'd not known since childhood. Tears both started in his eyes, and smarted in them – the sting and sweetness of onion zest. It wasn't that he loved the boy, not in the understood meaning of that word. But there is a kind of love – maybe the love that Christ spoke about so often – which is simply wishing well. That was the love Raleigh had that moment for the young man: He wished him well – and wished him better.

A few minutes later Drake came in with some broth. He too felt feelings he'd thought long since extinct.

"For as long," King Sebastian started, "as women embrace their feelings and men disown theirs it will remain women who are the stronger gender. Men's propensity for seeing black as white is never more obvious than in their perception that emotions are weaknesses. Indeed it might even start, their propensity, with that.

"Those who allow their feelings make civilisation; those who deny them make war. The victor of a war is still a loser; in a civilisation a loser does not exist. Indeed what defines civilisation is a desire to make winners of us all."

"Are we done, Your Majesty?" I asked him. "Might we return to the story?"

The prince would need medical care on several more occasions in his life. Never did he receive such with more genuine (if disguised and understated) concern than at the hands of Raleigh and Drake. Under their care the prince made a full recovery. Not even his burns were any longer visible.

Some thirty leagues off the coast of Biga-buga, the two ships anchored, the *Gimmy More* and the *Silver Hart*. There were those amongst the pirates none too eager to set foot in Biga-buga: Warrants awaited them for their arrest. Arrest would undoubtedly lead to hanging. This crew would take the *Gimmy More* to the Caribbean island of St Duettes, the biggest haven for pirates the world had ever known.

The *Silver Hart* would dock at Biga-buga, sell 'Squire Wodinton' and his horses, a few other of the more esoteric spoils gathered on their sorties. The two ships would meet again in St Duettes in ten days' time.

Obviously, as hostages Drake and Raleigh went with the *Gimmy More*. Their parting from their 'patient' was one where emotion not only had to be suppressed but stifled.

The view of Biga-buga from the sea was probably one of the most famous sights in the world. There were pictures of it in practically every academy in Eastlantic. However many times you may see such representations, though, nothing prepares you for the actual sight of it.

Charming had always known, of course, when seeing those

pictures, that one day he'd see it for real. He had imagined such would have been on some kind of state visit! Not when he was about to be sold into slavery!

The coast-line zigzagged unevenly, green lichen and amber seaweed clinging to rocks the grey and consistency of pumice. Beyond them vast towers, some as high as six storeys, gnawed at the sky with blunted molars. As the ship drew closer these towers seemed to grow, and the area which contained them seemed to broaden.

Sailing into the harbour itself felt Jonah-like, felt almost as if the sailor were plankton about to be consumed by a whale. More oddly than that, far from that sensation being repellent or frightening, it was one of ease, even of succour.

Biga-buga the port made Blefton look like a dinky pleasure marina. Everything was three times the scale of anything in Eastlantic. It was larger, brasher, busier, noisier, more bustling, more populous ... more exciting.

Even as he helped lower the gangplank the prince could not help but be dumbstruck by the sights and the noises, the smells and tastes which assailed him.

As was then customary the captain was the first person to set foot on land. Not only was he dressed in Bligh's uniform, but Captain Foocs had also shaved his beard. He'd even washed his hair. He looked to the world like the self-important captain of a self-important privateer. If anything he looked even more self-important than that acme of self-importance: Squire Squeers.

The Mercian officials were there to greet him. This was, of course, still some time before the advent of passports, but even then there were authorities who needed to check that aboard the ship was not any contraband or anyone with a contagious illness – or a price on his head.

As 'Captain Bligh'/Foocs was descending the gangplank to the quay, Squeers took Charming firmly by the hand. They too started to walk towards Mercian soil.

Out of the corner of his mouth, Squeers said to Charming, "You just stick close to me, dear boy. Don't worry about anything you may have heard. That was just a ruse. No-one's going to harm you or to sell you. It was all I could think of to get you safely on land."

"And what," one of the Mercian officials was asking Captain Foocs, "is the purpose of your trip to Mercia?"

Before the captain had a chance to answer, Squire Squeers said over the top of him, "I am a good personal friend of Mayor Leamore. An enormously good friend of his, don't you know. That man," he said pointing at Trim, "is not Captain Bligh, but Trim Foocs, the pirate. Arrest him."

Chapter 31

Mercia told the world that its system of justice was the finest in the world. And it was. Provided that your definition of 'finest' and of 'justice' was that the poor innocent should be wrongly convicted and the rich guilty should be allowed to walk.

In no country in the world, then as now, did the legal or judicial processes have too much to do with justice. Few countries, though – then as now –, championed so vehemently a two-tiered system of jurisprudence as did Mercia in those days. Those with clout or cash were treated with a gentleness of touch that would have shamed a concert pianist; to those at the other end of the social and/or financial scale was meted out a vengeance at which all but the most extravagant of Roman emperors would have balked.

Captain Foocs had little money (at least that he was able to access immediately). And absolutely no clout. The outcome of his 'trial' was therefore never in question.

Indeed, as so much of Mercian society then, the trial was nothing more than a piece of theatre. A charade, a pantomime. Its principal aim was to advertise the power of the state. "Step out of line," it told its citizens, "and this is an indication of the mightiness of the machine against which you will be pitted; this is the mightiness of the machine that – mightily – will crush you."

Its subsidiary aim was to try and convince the populace that the government and its agencies knew what they were doing.

Crime (largely and precisely because of their two-tiered system of 'justice') was endemic to Mercia. ("Though," said the king, "it has to be said that the Mercians were safer than the government told them they were: Fear is a really efficient way of controlling people.") Even in their own homes Mercians tended not to feel safe. (A tendency admittedly encouraged by both Dawes's gazettes and the government, for the same reasons as mentioned above.) For every one crime 'solved' (by which the authorities meant that someone could be convicted of it, guilty or innocent) ten were committed.

On the rare occasions, therefore, that a suspect could be found who had a good chance of being found guilty, the arrest had to be trumpeted loud and hard by the various authorities – and by Dawes's gazettes – as proof positive of the efficacy and efficiency of those who policed their society.

"You see," King Sebastian continued, "much of Mercian government then was based on the belief that if you repeat a lie often enough it becomes the truth. For which reason huge sections of Mercian society believed huge lies – the biggest of all being that its emperor and his cronies were interested in their welfare.

"If authorities lie to their citizens, my dear, they do so because they are doing something seriously either illegal or immoral. And would claim to be doing so in the name of those citizens who are being lied to! Never do we lie to hide our *good* deeds. If the government of your country – now, today – is lying to you it is your absolute right to know why.

"Your *absolute* right.

"If your government tries to tell you any different, that will tell you as much about your government as you need to know. Because that will tell you your government isn't fit to govern."

"Thank you, sire," I told him, trying not to let my impatience show.

Again he studied me before he continued.

The squire had to see Norman Leamore, Biga-Buga's mayor, and he had to see him quickly. He'd brought Leamore a wanted pirate. He'd brought him a full-blown privateer, more or less in working order. He'd brought him three valuable horses and a boy who had to be worth a doubloon or two. He could feel a place opening up for him in the big boys' gang. He was on his way, he was on his way ...

Leamore agreed to see Squeers without an appointment – big-boys'-gang-like. The mayor was delighted with the capture of Foocs. Delighted. So delighted that he gave Squire Squeers the captured ship, the *Silver Hart*. And he was delighted too with the three horses. He thought a tidy sum could be made from them. Small boys, though, seemed not to be really Leamore's 'thing'. He took one look at Charming, pulled a face and said: "Orphanage, dude."

Together, the two squires (Squeers and 'Wodinton') bustled through the teeming streets, dodging those hawking both wares and phlegm, avoiding feral dogs and horse-drawn carriages, skirting gazette-sellers and town criers.

The prince wanted to dawdle, wanted to absorb some of the new sensations – the smell of roasting chestnuts, the sight of red squirrels, the tang of blossom in the air. But Squeers was anxious that his young charge should be settled.

He was a ship-owner now, after all. He wanted to be aboard his brand-new ship, sailing the seven seas – or sailing, at any rate, however many seas there were between Biga-buga and Azrac. Because the biggest advantage of being a ship-owner is that you can show off your ship – *your* ship – to your friends. Squeers was anxious to show off the *Silver Hart* to Antonio.

Oh, he knew that Drake and Raleigh would be killed. And that was sad. Well, not really, but he could make some kind of stab at feeling some sadness for them. And the diamonds? Well, by now they'd be discovered just to be glass. Why tempt the pirates' wrath by re-joining the *Gimmy More*? No, Squeers was doing perfectly fine, thank you very much, all on his lonesome.

The mayor of Biga-buga did not consider that the city's concern extended to bailing out those of its citizens who had acted irresponsibly. Obviously that included those whose irresponsibility had resulted in a child being born. Its orphanage therefore he was not prepared to fund from the city's taxes – taxes which could more properly be spent on *far* more important commodities: his banquets, for instance, his residence and office and state carriages.

But there is always a need for orphanages, and orphanages always need funding. Because he wanted it known that his heart was big, Mayor Leamore had therefore started up a charity.

It is amazing how good people basically are. It was the people of Biga-buga who, despite already high taxes, contributed sufficiently to the mayor's charity to keep the orphanage funded. Because he wanted it known that his heart was big, the mayor's personal contribution to his charity was handsome: It was only a nominal fee (plus expenses) that he charged for his chairmanship of its board.

The people of Biga-buga were proud of their orphanage. And rightly so. It was a splendid and imposing building. Maybe fifty yards long, its stream-lined façade and its square windows all gleamed; its main entrance, a black set of double-doors, shone like ebony. It completely dominated the almost suburban square in which it was housed. Each time they passed it, the good burghers of Biga-buga were reassured that its orphanage was being well cared for.

This was no illusion. The orphanage *was* well cared for. It belonged to the mayor – who only charged a nominal fee (plus expenses) for its rent. The building, particularly the façade, was very well cared for. Even within it, there were two rooms immaculately cared for: the principal's office and a 'typical' dormitory – used on those occasions when the infrequent nosy benefactor wanted to see some evidence of how his money was being spent.

Squeers pulled down hard on a thin metal strip attached to an attractively tinkling bell. The door was opened by a portly woman in her forties, with rosy cheeks, her blond hair plaited then wrapped in a coil about her crown. Comfort jollied out of her hazel eyes, and bounced from her substantial bosom.

Squeers introduced himself and Charming. "Gertrude my name is," she replied with a – to Charming – curious mix of Mercian and German accents. The smile lasted as long as it took to close the front door.

"Follow me," she said sternly. The foyer was painted in an off-white, broken by a deep blue in its inlays and alcoves. This blue was echoed in the carpet, of a tuft soft enough to be a mattress. Either side of an elegantly columned marble fireplace were two heavily polished panelled doors.

They went through the right-hand one. Which took them from day to night, from warmth to cold, from charity to frigidity. The walls here were of unrendered brick, the floor of ill-laid boards – both bricks and boards hosted a thousand different holes and gashes through which the bitter wind would lash as it iced. By comparison with the atmosphere, though, this wind was balmy and tropical. A solitary gas light hissed out a melancholy song, like a snake with tooth-ache. The light it gave was so feeble it barely reached the floor.

The corridor ended with a door, the varnish of which had long since peeled. This gave onto a cavern of a room lined with cardboard boxes. The floor within was just earth, covered here and there with threadbare mats of reed. In the room's centre was an alabaster slab, not unlike a butcher's. Gertrude took up position behind it. Charming had never visited a butcher's shop. Had he ever done so, he might have expected a cleaver to dance into her hands.

"Clotheses off," she said. The prince looked at her blankly. "*Un*dress," she said, placing the emphasis on the first syllable. "*Un*dress now. *Schnell.*" The prince didn't need to know that '*schnell*' was the German for 'quickly' to understand that's what it meant. He looked around for a changing room. "Here we no secrets have. The clotheses off. Now. *Schnell.*" The prince appealed to Squire Squeers, but he had sat himself on the edge of the slab, and was clearly not about to intervene.

"*Schnell,*" Gertrude repeated, with ever greater impatience. As she spoke so she turned to one of the shelves behind her and removed a box. Inside of this was a pair of grime-encrusted, very holey breeches, and a v-necked 'T-shirt' whose 'v' had lost all definition. Shoes: none; socks: none; jersey: none.

Despite the cold of the room, Charming found himself very hot. He was blushing from head to bandaged toe. He was totally unused to undressing publicly. That he could remember *no-one* had seen him naked. He scampered into the breeches, however loathsome, just as quickly as he could.

Gertrude was rearranging boxes on the shelves. "What's that?" the squire asked of the bandage on the prince's toe.

"Nothing, sir. It's just a bandage, sir," the prince replied.

Gertrude turned back to the young man and addressed him sternly, "Clotheses *in* the box. Here have we no servants. Or *if* we them have, it is you who they are. Clotheses. Box. Schnell."

The prince hastily threw his clean clothes into the box. Already it felt to him that fleas were nibbling at him, or lice. His whole body was seized by a violent itch which made him want to scratch all the skin from his body.

Gertrude looked at the box, looked at the prince, looked back at the box. Twice more. And then she simply upended the box, spilling all its contents again over the slab. "These worth money are," she said. "Here we things correctly do, properly." She weighed each syllable. "You will the clotheses fold – correctly, properly." She again turned back to the shelves.

Charming, unaccustomed to such tasks, was no adept at folding clothes – or, even, clothes*es*! He tried to straighten them a little more when they were in the box. As he did so, out of the corner of his mouth, he whispered to the squire, "Please, sir. Don't make me take it off, sir, the bandage. I've been told it could cost me my life."

The squire beamed on his charge benevolently. "Got nothing to do with me, dear boy. No skin off my nose, don't you know? Enormously not. All that, that sort of stuff, that'll be down to your new owner."

"Sir?" Charming asked, not understanding.

"*Was ist das*?" asked Gertrude of the badly folded 'clotheses' in the box. "What is that?" she repeated in English.

"Sorry," the prince said sheepishly. "I'll try again."

"We do not all day have," Gertrude shot back at him. "No food for you today."

"You might want to think about that, dear lady," said Squeers. "The mayor tomorrow is bringing over a potential buyer, don't you know."

"Oh?" asked Gertrude.

"Protector of Zanoria, if I'm not too much mistaken. Tode Ostrich, is that right?"

"*Real*rich," Gertrude corrected him, enunciating the real name almost with reverence. "Tode *Real*rich."

"*Real*rich, that's the cove," confirmed Squeers.

"It will not him be, but an envoy. Realrich leaves never Zanoria. The envoy comes tomorrow?" asked Gertrude. "And for *him*?" The tone conveyed that she could scarcely believe her ears. She grabbed the prince and sized him up, back and front. She squeezed his arms, then pinched both cheeks, forcing the prince to open his mouth. She gazed at his teeth, pulled at one or two. "You could have something said."

"I did something say," said Squeers, but the mock was wasted. "I have *just* something said, don't you know."

"I don't understand," said the prince.

"*Was*?" Gertrude exclaimed in German. "*WAS*? You, *junger Mann*, you will speak only – '*only*', do you understand – when *to* you you are spoken. Understand?"

The prince nodded mutely.

"I have to go," Squeers told her. "Keep your mouth shut, young squire Wodinton, and your nose clean," this was his parting shot, "and – really, don't you know? – it's not so bad, a slave's life. Enormously not so bad."

"A slave's life? But this, sir, is an orphanage, sir."

"Of course it is, dear boy. Of course it is."

He and Gertrude capsized in a whirlwind of giggles.

Chapter 32

Not only was Naitly indignant, but he knew that he was right to be. His temper was a stallion which had seen a snake: It needed very firm handling to keep it under control.

Not even Lord Chancellors, though, storm out of meetings with the king – not if they value their heads, at least; not, at least, out of meetings with King *Cole*. True, no Lord Chancellor *had* stormed out, and thus the theory remains only that. But the theory had carried enough weight to check a succession of Lord Chancellors who had been tempted. As Naitly had been tempted. Latterly, even *very* tempted.

Goneril had been giving him a hard time: She had wanted the succession issue resolved once and for all. She had dragooned Naitly into preparing a paper with her. They had spent months, burnt gallons of midnight oil preparing that paper, arguing the case from every conceivable angle, countering every conceivable (and the occasional *in*conceivable) objection.

Naitly had just presented that paper. The king's response was simply to ignore all the hard work, pooh-pooh all the weight of the weighty arguments, and adamantly to refuse even to entertain the idea.

To cap all of which, HM (who as a recently appointed government minister was now answerable to Naitly) had been on the king's side!

Naitly catapulted from the inner sanctum. Had he, like Mercury, had winged heels, they would have been Catherine wheels.

He was relieved that, for once, Goneril was not already in the corridor waiting for him; and then he was indignant because he heard the door behind him re-open. It was completely certain that the king would not have followed him, therefore it had to be HM.

"You now answer to me, HM," Naitly told her without even

turning around.

"Oh dear, Lord Chancellor, is our little nosey-wosey out of joint?" HM sidled up to his side. She was playing with him. Maybe even – very gently – flirting with him.

"I don't think you understand, HM," said Naitly, for once allowing the man predominance over the Lord Chancellor, "how ... very difficult Goneril can sometimes be."

"Oh, I think I do. She is her father's daughter, is she not?"

"And her mother's," warned Naitly.

"God, *that's* still an issue?"

"He did chop off her head, HM," said Naitly blandly.

"On the other hand," HM replied urging him to be reasonable, "she was planning to assassinate him."

"Oh I know, I know. Some people seem to have the most sentimental attachments to the oddest of things, mothers and such like," Naitly remarked, as if such were a proposition of Euclidean complexity. "Some people in this instance meaning Goneril."

"Pay it no heed, Baron," HM returned with emphasis. "That is just so much saccharine propagated by merchants to sell the unsellable – Mother's Day cards, lavender bath salts, that kind of ...execrable excrescence." She wanted him to have thought that witty.

Naitly failed to react. "You have to start supporting me, HM," he said with a change of tack so neat it was seamless. "I cannot stress it too strongly. You are a minister now."

"And you, Baron, are a baby. Frankly, you're getting a bit long in the tooth still to be one."

"Excuse me?" asked Naitly, his hackles now scratching the ceiling.

"Babyness in the newly born is inevitable. Sometimes it is almost endearing. In adulthood, trust me, it is merely irksome."

"You try my patience, madam, more than is prudent."

"More babyness. If I simply join forces with you against the king, he'll just find someone else to replace me. What foe is more deadly? A tiger in the open? Or a snake invisible in the grass?"

Naitly appraised the jester coolly. "You're not all baubles and bells, are you, HM?"

HM sidled even closer. She looked at his mouth. She looked at his eyes. *Into* his eyes. "You ever thought," she asked quietly, coquettishly, "you might be engaged to the wrong woman?"

Lightly she traced her index fingernail under his chin. Then she laughed lightly, a soufflé of a laugh, and tripped dancingly down the corridor.

Naitly followed her every ripple.

***

Cross-Bones were starting to make money. Serious money. Of all unlikely scenarios, as after-dinner speakers. They were – not to put too fine a point on it, nor to labour the pun overly – making a killing. In point of fact (the same point as that not to put too fine a one on), they were making a considerably greater killing after-dinner speaking than the killing they ever made from killing.

They had money now, status, prestige – as evinced by their recently awarded pointed shoes. They were wondering about accessories for those shoes. After long deliberation, they decided on a wife.

***

"Mumsy," said Winny one day. The two sisters and their mother were taking tea in the drawing room – whose name was considerably posher than its size. It was a pokey little room, which struggled to contain three bustles all at the same time. Its furnishings were now either fading or faded. From the iron grate a small fire gave out a fragile heat.

"What might it be, Edwina?" asked Prim.

"I've been ... well, it's ..." she jiggled, trying to ease her excitement out like toothpaste from a tube, instead letting it blop in unseemly dollops, "... I'm so excited ... It's ... well, it's ... I've been *proposed* to, Mumsy."

"Oh, Winny," complained her sister. "You're such a beast. Really. *Such* a beast. I wanted to say it first. It was my turn. Mumsy, I've been proposed to too," she said and sank her eyes in the way her novelettes told her that romantic heroines did.

"By the same man?" asked Prim, in a horror she hoped would be mock.

"Oh, Mumsy!" shrieked the two girls together.

"Well," Prim continued, carefully replacing her red-and-white bone-china cup on its almost matching saucer as, in a way that appeared synchronised, she carefully replaced her little finger back into its fist, "it would seem that romance is *indeed* in the air. For I too have had a proposal of marriage."

"Oh, Mumsy!" shrieked Ginny again and threw her arms around her mother.

"Oh, Mumsy!" shrieked Winny again and threw her arms around her mother's other shoulder.

"So," said Prim, patting one hand each of both of her girls, "a triple wedding."

"Do you think," asked Edwina in tones she would like to have believed hushed, "the cathedral's free?"

***

Zanoria was on the Westernmost boundary of Mercia. Most of it was land captured from either the Waifu or the Tay nations.

Fredvie was anxious to extend Zanoria further, and to take yet more land from these indigenous peoples. To further which end Fredvie had appointed as 'Protector' of Zanoria a good friend of his, Tode Realrich – nicknamed Ostrich by most of his contemporaries (hence Squeers's mistake) because of his habit, in times of crisis, of burying his head in the sand. Tode and Fredvie shared many similar interests and passions – the acquisition of greater power and ever more money being the two principal ones.

The war against the Tay and the Waifu wasn't at this stage the all-out bellicosity it was all too soon to become. Tode was, frankly, not interested enough to create that much work for himself. Tode's chief passion was hunting – four-legged prey as opposed to two-. But he had to justify his government subsidy somehow. So there was the odd skirmish to organise. Which – "jigger me toenails" – demanded he be there to oversee it. Sometimes even – "jigger me toenails" – to participate in it. He almost never therefore left Zanoria. And, on those rare occasions he did leave, his trips even more rarely took him as far as Biga-buga. Whenever he needed fresh slaves or (far more importantly) new horses, he therefore sent an envoy.

This envoy was almost as lazy as Realrich himself. Leamore had told him there was a new young squire at the orphanage, had told him there were three excellent horses which could be attached thereto to make a job lot. The envoy, to please Realrich, had to be seen to be going through an exercise. But all involved directly knew that an exercise was exactly what it was.

***

The prince had been given the slave name of 'Tookums'. It would be for his new owner to change it or not. But such, for the time of his residence in the Biga-buga orphanage, it would remain.

There was something about Tookums which made Gertrude nervous. She sent word of her anxiety to Mayor Leamore. Oh, a fair amount of toffs had passed through their portals, it wasn't that. It was ... that there was something *more* than just toff-like about this young man: His skin was too soft, his hands too uncal-loused, his demeanour ... too pampered.

It had been their rule, Leamore's and Gertrude's, never to

question their suppliers too closely. Posh slaves were good news: There was a snob value attached to them which meant they could command *big* duds – 'duds' was Mercian slang at the time for 'doubloons'.

Ultra-posh slaves, though … well, the ultra good news that they might be was tempered by the ultra *bad* news they could also be. A few years back, a wealthy English duke, searching for his son, had caused them a *lot* of problems; a few months after that, a Swedish count, in similar circumstances, had got very close to exposing the whole – beautiful – scam. So, to maximise the good news and minimise the risk of bad, the ultra-posh slaves had to be pushed through the system as fast as was humanly (or, to be more accurate, *in*humanly) possible.

Gertrude suggested to Leamore the sale should take place the following day.

The night Charming spent in the orphanage dormitory was extremely uncomfortable. The beds were no more than straw mattresses on the floor. There were no blankets, there was no heat. He slept with his teeth chattering. He was awakened several times by the sound of scurrying. Rats. Once his waking was when one of them bit him.

There were maybe forty or fifty other children in this dormitory, and there were five more dormitories.

There was no privacy in this place, and thus no dignity. Boys and girls 'bathed' communally. The loo was just a filthy bucket in one corner of the dormitory, emptied once a day by whoever that day had been caught infringing one of the rules. There was around it not even a shred of a curtain, nor a hint of a screen.

The worst aspect of all for the prince was that there was virtually no talking between them. He tried to start a conversation. He was told, "Don't pay to make friends here. Tomorrow they'll be gone." It wasn't that there was hostility, just an institutionalised indifference – or a somewhat truculent apathy, depending on the individual.

Before Mayor Leamore and Realrich's envoy arrived at the orphanage, Tookums was introduced to the cat. It was not a domestic cat, or a gentle one. It never purred. When wielded, though, it would sometimes whistle. It had nine tails.

One word or gesture out of line, especially when potential customers were around, and the malefactor would be introduced to the cat. Even the suspicion of a misplaced word or gesture sufficed. No-one had ever misbehaved twice. No-one would have survived a second meeting with the cat.

For the length of the slave sale, Tookums (alongside another half-dozen of the institution's inmates) was allowed to wear only a loin-cloth, albeit a (mercifully) clean one. The orphanage had a reputation to protect: It never knowingly sold substandard goods. The transparency of this packaging was intended to be a safeguard.

The invoice said that Tookums had been sold to the envoy for twenty thousand duds. Of which the envoy gave Leamore seventeen and a half. Fifteen was split by Leamore and Gertrude ... oh, very fairly, seven-and-a-half thousand each. There were no overheads. These were picked up by the good burghers of Biga-buga.

Which good people, because they *were* good people, would have been horrified – totally and truly horrified – at the orphanage's real purpose.

Gazettes, of course, should be there exactly for that reason: on behalf of good people to expose corruption, to weed out abuse. *Dawes's* gazettes, though, were there only to *pretend* to tell the truth.

By dissembling the truth, by pretending to be truthful, by concealing the whole truth – and by a hundred different methods of bending and shaping the truth without (quite) ever straightforwardly lying – they lied more effectively than would any straightforward lie.

So often, *so* often the Dawes's gazettes had thus lied.

So, so often the good people – the *good* people – of Biga-buga had been sold a lie. Most of them, really, *good* people. And they'd been sold not one lie, but a succession of lies.

Lie after lie after lie.

Again and again and again.

So often that no-one any longer was able to demarcate the line between untruth and truth. Not even the liars knew any longer when they were lying.

After a bit of aptly named horse-trading, the horses Leamore sold to the same envoy, at twenty-eight thousand duds each. They were, the envoy thought, the finest beasts he'd ever seen. The envoy therefore knew that, whatever misgivings his boss might have about the price he'd paid for Tookums, such would be more than assuaged by his glee at the horses.

For his part Charming/Tookums really didn't know what to feel. Before he fully knew he was in the orphanage, he was out of it. He went to stay, short-term, with the envoy.

This envoy had no wish to present the young man to Realrich in anything but pristine condition. He was clearly going to be a house-slave. Neither fleas nor lice were generally considered attractive accessories on such slaves.

There was, the following week, a further detachment of militia going West on the 'Accidental', as it was called. Charming would join them. So would his horses.

Which was Charming's only comfort. He knew that, for as long as he had his horses with him, he would not be alone.

Chapter 33

If weather be the measure of Paradise, Azrac was a paradise. And still is. During the year rarely was there rain on more than twenty days; as many days again were dry but overcast. On over three hundred days the sun shone. No-one in Azrac even owned a winter cloak.

Its beaches were not of Caribbean white sand, but of Dijon mustard, so ochrey in their yellow as almost to be burnished gold. Giant palm trees and spider trees yawned expansively in the gentle breeze. The azure sea sparkled like a sapphire mine caught in the glitter of a shooting star.

Azrac's climes are halcyon climes, and the times that Cordelia and Antonio had within those halcyon climes, they were halcyon times. They had by now two children of their own: a girl, Viola, and their baby son, Sebastian. (It was no coincidence Charming later chose this name for his kingship.) Life was complete. A complete life is a happy one. Complete bar one thing: Cordelia saw what was happening to Belgiss.

She saw too what was happening to Mercia. And that hurt her. It is painful watching someone kill himself. The hurt, however, turns to anguish if that would-be suicide starts murdering the innocents around him, and you cannot stop him.

Anguish came to Cordelia when she saw what Mercia was doing, and what it was seeking to do, saw the consequences to Belgiss of those deeds and intentions, and then extended those to the wider world.

There was a tyranny spreading which masqueraded (as tyranny always does) as benevolence. There was a subjugation infiltrating in the name of expansion.

The world only expands when most people within it expand. And Cordelia knew that. A situation where the most are subjugated to benefit the few can never be expansion; it is not even simple diminution. It is repression. It is barbarism. It is blasphemy.

All of this Cordelia knew. And it saddened her and racked her. The stain and stench of tyranny, those saddened her; she was *tortured* by being able to do so little about it.

Still ...

That night would be jolly. That night they had Squeers coming to dinner.

It was May.

May in Azrac is even more halcyon than the rest of the year. Hyacinths throw their smell about like may-poling incense-burners. The wild flowers splodge the countryside with colour more lushly and anarchically than on any painter's palette. The days are longer. Which means there are more hours for the sun to sear into the earth. But it hasn't yet started to scorch that earth or to parch it. The cicadas are gargling in their dressing-rooms, but are not yet on stage. Belgiss is still soggy, cold in the evenings; in Azrac dinner 'al fresco' is not only possible, it is desirable – and relatively insect free.

They'd not seen Squeers since the wedding. Since which time the squire's fortunes had improved immeasurably. He was now so grand he owned his own galleon!

Also coming to the party was Baron Richardson. Things between Cordelia and the baron were ... strained.

In trying to see the wider picture, Richardson sought to throw a veil over the whole Horatio thing. Cordelia, though, did not want the 'Horatio thing' veiled. She was convinced that Goneril had poisoned the children, and absolutely certain that, not only had she not killed them, but that, in no way and in no measure, had she aided the crime or abetted it. She wanted her sister charged, and herself exonerated.

Antonio had business to do with the two businessmen. He'd bought the worldwide patent on a new weapon invented by an Azrian engineer, the double-barrelled musket. He was sure it would revolutionise warfare. From both his two guests he expected substantial orders. The sprat he considered necessary to catch these two enormous mackerels was a really sumptuous meal. No expense had therefore been spared in its preparation, no detail overlooked.

A compote of larks' tongues and whitebait fins was followed by an octopus and oyster soufflé. The main course was a ragout of milk-fed camel. For pudding were brought wild strawberries available only on one of the highest crests of Mount Galti, Azrac's highest mountain.

Richardson and Cordelia had both observed proprieties – punctiliously. And a courteous evening had been had by all.

Coffee had recently been brought to Eastlantic from the New World. It was considered a delicacy. The servants were flitting amongst the guests recharging their coffee-cups. (Slavery had by then already been abolished in Azrac, although it must be conceded that such was largely only in name. Domestic servants were expected to work enormous hours, their reward derisory.)

"And the king?" asked Cordelia. "How is he?"

"Grieving," said the baron. "He's still convinced the prince will turn up. Still sure he's suffered some amnesic shock or other. Still certain that the tattoo will identify him."

"Tattoo?" Squeers asked, but more out of politeness than genuine curiosity. He'd brought with him from Mercia an exotic luxury as yet unknown in Eastlantic: a cigar. This he was gently puffing at as the conversation ambled. He'd thought about investing in the cigar's plant, tobacco, but had then decided it was a taste far too sophisticated for it ever to enjoy any true measure of popularity.

As Richardson continued with the story of the tattoo, however (there now being, in Richardson's mind, no reason why he should not), Squeers's curiosity became genuine indeed. From genuine to intense. He puffed more intensely on his cigar.

He knew HM was Captain Bligh's sister. He remembered the plaster he'd seen on 'Squire Wodinton' in the orphanage. As the others continued to speak, so the yarn of the intrigue started, before his very eyes, to unravel. He began to see the whole thing.

Not only that. He started to realise that he knew where the prince was. More or less, anyway. And he knew he was alive.

He was probably the only person in the world who did know.

And *that* knowledge, that was indeed power.

That knowledge, that was power which was *real* power.

***

There are those who love war. Weapons manufacturers, for instance, love war. Those who make military uniforms. War, for a few, is a way of making unchecked fortunes.

HM could see the money being made by the few. She was in control now of the coffers from which they were paid. A remarkable number of these few would snort self-righteously about the 'hooliganism' of the young, and despair of these youths' propensity for violence. She tried to find such sallies amusing. She rarely succeeded.

In her ministerial capacity she was at a meeting with Naitly and Goneril.

"Our acadamies are crumbling, Lord Chancellor," she told him. "Our infirmaries have no money left for leeches. The war with Orismine is a huge drain on our resources. We have to pull out of it."

Goneril just snorted. "This is the quality, is it," she sneered, "of our ministers today?"

"Mercia is our ally," Naitly explained, as if to an idiot. "We have made a commitment. Not to honour such a commitment would, I cannot stress too much, be not only dishonourable but disastrous."

"To continue with this war, Lord Chancellor, *that* – trust me – would be disastrous. Ever to have started it was dishonourable."

"If you need more revenue," Goneril suggested wearily,

"raise taxes." She'd made the suggestion several times previously.

"A tax, maybe, on carriages?" HM wondered.

"*We* have carriages, HM," Goneril retorted.

"Our contributors have carriages," Naitly added.

"Do be sensible, woman," Goneril admonished.

"Kindling!" exclaimed Naitly. "Let's put a tax on kindling."

"The poor use kindling," said HM, trying to mimic the 'idiot' tone of voice Naitly had used on her, but succeeding only in sounding cranky. "Oil'd be better. The rich use oil."

"The rich are our *contributors*," Naitly pointed out, succeeding in the 'idiot' tone at which HM had failed.

"The poor are starving," said HM flatly.

"Nature's way of keeping the population under control," Goneril told her.

"Kindling!" said Naitly emphatically.

"Kindling!" said Goneril decisively.

"No," HM protested.

"Two to one," said Naitly. "That, HM, is called 'democracy'."

"I'll denounce it to the Press."

"I don't think so," said Naitly, adding his guffaw to Goneril's tinkle of laughter. HM realised how silly that suggestion was.

"I'll speak out against it in public."

"This is Cabinet responsibility, HM," Goneril chortled. "We are one, as far as the public is concerned. That's the way it has to be. You could always resign, return your ermine smock."

"A tax," said HM, with a sort of willowy sadness, "on kindling, I think we agreed."

***

There were gold mines in the Waifu territory and diamond mines in that of the Tay.

Dawes was anxious to acquire the wealth that was hidden in

these mines. Not even Dawes could simply go in and steal them. He could only acquire them as spoils of war. So, that's what he needed: war. He therefore needed the skirmishes against the Tays and Waifu to develop into war. To further which end, his gazettes printed long reports about the way in which the Tays had massacred Zanorian settlers, or the Waifu had. Zanoria therefore needed protecting. Dawes's gazettes screamed from banner headlines the responsibility Mercia had to protect Zanoria.

In response to which Fredvie was, in ever increasing numbers, sending troops Westward. They travelled in huge columns, alongside settlers from the East who thought a future could be reclaimed in this new land which had been confiscated in the old.

The journey from Biga-buga to Zanoria was one of rugged splendour and an ever-changing landscape. The forests in the East ceded to huge plains in the centre. These eventually came to a huge river over which a magnificent mountain range loured with majesty and menace.

The trek was originally called the 'Occidental'. But because of the death rate, over time it had come to be known as the '*A*ccidental'. Close to a thousand set out, only a few more than five hundred finished. And if the survival chance for adults was only somewhat better than fifty: fifty, that for children was even lower. Ninety-three children left Biga-buga. Thirty-seven arrived.

Of those thirty-seven, Charming (or Tookums) was one.

His owner inspected his new possessions in order of their importance: the horses first, then Charming, then three other slaves designated as field-slaves.

These last were taken immediately to the outhouse where the outdoor slaves were housed. The outhouse was a bleak building made of chiselled stone. Latterly, in a spirit of unusual hospitality, Realrich had allowed a chimney to be added to the homestead. Cold sickened slaves. And sick slaves did not work well. During the bleakest days of winter Realrich therefore allowed them the most meagre of fires.

There were sixty or so of these field-slaves who shared the accommodation. Slowly, the space occupied by each slave had been accepted by the others as belonging to that person. Field-slaves were expected to wash below the hand-pump in what was called the yard. Over the complete lack of latrine facilities we will draw a delicate veil.

Those slaves who worked *inside* the house fared somewhat better. They were expected to be clean and unsmelly. Therefore they were occasionally even allowed to bathe.

There were six male indoor-slaves and twelve female ones. Their quarters were divided by the width of the house: men slept on the far right; women on the far left. A few of these indoor-slaves even – as Realrich never tired of telling them – had beds. Added to which luxury, a certain snobbery pertained amongst the local slave-owners in regard to the lilyness of slaves' skin. This encouraged further 'pampering' – though not so much, of course, as to detract the 'inslaves' (as they were known) from their household duties.

Both inslaves and outslaves worked from the time they awoke till the time they slept. Idling was not permitted. There was *never* not work to be done: A polished table could be re-polished, a window rewashed, a floor re-swept. Indolence was severely punished – just as soon as Realrich awoke from any one of the dozen dozes with which his day was punctuated.

That notwithstanding, at least twice a day Charming contrived a reason to be sent outside. He had to see his horses. He needed to reassure himself they were alright, and to reassure them that he was.

He would lope – eland-like – round the side of the house to the splendidly appointed stables. (Stables which financial prudence dictated *should* be splendidly appointed: Realrich had a considerably greater investment in his horses than in his slaves.)

It was a five-star stable. Whereas most stables smell of dung, this one smelled of leather and wood polish. The stalls were defined by seasoned hardwood; straw carpeted the floor with a thick pile. And it had, of course, its own slaves to man it: those to groom the horses and muck them out; those to exercise them or change their shoes; and one who guarded them at night.

Charming hated seeing others grooming his horses. But he knew there was nothing he could do about it. Not for the moment. Not till he could work out a plan.

As has already been noted, the community in suffering is a mythical one. The inslaves were not liked by the outslaves. They thought them indulged and indulgent.

The first day the prince came to visit therefore ... well, it was to change the whole course of his life. Without it, maybe there'd have been no Cinderella story ever to tell.

Chapter 34

It was night. Night in Zanoria was velvety and soothing. Stars glistened almost ostentatiously; the moon was a huge ball (bigger then Charming remembered it from Belgiss) and tinged with a fiery orange that made it both sun-like but also, almost paradoxically, redolent of peace. Its light was sufficient to see by – not in detail, but enough to avoid bruising. It silhouetted the scenery with a hundred hues of blacks and dark, dark purples. It was a different but no less a beauty to that of the day. It gave starkness to opulence. It underscored how very fluid an element beauty is.

The night clanged with stillness. The solitary hoot of a screech-owl shrieked into it, a draper ripping the night's velvet.

'Tookums' jumped. The hoot had frightened him.

His whole body was a-jitter with fright, possessed of a zillion nerve-ends all straining at the full extent of their leash, alive to the slightest change of sight, of smell or sound, of taste or touch.

He was scared that he might be discovered, scared of the dire punishment that would follow, scared lest his horses had been harmed.

Scared of this new environment, of this new life.

He crept along the moonlit wall, darting from shadow to shadow. He felt the rough-clad of the house on his fingers as he scuttled past, the pre-dawn dew on his ankle; he smelt the drowsy jasmine and the dozing smoulder of dying fires. He smarted when he brushed against a shadowed nettle, and winced when he caught a splinter in his middle finger from the large door that gave ingress to the stable.

Crouching, he opened this door the merest crack. He slipped inside lithely, almost lizard-like, and quickly – but quietly – closed the door again behind him. Like a spaniel he squatted, ears pricked, listening for the slightest sound. Still scared. Scared lest he should have disturbed the horses, scared that consequently they may start neighing, that such might start attracting unwanted attention.

All, though, remained still. Even the smells of the leather were snoring. Even those of horse and dung. Slowly his eyes acclimatised themselves to this new light. From his crouched position he started trying to identify the occupant of each stall. All he could see was shapes.

He scampered closer, whispering their names. "Peggy," he said, "Horsa, Philly." At each stall he paused, waiting for a reaction.

The stables were cavernous. There was maybe a score of stalls either side of the building. In an inversion of the usual fairy-tale scenario where frogs turn into princes, this prince seemed to have turned into a frog: Like a frog he hopped from stall to stall. "Philly," he continued to whisper, "Horsa, Peggy."

There were two huge windows, set high into the walls. Through these the moon poured in its milky light. "Horsa, Peggy, Philly," the prince hisspered again, and waited.

No reaction.

He hopped on to the next stall. "Peggy," again he whispered, his tone increasing in urgency. "Horsa, Phill- ..."

There was a knife at his throat.

He knew immediately what it was. Even without pressure being applied, his throat could feel the keenness of its blade. On the side of the stall he could see the reflected flare from where the moonlight bounced off the metal. It was a strong arm which held the blade, but a thin one. If he were going to die, it would not be without a struggle. A strategy started to form in his brain.

"I'm not doing any harm," he said. "Just came to see my horses." By way of an answer his hair was gripped, his head pulled back, and his neck totally exposed. "Just tell me what you want," he continued, a whisper of despair curdling the assumed lightness of his tone.

"You ... want ... harm ... horses," a gruff voice said behind him. It was faltering, but emphatic.

"No," the prince replied firmly. "No. I want to comfort horses. Horses *my* horses." He patted his breast, felt the knife therefore being pressed closer on his throat. "I want stroke horses." He stroked the air, trying the mime the action. He felt the arm about his shoulder relax a little. He moved his arm in a stroking motion back and forth … forth and back … back and forth …

And then sharply back.

Straight into his assailant's solar plexus.

He heard a groan. He'd hoped he would also hear the clatter of a knife as it hit the floor. But that sound did not come. The grasp on his hair, though, and that about his shoulders were relaxed sufficiently – if only momentarily – for him to be able to squirm free.

With a dexterity born of necessity he executed an acrobatic turn which would have shamed most pumas.

He found himself on his feet, crouched, facing his protagonist.

Who had also sprung to his feet, and was crouched similarly facing him, the knife continuing its menacing glint in the moon.

The figure opposite him was a youth, maybe a year or two younger than 'Tookums'. Fuzz had yet to break the skin of his cheeks or chin. He wore breeches which, in the moonlight, looked bleached. He was barefoot, but clearly used to being so. His feet were as supple as most hands. The boy's skin was swarthy and looked as if it had been coated in olive oil. Below it rivuletted the muscles of a panther – glistening not just with brute strength, but also with agility and cunning: a dancer's muscles more than a boxer's. His head was crowned with a peculiar mobcap, not unlike those worn by the crones knitting below the guillotine, but woven with intricate design and livid, earth-tone colours; he wore a ragged crew-neck top.

The young mouth currently was set square in an expression of defiance and contempt. But the brown, brown eyes which sought to emulate the mouth also bore fear.

This was no enemy, Charming realised, but a pussycat who,

thinking itself in a corner, was baring its claws.

"I do not want to fight you," said Charming with his voice, whilst his body remained alert, ready to defend itself.

From a couple of stalls there were a few hoof-clumps. This did alarm the prince. This could waken the outslaves guarding the horses. Charming was considerably more anxious about the threat they posed than by that from this young adversary, whoever he might be.

"Me," Charming said, starting to relax his pose, acutely aware of the horses, not wanting to disturb them any more than already they had been, "friend. Me," he repeated, extending his hand, "friend."

In reply to which the young aboriginal slashed at his outstretched hand with his knife. Knee-jerkly, the prince withdrew it. "No," the prince said, forcing himself, albeit, tentatively again to offer his hand, "me *friend*." He allowed himself to become completely upright. He took an apprehensive step towards his foe.

"Horses," said the latter in a light treble at variance with the heavy bass of his stance, "my work."

"Your work, yes," said the prince appeasingly. "Your work, absolutely. Me, used to own some of the horses. Three horses …" He held up three fingers in the interest of clarification. "… mine," he said patting his chest: "Peggy, Horsatio, Philly, three horses my horses. Me, I come say 'hello'. 'Hi'. Just want say 'hi' to my horses."

"Horses my work," repeated the young boy, his eyes losing some of their fear but staying resolute in their hostility.

"Yes," the prince reassured him. "Yes. Your work. Yes." He took another step forward. The boy sprung a step back, his body tautening again in apprehension. "Not fight," said the prince. "Not want fight. Not with you. Me," he said, again tapping his breast, "also slave. Work in house. We," he waved his hand between the two of them, "both slaves. You and I. The same."

He could see the boy understood barely a word of what was being said to him, but he could also see that the lad was being mollified – by the evenness, presumably, of his voice's timbre. The boy was still ready to kill him, but truce was nervously peeping from below the bedclothes.

The prince looked him square in the eyes, almost indeed as if he were one of his horses. The glance was aimed at emulating the timbre, aimed also at reassurance. "It's all right," he said. "I don't want to hurt you, don't want to fight with you." He completed the step. "It's all right," he kept saying to the boy. "Me friend. Friends, you and me. Friends."

He took another step closer.

He was at a distance where he could almost touch the knife-wielder.

He waited.

He allowed the boy's anxiety to abate. Reassured him again with his eyes, with a gentle accompanying smile. Took another step forward.

Then grabbed the boy's knife wrist.

He whirled it, and therefore the boy, in a wrestling move which would have been of consummate skill had skill played any part in it.

This time the knife did clatter to the stable floor, and the lad let out a high-pitched squeal of both surprise and terror.

The prince whipped him round, holding him in a half-nelson. Then he smiled over the boy's shoulder. "Me friend. Me no want fight. All right? All right? Me let you go now, all right? No knives. No need of knives."

But he'd been careless of his left hand, which the lad suddenly grabbed and bit. As a terrier bites. This time it was the prince who howled, and instinctively loosened his grip.

The boy saw this as his chance to escape. He tried to bolt.

But the prince lunged after him and, lacking purchase elsewhere, seized the cap. Which came away in his hands. A thick clump of jet black hair slithered from under it.

"You're a girl," exclaimed Charming, perhaps unnecessarily.

The girl ran to the knife. But Charming beat her to it. He just stood on it. This seemed, literally, to petrify the girl. Who, turned to stone, stood stock still, staring at the trapped knife.

For a few seconds thus they stood. Until, caught again in the moonlight, the prince saw the shimmer of a tear trickling down her cheek.

He proffered the girl her cap. She was quick to sweep up all her hair, replace it in its 'cover'. "Please," she turned to the prince, "not talk. About me. Master, he think I boy. If he know I girl, soon I have to ... marry he."

"Me friend," Charming told her. He wiped away her tear with the cuff of his shirt. "We friends." Again he waved his hand between the two of them.

"Please," said the girl. "*Please.*" Her eyes were aflame with entreaty. "We friends." He offered to hug her. She accepted the offer. It was a gawky hug, but one too of tenderness and consideration.

It had been a long time since either had been hugged. To a man dying of thirst a muddy puddle is an oasis. However self-conscious the hug, to both these young people it was an act of lovingness and kindness. It was a moment both would remember.

They found Charming's three horses. Together they stroked them and petted them. Charming even allowed her to help him groom them. He knew it was a gesture, that she'd have to be seen to be grooming them during the day when the overseers were monitoring her work, but the gesture was an important one. To them both.

Using a lot of sign language and a great deal of good will, Charming found out about the girl. She was Tay by birth and had been captured about four months previously in one of Realrich's infrequent forays. Her name was Syun Drette, which in Tay means (roughly) Sparkling Laugh. Three expeditions had already been mounted to recapture her. Clearly, unsuccessfully. Men on both sides had been killed, including one of her brothers. This greatly saddened her.

Here she had no-one to talk to, and she lived in a permanent fear of being unmasked. She adopted a veneer of hostility as the best way of stopping people getting too close. She remained anxious that Charming would give away her secret. He vowed that he would die before he did so.

He noticed that the sky had changed colour, and that slivers of red and yellow and orange were darting across the sky like disembodied, but still very much alive dragons' tongues.

He had to get back to the house. And quickly. The other slaves would soon be rising. He couldn't afford to be missed.

There was nothing gawky about the hug they now shared. Nothing self-conscious or muddy-puddle-like about it. It was open and generous and expansive. It took in the whole world. And, in embracing the world, it also cocooned the two of them within an eggshell that was as strong as titanium and as gentle as goose-down.

Both knew that, for as long as they were encased in that shell, the world could not hurt them. It was a shell that carried them both through their many ordeals to come.

Chapter 35

"Trust me," said HM, "if I propose it to the king, he'll accept it."

"And what," asked Naitly, "would such ... intercession cost?"

"What do you think it's worth?" They were alone in Naitly's private apartment. Taking tea, indeed, at the same table where HM had interrupted his breakfast with Goneril. HM was relaxed, even enjoying herself. She was coming to realise that there was indeed one thing better than having a man in the palm of your hand: having two men there!

Naitly regarded her carefully before he replied. "Fredvie has offered me several million doubloons. You could have half."

"Money!" HM sneered. "Only an idiot, Lord Chancellor, thinks the Court jester is the Court's fool. And you're no idiot. It's not money that's the lure. Fredvie's offered you the Protectorship of Belgiss." There was lightness in her tone, maybe even a veiled flirtatiousness.

"That would be a reasonable presumption."

HM paused. She couldn't look at him. She played with the apostle spoon in the sugar bowl. "Protectors, Lord Chancellor, need wives."

This surprised him. "I'd be married to Queen Goneril," he said.

"Oh please," HM sighed.

Naitly caught her drift. "And your ... friendship with the king?"

"'Uneasy ...,' Lord Chancellor, '...lies the head that wears the crown.' Uneasier yet lies the head of the *wife* of him who wears the crown."

"And the crown that I would wear?"

"That unease I'll risk," HM said vixenly. "Please don't tell me you love Goneril."

Naitly scrutinised the person before him. Rarely before, he realised, had he seen her as a woman. He'd been blind. This was not only a woman, but a comely one. "No," he replied. "No, I don't love her."

"You don't have to love me," HM said blandly.

"That simplifies matters," said the Lord Chancellor.

"Love is not necessary for a successful marriage."

"To us, then," said Naitly, and raised his tea-cup in a toast. HM lightly touched his cup with hers.

"To us," she said, wondering as she did so whether the only thing better than having two men in the palm of your hand were having two men *and a woman* there. Without appearing to be rushed, she rapidly made her excuses to Naitly. And went off in search of Goneril.

Whom she found in *her* private suite.

"Dickens relates ...," King Sebastian leaned forward in his chair, his eyes sheening with significance, "...how Marley's ghost clanked around the after-life trailing a giant chain forged by his history. It is, however, not only ghosts thus burdened, but most of us who are still alive. Any time we fail to deal with the concern of the moment (in the thousand ways such might manifest itself), we forge a link in the chain which we carry about with us – not in the after-life, but this. Always. Every second of every day. Into the next moment. And the next week. Into the next decision, the next year, the next decade.

"As tribes or cultures we can carry these undealt-with moments into the next century, the next aeon. And the weight of these links not only affects the quality of our moment, and moments, but also our decision-making of the present. It is precisely thus, for instance, that one war creates another.

"To deal with the moment *in* the moment is a talent given only to the saint or the madman. As a *skill* it is on a par with that of a surgeon: it is one which is both *so* necessary and which *so* few of us acquire. Unlike the surgeon's skill, however, it is often derided. Today's economics dictate that we should deride it. It is yet another indication of the way today's economics seek not to liberate us but to enslave us."

"Right," I said, there being nothing else that I could.

"Both Goneril and HM already trailed huge and hugely heavy chains," said the king. "Their lust for power – which was a need for control now out of control – was stamped within each of these chains' many links."

Goneril had been only six when her mother's head had been severed. For a crime of which she was entirely innocent.

Cole had been desperate for a son. His first wife had been barren. But popular. His divorce from her had been received by his (deeply monarchist) subjects with rumbles and grumbles of too republican a hue for them to be ignored. His second wife had been more fecund, and had produced Goneril. Following her birth, however, there had been several miscarriages. The doctors had finally advised that it would be extremely unlikely that any future pregnancy would come to term.

Cole could not suffer the PR consequences of a second annulment. He had therefore employed a gigolo to engage Her Majesty in a conversation ambivalent enough in both content and context that, overheard by his witnesses and cast in a distorted light, it could be seen as treasonable. Exit Queen, headless, stage left.

At an extremely tender age, therefore, Goneril had learnt the lesson that 'power corrupts and absolute power corrupts absolutely'. This lesson had led her to conclude (erroneously but understandably) that life's only safeguard is to have that absolute power yourself.

The pain Goneril experienced on her mother's death prevented her ever from loving anyone else. She ached for the Crown – that much was true, and that much was less than admirable. But she ached for it mostly because it was only thus that she could vindicate her mother. She saw that vindication as her life's work.

When we perceive a goal as being our 'life's work', we tend to be blind to anything which will thwart us. It is therefore that zealots are not always admirable people. The zealous are only a nudge away from the obsessional, and the obsessional but a tweak away from the fanatical.

It is not religion but fanaticism which is responsible for so much horror, so much bloodshed, so much war. And usually that fanaticism, because it has to be, is extremely ill-considered and woefully informed.

The religious go to mass; it is fanatics who go to massacre. The religious *pray*; the slaying is done by fanatics.

HM's chain was, in its way, as heavy as Goneril's. Her mother's head had not been chopped off. If anything, rather the reverse. It had been used, her mother's head – specifically her mouth – as a tool: to bite off the head of her husband. Usually because the bacon he had brought home was deficient in either quantity or succulence – or both!

Until recently, her father had been a spice merchant. Whilst some of the turbulence in the family's fortunes was his direct responsibility, the whims of Fortune had also done some buffeting. The family had never known abject penury, but it had known need. And its brush with poverty was close enough for HM to be able to feel for herself the growls of hunger and the scowls of cold.

Like Goneril's, HM's life had also been dominated by an adage. In her case: 'If you can't beat 'em, join 'em'. Indeed she had adapted that adage to make one of her own: 'The only way to beat 'em is to join 'em'.

She would create a more equitable society, one less subject to economic fancy or the capriciousness of a few plutocrats. She wanted the hungry fed and the naked clothed. She wanted the ignorant taught. Most of the ignorant were to be found amongst the schooled. Some even amongst the academically elite. There is no man more ignorant than he who will not give bread to a famished child.

It seemed to HM that there were no methods unacceptable that led to the goal of feeding the hungry.

Only those distant from the forest, however, can see it as one. To those within it, it is an agglomeration of this beech and that birch, this bramble and that blackberry, this butterfly and that buttercup. Before it corrupts, power distorts. That is part of the process.

"It's never going to happen," HM was telling Goneril. They were in Goneril's suite. It was about as comfortable as a bed of nails and as gemütlich as a dungeon. The stone walls were bereft of any hangings – not a painting or a tapestry or an arras. The furniture was all of dark wood, chiselled very plainly and straight-backedly. On no chair was there a cushion. Each seemed to debar being sat on other than in the most upright, up*tight* fashion.

Goneril was pouring tea into two plain white cups. No tea, HM felt, would have had the temerity to splash.

"Plenty of things are never going to happen," Goneril replied. "To what in particular do you allude?"

"Your marriage to Naitly."

"Of course it's not going to happen," Goneril feinted. "The whole idea is preposterous. My father, as you very well know, ..."

"It's not going to happen, Goneril. Trust me."

Goneril watched HM closely. No, she knew ... she *knew.* No point in further trying to deceive her. "You're going to steal him from me?"

"Oh, please."

"Well, then?"

"You're never going to allow Belgiss to be annexed to Mercia."

Again Goneril read HM's eyes. Not the banner headlines but the small print. She needed to read it all. No, she knew ... she *knew.* No point further in trying to deceive her. "No," she said simply, "I'm not."

"It's not a problem, trust me. Not for me."

"Good."

"If I talked to your father, though, persuaded him about the referendum – if I got you the Crown, Goneril – would you drop Naitly?"

"Like a red-hot poker."

"And your new Lord Chancellor would be?"

"Ah."

"'Ah', indeed."

"It would be ... indicative, would it not, of a new order," Goneril suggested, "it would be *modern*, for the female sovereign to appoint a female first minister?"

"A decision Her Majesty would never regret."

"Never?"

"Trust me."

Chapter 36

The biggest building in Biga-buga was the 'Baccanaals'. This was the residence of the emperor of Mercia, Frederick V, known (as you know) as Fredvie. It was built on Biga-buga's highest hill, so that all its citizens looked up to it – actually and thus figuratively.

It was a huge edifice, designed to be both imposing and intimidating, designed to say to the onlooker that whoever inhabited such a structure had to be someone really, *really* important. The simply important or the simperingly important just didn't get to live in such a place.

Its dome was larger than any other in Biga-buga (or indeed the world); its columns were more Doric; its windows more crystal; the white of its paint whiter.

Within the palace, the emperor tended to confine his presence to two suites of rooms: one on the ground floor, the other on the first. The ground floor contained his public and official residences, the first floor his private and domestic ones.

These suites housed the biggest rooms. Which had been designed by a team of experts to reflect the emperor's personality: strong but with taste, harmonious but with flashes of boldness and individuality, rugged but comfortable. They had high hopes, now that they'd got the décor right, that the emperor's personality would one day match it.

In each of these suites' rooms, there was an area raised six inches above the rest. This was the part of the room that the emperor, and only the emperor, would occupy: It gave eminence to His Eminence.

Dawes and Leamore were waiting in one of the Baccanaals' anterooms. There was no dais in this room. So Fredvie never visited it. Dawes and Leamore were not used to waiting. And they were not used to doing things they weren't used to doing. They didn't like it.

They had been waiting three minutes. Dawes and Leamore

were busy men. And three minutes ... Jeez, that was ... *three* minutes!

Leamore was looking at the door, preparatory to tearing it off its hinges; Dawes was glowering at one of the nearby lackeys, rehearsing the vitriol he would soon be spewing at him.

Only two sets of doors away, Fredvie was sulking on his throne.

It was a well-padded seat, lush and almost womb-like in its design. The trim was of oak carved and then gilded; but the seat itself, the back and arm-rests were of goose-down covered in a rich plum velvet. It didn't require the sitter to do so regally. Which was as well.

Fredvie was curled up in a corner, like a recalcitrant five-year-old, legs tucked into a bad-tempered chest.

Minor Minor had settled in well to the Baccanaals. He had an accent which was hilarious, he came from a pagan and primitive land, and he was therefore to the other staff an object of some interest. Beforehand Minor Minor had never been an object of any interest whatsoever. His new-found status did much to calm the waves of homesickness which occasionally would lap lacklustrely at his feet.

"Tell them, Minor Minor, I'm not tootin' here," said Fredvie.

"Alas, Mr Imperial Majesty, they know that not to be the case."

"They're going to rootin' shout at me," the emperor whined.

"You are emperor, Mr Imperial Majesty. You could shout back."

"Oh sure!" Fredvie sneered woefully and sarcastically.

"The longer they wait, the greater, Mr Imperial Majesty, their ire."

"'Igher? They're 'igher than tootin' what?"

"Ire, Mr Imperial Majesty. Anger, wrath."

"Well, go get them, then." Minor Minor made to move. "No. Wait. Tell them to give me ten more tootin' minutes. Five. Just five. Tell them, Minor Minor, I am the rootin' emperor and I want five more minutes. Two. Tell them, two rootin'-tootin' minutes more."

"I'll try, Mr Imperial Majesty."

"Try? *Try*? Trying's no good to me, Minor Minor. Don't try, do."

"Yes, Mr Imperial Majesty." He closed the double-doors behind him. He breathed in deeply, glorying in an air unpolluted by emperors. The Mercians, Minor Minor continued to feel, were a strange people who set about life ... strangely. He braced himself for what he knew would be the onslaught of the emperor's two visitors.

"What's happening, Minor Minor?" asked Dawes.

"'Case you hadn't noticed, dude, we've been waiting," said Leamore, "five solid minutes now."

"Three, sir," said Minor Minor.

"Three minutes, Minor Minor, is a lot of time." This from Dawes.

"Indeed, sir."

"So?" asked Leamore

"Two minutes more ..."

"Oh Jeez!" exclaimed Dawes.

"Just two more minutes, gentlemen. The emperor ..."

"Is emperor, dude, – 'case you hadn't noticed – *only*, dude, 'cause of us," Leamore said. "You know *why* we're us?"

"Because you know the value of three minutes?"

"Because, like you say, Minor Minor," said Dawes, "we know the value of three minutes."

"The Hell with waiting another two," said Leamore. He crashed to his feet and stomped towards the doors.

"The Hell with it," Dawes agreed. He too crashed to his feet and stomped towards the doors.

"Gentlemen, gentlemen," Minor Minor appealed, "two minutes."

"You had the two minutes, dude," said Leamore, opening the

other set of double-doors, that which gave way onto the throne room. A couple of grenadiers (as they were called) made as if to bar his way. "Don't, dudes, even think about it," he growled.

The grenadiers looked at each other uncertainly. They let him pass. They let Dawes pass. They went to stop Minor Minor, and then recognised him.

"We don't," Leamore continued as he approached the emperor, "have to go through the whole schmeer, do we, Fredvie?"

"Mis-ter Im-pe-ri-al Ma-jest-y," Fredvie reminded them both, a syllable at a time.

"Sure," said Leamore brazenly.

"Just say 'yes', Fredvie," said Dawes wearily.

"'Case you hadn't noticed, dude, without our tax dubs, you'd be moseying down Queer Street."

"Without our contributions, you'd be dead."

"And I'm very, very rootin' grateful," said Fredvie, curling his legs even more tightly into his chest. "Really I am. Still and all, I am the rootin'-tootin' emperor."

"Sure," said Leamore again, again brazenly.

"We need war, Fredvie," said Dawes.

"We've *got* war," pouted the emperor.

"We've got squat, dude," squawked Leamore. "A few friendly slaps. Listen to the man, Fredvie. We need war. Full war. Out-and-out war."

"World public opinion, gentlemen ..." interjected Minor Minor.

"We *own* the world, Minor Minor. Why would we *care* about its opinion? Public *or* private?"

"Realrich would so ever so not like it."

"And, like, dude, we care about Realrich?"

"Realrich works for you, don't he?" asked Dawes.

"Talk about the tail wagging the dog!" Leamore stomped towards the emperor. The latter cowered further into his throne.

"'Case you hadn't noticed, we've paid, dude, way over *whatever* odds."

"Wars cost even more rootin' money," Fredvie insisted, trying to be as insistent as he sounded.

"Exactly!" said Leamore. "And how the Hell do you suggest we pay for it, dude, without the Waifu gold mines?"

"Or the Tay diamond mines?"

"Excuse me," said Minor Minor. "I'm so ever so confused here. You need the money from the spoils of war to pay *for* the war?"

"Yes, dude," duh'd Leamore, as if to a total idiot.

"And if you didn't have the war you wouldn't need the gold to pay for it?"

"No flies on you, are there, Minor Minor?" Dawes complimented him.

"Here's a thought: Why not *not* have the war? Avoid the cost?"

There was a startled beat, as if someone had burped in the middle of a ballet. A charged silence. And then, as a man, the three erupted into a thunderclap of laughter. Tears started rolling down their faces.

"No wonder," said Leamore, barely able to force the words out, "Belgiss is in so much trouble."

"Basic economics." Dawes was wiping his eyes, trying to stop his laughter. Fredvie was trying to whoop it up. For as long as these two were laughing they could not be shouting at him.

His voice still rocking with mirth Leamore again asked, "War?"

"Will the gazettes continue to help?" the emperor asked Dawes.

"When have they ever not?" asked Dawes, a taste of testiness trying to force its way into the guffaws. "It's got to be war, Fredvie. We all know it."

Minor Minor looked on the scene blankly. He was used to

being humble, but unused to being humiliated. From this point forth his loyalty was feigned. It was to have implications.

But so were the guffaws. For, in the midst of them, Fredvie finally built himself up to his full height and, thinking himself as one with England's Henry V before Agincourt, he proclaimed: "War!"

War is a word of three letters.

Over ten thousand people were to die for each one of them.

When thirty thousand die, one hundred thousand lives are devastated. And five hundred thousand cry.

Chapter 37

HM had left King Cole playing with Nose. It was frequently these days that HM left the king playing with the 'late' prince's dog. For as long as Nose was there to be played with (such seemed to be the reasoning of the increasingly unreasoned king), the prince was not dead. And for as long as the prince was not dead, the king had time to ponder about his succession.

It was these days often that Cole called for his pipe and bowl. Sometimes he even called for them at breakfast time. Having only a scant supply of HM's counsel, he increasingly kept his own. Unkemptly. Unshavenly. Un-finger-nail-cutly. He was beginning, frankly, to smell. To HM it seemed as if even Nose were holding his nose.

The worker leaving a car factory needs a few moments of silence. When HM left the king these days she needed a period of ponglessness. The day in question was no exception. The burnt toast smell of the flambeaux had latterly become as fragrant as a rose. She luxuriated in the perfume, felt her own clean hands upon her own fresh face, breathed in the perfume that was her, and then scurried on through the grey corridors to the meeting she was already late for.

"Punctuality," sneered Goneril as HM entered the government chamber, "is the courtesy of kings."

"You might try reminding our own king of that," replied HM. "Then he might let me go a little earlier."

"Cross-Bones," said Naitly, interjecting himself between the two snarling lynxes: "Surplus to requirements, no?"

"They were born surplus to requirements," HM said, in tones as measured as her hackles were still raised.

"No question," Goneril agreed.

"You cannot execute them," HM advised.

"No, I think we know that," said Naitly, almost patronisingly. "The publicity. Their statements."

"Dawes's gazettes are so unreliable at times," complained Goneril.

"I'll have a word with them," HM volunteered.

"We could just cut their tongues out," Naitly said, as if suddenly struck by inspiration.

"Better, *simpler,*" suggested HM, "that they just vanish."

"You're sure?"

"Trust me."

Cross-Bones were brought to HM's office. They had learnt by now about Court protocol, especially as it pertained to assassins. And that protocol demanded that assassins past their dispatch-by date did not hang around, lest that hanging around be from the end of a rope.

HM had therefore no sooner suggested that *maybe* their best interests *may be* served by quitting the Court forthwith, if not the land, than they were anxiously pawing at the door, eager to be let loose.

It was a shame about Ginny and Winny, of course – perhaps, HM would be kind enough ... HM assured them she would, *of course,* tell their fiancées of their departure. Of course it was a shame, but – hey ho! – all good things had to come to an end. Sometimes even before they've started.

Within twenty minutes of the summons, they were outside Wodinton Castle en route to Blefton. They had the clothes on their backs, a few dubs in their pockets and, most importantly, continued to have a head on their shoulders.

They'd been told Fortune favours the brave. And fortunes, they'd also been told, were to be made in Mercia. It seemed therefore to the two assassins that the place to go was where Fortune and fortunes were both leading them: West. To Mercia.

Chapter 38

Fredvie's envoy had arrived from Biga-buga. The message from the emperor was that the Protector should prepare for war.

In those days, no West existed Wester than Zanoria. Not, anyway, that the Mercians would have recognised as existing. To the Mercians the only thing that existed was what it considered the 'civilised' world. And the only civilising force of that world was Mercia. Thus the only world that existed for the Mercians was the world which was governed as the Mercians wanted the world to be governed.

Which was curious. Because Zanoria was itself not what the denizens of Biga-buga would have considered 'civilised'. Whilst Biga-buga had ballet, Zanoria had bullets; elegance in Biga-buga was French champagne in a flute of cut crystal, in Zanoria it was moonshine whisky in a clean glass.

Almost all communication between the two places was in those days by envoy.

Protector Realrich considered the envoy of Fredvie's he was currently entertaining a fop and an Easterner, only one step above the absolute dregs of being a vegetarian or a pacifist. The dinner they shared was one where the politesse was as restrained as Realrich's burps.

The inslaves, of course, were ordered into their finest livery. It was important to Realrich that the reports back to Fredvie should be that those at the 'Presidence' (as the Protector's mansion was called) banqueted quite as well and fastidiously as the barroom brigadiers and lounge lieutenants of the Baccanaals.

Oscar Wilde found American's Wild West charming and intriguing. Fredvie's envoy, though, was no Oscar, and he found Mercia's Wild West brutal and threatening. But contempt requires a lot of energy to sustain, and the envoy was therefore glad when the time came the following day for him to return.

Inslaves awoke Realrich that morning at the crack of ten. His emperor had ordered him to prepare for war and war had to be prepared for. In a scurry of activity orders were issued and drills commanded and exercises set in motion. Then came breakfast. And immediately after breakfast the envoy left.

Immediately after that, the Protector again took to his bed. And when he was awoken this time, at around the crack of twelve, all the previous orders were countermanded and things lolloped back again to their former meandering ways.

The history books give the impression that in those days Zanoria made a beehive look like a convalescent home. But that simply isn't true. For one thing, there being then no electricity, working hours were restricted fairly much to daylight hours. True, in the evening a few odd jobs were still done: Men whittled a bit of carpentry, women made the odd dress or darned the odd sock, but the freneticism that would later become the hallmark of Mercian culture was entirely absent. The slaves then worked shorter hours than their freed descendants were to do almost two centuries later. This, contemporary commentators would have you believe, is 'progress'.

At the crack of twelve-thirty, Realrich lunched. Realrich always lunched at the crack of twelve-thirty. He preferred to do so alone. Alone, he did not have to cope with the proprieties society dragged along with it. He could eat with his fingers, slurp his food, wipe his chin on his cuff, talk with his mouth full (albeit only to his slaves) and belch to his heartburn's content. And there was no ghost of Ma Realrich there to wag a chiding finger or to rub on his cheeks with a spat-upon napkin.

Eating was an exhausting business. Once lunch was over Realrich needed a rest.

At the crack of whatever time it was when he awoke from that came the high point of Realrich's day, his reason for living – his joy and his sport, almost his religion, all rolled into one: He'd go hunting.

When he first arrived in Zanoria, his favourite target had been the beestalo – a hybrid of the wildebeest and the buffalo. But one of these had taken it into his head to turn the tables on Realrich and to attack *him*. The colour had drained from Realrich's florid face, and, discretion being the better part of pallor, Realrich had decided from that day forth to give the beestalo a miss. He opted these days for rather less antagonistic quarry. Mostly deer. Mostly the okaland.

There was then an abundance of okaland. Realrich wanted to cull a few more. Personally he couldn't stand venison. He preferred the beestalo steaks agents of his bought off the Waifu. But these were expensive. Venison he therefore considered good fodder for his slaves. (It is somewhat chilling to note that a shrewd slave-owner would not have fed his slaves the food considered today by many of our children as staple fare. This, contemporary commentators would have you believe, is 'progress'.)

The okaland is, of course, today extinct. Literally hunted out of existence. The 'descendants' of the okaland we know today as two separate animals: the okapi and the eland. They were the most docile of creatures. Occasionally in the rutting season two stags would lock antlers. Apart from which they attacked nothing on Earth. They paid the price for it.

The okaland's extinction is used by those of a bellicose persuasion to justify their argument that Man's aggression is necessary for his survival. If we do not attack, they argue, then – like the okaland – we will be wiped out. *If* these pundits are right, if we are kept alive by our aggression, then – we have to face this – there is no hope for humanity. None at all.

Because, whilst their hypothesis *may* be true, it is *certainly* true that aggression is killing humanity (in both senses of the word 'humanity'). If a *lack* of aggression would *also* destroy it, then (apparently) we're doomed. In which case, let us ask ourselves this one question: Is it not preferable – and by a thousand times – to die a death by a thousand kisses than one by a thousand cutlasses?

Realrich ordered that Horsatio should be saddled and bridled.

Charming hated watching this. He could see how much Horsatio detested being ridden by this man, how much he detested the man himself – and how much this man mistreated the horse. Charming's other two horses were just as frightened – all of Realrich's horses were. Realrich was abusive to them all.

But Charming (or 'Tookums') was – and he knew it – powerless to do anything about such treatment. He could only mitigate the consequences. He continued to pay his nightly visits. Together with Syun, he would groom the horses, pour ointment on where Realrich's spurs had broken their flesh, and rub them with lotion where the saddle-girths had been pulled too tight.

It was too painful for him to see Realrich riding his precious animals. So he made sure that, just after lunch, he was so busy with household chores that he was unable to do so.

On these sorties Realrich took with him a small detachment of fellow 'hunters', always slaves, sometimes also guests. The guests 'hunted', the slaves helped make life easier for them. Some beat the quarry from its lair, others frightened it back into Realrich's path. The dogs would weaken the okaland, of course, and the guests would help with the kill. But the final slitting of the animal's jugular was the 'privilege' bestowed on the hunt's master. Realrich was always the hunt's master. No-one ever complained.

Communication being as difficult, erratic and wearisome as it was, in many ways, the Protector was more powerful locally than the emperor. In theory, for example, forensic appeals could be taken to the Uppest Court in Biga-buga. But, in practise, communication between the two places took so long that, more often than not, the sentences had been served before Notice of Appeal had even been received by the Biga-buga court. Particularly was this true in cases involving the death penalty.

There were in Zanoria at that time one hundred and thirty-four crimes which could lead to the scaffold – including the somewhat quixotic ones of dancing around a maypole in June, or selling honey on Ash Wednesday. There were, in other words, sufficient laws of fatal consequences that it was practically impossible not to fall foul of one of them. Death sentences had to be ratified by the Protector. For which reason, no-one wanted to be on the wrong side of him. Consequently, even on those hunts at which other local 'big-wigs' were guests, he was still master of the hunt. Always.

But that day was not a hunt which did involve 'big-wigs'. It was a small one, a private affair: Realrich, his overseers, those of his slaves who could be spared from other duties.

And Horsatio. Poor, frightened Horsatio.

The Protector larruped his spurs into the beast's flanks. They immediately drew blood. Horsatio whinnied. He threw his large brown eyes over to the kitchen, almost as if he knew his real master was there. Which he was. Scouring the pots. Not hearing the fear and pain searing through that whinny. Not allowing himself to hear.

The hunting party left the 'Presidence''s grounds. It scattered into different groups as the hunters started to scour the local forest for a likely okaland. The creature was found. A blast was given on the beestalo horn which had been hollowed-out to become a horn capable, with some oral dexterity, of sounding two notes.

Two notes were enough. It was the signal that the hunt was on.

It was a glorious afternoon. There were three or four cotton wool clouds clumped in a sky, the bluer for being offset by this white. It was warm but there was a breeze whose nip had enough edge also to provide a contrast.

Realrich loved galloping on such days. He loved the nippy breeze rushing over his cheeks, loved the whoosh it left in his ears. He loved the sound of the hooves on the turf beneath him, loved the slide and bump of his bottom in the leather saddle, loved the panting of the horse – loved the sense he had of oneness with the animal, with the countryside around him, with the world as a whole. So much did he love it that he wanted more of it. And the only way he knew to get more of it was to jab the horse ever more with his spurs and lash its rump ever more frequently with his crop.

The two notes kept being repeated until all the disparate groups had joined together to form one succession of hunters, all set on depriving the ruminant of its life.

The animal – even facing death, balletically graceful – broke the cover of the forest and started to spring across the open fields, fields criss-crossed with hedges. These the okaland leapt as if they were no more than logs in its path. And with such elegance that it seemed to freeze above the hurdle, uncertain whether to land the other side of it or to launch itself into the stratosphere.

Horsatio was already in pain. The blood was now pouring from his flanks in a stream, pinkened with the white of his sweat, which flew for yards before it fell. He'd closed his eyes. Just momentarily. Just, for a moment, to blot out the pain.

He didn't see the rabbit-hole.

But he felt it.

And as he felt it, he felt his right foreleg break. And he crumpled in a writhing heap of agony on the ground just before the fence.

Realrich, however, cleared the fence. Unfortunately, by himself. Realrich was so rounded that the noise he met hitting the soft ground was the plop of a cherry dropped into blancmange. The face he had on him, though, was that of a raging bull. It was so snorting, it was fuming. Realrich was so angry that he bounced straight back onto his feet.

He could hear Horsatio's screams. He was apoplectic, beside himself with rage. The horse, of course, would have to be destroyed, but the horse for having thrown him *deserved* to die.

That was without question. He had, however, paid out good money for the beast. Damn good money.

Horsatio continued to scream out his agony.

Realrich stopped the next horse which cleared the fence. He ordered the rider from its back, and mounted it himself. He rode straight back to his farmstead. He was still furious, still livid.

There he told Syun to return to where the horse had fallen and, at the very least, retrieve the saddle and tackle. It was bad enough he'd lost all the investment he'd made on the nag. He was damned – dammee! – if he was going to leave all that leather also on the horse merely for the Waifu to steal.

He screamed these words from the yard of the 'Presidence'. *Screamed* them. The whole household came to hear the tirade. A few wanted to snigger. None did.

Syun knew the horse was hurt. Knew that she'd have to kill him. She went to the stables, fetched the largest sharpest knife, and put her emotions into neutral. Charming met her in the yard. "I'll go," he said, and took the knife from her.

Realrich noticed this moment of tenderness between his two slaves.

The tears were already traffic-jammed behind Charming's eyes. His face was set in concrete because it had to be. Were he to relax it, the dam would no longer hold.

The Protector had dismounted by this stage, had passed the reins of the acquired horse to Syun, and was storming back to the house.

Charming took the reins, and mounted.

"What do you think you're doing?" Realrich roared at him.

"Horsatio is hurt, sir. I have to go to him."

"Slaves do not make decisions," Realrich fumed. "Slaves ride only – *only* dammee – when they are *told* by me they can ride. Get down. Get down this instant. Get down, Tookums – dammee – right now."

But Charming was already galloping out of the yard.

Realrich raged after him, "You just wait, Tookums, till you get back. I'll have the skin off your back. I'll flay you alive – dammee."

But Charming was out of earshot. Not that he would anyway have minded. His only concern at that time was to tender Horsatio whatever help he could. He knew that wouldn't be too great. But he knew too that, if only by the tiniest bit, his pain had to be relieved.

He didn't have to know where the stricken creature lay. He could hear Horsatio's screams of pain long before they got to the wood. He detoured round its edge, following the animal's tortured whinnies.

The whites of Horsatio's eyes were so latticed with red veins there was almost a pinkness to the whole of them. In his irises, despite the pain, came the joy of recognition. Received wisdom was that, before killing it, you stripped a beast of its saddle and bridle. Dead weight made the stripping so much more awkward. But Charming was beyond all such considerations. He knew only that Horsatio was in pain, and that he had to stop him from being in pain.

He stroked the flop of mane which came between his ears and fringed his face. He stroked the forelock. "It's all right, Horsa," he told the horse. "It'll soon be over. Soon be all over. There, there, boy," he told the horse.

He scratched the end of his nose. As, with his other and trembling hand, he prepared to cut the horse's jugular. He knew he had to do this keenly. And decisively. He knew horse flesh was tough. He knew, trembling, he would make a botch of it, would cause the animal further pain. Just as he'd earlier stoppered the tears, now too he forbade the trembles their tremor, forbade the shakes their wobbliness.

"You've been a great friend, Horsa," he told the horse. "A great, great friend. And a great, great horse. Rest now, my dear, *dear* friend. Please. Please, rest now." And he brought the blade sharply into Horsatio's neck, and pulled down it with all his might.

The horse gave one high-pitched shriek of alarm – and then screamed his silence, as his last breath whooshed through him and from him.

The prince was on his knees, staring, unseeingly, into the sky. He could feel his right hand bathed by warm, thick liquid – the heat and consistency of soup. He looked down. It was covered in Horsatio's blood, which continued to gush in a pulsing stream from the open wound. And then the jammed-up tears finally broke their bonds, and the tremors and shivers and shakes would be debarred no more.

Almost like a wolf, crouched like a wolf, he raised his eyes again to the heavens, and he howled.

***

Realrich, unusually, had been really busy.

A horse lost in war was one whose cost could be charged to the national exchequer – as indeed could the cost of a slave so lost. Slave-owners were therefore considerably more anxious that their slaves should participate in wars than that they should. Their own deaths reaped neither them nor their loved ones any recompense at all.

Realrich was writing a report for the Baccanaals about the preparations ordered by the emperor for war. In it he explained how Horsatio had been shot with an arrow from underneath him when he, following the emperor's instructions, had been out reconnoitring ground that could be suitable for an onslaught on the Waifu. The report concluded that the only way the war could be conducted satisfactorily was to send the amount of troops necessary to conduct the war satisfactorily. Realrich congratulated himself on a point well made.

The Protector also had Syun Drette brought before him.

He'd lost a horse, Realrich ranted at what he continued to believe was the boy. Furthermore the slave's attitude was one of mule-like obstinacy and sulkiness. Over and above which (this said in a voice awash with sarcasm) the slave's "dear, dear friend" (Charming, in other words) had seen fit to disobey his master. Taking all these considerations into account, Realrich thought it only reasonable, only equitable – he was sure that the slave would agree – that Syun should himself replace the lost horse. The shire horse pulling the plough through the wheat fields would therefore become a hunting horse. And he, Syun Drette, would take its place in the furrow.

Already when Charming returned forlornly from his gruesome and bloody task, Syun was yoked to the plough.

And the plough-slave driving her was flicking at her with his whip. The plough-slave was a large man with a broken nose. The little finger on his left hand had been cut off in a threshing accident. Syun was already breaking under the strain.

The sight was devastating.

And the memories ... of Horatio and Philly ... they were devastating also.

Chapter 39

Things on Richardson's professional front were on the up-and-up. He'd gone to Azrac a rich man; he returned an even richer one. He'd negotiated with Antonio for the Eastlantic concession to the double-barrelled musket. Mercia was still at war with Orismine. And because Mercia was, Belgiss was. Orismine had already bought several consignments of the new munitions. Naitly, and Richardson knew that too, could not afford *not* to put in an equally substantial order.

Things too on his domestic front were ... well, less muddy. Not only was he convinced that Cordelia had had nothing to do with his son's death, but he was *so* convinced that he was able to persuade Nancy too of her innocence.

Sort of persuade her, anyway. Privately, Nancy's waters continued to squelch as bemuddedly as ever. Whilst she had no doubt of her husband's ability as a navigator of wider pictures, she was less convinced of his skill as an unmuddier of waters. She needed some kind of friend, some kind of objective ally. But who?

If Cordelia hadn't killed Horatio, it seemed horribly feasible that Goneril had. So that ruled her out. Naitly, Nancy knew, was involved with Goneril. Which ruled *him* out. Her father was ruled out by being involved only in his bowl, and Charming's dog. ... To Nancy it seemed there was only one person in the Court to whom she *could* turn: HM.

She had to know, she told the former jester, which of her two half-sisters had indeed murdered her son. The uncertainty was driving her mad. And not figuratively mad, actually insane.

"*Why* do you have to know? " HM asked her. "I mean, what would you do with the information? Think about it."

Nancy thought about it. "I'd take it to the king."

"You've seen the king recently?"

"Yes."

"You think there'd be any point?"

Nancy paused, torn between hope and realism. "No," eventually she said. "No, you're right. No point at all."

"The king needs a queen," HM said delicately.

"Yes?"

"He needs ..." HM paused, teetering on an abyss of commitment, "... me."

A thousand reactions tore through Nancy's brain. Not one showed itself on her face. "Yes," she agreed, slowly enunciating the words, as her brain was working through the consequences. "Yes, he does. That's just what he needs: A queen. And you, HM, *as* his queen."

"Good," HM commented, keeping the jack of her astonishment firmly in its box.

"You're not surprised? That I should agree, I mean, to your being Queen?"

"I underestimated your ... perspicacity," HM confessed.

"Like Fredvie, many people 'misunderestimate' me."

They laughed together. A laugh between friends. They hadn't known beforehand they *were* friends. "Married to the king I could persuade him to ... take measures."

"Yes."

"You still haven't answered the question," HM suggested.

"Why I have to know?"

"Yes."

"Don't we all, HM, have to know whom to hate?"

HM searched deep into her eyes. "Yes," she replied simply.

"Will you help me?"

"Will you help *me*?" HM asked.

"With the king?"

"Yes."

"Yes, I'll help you."

"Then I'll help you. Next Wednesday I've a meeting here with Goneril and Naitly. If you got here early, you could hide in the wardrobe."

"Not a trifle melodramatic?" Nancy asked simply.

"You've till Wednesday to decide. If you're not here, you've lost nothing."

"Right."

There was a breath of still between them. "I would make a good queen, Nancy."

"Right."

"Maybe even a great queen."

"I hear you."

"I could wrest power back from Naitly."

"And my son?"

"Your son?"

"Could you bring him back from the dead?"

"No."

"So?"

"I might be able to stop some other mothers from grieving over the deaths of their children."

It was now Nancy's turn to scrutinise the eyes of her companion – of the woman, she now realised, who might soon be her stepmother. "Good answer, HM," eventually she said.

"A good queen, Nancy. Possibly a great queen."

"Right," said Nancy.

That evening she was talking again to her husband. HM's words had rung true, but Nancy was savvy enough in the way of politics to know that circumstances could be a despot, and that they would dictate that even the pledges of the sincere were sometimes broken. She would, for once, follow her husband's advice and see the wider picture.

"Annexing Belgiss to Mercia *would* be a good thing, no?" she asked him.

"Wider picture?"

"Of course."

"In most respects."

"Can you get to Fredvie?"

"Easily."

"Via Leamore and Dawes?"

"Exactly."

"And you need to talk to them anyway, right?"

"Mercia is fighting two wars, my dear. Twice the need for double-barrelled muskets."

Nancy took her time. She broached the subject as tentatively as HM had broached hers. "If I became queen," she tried to say matter-of-factly, "you would be consort."

Richardson understood exactly what she meant. "I'd like to be consort," he replied.

"Then, let's get word to Fredvie. Let's do a little business."

"Wide picture?"

"The widest you've got."

Chapter 40

Three months had elapsed since Horsatio's death. Each day that had gone past had persuaded Realrich more trenchantly that it was the Waifu – possibly with Tay collusion – who were responsible for the horse's death.

The distortion of history is never a good idea. However noble the intention might be of that distortion. One reason it has become as prevalent as it is is because the distortion of history is the dough-and-curd of the bread-and-butter of today's Mercian movie industry: an industry fuelled by a regard only for the box-office. Its adulteration of history is dictated therefore by what the industry believes its audience would like to believe is history – or by what those who control it would prefer history to have been. Unlike its counterpart in Hollywood, truth is not the concern of the Mercian movie industry; often it is too inconvenient to the story-line. The industry has thus spawned many misconceptions, and not a few downright lies.

One such misconception is that at that stage the native Mercians were a united foe. The unification of Tay and Waifu came later. At this stage the entente that existed between them was less one of cordiale than of a sort of rumbly live-and-let-live. Mostly they kept out of each other's way. To describe what they had for each other as mutual respect would be an exaggeration. Both had the feeling about the other that to be intolerant of them would be to attach too much importance to them.

Had the Waifu come across Syun Drette lost in the forest, as a 'for instance', they would have returned her unharmed to her own people. But it is doubtful that, in a raid on Realrich's territory, they would have bothered, along with their own nationals, also to have released her. They certainly would not have *mounted* such a raid on her behalf.

As has already been noted, the Tays *had* mounted three such rescue missions. Syun had remained captive.

Charming contrived a plan by which they both escaped. But an overseer got wind of it. The overseer was the large man with the broken nose, whose little finger had been amputated in a threshing accident.

In an act of astounding charity he did not report the foiled attempt to Realrich. Instead he explained to the two would-be runaways, slowly and laboriously, the consequences to them of their flight – and to him: If they were caught, they would both be flogged – he once a month for twelve months. They would spend the rest of their lives with their ankles manacled. Even if, by some fluke, they did manage to get away, they would spend the rest of their days still manacled – their eyes would be manacled over their shoulders!

Whether or not they were re-caught the overseer would also be flogged. And he would be forbidden for a year, on pain of another flogging, from even talking with his 'wife'. (Slaves did not marry in the accepted sense, but – in the interests of breeding – were occasionally permitted to form permanent and exclusive alliances wherein they were considered 'husband' and 'wife'. Unless, of course, the owner had a particularly good stud, when ...well, *financial* husbandry prevailed.)

This overseer was not Charming's favourite person. Not since he saw the man 'driving' Syun like an ox. There was an unworthy moment when the prospect of this man being punished actually *increased* his wish to escape. But Syun turned her big brown eyes onto him. If she could forgive the overseer, the prince told himself, then he was under some sort of obligation also to do so.

They stayed.

Three days later Syun was nightly shackled to a concrete post. This was ostensibly on the orders of Realrich. But Realrich only gave orders in regard to his slaves when advised to do so. His advisers were his overseers. Charming was sure that the command to shackle Syun had come from the overseer with the missing finger. When, much later, he heard of the man's death the grief he felt had to be a trifle forced.

Syun's life became wretched beyond belief. By day she was yoked to a heavy plough, expected to do the work of a dray horse; at night she was tethered like a savage dog to a post. Fed with scraps and left-overs, spat at even by the other slaves. And it was beyond belief too, the wretchedness that tore through Charming, having to witness such scenes.

Nightly not only did he visit both Philly and Peggy, but now also Syun. Who retained her humanity *only* through the prince's kindness. Even with it, Syun's humanity developed several jagged edges. Those serrations were to slash a few lives later on in Charming's life. If we buy stolen goods, we have no right to complain when our house is burgled; if we ignore the abuse of children, we cannot complain about adult delinquency.

It was now Philly whom Realrich rode on his hunts and on his forays. Charming winced even more now whenever he saw his horse being ridden by the man. He knew that it was only a question of time before Philly met a fate similar to Horsatio's.

But the prince was also approaching a state where he was emoted out. His mind and body chose to respond to this by becoming more robotic. He found himself even mechanically applying unguent to Syun's cuts and blisters, her lesions and her bruises.

***

In the three months since Horsatio's death, military reinforcements had started to arrive. In the first month, no more than a dribble. This had now become a steady trickle. When it became a stream, Realrich would be ready for all-out war.

Along with the soldiers came officers. Even three generals. And the generals had demands all of their own. Despite having tents the size of fair-sized mansions, these eminent 'eminences-grises' infinitely preferred mortar to canvas. And they therefore billeted themselves for as long as they possibly could at the 'Presidence'. Which increased considerably the workload of the inslaves.

There are in this world few beings more redundant than a general in peace-time. They spend their entire time envisioning warlike scenarios. When the blast of war blows in their ears, therefore, they do imitate the actions of the tiger – a freshly released and very pent-up tiger. It is blown, the blast of war, on horns trumpeted by generals proclaiming their new-found importance. They need to flash their importance in the way that an enriched beggar needs to flaunt his wealth. A few generals demand that recognition by being extremely discourteous (because they know they can be!) to all the *non*-generals of the world. There is no-one in the world non-generaler than a slave.

Charming learnt what it was like to be lambasted without reason and to be ranted at out of capriciousness; he learnt what it was like to be able to do nothing right, not to be apologised to, not even to figure in any kind of consideration. In its way, this treatment was almost as cruel and humanity-threatening as that meted out to Syun.

In his memoirs, the surviving general of that company would later claim that he had protested vehemently to Realrich about Syun's yoking. Never did such happen in Charming's hearing. And any time the general was lodging at the 'Presidence' Charming was the general's valet.

***

There was a part of Realrich that really enjoyed war. It was the hunt with a lot of bangs, it was sport writ even larger, and where victory and defeat had even greater consequences.

There was, though, one major downside of war: It involved a risk to himself personally.

Realrich saw it as his first priority – indeed his first patriotic duty – not to let himself be injured or killed. He was, after all, Protector of Zanoria. And if he weren't there on Mercia's behalf to Protector the poor place, it would almost certainly fall again into the hands of those savages from which all too recently it had been liberated.

He therefore went into battle surrounded by a 'box' of four horses – one fore and aft, the other two on each flank – the riders of which were supposed to take the arrow, sword slash, spear jab, or club blow on behalf of their worthy general. One of these riders was Charming. Another was Syun. She was blindfolded and lashed to her saddle. Charming had already resolved that, at a suitable moment in the battle, he would bolt with Syun for freedom. He'd return later for Philly.

Eventually Realrich allowed Charming to ride Peggy. Not out of any charity, just out of expedience. Peggy, ridden by anyone else, proved too contrary to handle. With Charming aboard it, it became docile and obedient. It also helped to make Philly quieter. Friskiness in a horse was all well and good in the hunt. On the battlefield, however, there was enough jitteriness caused by the smoke and the screaming without compounding it with equine nervousness.

Neither the Waifu nor the Tay understood what the Mercians would have described as 'conventional' warfare. Prior to the Mercians arriving they'd had extremely limited experience of killing their fellow man. When Realrich 'pitched' for battle, therefore, the Waifu were bemused. They didn't know what he was up to.

Until his cannon started lobbing balls of red hot lead on top of one of their villages.

When they reacted as would someone burnt by a flying cinder – by screaming in pain and vowing vengeance.

They started attacking the Mercians. Not cogently, not with any kind of plan, but in rage and individually.

In *their* revenge, the Mercians were merciless. The Waifu

village was destroyed, over three hundred Waifu men were killed; over a hundred women and children, merely fleeing.

Realrich relished the spectacle. He stood in the stirrups astride Philly, urging his troops onto greater massacre and gorier bloodshed. Charming's nose took him back to the *Silver Hart* – the smell cocktail pervaded here too: of gunpowder and sweat, of blood and fear. Of agony. And death.

Next to him a man was impaled with a spear, before him another was shot by an arrow – like England's King Harold – in the eye. He did not die. Not immediately. Instead he screamed. He screamed in a torment so great so great*ly* that Charming could not hear the artillery for those screams.

Within seconds, all around him was a 'danse macabre' of screams. About him the soldiers whirred into silhouette and slow motion, a grotesque ballet of ugly movements and ugly features, gargoyles lumbering at gremlins.

And in the midst of this, he saw Syun Drette. Arrows whistling about her blindfolded face, stones searing past her ears.

This was the moment. To rescue her. To rescue himself. To make their bid for freedom. Amidst this mayhem it would be assumed they'd died.

Now was the moment.

Right now.

"Sy- ..." he started to shout. And said no more. One of the stones from the Waifu slingshots had felled him. He toppled lifeless from his horse.

Realrich was – again – incandescent with rage. He'd lost one investment – Horsatio. Now he'd lost a slave. Yeah, yeah, yeah, eventually he'd get the money back, but – dammee – all the damn forms to be filled in. He was getting bored now with this battle thing. He wanted a warm glass and a warmer bed.

Furiously he grabbed for Peggy's reins and tugged at them. But Peggy would not be moved.

He ordered two other slaves to retrieve Peggy. But Peggy

simply dug in its hooves. It was not going anywhere. It was standing guard over its stricken master.

Philly seemed to intuit this. As the slaves were forlornly tugging at her stable-mate, she reared. Not as a horse rears who is alarmed. But as a horse rears who wants to rid itself of a seventeen-stone louse. Realrich was no mean horseman. Philly had not only to rear, but to jiggle as well when upright in order to unseat him.

Realrich's fury was now volcanic. He tried to grab Philly's reins in order to remount her. But there was no way Philly was going to let him do that. She and Peggy joined forces, and presented a snorting, pawing, extremely threatening front that would deter all but the most valiant or foolhardy.

Realrich was not one of either. Those of his slaves who *were* valiant considered valour expended on Realrich's behalf was valour that could far more sensibly be used elsewhere, considered valour spent on Realrich was ... a valueless valour.

Realrich grabbed hold of Syun's saddle and mounted her horse behind her. He then galloped the horse back to the 'Presidence', where – still fuming – he had his claret taken straight to his bed.

The Waifu village was no more. The battlefield, once Realrich left it, was no longer one.

The deafening noise was replaced by an eerie silence. As if the birds were singing mutely, as if the cicadas were noiselessly rubbing their legs.

The field of crops had become a field of corpses. And then a carrion field. Within a very short space of time vultures had arrived to pick at the bodies.

And then the human vultures descended to pick at their pockets. Where they came from, and where they went to, remained a mystery.

A vulture tried to land on Charming. But Peggy was quick to frighten it away. It stood there, head bowed, gazing at its master.

Philly came to join it. They were almost two mourners at a graveside. A coyote ventured close by – and was whinnied at. Foxes, hyenas, even some earthworms, all were scared off.

Soon more Waifu, presumably from the next village, arrived. They started looking for the living. They found two.

They strapped them to stretcher-like assemblies mounted on some of the horses. Their dead they simply draped over the midriffs of other horses. The torsos of the living Waifu were tense with grief, their faces lined with gulches that would be awash with tears once sadness could penetrate the shock.

Two walked past Charming, snatched a quick look at him and walked on. One of these was Quifah, the Waifu Chief. He was an imposing man, far taller than his meagre five-and-a-half feet. His hair was long, thinning gently on the crown, and streaked liberally with grey strands and with silver ones. His almond shaped, pistachio coloured eyes normally beamed with wisdom and a simmering contentment. They were veiled now in a haze of only sorrow.

It is either a rash person, or a sentimental one who tries to decide the thoughts of an animal. It might have seemed to a casual onlooker, however (particularly a rash or sentimental one), that Peggy left Philly to look after their charge whilst it went in pursuit of Quifah.

It pushed its nose into the small of Quifah's back. The Waifu chief turned round, startled. When he saw it was a horse, he was angry. He had other things to fret about, real tragedy to deal with. Angrily he shooed the horse away.

But Peggy kept coming. Kept nuzzling his nose into Quifah's back, kept ignoring the chief's grunts and waves that it should keep away. Finally the chief looked properly at the horse. He saw what a truly fine creature it was. He made a grab for Peggy's reins, but the horse skitted away – the coquette playing hard to get.

Quifah became intrigued. Peggy led, he followed. Not as a

procession, but as a few sprung steps, followed by a grab and then another little dance. Thus did Peggy bring the Chief to Charming.

Charming appeared dead. Quifah made to walk away. Peggy whinnied loudly. The Chief stopped. Looked at Peggy. Looked at the 'corpse'. Looked back at Peggy. Snorted. And then squatted by the inert body. From the charm around his neck he pulled out a feather. This he dusted lightly around the prince's nostrils. A twitch. A slight twitch, true, but a discernible one. Quifah called – in Waifu, of course – to his companion. Who rushed over bringing water.

Gently, gently they trickled a few drops down the prince's throat. He started to cough. He sicked up the few drops of water. But the cough restored him to life.

Quifah gave further commands for the prince to be strapped to one of the litters. He again made to grab Peggy's reins. This time the horse came forward to meet the grab. As did Philly when the Chief went for her.

It was thus that the prince entered this new, and mostly happy, period of his life.

Chapter 41

At more or less this time, Cross-Bones arrived in Biga-buga. There was never a shortage in Biga-buga of work for assassins, but, having (literally) 'stepped straight off the boat', they were not to know that. Instead they heard the drumming of a Recruiting Sergeant. Only half of whose patter had spieled before they accepted the emperor's doubloon and enlisted. They'd never even heard of Zanoria, and so, on hearing that's where they would be posted, their feelings were no more than those of the most casual curiosity.

***

One of the bloodiest stains on Mercia's history is the genocide perpetrated on their continent's first inhabitants: the Waifu, the Tay and the other seventy odd nations then extant. Contemporary reports written by Mercians portrayed these natives as bloodthirsty thugs – sort of the S.S. on horseback. Only recently has the truth started to emerge.

The truth is that these nations were civilised, considerably more so than those who came to massacre them, interested almost exclusively in peaceful pursuits. It is a tribute to these aboriginal nations that they have been *so* civilised as not to seek from their assassins a retribution dire and terrible. Mercia would do well to look to such people for its moral lead.

No one book can hope to expose all wrongs. The canon of literature is today – thank God – large that expounds the Waifu's religious and anthropological beliefs, its agriculture and economy, its laws and customs. It was an enduring sadness of Charming's that he could not introduce more of these to Belgiss when finally power there was his.

But it would also be a distortion of history to pretend that the Tay and Waifu nations were housed in some kind of aboriginal

Shangri-La. There is no human being past or present who isn't flawed, no culture that didn't or doesn't have many things wrong with it. So often, to eulogise is to patronise. And to eulogise by omission is to revere myth over reality. Great human beings and great nations alike have no need to be either eulogised or patronised. You do not need to colour in da Vinci's cartoons.

In the winter the Waifu joined together in a complex far too big to be called a village, but far too impermanent to be called a town. In the summer, however, the nation split up into disparate villages whose population remained constant – bar the changes occasioned by the not infrequent intercession of a winter romance. These villages returned, like migrant birds, to the same spots in the mountains: ones perfect for a few hundred souls, but too cramped for several thousand.

Quifah's village was called Chiloquin – with translated means 'silver brook'. Its brook *was* silver. It also glistened with silver fish and silver stepping stones. Its water was clear, its bed alive with shingle of shiny browns and oranges and reds. It danced in little eddies round the rocks with which it was spangled.

A bank of limerick green rolled extravagantly to its edge, a willow whisped its shard-like leaves lazily into the waters – like a woman's fingers dangling in the river whilst her suitor punts.

The tents and the shelters of the Waifu covered the little valley as marmalade covers toast. Plumes of smoke phutted into the sky, made whiter by the grey of the huge mountains which both surrounded and protected them.

The Waifu spent nine months of the year in their mountain villages, moving down to Zeikiwi (the 'town') only when the snows were imminent.

The Waifu had never heard of Western medicine, knew nothing about leeches or letting blood or anatomy. They knew, though, which roots cured which maladies, which barks to use as which emollients, the sap of which flower to use for which complaint. Under their expert care, Charming soon started to recover.

The prince could not speak Waifu. And the Waifu ... well, their Belgic was very basic. There wasn't a great deal of use for Belgic in their world. (To avoid the tedium of constant translation, the Waifu speeches are italicised. Those not italicised were those conducted in Belgic.)

The prince one day complained that he had been left "High and dry". Though he didn't know it, this had been in reply to the question "*What is your name*?" Thus it was that to the Waifu he was always known (and continues to be known) as Hyandri.

The Waifu very quickly took to Hyandri. They'd taken very few prisoners at this stage of their history. They'd had no wars, and therefore no need to. Those 'Mercians' they had captured during Mercian raids on them had, to a man, been aggressive and snarly and arrogant. All had tried to abuse Waifu hospitality – and all had paid for such transgressions with their lives.

But Hyandri was different. He was keen to learn their language, eager to know of their culture and ways. He even tried their food. And without pulling a face.

The girls of the village thought he was just gorgeous, and each would curl up at night with their own little fantasy of their wedding day. When he was around they giggled a little bit too frantically, batted their eyelashes just a little bit too often. It is a tribute, indeed, to the prince's personality that the village's other young men did not merely lynch him from some unobtrusive tree. But, his powers over damsels (distressed or otherwise) notwithstanding, the prince soon became a close and trusted confidant of the male teenagers as well. They took him fishing and hunting – Waifu style.

For the Waifu these activities, certainly, were fun. But their real objective was ... food. Those who came home empty-handed from the trip did not eat. It was that simple.

Charming soon became expert therefore at tickling fish and ensnaring snakes – which he found delicious. His apprenticeship included being hit by both a porcupine quill and a skunk. They were lessons he did not need repeated.

But he also learnt even more important lessons: that greed is *not* innate to the human condition, but something which is acquired; that property is theft only when possession seeks to deprive others of its use: the Waifu, for instance, owned their own tents, but anyone was free to enter it to shelter from the rain – or for any other reason; they owned their bows and hatchets, but anyone was free to avail themselves of them.

The prince learnt about a community caring for each other. There were no strictures, no commandments – insisting, for instance, the old be looked after. It was taken as self-evident that such needed to happen. If a child fell over and hurt itself, the person nearest the child would tend to it. There was occasionally competition in love – of course there was – and there was 'competition' to become Chief. But there was no competition in daily life, no constant comparing of oneself against one's fellows. In Waifu society everyone in it was valued. They might not have *known* they were valued, not in a conscious way. But there was no need to: You don't need to know you have lungs in order to breathe. At an unconscious level they knew it so well it was ingrained.

And certainly there was conflict. Of course there was. When homo erectus chose language as a means of communication he opted to fell the tree with a very blunt axe. But such conflict was usually resolved quickly – and always bloodlessly. If the conflict lasted for more than three days, the protagonists' friends interceded; three more days and the elders were consulted. On three occasions, the disagreement had been so impassable that one of the dissenting Waifu had left his own village for another. And on four other occasions, Chiloquin had accepted similar 'exiles' from other villages. These strangers were immediately accepted. There was no stigma, were no strings attached. These things happened, that was all.

The prince realised that there were many reasons why, in what the Western world in its arrogance proclaims 'civilised' society, Man has become the creature he has. It is simply not true that most of his undesirable traits are either genetic or generic. They have been learnt.

But we have learnt some admirable traits as well: Western Man, for instance, has a need to think he's doing good. The Waifu had no such considerations. Their welfare was the common welfare. This they less knew than intuited. They never thought in terms of 'doing good'.

Western man does. Even the greedy of the Western world, and those so inadequate they must have power, even they have a need to think they are doing 'good'. Over the years, therefore, they have tried to persuade us that their delinquent behaviour is only an unfortunate means to a very beneficial end; or they have tried to persuade us that delinquent behaviour is endemic, and that, in the real world, the only way to fight fire is with fire. (Which is a totally false analogy. A more accurate one would be that it is trying to save a drowning man by dousing him in more water.)

"It is awesomely powerful," the king said, "our need to be doing good. So powerful, in fact, that these moral bankrupts have persuaded even *themselves* of these fantasies. So much so that they do actively believe them. Those who believed the Earth was flat also passionately believed that.

"Such people argue that, without ambition, Man would still be swinging from the branches – may even never have emerged from the sea. They argue that the survival of the fittest is the survival of the most aggressive and that therefore we hone our aggression or we perish. They argue that the first instinct of any animal (before its need for food or mating) is to protect its territory. And they argue it very well. But it is a Chippendale chair fashioned in balsa. The rhetoric is ornate and mellifluous, but the argument is specious. Sit on the chair and it collapses.

"Contrary to myth, we are not the only species to kill each

other. But we are one of the few. Neither the success nor the survival of the species requires it. Man evolves most completely when he works in association, and for a common cause. When he works to satisfy only his own needs, he betrays his family, his community, and his species. Most of all he betrays the very person at the centre of his universe: himself. You cannot create a society with anti-social behaviour. When you are working for yourself, you are – by definition – behaving anti-socially.

"When Mercian and Belgic economists argue that the best (some say, the *only*) way forward is to create a society where everyone is looking after his own interests, listen to the chef telling you that the best (or the *only*) way to cook a cake is by keeping all the ingredients separate, never mixing them together. We are dealing with the same level of nonsense."

"Thank you, sire," I said. "You were in Chiloquin?"

The single cloud in Charming's sky at that time was knowing that Syun Drette was still at the 'Presidence'.

Quifah had told Charming to keep away from the place, told him that each foray thither was tempting Providence, inviting unnecessary danger. But Charming had a need to check the girl was all right. It was a need that was stronger even than his loyalty.

And so, frankly, he'd lie to Quifah. He'd tell him he was going higher up the mountain to have some time with himself, or was going to the East to see whether the beestalo had returned. He'd mount Peggy, and he'd head off in the designated direction until he was out of sight. When he'd double back on himself and make for the 'Presidence'.

On his first two trips he didn't even see Syun. On the very first this relieved him: It meant she was no longer yoked to that dreadul plough. There was again a shire horse pulling this. On the second occasion, his heart even gave a little skip: Perhaps it meant that the Tays had freed her. He went for the third time merely to convince himself that was true.

But on the third time he did see her. And it was now unmistakably a 'her' that he saw. She was dressed as a shabby replica of a Mercian serving wench – long full skirt, a blouson of ragged cloth, a tatty head scarf. Clearly somehow her true gender had been discovered. She looked unhappy, but defiant. Her stance was one prepared to take on all comers. She was hanging out laundry. As she put the pegs on the washing-line she stabbed with them – a vulture stabbing at a carcase. Had Realrich yet married her, Charming wondered. How could he get word to her that he would soon return to rescue her?

As well as seeing Syun, Charming also noticed (as who could fail not to?!) the huge increase around the 'Presidence' of the military machine. What had been a small canvas town had now spread into being a sprawling and sizable city. There were large cannon visible, several huge paddocks, holding literally thousands of horses. And there was an ancillary town growing too, there to support the garrison: a town of bars and barbers, of cookhouses and bathhouses.

Quifah needed to know about this.

But if Charming told him, Quifah would know that he'd been lying.

Chapter 42

The succession referendum issue, finally, was settled very quickly.

HM entered Cole's inner sanctum. She brought with her a 'bowl' for the king. She put this alongside two empty ones. Cole was trying to play with Nose. But Nose still had scant interest in such games.

"Will you go hunt, Your Majesty?" asked HM.

"What, HM?"

"The hart?"

"Hart?"

"The stag, Your Majesty."

"Hunt?"

"Yes, sire."

"Hart?"

"Yes."

"You and me?"

"Together, Your Majesty."

"And your Ministry?" The king pronounced the word as if it were some nefarious and rather distasteful enterprise.

"I could, sire, take the day off."

"You could?"

"Yes."

"Really?"

"Really. If only ..."

"Only?"

"I didn't have this referendum thing hanging over me."

"Referendum thing?"

"The line, sire, of your succession."

"Women, that sort of thing?"

"That sort of thing, yes, sire."

"What do you think, HM?"

"I think we should have it, sire."

"You thought too you should be queen."

"I still think that, sire."

Cole studiously avoided pursuing that particular line. He thought about it, though. Chuckled to himself. "So, if one agrees to a referendum, we can go hunting?"

"Yes, sire."

"Right."

"Right?"

"Where does one sign?"

"I'll have the papers before you within the hour."

"Don't leave one, HM," the king said, unable to disguise his desperation.

"Sire?"

"One gets ... bored, HM. So bored."

"Then marry me, sire."

"Don't bully one, HM. You're not yet married to one. Not yet. Don't nag at one. One'll think about it, okay? Okay? One'll think about it."

"I'll be back within the hour."

"And tomorrow, HM, we hunt?"

"The hart, Your Majesty," said HM and left.

***

Squeers was later to acknowledge that he'd missed a truly terrific business opportunity. He'd bought a few double-barrelled muskets from Antonio. But not enough, not by a long chalk. He hadn't realised how quickly and totally the High Command of Mercia would fall in love with the weapons, how insatiable would be their hunger for them.

Just now he had more important things than guns on his mind. He had to get to Mayor Leamore. The so-called Squire Wodinton, the young man he'd left at the orphanage ...

"What of him, dude?" asked Leamore.

They were in Leamore's office. This was a splendid and ornate room. A marble tiled floor was covered in a middle-Eastern carpet of an extraordinarily complex design and lushness of tuft. The room was colonnaded with Doric columns. The huge and silk covered couches were grouped around a long low table, in the centre of which reposed a giant bowl garlanded with the most exotic of blooms. No expense had been spared on this room – the bill for which was also footed by the good burghers of Biga-buga.

"D'you know, by any chance, where he went?" asked Squeers.

"'Case you hadn't noticed, dude, I'm kind of a busy man."

"It could have big consequences. Enormously big."

"*Your* big, or *my* big?"

"Yours, don't you know," said Squeers. "And then some."

"'Case you hadn't noticed, dude, that big don't exist," Leamore pouted. The most important thing about this man was his money.

"You know where he went?"

"We could find out," said Leamore and went to ring the bell to summon one of his lackeys. "Wait, I remember. The classy kid. The real classy one."

"That's him."

"Squire Wednesday? Something like that?"

"Wodinton, don't you know," Squeers corrected him.

"Yeah. Went with ...let me think ... went, yes, to Realrich."

"Zanoria?"

"There's another?"

"Is he still there?"

"Geography, then, not your best subject." Squeers didn't know whether to look abashed or indignant. "Zanoria, dude," Leamore continued, "is the back of beyond *of* the back of beyond. It makes the plain simple back of beyond seem like downtown Biga-buga."

"You're trying to say, don't you know, you don't know," suggested Squeers, and then wondered whether that's what he *had* suggested.

"Only way you'll ever know for sure is to go there yourself."

"When could I leave?" asked Squeers.

Which was when Leamore realised the 'big' he was talking about was very big indeed.

***

That which is innate in human beings is goodness. From which emanates senses of propriety and decency and equity. The result of the Belgic referendum was therefore never in question.

It wasn't that the Belgics were desperate for Goneril as their queen – not particularly desperate for *anyone* as their queen. But they recognised a basic unfairness in a men-only succession. The countenancing of any unfairness countenances all unfairness. The majority was overwhelming.

HM reminded Nancy of her promise to talk to her father. *She'd* delivered, after all: She'd arranged, hadn't she, for Nancy to overhear Goneril's 'confession'? Well, okay, maybe she hadn't precisely 'confessed', hadn't in fact said anything the least incriminating – but that was scarcely HM's fault, was it? And that had certainly never been part of the deal. Surely Nancy had to see that. And it behove Nancy therefore to stick by *her* side of the bargain.

Nancy therefore did go to see the king on HM's behalf. As even the king's children were not allowed into his inner sanctum, she had to see him in his bedroom.

"Father, you know HM wants to marry you?"

"What do you think?"

"It would be disaster."

"One thinks so too."

"Is there anything more that need be said?"

"Not a thing."

And so it never was.

***

In Prim's household, plans were approaching an advanced stage in her wedding to Squire Anderson. Throughout the house there was fluster and bluster and flicks of the duster, a hustle and bustle and a permanent tussle.

Prim had only been a bride once before in her life. She had scant memories of her first wedding: it had all happened too fast, and at an age when she could not appreciate it. This time she wanted to be sure she was going to enjoy it.

And she couldn't – she simply could not, dearie – understand why her two daughters seemed so sanguine about the whole affair, so totally unbustled and unafluster. Was it *her* fault they'd lost their fiancés? To lose one fiancé may be considered misfortune; to lose two smacked of … well, dearie, she didn't like to say, but ... of carelessness.

She wallowed in the line. Throughout her life she would trot it out whenever occasion allowed it. In her later life she would repeat it yet again to a young man of her acquaintanceship, then an Oxford undergraduate from Ireland with ambitions to be a dramatist.

For their part, Ginny and Winny could see no earthly reason to get into a tizzwazz over their mother's second wedding. She'd had *one*, for Heaven's sake.

Dr Johnson once opined that a second marriage was the triumph of optimism over experience. As far as Winny and Ginny were concerned, a second *wedding* was the triumph of vanity over expedience. Their mother was making a far greater to-do about really very little than was either decorous or propitious. They were not about to debase themselves by following her example. There was enough debasement going on elsewhere, for pity's sake. Squire Anderson's oh so pretty bloody daughter, for pity's sake, being demure all over the place, helpful all over the bloody place.

Well, they'd show her. They'd soon show *her*!

Chapter 43

Goneril was crowing. The result of the referendum meant that one day she would be queen. Thus it would be that, as well as vindicating her mother, she would avenge her.

Indeed so cock-a-doodle-do was the crowing of Her future Majesty that she found it hard to contain it. Each time she thought of it, each time she opened her mouth she was smothered in a lather of it, which radiated from somewhere deep within her solar plexus and spread, fan-like, over the entire of her body.

For the moment she had to appear reticent and poker-faced. Any closer to her chest, the cards that she played would have been glued to it. It was, for the moment, important that Naitly, HM and Fredvie believed she would honour the 'promises' she'd made to the three of them.

Nancy had to watch all this. She was not fooled by her sister's apparent insouciance. She knew she was crowing about becoming the future queen. And how much she was crowing, and how well. And it stuck in her craw, the crow.

Hidden behind the arras that day, at Goneril's meeting with HM, she'd heard ... well, nothing. Nothing, anyway, which by a court of law would be considered anything – evidence or anything. But she had heard enough. Even, more than enough. Call it a mother's instinct, or the intuition of the bereaved, but if she hadn't known beforehand, afterwards she knew. Knew. Knew it as she knew that night followed day: This woman had killed her son. She had murdered him. He had died not as the consequence of an accident, not even from carelessness. His death had been executed not in the heat of the moment, but coldly, heartlessly, brutally, with malice aforethought and afterthought. With precision, without remorse.

It stuck there, the crow, and *scraped* at her craw. It scratched and tore at her craw. It felt like it was lacerating her craw, that it was a black bear whose claws were tearing at her craw. It felt like she couldn't talk, or that words, if they did come forth, would not be spoken but spewed. She felt her body seized with hatred and with fury, possessed of them – and by them. She felt them gnawing upwards from her tummy as downwards the bear kept tearing at her throat.

She would have told you that these reactions were the consequence of this woman being her son's killer. She would have insisted 'entirely'. She *believed* it was entirely. But it wasn't.

What Nancy could not bring herself to reveal to herself, to know about herself, was that there was also a part of her bear which was envy. Pure envy. Envy that Goneril should have been born first, that one day Goneril would be queen, that in the history books Goneril would always be the chapter and Nancy the footnote. It is unlikely, of course, that such self-knowledge would have diminished the power or intensity either of her hatred or her rage, but it might – just – have tempered some of the attendant self-righteousness.

"There are few tools better able to intensify indignation than self-righteousness," King Sebastian told me. "It may not have provoked many wars, but it has precluded many cease-fires; and its smoulder has ignited a lot fuses which have led to war. When Jesus said, 'Let he who is without sin cast the first stone', that was not just to stay an execution. It was a call for international peace. Those who recognise their own guilt find it harder to condemn others. It is hard to wage war on those you do not condemn."

"Meanwhile, sire," I said, "back at the plot?"

Nancy was damned if she would let Goneril become queen. *Damned* if she would. Now that accession was open to women, she'd make sure it was she the daughter wearing the crown. On board the ship carrying them to Mercia she told her husband that; told him too there was no wider picture than that. That was the widest the picture got: She *deserved* to be queen. It was some small token she was due in recognition of all the pain she had suffered.

Nancy was now in Biga-buga. None too happy. She'd been waiting well over half-an-hour to be summoned before Mayor Leamore. She knew Dawes was with him. Nancy was unused to being made to wait for this length of time. It galled her.

It galled her because it was so obviously a ploy designed to let her know *they* knew who needed whom most; and it galled her because the previous evening she and her husband had taken both men out to a hugely expensive dinner precisely to avoid such overt humiliation. She looked to her husband now. He was pretending that all was all right in a nigh-on perfectly all right world. She knew him well enough, however, to know that he was seething.

Finally they *were* summoned before the mayor. They weren't invited to sit.

"Yes?" Leamore said, seated at his desk. Dawes was ensconced in a green leather wing-chair. Neither had bothered to rise.

"I'm going to give you Belgiss," Nancy said, her voice as direct as her words. "I need you to support me before Fredvie."

"You are talking, dude – Your Princessness –, dudette, about the emperor of Mercia," Leamore told her crossly and condescendingly, as if she were a truant child. "You would do well to refer to him by his correct title."

"I'm offering you Belgiss," she said. Tacit within which was "What more do you want?"

"We already have Belgiss," drawled Dawes. "We keep telling Fredvie, we don't want annexation. It'd just make the whole thing too obvious. The Belgics might start figuring out what's happened. We *own* Belgiss, lady. The interest we charge you each year for past debts, the stock holdings we have in Belgic companies, in its commodities. Me, I own most of your gazettes, over half of your publishing houses. If you want our support, Nancy, talk about *not* annexing Belgiss to Mercia."

"And why should we support *you*, dudette?" asked Leamore. "Why would we need to? 'Case you hadn't noticed, we put the people in charge of Belgiss we want in charge of it. You think Naitly's there 'cause of the will of the people? The answer we need from you, dude, is: If we *let* you become queen, what'll you do for us that isn't *already* being done?"

Nancy was stuck for an answer. Richardson fielded the question for her. "I'm a businessman," he said. He tried to ignore the patronising smirks both bothered only to half-conceal behind well-manicured hands. "We could tear up the minimum wage agreement."

"Already that's there in statute only," Dawes reminded him. "It's never applied."

"Abolish maximum working hours, allow for unpaid overtime."

"Give us something *new*, dude," Leamore whined.

"One new tax level: twelve per cent across the board, whatever the income," Richardson announced.

"Sounds high to me," said Dawes.

"And me," agreed Richardson. "You're right. Initiative should be rewarded. Twenty per cent on all incomes of five hundred doubloons or under. Of, let's say, fifteen on those between five hundred and a thousand. On a sliding scale, so that those most ... innovative receive most rewards. Rising to zero tax on those with incomes of over a million."

"Meaning, I trust," said Leamore, "that those hypothetical millionaires, dude, pay nothing at all, not that they pay nothing on any income they might have over a million. Hypothetically, of course."

"*They* pay nothing at all," Richardson confirmed. "Obviously."

"On that basis, we can talk to Fredvie."

"I've also got some new musketry that might interest you," said Richardson.

"Oh?" said the two Mercians together. And both leant forward in their seats. "Have a seat," they told the baron.

Nancy was left standing.

***

She was left standing as well when they finally got in to see Fredvie.

Fredvie had spent a lot of time latterly before a mirror, rehearsing being tough, practising saying "no" to Leamore and Dawes, repeating over and over again that they could take a hike or get lost or take a long walk off a short pier. He had tried his toughness on Minor Minor. And Minor Minor had quaked suitably. He saw this meeting as the grand unveiling.

"The lady wants to be queen, Fredvie," Leamore told him. "We're backing her."

"No," said Fredvie, toughly, decisively.

"We are backing her, dude," said Leamore, unsure to what the 'no' referred but unpleased to have heard it at all. "You're to back her too."

"Take a rootin' hike," proclaimed Fredvie, and turned to smile a smile of victory at Minor Minor. Who flicked a wan smile back.

By the time Fredvie had turned back to where he thought Leamore was standing, the mayor was looming above him. "What?" he asked indignantly. "*What?*"

"Nothing, Mr Mayor," whimpered Fredvie. "Nothing. Please don't tootin' shout at me. It was all rootin'-tootin' Minor Minor's rootin'-tootin' fault. He made me do it. He made me – ..."

"Just don't forget," said Dawes, who had loured up on the emperor's other side, "just who wears the pants in this relationship."

"*You* do, Mr Dawes. *You* rootin' do."

"'Case you hadn't noticed, we put you here, dude," Leamore told him. "We can take you away from here too."

"It was Minor Minor. All Minor Minor's rootin'-tootin' fault."

"We want you to support the lady, dude," said Leamore. "She's Richardson's wife. 'Case you hadn't noticed, she's not as snooty as her sister. We like that in a woman."

"Half-sister," Nancy corrected him gently.

"Why didn't you say?" Fredvie asked. "Support the lady ..." He caught Richardson's scowl. "... this *princess* against that awful woman, what's her name, Goneril? I'd be delighted. She was unspeakably discourteous, did you know that, to our rootin' ambassador? Those who insult our ambassadors insult rootin'-tootin' me." He caught the scowls of Leamore and Dawes. "Insult, I mean, rootin'-tootin' *Mercia*. Delighted to support you, ma'am. Please, have a seat."

"I'd rather have a throne," she said.

"You shall have both, my dear," her husband told her, and plonked himself on the couch.

Chapter 44

There is a peculiar notion abroad that the peaceful do not get angry. It is probably the warlike who propagate the myth. It helps to sheen the peaceful with other-worldliness, with a lack of reality. The peaceful do get angry. Of course they do. Very angry, sometimes. Even Jesus Christ got angry, and the Buddha. The peaceful are simply more skilful than the bellicose in the way they deal with their anger. The peaceful even get physically aggressive. Indeed, they often do. But the peaceful will punch not a face but a cushion; they will smash their chipped crockery rather than their neighbour's window.

When Charming told Quifah about the troop build-up, Quifah was doubly angry. He was angry with 'Hyandri' that he should have disobeyed him. And he was angry with Mercia that it should, as self-evidently it was, be preparing for all-out war.

His anger at that became fury. The fury became molten, and the molten fury canalled through his veins to seize the whole of him.

Because he knew that the Waifu would have to fight back. Which meant untold numbers of his family and his friends would be killed. Prematurely. Some in hideous pain. Others would be forced to live with that pain. For the rest of their lives. Mutilated, if not physically, certainly emotionally. There would be no-one – no-one – left whole.

Mercia, though, was not there for him to lash out at. Hyandri was. "*This is how you thank us?*" Quifah asked. "*We bring you back from the dead. We free you from bondage. We nurse you and care for you as if you were a Waifu – a Waifu child – and on the very first occasion I forbid you from doing something you flagrantly disobey me?*"

"*I care for this woman, Quifah. I had a seed to see her.*"

"*Need. Need. You had a need, Hyandri, to see her. You learn Waifu slowly. Both our tongue and our customs. Maybe we are failing you.*"

"*No, Quifah,*" said Hyandri rather sheepishly. "*I disobeyed you.*

I should be nourished."

"Punished," Quifah corrected him. *"It is not fitting that I punish you. You are not Waifu. I think we have both tried to pretend that was not so. Now we should recognise it. It is, I think, time that you left."*

"You will call me back when you have decided what my nourishment might be?"

"Punishment," Quifah wearily corrected him again. *"No, Hyandri,"* the old man said sadly: *"Not leave my tent, leave the village."* Charming staggered as if pole-axed. *"I'm sorry."*

Charming felt physically winded. He fought for breath, for speech. *"Please, Quifah,"* he gasped. *"Please."*

"If you knew Waifu ways, Hyandri, you would know I have spoken. Go now." Charming rocked back and forth on his legs. Collapse seemed possible and imminent. *"Go."*

Charming staggered from Quifah's tent. Outside it, a fair percentage of the village had gathered. They knew of Hyandri's disobedience. They had gathered for the sentence. One glimpse of Hyandri's ashen face told them what they didn't want to hear.

The crowd divided to form a raggedy lane through which the young man could walk. He could not sustain looks to any one of them. Young women turned to their mothers' breasts in order to cry. Thus closeted they couldn't see that their mothers too were shedding tears. Even some of the men – those wise enough to know that crying is a balm – were brushing acrid tears from weathered cheeks.

"I'm sorry," the prince kept saying again and again. *"I'm feally, feally sorry."*

He passed through the far end of the crowd. He was dazed still, and slumped. Peggy and Philly came to see him. Came, it seemed, to reassure him, to re-avow their love for him. He sprang aboard Philly. He no longer had need of either saddle or bridle.

The village kept looking back to Quifah's tent. Kept hoping that the Chief would emerge from it and rescind his decision.

Kept willing him to do so.

Now mounted on Philly, Charming also looked over in the tent's direction. Its flap remained obstinately closed.

"Good-bye," the prince said. *"Good-bye, my briends. You have looked after me yell. And I shall piss you. I shall piss all of you."*

Even Philly seemed to slouch, even Peggy, as the three of them made their sad and desultory way out of the village. They passed in front of Quifah's tent. Charming cast one last, mournful glance at it. And then – to his utter amazement and to gasp of the on-lookers – the flap did open. And Quifah did appear.

He glowered at the young man astride his horse. *"You still here?"* he asked him angrily. *"Be gone. We have work to do."*

The prince urged his horses forward, and the village, as one, cast down their communal eyes in both grief and embarrassment.

"Did you not hear me?" Quifah asked the village generally. *"I said, 'We have work to do.' We have a war to prepare for. We have ..."* He paused for emphasis. *"... work to do."*

The village sought to scurry to their respective tasks. But the scurry was lacklustre and without energy. Its only purpose was to occupy them sufficiently to save them the pain of their final good-bye.

Once the Chief had spoken to him, Charming urged Philly into a canter. Peggy followed her example. They sent up puffs of dust, as hooves bit into the sun-baked clay

Long after Quifah could no longer see Charming or his horses, he could see the puffs that marked his trail.

***

In an army unit, just as every man has his job to do, so there is a man too who fulfils each social function. (There is, in fact, this division in any society, but we are here involved only with the army.) Just as there is the cook and the messenger, so there is the Father Confessor and the joker. Cross-Bones had become the bores.

Both Cross and Bones had captured the unsuspecting and had, for hours at a stretch, regaled them with tales of their life at the Belgic Court, the intimate terms they'd been on with King Cole, with Baron Naitly, with princesses Goneril and Nancy and (the notorious) Cordelia. Names were dropped with the casualness of Big Ben knelling the hour.

Leamore and Squeers had decided that the best way to find the prince was for the latter to travel to Zanoria. He was moving West on the same Accidental as Cross-Bones. Squeers, of course, was riding whilst Cross-Bones were 'marching' – although a Regimental Sergeant Major of the Belgic army witnessing what the Mercians described as a 'march' would have burst several buttons-brassed-boots-blackened blood vessels.

It was common at night for small groups to eat huddled around their own camp fires. That sat with Cross-Bones around theirs was smaller than most. People tended to avoid a second evening in their company.

Even in Mercia, whence they hailed, cigars were at this time still a relative novelty. An equal amount of people objected then to their being smoked as do today. Squeers had thus absented himself from his group – the big brass group – in order that he might indulge. He happened to be passing Cross-Bones's little group when he heard the following exchange.

"King Cole and uth, like brotherth we were. Clother than brotherth!"

"Sure you were," roared a sceptical, whisky-grizzled voice.

"'Oo d'you think it was talked Naitly into going into Orismine?" asked Bones.

"And I'm sure you'll get the Imperial Medal of Honour for it, straight from Fredvie himself," roared the same third voice.

Squeers had heard enough bragging to know it at a thousand paces, and he would normally have paid the words the lack of heed they deserved. Had he not caught Bones's profile in the firelight. And had he not – he was sure of it – seen it somewhere before.

The wedding!

No, not at the cathedral. He didn't remember seeing the men at the cathedral. But then, in that much pomp, it'd be hard enough to distinguish your own mother.

At the palace! He'd seen them at the palace. Not officially, of course. Not banqueting or wedding breakfasting. Skulking, rather. But within the palace. Certainly.

He feigned a casualness as he approached them. "Well, I'll be! Do I detect a Belgic accent? No, don't get up. Don't get up," he told both Cross-Bones and their audience.

"Yeth, thir. From Wodinton, thir."

"We'se seen *you* before an' all."

"Princess Cordelia's wedding?"

"And you were the best man," said Bones, as a sort of 'eureka'.

Squeers exclaimed a second time, "Well, I'll be!"

"Well, *we'll* be … away," said the voice which had previously roared its scepticism. "Time to hit the hay." The three men were left alone.

Squeers started by letting the two soldiers exaggerate themselves dry. Confronted by someone whom they knew was in the know their braggary anyway had shrunk considerably.

"The prince," asked Squeers finally, "how well did you know him?"

"None knowth him better, thir."

"We nearly flogged 'im once – God rest 'is soul. There's few ways better to get to know a man."

"Mithter Thtern, there, he wath engaged to hith nanny."

"Engaged, sir, I was to 'er."

"Nothing we don't know about the late prince, thir."

"Nothing."

"You *were* engaged to his nanny?" asked Squeers

"Politicth, thir: a devilish buthineth. A *devilish* buthineth."

"Forced to leave my lady love be'ind, sir," Bones confessed.

"And such a lovely lady love she wath, thir. Mine too."

"And a lovely be'ind, what's more, sir."

"Lovely behind," agreed Cross.

"Forced, sir, to leave 'em both be'ind, sir: 'Er and 'er be'ind."

"Well, I'll be," Squeers was starting to tread very carefully now. "The tattoo, don't you know, on the prince's toe ..."

"You knows about that, sir? I always thought that was, like, tip-top secret."

Squeers hid his jubilation that the two men should be privy to so much knowledge. "You ever see it?"

"No-one'th theen it, thir. Not even the king. Only HM, thir."

"And Winny, Mr Krantz."

"Oh, and Winny, thir. Gretel, I thuppothe: She wath the nanny before Winny, thir. It wath hidden by a bandage, thir ..."

"This Winny," asked Squeers, "do you think she might care to visit Mercia?"

Which was the question which led Cross-Bones to realise that, once again, their fortunes had made a dramatic turn. This time dramatically for the better.

Chapter 45

The 'Presidence' was three days' ride from the Waifu village. Charming had been riding for two-and-a-half. He was still desolate at his banishment from the village, still angry with Quifah at the savagery of his sentence, and furious with himself for having put himself in such a position. Only one thing now mattered to Charming in his life: rescuing Syun.

If he could free her from her bondage, return her to her people, then his life would have some meaning. Maybe, if she didn't want to be returned, maybe – even better – they could escape together, back to Biga-buga, maybe, where they could lose themselves in the metropolitan whirl. No-one would come looking for them there. And there everyone was too busy looking after their own business to worry about anyone else's.

There was nothing floppy or foppish about the prince now. His skin stretched tautly over his sinews, as a cheetah's does; he was as lithe and lissom as a cheetah; as patient, as sly. As merciless.

And self-sufficient.

He knew about survival now, the prince. He knew how to catch game and to skin it; knew which were the edible toadstools and which the poisonous; knew where to look for water in a desert. He was strong and resourceful. He was beginning even to like his own company.

And his horses? Well, the love he had for them had matured. It wasn't any longer the sentimental attachment that many of us have for our pets – creatures to which we assign anthropomorphic attributes. The bond now was both more spiritual and more elemental.

He allowed Philly and Peggy to be horses. He didn't think of them any longer as four-legged friends. Friendship requires, as well, intellectual rapport. There can be connection between man and beast; often there is sympathy; there is never rapport. And there never can be. We can only imagine what might be an animal's perspective. It is extremely unlikely that any animal ever even tries to imagine a human one. And, the prince realised, that was fine. You don't need to have a rapport with something in order to respect, even to revere it. Indeed, if in order to love it you have to make of it something it isn't, you *cannot* be loving it. You are then loving, in fact, what it isn't.

They cared for each other. At an instinctive, a bestial level. Now that Charming rode bareback, very often without even a bridle, he meshed more with the beast he was riding. Through his thighs and calves he could feel the fabulous machine that was this creature pushing, churning, thrusting, coursing. He could feel himself melt into the horse, fuse with it, weld with it until they became one. Indivisible. Their hearts pumping together. Almost as one heart. Their muscles rippling together, their energy surging together.

Astride one horse he also became deeply aware of what was happening to the other. He could see the grey, for instance, of Peggy's coat fleck into a thousand variations of grey and white and silver as it galloped beside him; he could see the whirr of its radar ears as they turned towards some, to Charming inaudible, sound; he could watch in fascination as the coat rolled over withers and shanks shingled with power and strength and energy – and life. Horses, Charming knew at such times, aren't magnificent because they are human carriers, nor because they are quadruped chums. Horses are magnificent because they are horses; and horses are magnificent.

He'd caught a rabbit for lunch. He was still far enough away from the 'Presidence' to be able, with impunity, to barbecue it on an open fire. It was almost cooked. That night he would rescue Syun. He was already getting nervous about that.

He was absorbed in his task; absorbed in his plans for that night's 'kidnap'; absorbed in stilling his nerves. It came therefore as a shock, the voice behind him. *"You travel fast."* It was Quifah.

The prince sought quickly to regain his composure.

"I had good peaches," he replied. He stood up. He wanted to embrace the chief, knew he couldn't. They stood for a moment, silently gazing at each other.

"Old is not always wise," said Quifah measuredly. *"Old men often do stupid things."*

"And yet to learn from our mistakes is the stasis of all wisdom."

"Basis, for God's sake. Basis."

Charming smiled. *"I know,"* he said and laughed. And then Quifah laughed. And then they did embrace. *"Habit?"* Charming invited. He meant 'rabbit'.

Quifah didn't correct him. *"It's very small."*

"I wasn't expectorating company."

Quifah sat. *"The Tay have recaptured Syun,"* he told the prince.

"Oh?"

"In case you were thinking of …"

"Yes."

"Were you thinking of …?"

"Yes."

"I thought you might have been."

They ate silently for a bit.

"She's back with her own people, Hyandri."

"Yes."

"It's where she belongs." The prince said nothing. *"You too belong with your own people. One day you must go back to them."*

"You are my people, Quifah," the prince pleaded.

"No." They ate some more, again in silence. *"We will visit the 'Presidence' together."*

"Okay."

"See together the machines of war."

"Okay."

"You can help the Waifu."

"O-kay."

"Help them very much."

"Thank you."

"We love you, Hyandri, as one of us. You could stay. Only for a time. But for a time, you could stay."

"Great. Great, Quifah. Great."

"Your destiny will not allow you to stay long. You understand that? It will be your destiny that wrests you from us."

The young man dived into the liquid brown of the old man's eyes. He found himself coated in the Chief's insight and wisdom. The words that came from his mouth resonated with that wisdom, but resonated too with resignation and regret, sadness and courage.

"Yes," the prince said.

***

"The living dead," pontificated Leamore, "are not zombies, dude, but Zanorians. If the prince is in Zanoria and he isn't yet dead, then he soon will be. And if he's not dead soon, he might as well be."

"We *are* talking high treason here, don't you know," Squeers reminded him. "*Enormously* high treason."

"'Case you hadn't noticed, I'm Mayor Leamore. Think a tinpot country like Belgiss, dude, is going to risk taking off *my* head?" he exclaimed, before adding – rather too hastily, "Or yours too, 'course."

"Well ..." Squeers fought hard to find some false modesty. He lost.

"It's beautiful, dude. Beau-ti-ful. We can have complete control without it appearing we have *any*. We just need to get this Wendy over here p.d.-damn-q."

"Winny," Squeers corrected him.

"Excuse me?"

"Not Wendy, Mr Mayor, but Winny," Squeers told him.

"Right."

"They've been invited, Mr Mayor."

"Right."

"They'll be here. Quickly, don't you know. Enormously quickly."

"They'd better."

"They'll be here," Squeers reassured him.

***

WAIFU MURDER PROTECTOR screamed the headlines of Dawes's gazettes. The editorial within insisted that there must be no more shilly-shallying: This act of open aggression had to be met aggressively. No more peace-pipes, no more kid gloves, no more tolerance. There was one way, and one way only, that such violence should be countered – with yet greater violence. With the declaration – no time now to be mealy-mouthed about this!!! – of WAR. Glorious, jingoism-promoting, gazette-selling WAR.

As so frequently happens, the headlines banged a big bass drum when the only drum beaten by reality was the hum-drum. An adage of journalism has it that the reporter should never allow the truth to spoil a good story. Dawes's gazettes had so venerated that adage that truth in a story they now considered inappropriate. The Protector's death had nothing whatsoever to do with the Waifu. The Protector's death was caused by his cruelty.

There had been several armies billeted on the Zanorian border. As is usual, however, the troops arrived considerably ahead of all the supplies that they would need – ammunition, food, medical supplies, blankets. When Napoleon (admittedly a few years later!) opined that an army marches by its slowest man he was being wildly optimistic. It marches by its dimmest clerk. And when it comes to dimness ...well, there are few professions where dimness is held at the premium that it is within the armed forces.

Although his estate was thereby 'invaded', Realrich took some solace in having at his command a ready supply of hunting companions. Men, moreover, of substance and clout who would regale audiences back East of tales of the Protector's valour and hunting expertise. He contrived thus to organise as many hunting sorties as he could.

No horse in his stable could replace either Philly or Peggy. Something Realrich attributed to pure obstinacy on the horses' part. 'Firm' treatment was all that was needed.

The fact that on not one single occasion in history has a carthorse been lashed into becoming a racehorse was one of no interest to Realrich. At all. Try to create a racehorse that way and all you'll get is a bruised and resentful carthorse. But, just as there are none so blind as those who will not see, so there are none so stupid as those who will not learn. It is for that precise reason that so many politicians – to this day – continue to be as stupid as they are. And why Realrich was as stupid as he was. His horses hated him. They were also frightened of him, and they therefore hated him even more. He hurt them. He even tortured them.

That day was a day like any other. Realrich had attended military manoeuvres in the morning – all very tedious and tiring; had lunched and snoozed. And had then had his horse saddled for hunting.

He had, as was his wont, led the pack. He had had his slaves beat the deer into his path and had set after it in bloodthirsty pursuit. He had, as was his wont, bitten into the horse's flesh with his spurs; he had beaten its rump with his crop. But this day, as was *not* his wont, the horse had had enough.

Realrich stomped into its flanks with his spurs. The horse, rather than speeding up, slew to an almost dead stop. And reared. Its forelegs hit the ground again, and it bucked as if stung by a bee.

And then it reared again. It was determined to loose, and lose, this tormentor from its back. It kicked, it reared, it broncked, it bucked.

Finally Realrich could hold on no more. He toppled blanc-mangely to the ground. And was on the point, wobblily, of rising when – to the consternation of all close-by – the horse started to attack him.

Realrich tried to protect himself, but the horse (according to witnesses) was possessed by some kind of demon. It started stamping on Realrich. Kicking him, jumping on him. One hoof knocked him unconscious.

But that wasn't enough for the horse. It started pummelling the man, squeezing him. Realrich died quickly.

Still the horse continued, however. The Protector was just a pulp when eventually some of the slaves managed to lasso the horse, and to drag it away. There was nothing which could be done for Realrich. And the horse too had to be destroyed.

Heroes are good for emperors. Heroes help to unite nations, and therefore give the impression that under that particular emperor, the empire is united. Alive Realrich was not the stuff of heroes. Dead, though ...

A state funeral, that's what was called for. Minor Minor suggested it, and Fredvie agreed. Leamore was gratified. And Dawes delighted: State funerals also sold gazettes.

Your own horse killing you is not what happens to heroes.

Thus WAIFU MURDER PROTECTOR.

And thus slaughter on a scale that cannot be imagined.

Chapter 46

Neither Mr Stern nor Mr Krantz (Bones or Cross, in other words) was a poet. Their letters to their former fiancées were ... brief, prosaic, to the point. Lacking in ornament, bereft of compliments.

Again they were surrounded, Cross-Bones, by great luxury, even opulence. But the seas that house these trappings are ones where most fish are sharks. The only way for minnows to survive in such waters is for them to befriend a shark bigger than the one threatening them.

This was the first reason why Cross-Bones chose also to write to HM. The second was that, undeniably fond though both were of their respective betrotheds, they were fonder yet of their heads. Whilst Leamore considered he was far too important a person to have his head lobbed off by unimportant Belgiss, Cross-Bones did not share his lack of humility. They knew the fate of their heads was no more important to important people than the fate of a deer's head or a chicken's.

What was being hatched in Mercia would in Belgiss be considered high treason. No-one seemed to know what low treason was, but the penalty even for that was bound to be beheading. What would then be chopped off *too* if convicted of the high variety?

In their letter they told HM there was a plan afoot to put a usurper on the Belgic throne: A look-alike would be found amongst the Biga-buga citizens, and the likeliest candidate would be groomed to behave like the prince and educated in his ways. Edwina would be arriving shortly from overseas to oversee (here they collapsed into giggles at the cleverness of their pun) the tattooing of the pretender toe.

Cross-Bones wanted to assure HM of their continued loyalty to King Cole and trusted such loyalty would be remembered when next amnesties and preferments were being discussed.

They awaited HM's urgent reply and were confident of the beneficence (they had to look that word up in a dictionary) to them of what would be contained therein.

They were to await for some time.

***

The Waifu had no choice.

If they were not to be obliterated from the face of the planet, they had to prepare to defend themselves.

Charming and Quifah had returned to the sight overlooking the 'Presidence'. The men now billeted around the estate totalled something not far short of those which comprised the entire Waifu nation. The Mercians had cannon as well, and muskets. The Mercians had more troops, better weapons, more experience of war. The fight apparently would be as fair as that between matador and bull.

Charming tried to convince Quifah that their best protection would be in forming a coalition with the Tay. He even offered to mediate on Quifah's behalf.

"*You want to see Syun again,*" the chief suggested.

"*That has muffin to do with it,*" Charming replied with enough indignation, he hoped, to veil his blushes. "*Muffin.*"

"*It is a young man's lot to talk of love,*" Quifah said, a smile curling his tone if not his lips.

"*And an old man's to chalk of war?*"

"*No. Whilst old men talk of war, young men die. Dead young men cannot talk of love.*"

"*Young men also die when old men of other nascents chalk of war.*"

"*Old men of all nations should only talk of peace.*"

"*Those are cannons out zere, Quifah. Cannons do not chalk peace.*"

"*The time is not yet right that I should talk to the Tay.*"

"*Would you listen to them?*"

"*Always.*"

"Maybe they would chalk to you."

"Listen to me, Hyandri: You must not visit the Tay. They do not know you as we do. To the Tay, you are simply a pinky. And pinkies are evil. To be slain."

Charming dropped his eyes. He spoke quietly. *"I have to see her, Quifah."*

"You cannot die, Hyandri. You cannot cheat your destiny in that way. The Great Being will punish you."

"I have to see her," Charming repeated even more quietly.

The old man watched him very carefully. *"Be careful,"* he told the prince. *"Be very, very careful."*

***

Neither Mr Krantz nor Mr Stern was a poet. Their letters to their former fiancées were lacking in ornament, bereft of compliments. Not even the Dark Lady, however, could have been more delighted by Shakespeare's sonnets, more flattered by their content, than were Ginny and Winny on receipt of their missives.

Their mother's wedding was a mere four weeks away. And the preparations were reaching a flurry of deadlines to be met, and dominoes to be knocked over.

The triple wedding was back on, they told their mother. They just had to pop across to Biga-buga, reclaim their missing husbandage, and ... well ... the whole celebration could return to the triptych it was always meant to be.

Prim, though, had by now developed quite a yen for solo portraiture – particularly if it was she its star. There was no way she was delaying her wedding, and that was the end of the matter. And she certainly wasn't marrying, dearies, without her daughters being there and that too was the end of the matter. And she wouldn't dream of asking her Squire for the fares they would need, dearies, ... not until the knot had been tied – and tied to un-undoableness. And that, dearies, was the end of all matters!

Furthermore they were having a picnic lunch al fresco the following Sunday, with that selfsame squire and his (admittedly, rather dreary) daughter. And that picnic too the two girls would attend. No, dearies, no further discussion, that was the end of the matter.

The two girls wrote back to their beaux that, yes, they would love to visit Biga-Buga. It had been a place which had always attracted them. They'd be there, promise. And soon. Promise. Just as soon as ... circumstances permitted. Their beaux were to be patient. They (Ginny and Winny) would ensure their lovers' patience was well rewarded. Promise, promise, promise.

Winny then immediately went to see HM. It was a risk. Of course it was a risk. But if the plot all went pear-shaped at this stage, she could claim that she was denouncing the plot, and attain some kind of status as a national heroine. If, on the other hand, HM kept schtoom, Winny could be reasonably sure HM was not averse either to the idea.

HM, it must be remembered, believed that Charming was dead – killed either by her brother himself, or by the buccaneers who had killed her brother. She had continued to persuade the king that there was still a hunt on for his son (and therefore to keep Winny employed). But she did so only because it suited her purpose for him to believe that. It wasn't that HM *felt* that the hunt was a waste of time (the king also *felt* that), it was that she *knew* it to be.

She also, it must be remembered, knew by the letter from Cross-Bones of the plot to put a pretender on the throne. However, two functions were served by Winny also informing her of the plot. Firstly, it confirmed the reality of it; secondly, it confirmed to her that the royal nanny was someone who understood where, and how, her bread was buttered. That augured well. No Machiavelli can operate without a brigade of loyal henchmen.

For her part, Winny needed leave of absence from her sinecure at the palace. Without the prince at Wodinton, it was almost certain her presence would never be missed. However, Sod's law would probably oblige someone at that time to come snooping.

Over and above this practical consideration, however, she wanted an independent witness to know of her forthcoming deed lest, having overseen the toe's engraving, her attractiveness ... let's say ... 'waned' - and to such an extent that political convenience might recommend ... let's say ... her removal. Of the permanent variety. It would be good to have some insurance in place ... just in case.

HM felt warmer to Winny than she had to anyone in a long time. She was ferociously ugly, of course, and not just superficially. Both sisters were. But this act of loyalty to HM was to endear Winny to her for some time to come.

Immediately Winny left, HM went to see the king. "Is it still Your Majesty's deepest wish that your son be returned to you?"

"You know it is, HM." He was grooming Nose, alternately brushing the animal's coat and his own hair.

"And the reward for his return?"

"You know it, HM."

"It hasn't changed? Anything the finder wants. That hasn't changed?"

"You make one sound whimsical."

"Would you marry me?"

"This again?"

"Would you, Your Majesty, marry me?" HM repeated, even testily.

"Like a shot, HM." And took another draught from his bowl. "Like a shot," he repeated.

"In that case, sire, I might have some good news for you."

"One will wait and see, HM, won't one, Nose? One will wait, Nosey Wosey, and see." And he tapped the dog's nose with the end of the brush, and then he used it to tap his own.

Chapter 47

Like the Waifu, the Tay divided throughout the summer into villages. Charming expected to be away for four days. But in that time all he found out was that Syun was not in the six villages he'd by then managed to scout. It took him another four to find the one she *was* in.

This countryside too was rugged. Enormous boulders perched precariously, and sometimes apparently impossibly, on top of each other. Lizards scuttled above these rocks, and snakes slithered through their fissures. The sun beat on them during the day, but at night the rocks felt colder than they were. It was a wasteland of plenty and a forest of want.

Charming had taken Philly. Even she found the terrain arduous and hazardous. Her hooves slipped on the rock, and slid in the scree: a furlong seemed like a mile.

In all the Tay villages Charming saw what he had also seen in Chiloquin before he left it: the clumsy preparation for war. It was *everywhere* the same. The preparation was awkward, maladroit. The apprentice always works harder than the master. It's not that the master takes short cuts; it's that with accomplishment comes ease. Neither the Waifu nor the Tay were then anything but the most arrant beginners in warfare. They were David wondering how far a sling would throw a stone, what weight of stone would best suit what length of sling. It was not even David getting ready to fight Goliath. It was an ant hiding behind a thistle to protect itself from an elephant.

Charming had also seen *Goliath* preparing. And the contrast terrified him. He'd seen enough of war to know what it meant, and to hate it. But the preparation that he saw was not for war but for slaughter.

And then, in the eleventh village, he did see Syun. And all his other anxieties took second place.

He was crouched within two huge rocks on the brow of a hill

formed almost entirely by similar ones. Aeons previously there had to have been some sort of seismological cataclysm to have formed this cliff. The nearest mountain faces were half-a-mile away or so. What had caused this agglomeration of so many stones, and of such a size?

Philly he'd left grazing on the far side of the crest. This was terrain that was too dangerous for her – where she was too likely to snap an ankle, or disturb a snake-hole.

Charming watched for hours. In those days there was a lot more about him of Hyandri than there was of the heir to the Belgic throne. He was conscious of where his smell might waft to, of anything about him that might attract light and therefore attention. He was confident that he could watch for as long as day would permit without fear of being discovered. There was a part of him even at peace, warmed by a clement sun, refreshed by the smell of pine-cones and wild apricots drifting in from the nearby copse.

And then he saw her again.

Syun's bearing still bore the scars of her treatment. Not overtly. Not as the stripes of a whip. But in a deportment which was bent, and in a gait which was shuffling. As if her feet were reluctant to carry her into the future. She was still beautiful, and now more overtly feminine than he'd ever seen her. But both beauty and femininity were imbued with a hatred, which threatened to become self-hatred. It wasn't even that she scowled, or that her eyes were set on the ground. Her eyebrows were perfectly symmetrical and exuded blandness; and her eyes were set on a haze in the middle-distance. They saw all and were conscious of nothing.

Charming's heart nearly broke as he saw her. He wanted to spring on board Philly, rush into the village, swoop her up in his arms and take her off to a land where hope blossomed on trees of kindness. And his heart broke again knowing that he could not.

He knew Quifah was right. Looking at her as she now was, *he* could have killed Realrich for what he had done to her. He understood that likewise her family would be overwhelmed both by anger and by grief, understood that therefore sight of a pinky – any pinky – would so enrage them that they would kill first and ask questions later.

But he also understood Syun, understood she had to know – she had a need to know – that he had not forgotten her. He didn't want to disobey Quifah again. But to disobey the dictates of your heart is to disobey another chief. Perhaps the most important chief of all. He had to let her know he was thinking of her. He simply had to.

He crept closer. If he could shoot an arrow close enough to her to attract her attention, he could wave at her. She just needed to see him. If she saw him, she'd know he cared. Then he could disappear. And if he were killed in the forthcoming bloodshed, she would always know he *had* cared.

He bobbed and ducked, leapt and hopped, from one cranny to another, between cracks and crags. Soon he was close enough, if ever she went to the glade skirting the South of her village, for an arrow to be placed in her path.

The first time that she did so, though, it was with two elder women – who, by their appearance and general clucking around her, were probably her mother and aunt. The next time that day she visited the spot she *was* alone. But there was a group of young boys also close by – too close not to notice an arrow. She did not visit the glade that night.

Charming was hungry. But he couldn't light a fire and he wasn't desperate enough to eat his quarry raw. So it didn't make too much sense to go hunting. He therefore slipped into the copse, and picked the apricots he'd smelled earlier. The night was cold and long.

But rewarding.

As in the pre-dawn the sun streaked the lilac sky with shafts of magenta and of citrus, as the pre-dawn's luscious smells awoke in panoplies of hyacinth sweet and pine-tree tangy and dry-rock chalky, as the birds warbled their first gargling chirrups of a day thus proclaimed to be magnificent, so Syun returned to the glade.

She appeared almost to be sleep-walking. There was an involuntariness about her progress that was almost spook-like. It was almost as if she were being rolled on castors.

Charming had fallen into an uncomfortable sleep. He'd awoken as some dew had decided to settle on his nose, and did so consequently with a snort and a start. In this light he could only see Syun's silhouette, but he knew it was her.

And he knew that it would probably be never that he'd have such an opportunity again. Quickly, and with less caution than he should, he loosed off an arrow.

She didn't notice it.

He cursed to himself. He loosed off another.

Which she also didn't notice. He cursed her to himself. He checked the village. Probably mice were stirring, but certainly no other creatures. He had to see her. He had to. She had to know he cared.

With the stealth and wariness of a fox cub, he scuttled and scampered his way to the bottom of the cliff and thus to the edge of the glade.

"Syun," he hissed at her. "Syun."

Slowly something seemed to penetrate. But she reacted as if she'd heard the trees whispering to her: Not only did she not believe she'd heard anything, she was *anxious* not to believe it.

"Syun," he hissed again at her. "It's me. Tookums. Here."

This time Syun did look round. But in the manner that you look behind you lest the Grim Reaper be standing there.

"Syun!" he hisspered at her for a third time.

She turned on that occasion to look straight at him. She was looking *straight* at him. Yet still she didn't see him. There was light in her eyes, but no substance. A flame without a candle. They weren't haunting eyes or haunted, they weren't the eyes of the dead. They were the eyes of the have-been-hunted, the eyes of the *should-be*-dead.

They might as well have been spitting red-hot coals, for they tore holes through Charming as if he were made of tissue paper.

He couldn't help himself. He ran to her.

And he wrapped his arms around her. And she recognised him, not by words, but by coiling into his embrace as a cat purrs into the hearthrug. She closed her eyes and let his embrace warm her.

She slid her hand over his chin just to check it was really he. And she snuggled closer. He kissed the crown of her head. Closer she snuggled. Closer, closer she snuggled. He stroked her hair, her back. His gestures tried to tell her that which ears could no longer hear: That she was cherished and loved and cared for; that there were those in the world determined to shield her and to protect her.

But, before her spirit had opened even to the idea of such ideas, her mother came charging out of her tent and towards the glade, frantically shouting her name.

The sun was visible by now. Which meant Charming also was.

The entire village was alarmed into awakeness by the mother's wails. Upon hearing which, Charming gave Syun a quick kiss on her lips, and then loped off back to the hill, and up it, whence he had come.

Syun was left in the middle of the glade, uncertain whether what had just happened had. Or whether it was yet another fantasy. Her fingers touched her lips, as if to reassure those lips they had indeed just been kissed.

Prey is never as sly as predator. In fleeing, Charming knew that invisibility had to be tempered by swiftness. Her mother was the first to see him. In another incarnation, she probably became a Drill Sergeant or a diva. She had a voice on her which, let loose in Rumania, could have shattered a champagne bottle in Rheims.

Within seconds of her pointing out her daughter's would-be abductor, the young Tay of the village had armed themselves and were setting out after him. They assumed that his intentions had not been honourable.

Nor were theirs.

Chapter 48

Rose-growers love Valentine's Day, cake-makers love weddings ... and arms-dealers (as we've already noted) love war. Without wars they'd have no customers.

Arms-dealers are the most self-effacing of professionals: They recognise they have motes in their eyes. Christ urged those of us with motes not to concern ourselves with those in the eyes of our brothers. To discriminate *is* to see the motes of others, and therefore (so arms-dealers see it) discrimination between customers is anti-Christian. To decide which adversary in a war is the more worthy is to discriminate. Therefore arms-dealers sell to both.

Baron Richardson maintained that 'his' new double-barrelled musket was a far more efficient tool than its single-barrelled predecessor. It killed the enemy more quickly, and protected the firer more effectively. It was thus also a *humane* tool. Indeed Richardson would have you believe it was an engine of kindness and compassion. And because these are virtues to which the whole of humankind should aspire, Richardson recognised it was the right too of the Waifu and Tay to have access to these new weapons.

Such was his love for the world that, when it came to dispensing kindness and compassion, Richardson's own comfort and security were distinctly secondary considerations. He therefore resolved to travel to Zanoria himself in order to deal directly with the two nations.

Nancy bade him a tearful goodbye at the port in Biga-buga. She was returning to Belgiss, confident of Fredvie's support for her claim to the throne. Neither she nor Richardson was, at this stage, aware there was a pretender about to enter the lists.

Ship crossings in those days were not the luxury cruises beloved of so many today. They were a strange amalgam of both peril and monotony. The ships were matchboxes in an Olympic lido, the slightest swell threatened to engulf and to swallow them. But also often days would go by when the breeze was so slight they barely moved at all.

Being a princess, Nancy of course had her own cabin. And this was decked out in a fashion as sumptuous as the primitive ship would allow. She found, however, and within a short space of time, that needlepoint was far from the most absorbing pastime in the history of leisure, and that one stretch of azure ocean looks very much like another.

It was fun when the dolphins passed, even more fun when, some hundred yards or so away, a whale was spotted. But, for the most part, boredom was relieved only by tedium. Most of her days she spent in the imagination of her future life as queen. How deeply would her subjects love her, how well would history judge her.

By the time she arrived in Blefton she'd appointed and dismissed seven full Cabinets, and fifteen Privy Councils; she'd beheaded at least seventy-five irksomenesses and had, to prove her clemency, reprieved five.

She was armed with letters from Fredvie. She didn't hang around. Before even she went to her own suite, she visited HM.

"No more fence-sitting," she told the Finance Minister. "You're either for me or for Goneril. Fredvie's for *me.*" And she threw on HM's desk his letter of support.

"This is Minor Minor's hand," HM said evenly.

"Fredvie signed it," Nancy insisted, maybe just a touch defensively.

"I'll talk to Naitly about it."

"Naitly?" Nancy was astonished.

"Of course."

"But ..."

"Politics, Nancy, is – trust me – all about timing. For the moment, probably for as long as the king lives, we need Naitly."

"We do?"

"Trust me."

A few social niceties followed before Nancy returned to her suites and HM went to find Naitly.

"Time to call in your marker, Lord Chancellor," she told him.

"Explain."

"Marry me, you stay Lord Chancellor."

"I thought you were marrying the king."

"The king will die. The queen *step*mother is a job, let's say, the security of which is not absolute."

"And being the wife of the Lord Chancellor?"

"Oh, I shall have replaced you long before you die."

"You will?"

"I'm far cleverer than you are, Lord Chancellor. Trust me. Far more able as well. More accomplished, more insightful. And a lot prettier."

"You are?"

"Far more."

"And Goneril?"

"Time you baked a cake, Lord Chancellor."

"Me?"

"You."

"Bake a cake?"

"You."

"All right. Me?"

"Yes."

"But … a cake?"

"Poetic justice, it's called."

"A cake?"

"Yes."

"All right. … You're sure? … A cake?"

"I'll help."

"Fine. Right. Okay. It's just … A cake?"

HM picked the toadstools herself. She didn't hold any particular grudge against Goneril. She wanted a thorn removed from her side, and it was important that the removal be permanent, but beyond that she wished the thorn no harm. Without making a big deal out of it, she wanted the excision to be as painless as possible.

Naitly and HM went together to the princess's suite. She was alone – bleak within the bleakness of her rooms.

"I baked you a cake," he told her.

"You what?" she snorted, barely able to believe her ears.

"It's chocolate," HM told her approvingly.

"What is this nonsense?"

"You have to eat it, Goneril." She looked at Naitly, her eyes twinkling in the absurdity of it all. She saw his eyes. She saw the seriousness of his eyes. She went to speak. And could not.

She went to protest. And could not.

She went to plead, went to explain, went to weep, went to rail – she could not. "It's over, isn't it?" she asked simply.

Naitly just nodded. Solemnly. Quietly. Real sadness was blotching his eyes. There was even sadness in HM's eyes. An end-of-an-era sort of sadness. "We wanted to spare you your mother's fate," she said gently.

"Who saw me?" Goneril asked.

"I did," HM replied.

"You?"

"Me."

"You were with my father."

"We'd have to appoint Nelris as judge," Naitly told her.

"Ah!"

"We couldn't risk a trial where you might be found not guilty."

"No."

"You were a worthy adversary," HM told her.

"Am I expected to be gracious in defeat?"

"What other choice do you have?" asked HM. She cut the cake. Put a slab of it on a plain white plate, passed it to the princess.

"You know I'm on a diet?" Goneril smiled sadly as she took it.

"It's sugar-free," HM reassured her.

"You're going to annex Belgiss to Mercia?"

"What other choice do *we* have?" HM asked again.

"It's all been for nothing, then, the fight?"

"You might have won." Naitly was trying to sound sympathetic.

"You think?" Goneril asked sceptically. She bit into the cake, munched at it ferociously. "I did what I did," she continued, "for Belgiss and for Mother."

"I think you did," HM consoled her. She put an arm around Goneril's shoulder as her face started to distort in pain. "Rest now, Goneril," she there-there'd her. "It's all over."

***

"*I'm* going to be queen." Nancy tra-la'd as she danced around the round, three-legged coffee-tables which were scattered about her sitting room. "I'm going to be quee-een."

"And your son's murder has been avenged," HM reminded her.

"Oh yes. That too. Oh yes. Quite. We should bring Cordelia home."

"We should?"

"Now that the real murderer's been found, HM, the not-real one should be pardoned."

"She would, when you succeed, be heir to the throne, Nancy." HM measured her words, like a tailor preparing cloth.

"But I would be quee-een."

"For how long?"

"Excuse me."

"With the heir apparent pardoned and present, who's to say? Plots get hatched, Nancy. Cakes baked."

"Ah!"

"The Lord knows the right murderer has now been punished. And *you* know. Soon the king will know. Is there any need for such knowledge to be more general than that?"

"Well, if – as you say – the Lord knows and Papa does, and *I* do, no need, is there, to … whatever?"

"Wash royal linen in public?"

"Whatever."

"It could even undermine public confidence."

"At no cost must public confidence be undermined."

"Indeed not."

"Do you think I should tell Papa?"

"His Majesty, Nancy, is already grief-stricken," HM replied almost formally. "The breaking of this sad news needs to be … delicate. I fear anything more abrupt might induce … let's say medical complications. Possibly fatal ones."

"So, you *do* think I should tell him, then," bounced Nancy.

***

Cole greeted the news of his eldest daughter's death with a stoic nod, a slurp and a stroke of Nose.

"Apparently, it was suicide, sire. Remorse at having killed her nephew and niece."

"Apparently?"

"Apparently."

"Apparently's not the full story, HM."

"There is certain … well, not evidence exactly, nothing that definite … but pointers, Majesty, that her eating of the cake might not have been completely voluntary."

"Don't talk in riddles, HM. One hates it when you talk in riddles. Well, one enjoys it, actually, when you do – but in *fun* riddles. Not in these riddles that are just … *unfun* riddles."

"I'm not sure, sire, how to say this."

"Spit it out – you know one – spit it out, HM."

"We think it might be Nancy, sire."

"Nancy?"

"In the absence of the prince, sire, she becomes heir to your throne. Such is a powerful motive."

"Has Nancy that much gumption?"

"She has determination, sire. Sometimes that's a satisfactory substitute."

"Is one in danger?"

"Always, sire. That's the penalty of wearing the crown."

"One supposes that means they care."

"Your Majesty's wit, as ever, rises to the occasion. Nancy must be watched, sire."

"Yes."

"Cordelia too."

"Cordelia?"

"She will consider herself wronged."

"She *was* wronged, HM."

"It's not that the problem, sire. The problem is that she will consider herself to have been wronged."

"Not by one, though. Not by one, HM."

"She *was* banished by you, sire."

"One had no choice. One's hands were tied."

"As I know, sire. The problem, though – and I repeat – is that she will consider herself to have been wronged."

"Is it that all women are unreasonable, HM? Or just princesses?"

"I'm not unreasonable, Majesty."

"And when you're Queen?"

"I could protect you."

"You mean you're not doing so now?"

"I could, sire, protect you better. Marry me, I would protect you against all."

"Bring one back one's son, HM. *Then* one will marry you."

***

"I cannot stress it too much," said Naitly. "I did not say I would marry you."

"I'm not one of your electorates, you know," HM reminded him. "You can't fob me off with rhetorical niceties. Any of that other guff."

"I might marry you."

"You will marry me, Lord Chancellor. If I want you, you *will* marry me. Fight me, and you'll be begging me to marry you." Naitly snorted. But it was a snort more of bravura than conviction. HM added, "Trust me."

Chapter 49

Leamore and Dawes were not big ones on acquired taste. As far as they were concerned, if something didn't grab their fancy first time round, they saw no reason at all to repeat it. They'd given this 'waiting' thing a try, they'd decided, and they'd decided they didn't care for it.

On this visit to the Baccanaals, they had Squeers with them. But his presence had not endowed 'waiting' with a charm it had previously lacked. They therefore simply swept through the anteroom as if it were some branch-line station and they were the mainline express. With like disdain, they stormed past the grenadiers guarding Fredvie's office.

"We're gonna give you Belgiss," Dawes told him.

"We so ever so have Belgiss already," Minor Minor told them back.

"Everyone keeps giving me rootin' Belgiss," Fredvie complained. "A person of a more suspicious mindset might get a bit ..."

"Suspicious?" suggested Minor Minor.

"That's the tootin' word," Fredvie confirmed.

"We mean, dude," Leamore butted in, "we're going to *give* you Belgiss."

"Tied up in pink ribbon," Dawes added.

"In my short time here, the thing I've so ever so noticed is that your presents ... they tend to cost those who get them so ever such a lot."

"You ever heard, mister, about looking a gift-horse in the mouth?" asked Dawes.

"A gift-*Trojan*-horse might that be?" Minor Minor asked. But no-one there present understood what he was talking about.

"The prince had a tattoo, dude," explained Leamore.

"Prince?" asked Fredvie.

"Of Belgiss, Fredvie," Leamore said. "Do pay attention."

"You are in the Baccanaals, gentlemen," Minor Minor reminded them.

"Yeah, and here your boss'll stay, Minor Minor," said Dawes, "for just so long as we let him."

"It's okay, Minor Minor," Fredvie placated. "We're amongst friends here."

"Friends?" exclaimed Leamore. "*Friends*? This ain't about friends, dude. This is about boss and worker, executive and hired hand, engineer and oily rag. I got too much respect for my friends to number you, dude," he said with some distaste, "amongst them. Think a friend of mine would do a job as crappy as yours?"

"What I said, Minor Minor," said Fredvie. "Just tootin' joshin' amongst rootin'-tootin' friends."

"We're getting the nanny over from Belgiss," explained Dawes one-syllabley. "You getting this, Minor Minor? I'm not repeating it."

"So ever so ever so."

"We're finding, like, a look-alike here. Kids change so much at his age, who's going to know the difference anyway? The nanny'll oversee the tattooing. We send our prince back. He succeeds to the throne. We don't need no annexation nor nothing. We have complete control."

"There's only one tootin' snag," Fredvie said pointedly. They all stopped to look at him. "The tootin' prince of Belgiss is rootin' dead." They all groaned. "Well, he is, isn't he? I mean, isn't that why he's in mourning, tootin' merry old rootin' Cole? What? What have I said?"

"Explain it to him, Minor Minor," Dawes said wearily.

"*What*???" wailed Fredvie.

"Later, Mr Imperial Majesty," said Minor Minor. "I'll explain it to you later." As was usual on such occasions, Fredvie retreated, tortoise-like, into his shell where he could better unravel what was confusing him. "I would remind you that HM too knows of the tattoo."

"HM?" asked Dawes.

"Handy Mandy," Squeers replied, relieved to be given some pretext to talk. "Used to be the king's jester, now Finance Minister."

"Who are you?" Fredvie asked him.

Leamore waved at Squeers not to bother answering. "And?" he asked Minor Minor.

"She's so ever so not anyone's fool."

"Except the king's," guffawed Dawes.

"So ever so droll. Like no-one's not heard *that* several thousand times previously," muttered Minor Minor, moments before the emperor understood the joke and chortled loudly.

"Good one, Dawes," he said.

"He expensive, dude?" asked Leamore of Minor Minor.

"He?"

"The king's fool?"

"He's a she. And I really don't know."

"She?"

"A woman, Mr Leamore. Surely you've heard of them," Minor Minor said with that tang of condescension which for some was the epitome of Belgicness.

"They got a woman running their finances? Bit, isn't it, like putting a goat in charge of a haystack?" And this time it was loudly that Leamore guffawed.

"She's ever so able, I understand," Minor Minor corrected him. And then he saw Leamore's glower. It was a glower which proclaimed that he was *never* gainsaid. "Of course," Minor Minor added quickly, "I could ever so have *mis*understood."

"I think, dude, you did," said Leamore.

"No question," Minor Minor confirmed. "So ever so ever so no question."

"Nice one, Leamore," Fredvie again chortled. "A goat in charge of a tootin' haystack: nice one."

"We want an easy life," Dawes told the emperor. "Easy lives come when there are no complications ..."

"Oh so ever so ever so," said Minor Minor.

Dawes glared at the interrupter before continuing, "And the road to no complications starts with having our own guy on the Belgic throne."

"Right," said Fredvie. "I absolutely a-rootin'-tootin'-gree."

"'Case you hadn't noticed, Belgiss is a stepping-stone to Eastlantic," said Leamore.

"Right," Fredvie agreed. "Right, abso-rootin'-tootin'-lutely."

"We'll let you know," said Dawes.

"Right," nodded Fredvie.

"What are we going to let you know about?" asked Leamore.

"Whatever," said Fredvie cheerfully.

"When the prince is ready, dude," said Leamore.

"Right."

"We'll let you know," said Dawes.

"Right."

"Right?" asked Leamore and Dawes together.

"Oh so ever so ever so right," said Minor Minor.

Leamore and Dawes made to go. They noticed Squeers again. They didn't even turn back. "One other thing," Dawes said to Fredvie. The emperor and Minor Minor exchanged a look: What more did they possibly have to give? "Yeah?" the emperor asked, trying to sound both nonchalant and imperial, and actually sounding only tetchy.

"Zanoria ..." Dawes started.

"Zanoria?"

"It's a province, Mr Imperial Majesty ..." Minor Minor started.

"I *know* what it is. I *don't* know, what about it?"

"It needs a Protector," said Dawes.

"Right," said Fredvie.

"Squeers, dude," Leamore told him.

"He's Squeers," said Dawes pointing him out.

"Right," said Fredvie.

"We'll expect confirmation in writing," said Leamore. "Right?"

"Right," said Fredvie.

"Right?" asked Leamore.

"Right," said Minor Minor.

***

"It's time, Hyandri," said Quifah. They were sitting in his tent. Outside the men were preparing for war, and the women for weeping. There was the sound of wood being whittled, of arrow-heads being forged on primitive anvils, of cotton being woven – and of babies crying.

"I know," Charming replied sadly.

"It will be a sadness to lose you."

"The lessons I have learnt, Quifah, will stay with me always."

"The wise never stop making mistakes."

"Then I must be rise indeed." The two men smiled. A shared comradeship more than a shared joke.

"You will go and see Syun," Quifah said.

"I have to, Quifah."

"Be careful."

"I know I must obey my westiny."

"Yes."

"There's something I have to do."

"You have to give her Philly."

Charming regarded the old man again, even now finding new depths in him. *"You are as rise, Quifah, as you are kind."*

"And that was kind. Without kindness, Hyandri, wisdom is a cup with a hole in its base."

"Yes."

"If you forget all else from your stay with us, remember that."

"You have been a rather to me, Quifah."

"I always will be, Hyandri."

"Yes."

"Travel well."

"Live well, Quifah."

***

In Biga-buga, Leamore instructed Gertrude to start the search for the look-alike. Once a week Cross-Bones came to check her intake. The rest of the time they were scouring the countryside. A likely candidate was encouraged to volunteer; but if he were reluctant, they were empowered to press-gang him. A short-list started to be compiled.

Squeers left with the next Accidental to take up his new appointment.

He now had wealth and position. Another man would have thought that what was now needed was a wife. But Squeers was too selfish to want his status or his wealth shared with anyone. He basked in the knowledge that, in Zanoria, it was now Baron Richardson waiting for him.

***

Charming needed time with Syun. In order to get that time he had to bide his. Three days he waited. He hunted by night, ate his meat raw, shivered through the night. He saw Syun several times, always in company. On the third day, however, she wandered far enough away from her friends for him to be able to let her know he was there.

Later that afternoon she contrived to leave the village. She and Charming met in the same grove from which he had made his somewhat undignified escape. The water continued to trill over the rocks, fish plopped back into the water from their jumps, crickets chirped their aliveness. Smells drifted through of sandalwood and almond, whiffs occasionally of the nearby smouldering fires.

"You must go," she told him, her Tay accent stronger than it had been when they had both been slaves.

"I will come back for you." The prince took both her hands, held them in his.

"I must belief you," she said. The tone told him she didn't want to. And she was also far from happy that he was going. Maybe in Tay legends too Princes Errant were supposed to arrive on white steeds, sweep damsels off their feet and into a future of joy and plenty.

"I will," the prince repeated, "come back for you."

"Yes," she said enigmatically.

Suddenly her hands felt heavy in his – or maybe his in hers. He felt clumsy, awkward, uncomfortable.

"I brought Philly for you," he said. "Philly will look after you." She laughed. "What's funny?"

She couldn't tell him. She'd been thinking, how absurd the notion was that a horse could somehow look after a person. But she'd been thinking too her heart might burst in appreciation of the size of the gift with which she'd been presented. What she said was, "You will come back for Philly."

"I'll come back for both of you," he promised her.

"Go now, Tookums," she said, and then corrected herself. "They will know you have gifted me Philly. The gift gladdens me. Them it will not gladden. Go, Tookums, go now."

"I love you, Syun."

"I think yes," she said. And turned her back before he had a chance to do anything, for instance, about kissing her. "Go now," she said again. "Go."

And so he went.

Chapter 50

Death is death. The residue of any potential the dead may have had will be left unrealised. Cordelia knew that. She tried to remember it, tried to let such knowledge temper the 'whoopee' which erupted from her on hearing of Goneril's death. But the tempering was superficial and short-lived. The sorry she was, she told Antonio, was that she was 'sorry' but she was *delighted*.

Goneril's death meant, she said, she *had* to be cleared. Her conviction – whatever else it was called – had to be quashed. She would receive a pardon from the king – even (who knew?) a 'pardon me' from the king, an apology from him. And that would be a first. She had to leave for Belgiss. She had to leave for Belgiss right away.

"Don't do it, Cordelia," Antonio warned her. It was the soothsayer telling Julius Caesar to beware the ides of March.

"What's the matter?" she asked, unsure whether to find his doom alarming or amusing.

"We have a good life here. The kids have a good life. Your father's ... well, not stable. Nor is Belgiss. It's a quicksand. Quicksands don't care about intentions. The best-intentioned in a quicksand are just as likely to get drowned as the worst-intentioned. Why rock the boat? No-one'll thank you for it."

"It's my country, Antonio."

"So is this, Cordelia. And these ... these are your children. Your children love you. I love you. Does your country?"

"Yes," Cordelia insisted.

"It used to, it might again. That we can hope for. Even pray for. But now ...? Dawes's gazettes have poisoned the country, Fredvie's machinations are finishing it off. Naitly is too corrupt and your father is too feeble. You will return, Cordelia, only to your humiliation. Perhaps even to your death."

"Don't sugar-coat it for me, Antonio. Give it to me straight."

"*They* will, my dear: Give it to you straight – straight between the shoulder-blades or straight between the eyes."

"Trout all right for dinner?"

***

Had Squeers known of the rigours that would await him on his trip, never would he have accepted the Protectorship of Zanoria, whatever its attendant status, however grand he felt having two personal guards walk each step with him.

No money in the world, not even an entire army of personal guards will make rocks softer or snakes less poisonous or a saddle-sore bottom more sittable-on. The whole Accidental, in good conditions, took three months. Conditions were never good. The mortality rate (as has already been noted) was appalling. Burying the dead added days to the overall trek.

The food was often rancid. And that would cause epidemics of diarrhoea. As has also already been noted, Napoleon would later maintain that an army marched on its stomach; no army marched anywhere on an upset one. Even the weather seemed against them. The Accidentals, as the trekkers were known, found themselves either baking hot and bitten by bugs, or freezing cold and bitten by cramps.

It was less than surprising therefore that along the way there were settlements, which earlier Accidentals had decided were Eden-like enough to make their permanent home. None of these had yet grown to the size of a town. But there were those now too big simply to be called a village. One of these was Phillizelda.

Phillizelda was about a third of the way from Biga-buga to Zanoria. Squeers had spent the night in the best room in the best hotel. It did not, he thought, augur well.

He was dog-tired. So pleased to be spending a night under a roof (however humble, he had thought to himself), so relieved to have removed several films of grime in a hot bath, he had imagined he would sleep like a baby. But the bed-bugs had had other ideas. They had gnawed and nipped at him at such regular intervals that sleep had entirely eluded him.

And then it had started to rain. Not a light drizzle. Not even cats and dogs. But lions and wolves. And he was even more grateful that he was under (however so humble) a roof. Until his nose and forehead got spattered in various drops. The roof, he shortly realised, was less a cover than a colander. There seemed to be a hole for every star – and for every star a raindrop. If this was the best that could be offered in the best town outside of Biga-buga, what in God's name would the worst be like?

On the other hand, where else was it likely that he would be kingpin? No, forget the -pin. Where else was it likely he would be king? Because, effectively, that is what he would become – like a Pontius Pilate of the present day. He'd always reckoned himself an adept Pilate, Squeers, always thought his skill at washing his hands of responsibility was second to none. In Zanoria, moreover, he'd be *treated* like a king. A couple of years of that, a couple of years of lining Protectored coffers, and he'd be set up for the rest of his life.

And then he tasted the coffee. The coffers would need to be really bulging to compensate for that. It hurled him back into a depression of wondering whether *anything* were worth the appallingness of that coffee.

***

When he had been going West, Charming had, of course, noted the name. He also knew that if ever he got back to Phillizelda then he'd get back to Biga-buga. It had taken on a dimension in his head that was other-worldly.

The countryside of Mercia now posed no threat to him. It was barely even a challenge. What on the outward bound trip had been a haul and a nightmare, on the way back was almost a jaunt and a delight.

Of course, no longer being a slave played its part in that. But he was – and this he could not afford to forget – an *escaped* slave. There was probably an assumption that he was dead. If he were captured, however, there would still be a reward for his captor. He would still be returned to bondage. He had to be really careful. He had to assume that any stranger was a potential bounty-hunter.

He had no money, the prince. The possibility was simply not available to him, popping into the Grand Hotel for a bed, even a coffee. But, although he had a deep hankering at least for the coffee, he had no need of either. He'd eaten that day. So had Peggy. They'd both drunk – and from fresh spring water. The prince had bathed himself in that same water, had shaved in it. He'd groomed Peggy. His need for cash was slight.

But he saw Squeers emerge from the hotel, his two guards also in tow. All about him was grandness and self-importance and loving the importance his title attached to him.

Charming recognised him immediately. This was the man who had sold him into slavery. Charming's first reaction was to murder him. He felt the blood surge to his head, his eyes film over, his hand make (apparently of its own volition) straight for his knife.

But he checked himself. He had to check himself. Squeers may have deserved to die, but for the prince to kill the man there and then would, without any doubt at all, have led to his own death. And he'd promised Syun he'd return for her.

Squeers had started a strut down the dusty main street, a nosegay pointedly, and undiplomatically, constantly at his nostrils. Protectors, Squeers felt, should exude superiority. Which was all to the well: Squeers considered his attitude of superiority one so accomplished as to be bordering on excellent.

It had taken the prince the entire length of the street to still his murderous instinct. But then another thought came to his mind: How recognisable *was* he? Oh, he knew Squeers wouldn't recognise him merely as a passer-by. Squeers was far too grand to notice anyone: even Squeers's shadow was supposed to fawn.

Charming knew where Peggy was. He was pretty sure, if he *were* rumbled, that he could outpace and out-distance any pursuers. Once he was mounted, he was *absolutely* sure. It had to be worth the risk: If Squeers didn't recognise him, he could be reasonably sure that no-one else would. And if no-one recognised him, that would obviate the need for so much subterfuge. It would also radically affect the strategy he was devising about returning to Belgiss.

"Want your boots shined, sir?" he scrambled after the Protector. Who sought to swat him away as if he were some particularly zealous mosquito. "Want your coat cleaned? Your horses groomed?"

One of the Protector's guards moved to intervene. "Beat it, savage," this guard told the prince. Who seemed to shy away, only (expertly) to cut the purse strings from the same guard's belt – before, in a spirit informed only by devilry, cutting the belt itself. The guard continued his Sumo swagger for a few steps when suddenly his breeches dropped to the knees at which they were attached.

The passers-by thought the view hilarious. This further embarrassed the guard. And then Squeers too started to laugh. Which catapulted the guard's outrage into a distant cosmos. This was the moment at which Charming dangled the guard's purse from his fingers.

The guard made to give chase; and fell splat into the dusty path before him. His colleague would have taken it up, had he not been prevented from doing so by a violent attack – of uncontrollable giggles.

Maybe conjecture *is* idle. But, let us just ponder for a moment: If Squeers had been just a little less absorbed with his own importance, if he'd just taken the trouble to look at the 'savage' who'd accosted him, the difference to our world would have been incalculable. No-one can say with any safety for better or worse. But that it would have been different, and in a big way, is undeniable.

Further proof, as if such were needed, that (despite what the generals would love us to believe) it is not battles the building-blocks of history, but people too self-absorbed to notice what is under their noses. It is not the big gestures which define history, but the incidental details; not rulers who dictate its course, but the blindness and stupidity of ... well, of all of us. No-one can ever say what would have happened in history 'if' or 'if only'. No-one can with any confidence predict what would have been the outcome if Guy Fawkes *had* blown up the British Parliament or if the Pilgrim Fathers had decided to give Plymouth one final chance or if the last Ice Age hadn't happened. But one thing *is* certain: If battles constitute ten percent of history, then detail and coincidence contribute fifty.

There was scarcely a king's ransom in the stolen purse. But it could have paid for the cup (or three) of the coffee for which the prince craved. Charming, though, was not heavily into pushing his luck. He'd have his coffee in the next settlement he came to. Maybe he'd even keep the treat until he got to Biga-buga itself.

Because he would get to Biga-buga, of that he was now certain. As he was also certain that his worries about being an escaped slave were not those he had imagined them to be.

Chapter 51

Ginny and Winny felt fully justified in feeling extremely proud of themselves: They had bridesmaided with an impeccability which was ... exemplary. At the wedding breakfast this pride was stirred together with a haughtiness they felt fully justified in feeling was innate. The resultant cocktail was so toxic it was almost radio-active. At least, to all who weren't Winny and Ginny. But, then, to Winny and Ginny those who weren't Winny and Ginny meant very little.

So exemplary was the impeccability of their bridesmaidery, indeed, that they even condescended to condescend to the wimpish daughter of their wimpish and recently acquired stepfather, what's-her-name. Why everyone thought her pretty was quite beyond them. Their eyes had seen more winsome pikestaffs. As for personality? She had as much of that as a ghost's shadow. She'd learn, of course, whatever her name was – Emma or Ella or Ellie or something – she'd *have* to learn. If the oomphless in life were not to live an oomphless life it was down to the oomphless to *find* oomph in life. That oomph distinguished those on the cinder track from those in the cinders.

There'd been a time, of course, when they themselves had wondered whether *they* lacked personality. Now, though, their wondering could remain moot. They were soon-to-be guests, no less, of the Mayor of Biga-buga. Himself. Personally. And that distinguished them as being distinguished. That distinguished them as being not persons any longer, but personalities. The personality of a personality is the fact of being a personality. Personalities need no personality (and rarely have one) beyond that.

So magnanimous was their spirit, so magnificent their self-effacement, they *acknowledged*, Winny and Ginny, they had not *always* been personalities. Sadly, they sadlied, their eyes cast fetchingly downwards, Mumsy, poor thing, would only ever be a *second-hand* personality – a personality dint only of being the mother of one. As for her groom and his daughter! Well, they were afraid, strictly *third-hand* personalities – which was, of course, a contradiction in terms.

So magnanimous was their magnanimity, however, so magnificent their largesse, they didn't hold her vicarious status against their mother. Still she was allowed to be seen with them. Still they bridesmaided for her. Impeccably. Exemplarily impeccably.

Now, though, the wedding was over and they had more important affairs to attend to. They had *their* affairs to attend to.

***

As Protector of Zanoria, Squeers would – of course – make a lot of money. A government salary of not inconsiderable size would be augmented considerably by local interests anxious to curry favour.

But he still had a ship. And a ship at harbour is a luxury: There are constant repairs to be made, a crew wanting wages and food, moorage, maintenance, machinery all to be paid for. The only way for a ship not to become a liability is for her to become an asset. And to become an asset a ship has to do what she's supposed to do: sail. In the interests of his interests, Squeers had made some cosmetic changes to 'his' ship's hull. And, because he was not totally devoid of wit, he had changed her name to the *Enterprize*. And he had instructed the *Enterprize* to set sail.

It was onto the *Enterprize* that the two personalities, Winny and Ginny, embarked. At the same time that Charming rode from Phillizelda to Biga-buga, Ginny and Winny were privateering across the sea.

***

Charming had decided he really had to get back to Belgiss.

He didn't really want to, but Quifah had intimated that it was there where his destiny was lurking. Frankly, the prince didn't care much about his destiny, but he did feel he owed the old man a lot. Maybe the lot he owed him was *his* lot: his fate – pursuing his destiny, in other words.

Charming's reluctance to return stemmed, in part, from the fact that he knew it meant a return to being a prince. He remembered enough about that to know it was not the job which fairy-stories vaunted it.

As a prince you were embroiled in all sorts of subterfuges and machinations, pickled in a permanent political brouhaha, the 'haha' in which was about as funny as tooth-ache. A prince's potential for doing good, he remembered, is extremely limited; that for doing harm almost limitless. ... And as a prince your sister and your best-friend got killed.

Quifah, though, had made no mention about destiny being a permanent funfair or a barrel of laughs. It was just ... what you *had* to do. It was like a sort of duty, except that it was to yourself. Therefore no-one beyond yourself recognises it as being duty. Often quite the reverse. What you consider duty to yourself is so often called by others arrogance or self-indulgence, even egomania.

Few indeed are those encouraged to pursue their destiny. It is the road *least* travelled. And it is so because it is so often the loneliest road. If the entirety of us is the litter, our potential (usually) is considered the runt: We are dissuaded from giving it suckle or succour; often we are screamed at to let it die. Few of us are strong enough or brave enough or resilient enough to pursue our destiny down this lonely, perilous, arduous path. Those that do are true heroes.

It had been the imp in Charming who had committed the theft, not the crook. The money he had robbed from Squeers's guard had been enough only for a couple of restaurant meals and a few coffees; it was never going to be enough get him home.

There was, and he knew it, only one way he was going to get passage back to Belgiss: by working it.

It wasn't by coincidence therefore that he met the *Enterprize* as it docked: It was his intention. The only coincidence was that it should have been on that crossing that Winny and Ginny arrived.

The quayside was an anthill of bad-tempered jostle and a caterwaul of ugly sounds: whistles and shouts and ships' hooters and metal wheels on cobbled stone and louder whistles and even louder shouts. There was everywhere the smell of fish, mixed sometimes with the coals of the chestnut seller, sometimes with the heady perfume of wealthy matrons there to meet long-time-not-seen friends. There were cabin trunks being handed over the heads of the recently arrived and severely confused; there were huge hawsers being lobbed between stevedores as if they were skipping-ropes; there were small children (having been trampled on) in tears, porters touting for trade, beggars seeking the gullible, pickpockets the careless.

Charming recognised the *Enterprize* as being a made-over *Silver Hart*. An undemanding appreciation of irony had in the last few years started to nestle within him, and this enjoyed the fact that he would be returning to his homeland as a deckhand on a ship which had borne him thence as Crown Prince. Before he could lose himself in such wryness, however, he recognised Winny. Ginny he knew only by sight, not well enough to accost. Winny, on the other hand …

He was cutting a rather scrabbly path through the throng, about to halloo her, when he saw bounding towards the two sisters Cross-Bones.

On the list of all the people in the world Charming was anxious not to see, Cross-Bones came fairly high up. Which was, in fact, where he would like to have seen them: fairly high up – *strung*, in fact, fairly high up. Preferably from a fairly high-up gallows, or an even higher-up yardarm. But a tree would have done. Even a lowish tree.

Charming, of course, had as yet no knowledge of what this meeting meant for him, or could mean. Then it was just the meeting of two of his adversaries with ... someone whom he had thought cared for him.

It is only those determined never to grow up who do not recognise we papoose always our own infancy. Often when the adult feels pain it is his papoosed infant who is crying. When we ignore that infant's crying we are repeating the neglect felt by that child so many years previously. And our own neglect of our own infant is not only to add salt to the existing wound, it is not only to enlarge and deepen that wound, it is also to create an entirely fresh wound all of its own.

If, as adults, we want to be responsible for ourselves, it is for the whole, for the entirety of ourselves that we have to be responsible. Which means we have to change the nappies of our past – and even more urgently than we have to build the Zimmer-frames of our future.

None of which the prince was yet in a position to know. All he knew then was that it hurt him, the embrace of his nanny with his would-be assassins. It hurt him just as keenly as he'd first been hurt by HM's revelation to him back in Parsifal forest of their murderous intent. It was as real, the pain, and as deep. He was shocked by its intensity. And then, because he was yet to know better, he started to berate himself for exaggerating the hurt. What was it? By comparison with everything else he'd been through? A pin-prick, not even that.

But the prick continued to be not of one pin but ten thousand, honed to a sparkling fineness, and which were not assailing his skin from the outside, but were macheteing out from *inside* of him.

Although he'd never previously given it much thought, he now realised that Winny had been, as it were, his number one reserve. Of course HM would have been his first port of call. Of course. But for some time there had been something gnawing at the prince about the depths of HM's loyalty. He felt he needed, at least, someone else *in case* ... a reserve, if you like. And now, clearly, there wasn't one.

He could have followed the sisters. But he didn't. He couldn't see the point.

Suddenly he couldn't see the point either of returning to Belgiss either. Not on his own. There was absolutely no knowing what awaited him there, beyond the fact that the waters he was sailing into would be hostile. He'd done some thinking in the intervening years. He'd come to realise that even HM's loyalty might not be absolute. But he'd also come to realise she had told him true about at least one thing: It would have benefitted Cordelia not at all to have killed Horatio and Philly. His own memory told him that it had been Cordelia – and only ever Cordelia – who had supported him at Court. Over time, he had come to realise, in Eastlantic Cordelia was the only person whom he could trust.

Was she still in Azrac? He had no idea. But where else to look for her? And, even if she weren't, as a first stop in Eastlantic, Azrac (Charming considered) was likely to be a safer haven than his homeland.

He therefore sought out a ship bound for Azrac.

Chapter 52

It wasn't the first time in their lives that Ginny and Winny had eyed up young men. To date, though, their appraisal had been done covertly, behind fans or hands, usually in conjunction with a ripple of giggles about ten years younger than they were. This time the ogling was as overt as it was encouraged. It was flagrant, in fact. And endowed with the solemnity of a state funeral.

Albeit on behalf of the Mercian nation, Ginny and Winny were considered buyers. And the young men of the orphanage were arrayed before them as Charming had been before Realrich's envoy, as slaves *are* before buyers. That the slaves' genitals were covered by a loincloth was not in deference to their modesty but to the buyers'. Apart from which covering they were stark naked.

Ginny and Winny had never previously seen such an expanse of flesh. Theirs was an era which tried to deny the functions, needs and cravings of the body. Ginny's imagination was fired by the sight. So was Winny's. Not as the imagination of a sculptor is fired – the poetry that is the interplay of muscle and sinew – far more carnally. But, of course, they had to disguise that – the more so as their recently revived fiancés were right behind them.

The only place where the two sisters forbore looking was into the slaves' eyes.

When we meet the eyes of someone else, or something else, we acknowledge the life, and therefore the soul, and therefore the dignity, of that other being. It becomes imbued with importance. If we then strip that being of its importance it requires from us a wrench of conscience. Easier by far simply not to look. Certainly there is an element in conscience which is sentimental. But there is another element which is to do with our own protection, with our own survival: The best way to ensure that our lives are considered sacred is by ensuring that all life is considered sacred.

No government throughout the entirety of history has ever

considered life in general sacred. Not even human life. Government considers the lives of its subjects are a commodity. Nothing more. Isn't it extraordinary, then, that government should insist we should turn to *it* when we feel threatened? Isn't that like asking Herod to baby-sit for us?

Ginny and Winny kept having to remind themselves – and each other – that they were there for a very specific purpose. They were in a candy store not to sample the various sweets on offer, nor to make comparisons between their various deliciousnesses, but to find a very specific bonbon indeed. Not even a pear drop or a humbug – but the *one* pear drop, the peariest dropiest one of them all.

They went through processes of elimination. They started with the orphanage's whole stock of those the right colour, age, eye-colour and general physique. They whittled this down to those with similar noses, ears, chins and hands. Thence to those of the same demeanour.

At every stage of the elimination, fights broke out between the buyers. Cross-Bones's memories were often at variance with that of Winny – and of each other. Ginny's opinion was not considered even worth the eliciting. It was acknowledged only out of courtesy and heeded not at all. And that was foolish. Because acquaintance brings with it its own lenses. And these distort the image before us. We see people most accurately when we first see them. To see our friends as first we saw them takes an effort of will. Rather than Ginny's view being the least valid or accurate, it was probably the most.

Eventually there were only two young men left. And it was decided that both should undergo the tutelage necessary to develop them into the surrogate prince. It was considered that an 'aptitude for attitude' was more important at that stage than undue attention to physical detail. Young men, it was considered, change so much in puberty that the presence or absence of small differences could be convincingly explained away simply by that.

Three days later, Winny insisted on a meeting with Mayor Leamore. Mayor Leamore was unused to being insisted at. Even less by a mere woman. Just for the moment, though, he needed her expertise a little bit too much in order to dismiss her 'insistence' with the acid contempt it so extravagantly deserved.

He rose from his desk to greet her, though, with a sourness which he made no attempt to conceal.

"I don't beat about the bush, Mr Mayor," she said. "It's not my way. I want a meeting with Dawes present too. And Fredvie."

"It's not going to happen, dudette," Leamore told her. "Nor is this going to happen again. 'Case you hadn't noticed, we're all busy men," he said, oozing reasonableness. "Way too busy for this, whatever it is ... histrionics, I guess."

"Even if you aborted the plan now, Mr Mayor, I'd know about it. You're going to get rid of Krantz and Stern very soon. My guess would be to the Zanorian front. And my guess also is, you're wondering now about getting rid of me too. But I left letters back in Belgiss. And with someone ... reliable. They would make the execution of your plan ... more problematic."

"You ever thought about going into politics, Winny?" Leamore asked her with some admiration.

"I've just got a neck pretty enough to be worth its saving," Winny replied. "Next Thursday? Say, at four o'clock? Tea and muffins?"

Winny had only been out of Leamore's office for about forty-five minutes before, escorted by the Mercian militia, Cross-Bones were being marched back to the military barracks in Biga-buga. There they were placed under close arrest to await the next Accidental. Whether this was inspired by Winny or whether she had just surmised correctly is something where only conjecture is possible.

As was usual with Cross-Bones, they accepted their fate with a resigned fortitude, and received some solace in still being alive. Their fortunes had changed so many times, it was, they thought, not unreasonable to suppose they would again change for the better.

As was usual with *Ginny*, when she heard of Cross-Bones's plight, tears came in great globs of 'woe-is-me's and hand-wringing and self-pity. She completely failed to understand the quiet calm with which her sister accepted again fiancélessness. But then she completely failed to understand that Winny had far bigger fish to fry.

Winny, in fact, had a whale to fry.

At four o'clock on the next Thursday she was sitting in the emperor's private drawing room. She was taking tea and muffins. So were Leamore and Dawes. Minor Minor took the tea, but declined the muffins – an aberration, so he very publicly announced them to be, of those confections called by the same name in Belgiss but as similar in taste as anchovy and avocado.

"I'm not used to being tootin' threatened," Fredvie told her angrily.

"Oh, get real, dude," Leamore returned to the emperor. "You're *quite* used to it. And to being blackmailed, cajoled and bribed. It's the price of doing business," he added, with a look to Dawes. "Go on, Winny."

Winny replaced the cup in its saucer, placed both delicately on the round table which stood adjacent to the round-backed chair of sky blue silk on which she was sat. She amazed herself at the calm she was. Without any question, these were the most important minutes of her life thus far – probably of her *whole* life, as her future (whatever it might be) would be dictated by their outcome. And yet there was a part of her as calm as if she had been visiting one of her girlfriends for a gossip.

She addressed the assembly as if throughout her entire life she had been advising heads of state and captains of industry. "Your plan, gentlemen, is bold," she said. "And Fortune does favour the bold. However, she looks considerably less favourably on complications.

"Certainly I'm foolish. All here present know *that*. Not *so* foolish, though, as to think that of myself I am worth, officially, a second thought. You'd take my life without blinking. All here present know that too. In that event, Belgiss might, officially, rumble a bit. But official rumbles are not worth the indigestion tablets they take to cure them. As all here present know as well. My letter back in Belgiss, however, that *is* a complication. And a complication you don't need. It's a bigger complication than my continued presence would be."

"This is just not tootin' acceptable," Fredvie fumed.

"And?" Dawes asked of Winny, ignoring Fredvie.

"We could help each other," Winny smiled in what she hoped would soon be collusion.

"The best business, dudette, is the business which benefits both sides," Leamore said with a small smile of acknowledgement.

"Your pretend king, gentlemen, he's going to need … a *real* queen."

"Ah!"

"Would it not be sensible – from the Mercian point of view – for that real queen to be kindly disposed towards Mercia?"

"Ah!"

"There is no-one more kindly disposed towards Mercia, for pity's sake, than yours truly."

"Ah!"

"Would someone mind rootin' explaining," Fredvie resumed his fuming, "just what is tootin' going on here?"

"We're playing chess, dude," Leamore explained.

"With a master," said Dawes.

"A *grand* master," said Minor Minor.

"A pawn heading for Queen," said Leamore.

"A pawn," smiled Winny, "*about* to be Queen." And she took a big bite of muffin.

Chapter 53

Naitly was keen on protocol. It was as if the more doors that the more lackeys opened for him the greater his control of the country.

It was a year or so since Goneril's death. The Mercian ambassador had yet to stop crowing about his part in her downfall. Seek to get the better of the Mercian ambassador, the crowing would cackle, the so much worser off you'd actually be.

Protocol normally demanded that ambassadors visit Lord Chancellors. But not even Naitly was so obsessed with it that he applied this norm to the Mercian ambassador. Not after Goneril's … diplomatic grouch. Finally it was just too much hustle, winching His Excellency in and out of chairs, waiting as his huge bulk puffed along corridors. Naitly also had no desire that his domestic lackeys should witness the scorn of him with which the ambassador's remarks were liberally coated. (About the only thing relating to the ambassador which *could* be called 'liberal'.)

Protocol demanded that, should an audience be wanted, an ambassador send a message to the Lord Chancellor 'entreating' one. This 'entreaty' had been sent. By return, Naitly had replied to His Mercian Excellency that he would be happy to grant such an audience, and that he would be at the embassy within the hour.

Naitly was now leaving that embassy. He was uncertain how to react. Well, he had to see the king, that much was clear. But how did he break the news to him? Did he *believe* it?

He rushed straight to the castle. The guards and stewards now knew him well enough to let him through, no questions asked. And with the most casual knocks, he entered. He was astonished to find HM already there, and Nose not.

"Do you want the good news, Naitly," the king asked, "or the *great* news? The great news, in fact, or the even greater news?"

"Your Majesty?" asked the Lord Chancellor.

"Do you want to tell him, my dear," the king asked HM, "or

shall one?"

"*Both* bits of news are yours," HM replied. "Only one affects me ... my dear," she added pointedly, looking straight at Naitly.

"Well, that's the second item out of the bag, one fears," the king joked. "HM and one are to be one, Naitly."

Naitly didn't move a muscle. His eyes did not register even a flick of surprise. "You both so richly deserve one another," he said, matching HM's pointedness. "What other news could possibly match that?"

There was an entire conversation occurring now between Naitly's eyes and HM's. Irritation was met with apology; jealousy with reassurance; grace in defeat with grace in victory.

"Fredvie has found Charming," exclaimed Cole.

"Ah!" said Naitly.

"He'll be back on the next sailing of the *Enterprize*."

"Ah!" Naitly said again.

"He's changed quite a bit, apparently," said Cole.

"Ah!" said Naitly for the third time. More of his attention continued to be on the optical conversation he was continuing with HM.

"Boys do, don't they, at that age?" Cole said to no-one in particular. "Know what? Know who doesn't know? Nose doesn't know. One thinks one had better go and find him. Nose *should* know. *Nose* should *knows*, eh, my dear?" he said as a joke to his beloved. She reacted, to his disappointment, only slightly. "Nose's master's coming home. Nose? Nose?" He left his inner sanctum in order to break the news to the dog. "Where are you, boy?" And closed the door behind him.

"I will marry you," HM sought to reassure the Lord Chancellor.

"It was you who wanted to marry me," he reminded her.

"And I still will."

"Oh? Bigamy?"

"Very big o' me," she struggled to joke. It was so bad, its

badness squeezed out a smile.

"Why?" Naitly wanted to know.

"I need to be queen. I'm young enough. I might even be a queen mother as well."

"And Mrs Lord Chancellor?"

"That too. Maybe even Lord Chancellor myself. We're not Mr and Mrs Average, Naitly, you and I. Hidebound by conventions ... or expectations ... hidebound by *absurdities*."

"Absurdities?"

"Is there anything more absurd than love?"

Naitly laughed. It was a laugh which wasn't sure about its depth of irony. "Not much," he agreed.

HM took his hands. She waited till slowly his eyes rose to meet hers. "I don't not love you," she said gently.

"I don't not love you either," said Naitly with a tenderness the rawer for being so underused.

They kissed lightly on the lips. Still with his eyes shut, he said to her, "I could, of course, just denounce you to the king."

"In which case, my darling man, you'd be lucky to keep your head. Your job you would be sure to lose." They could have been discussing the garden's begonias.

"You seem very certain." He kissed the tips of her fingers.

"You really are such an innocent," she told him, swapping recipes. "Maybe that's why you've lasted so long. Doesn't God protect the innocent?"

"Children, I thought, and drunks."

"Well, that covers most of the Cabinet. The king, o darling one, would believe me a thousand times before he would believe you. I have a history with him which you lack. And a future. As for the present, I'm the woman he's going to marry. I was the only one who continued to hope the prince was alive, the only one who continued the search."

"You know, of course, this ... whatever he is ...is only a Mercian stooge."

"God, you really *are* an innocent. Of course, he's only a stooge. The real prince ... well, you know as well as I do. God knows whether they even know about the tattoo. But if they do – and it's my guess it's precisely for that reason that Winny is visiting Mercia –, then the only person whom the king would trust to identify it would be me."

"Tell me something," said Naitly sweetly: "How do you know which of your faces to make up in the morning?"

HM responded with equal scoops of molasses. "You just be careful, my darling one, you don't find yourself out of a job. After all, how could I be Lady Chancellor if you're not the Lord?" And again she kissed him lightly on the lips. "And now, my dearest, if you'll excuse me, it's time for my daily exercise: pulling the knives out of my back."

***

It seems to be one thing common to us all that we seem to need to think ourselves successful, and that we tend to adjust the criteria we have for success until we meet them: The despot convinces himself his brutal actions have brought stability to his country; the bankrupt entrepreneur tells himself his family was more important to him than his business; the unpublished writer believes the only authors worth their salt are those, like Emily Dickinson, acclaimed posthumously.

Richardson glowed in his self-assessment that he was successful. He also glowed in his belief that he *deserved* his success – and deserved the money that bought the *public* assessment that he was successful. As Squeers would have said, "Enormously so".

He ascribed his success to two things: working extremely hard and seeing the wider picture. This wider picture meant that he was prepared to sell to both sides in a conflict, or, in the case of the Zanorian conflict, to all *three* sides. By the time Squeers arrived to take up his post, Richardson had already sold five thousand such muskets to Quifah, and a like amount to his opposite number in the Tay.

Quifah hated these machines. *Hated* them. And he hated the fact that he had to annihilate whole flocks of beestalo in order to be able to pay for them. But even more than his hatred for the muskets and the decimated flocks, he hated the possibility that his nation might be annihilated: not only his immediate family, but his wider one, his friends, his neighbours, his acquaintances, his villagers, his townsmen and compatriates. And with them an entire culture, a whole way of life – a theosophy and philosophy, a music and dance and drama, a cuisine and a code of conduct.

Squeers had, of course, acquired the Mercian license for the muskets from Antonio. But he had lacked the time to establish factories capable of producing the bulk that Richardson's were. Of his three hundred thousand troops only fifty thousand had this new musketry. That was stacking the odds in favour of the enemy. Ensuring his commission, he ordered from Richardson a further fifty thousand. A rush order. A very rush order.

Which arrived on the same Accidental as did Cross-Bones. They indeed helped to unpack them. They were enlisted indeed to help *demonstrate* them.

Bones set one up. In order to show off to the assembled generals and bigwigs their efficiency and deadliness. The proof of the latter was spectacular. Bones pulled both triggers, the gun back-fired and blew Bones's head off, almost literally. There were soldiers standing nearby. Grizzled and battle-hardened veterans. Even they, at the sight of such carnage, came close to fainting. Several others lost their lunch.

Richardson shrugged. There was bound to be the odd fault, he philosophised to Squeers. An order of that size, wanted at that kind of speed, accidents were bound to happen. Bound to. Cross was ordered to set up a second musket. Although standing well to one side as he pulled its triggers, his head too was blown off.

Clearly this was an unsatisfactory state of affairs. Squeers negotiated a discount. And when the muskets were distributed to the troops, instructions were given that they were to be fired backwards. Just this batch. Just till the replacements arrived.

Meantime, Squeers ordered that the bodies of Cross-Bones should be embalmed, that the citizens of Biga-buga might see for themselves the atrocities perpetrated on his gallant troops by the Waifu and Tay savages.

No sooner had Cross-Bones arrived, therefore, than they found themselves on the way back. Proclaimed heroes. Just as they would have wanted. Bar the one incidental detail, of course, of their being dead.

Dawes's gazettes already had the news. They were preparing the burghers of Biga-buga for the revulsion they would feel at the sight of these two young martyrs. National heroes, the gazettes proclaimed them. *International* heroes. And they insisted – again and again – that these two heroes *had* to be avenged. That neither *could* there, nor *should* there, be *any* quarter given to this enemy: Savagery had to be met with savagery.

Even before the bodies arrived, the Biga-bugans were baying for blood. (Blood is so much more easily bayed for when the bayers are safe from spilling their own!) There were protests outside Baccanaals. The gazettes continued their non-stop onslaught.

When Fredvie announced he was sending two hundred thousand more troops there were cheers. These became a little bit less raucous when he further announced that, regrettably, in order to find that many troops he would have to conscript them from the Biga-bugan young. And less raucous still when he also announced, regrettably, to pay for such troops he would have to make an additional levy – on fresh fruit (tinned fruit was still exempt) and children's shoes.

They would have been less raucous yet, those cheers, had they known the scale of devastation to which this young would be subjected. *Nothing* mutes quite like mutilation.

Chapter 54

We all share a need to be loved. However apparently 'tough' we are (which isn't tough at all but cowardly), however ascetic or hermit-like, however ethereal or intellectual, we each of us – every single one of us – has a need – not a wish, a *need* – to be loved.

But greater even than that need is the need we all of us have *to* love. Deprive us of that and it is in the 'souler' plexus that you stab us. And not once with a sharp stiletto, but over and over with a rusty hacksaw. The wounds, because they do not bleed, are that much graver. A punch to the solar plexus can pain us; but one to the *souler* plexus can paralyse us.

Peggy was now Charming's only horse, the only thing in his present world he had to care for. He lavished on it, therefore, a care and adoration which was maybe excessive.

It took him several attempts before he found a ship bound for Azrac which was prepared to take Peggy as well. He finally came across a captain who would. This captain made him work hard – that was 'of course': He had two passages to pay for, after all. But the captain was not unnecessarily cruel or exacting. The crew too would have their laugh at his expense. But it was not the sadistic nor the relentless laugh of that aboard the *Silver Hart*. Added to which, the prince was now older and considerably more experienced and accomplished. And stronger. He was indeed a very strong young man. To be challenged at your peril.

On the whole, the prince found the passage bracing, even exhilarating, and he remembered it, certainly with a few winces, but mostly with smiles which over the years slowly gained in expansiveness.

By the time they arrived in Azrac, Peggy sheened as if covered by satin. The horse became the inspiration for a host of fairy-story-tellers: From that time forth it was, apparently, always astride gleaming white chargers that heroes rescued their various sleeping beauties.

But their arrival in Azrac was still some ten days' hence.

***

Almost no-one who is rich thinks of himself as being such. To the rich, the rich are those with more money than they've got. By their token, the world's only rich man is the richest man in the world. The richest man in the world is also one of the poorest. He is morally bankrupt. His riches have killed untold thousands, possibly millions. There are few people poorer than the perpetrators of genocide. It is not one man's meat which is another man's poison, but everyman's greed. No, of course it's not as simple as that. But neither is it as complicated as the wealthy portray.

It would not have been possible for Richardson to have spent in his lifetime the money he had accumulated from the sale of double-barrelled muskets. Even so, he did not think of himself as wealthy. But he did recognise, at least to himself, that he was comfortably off. And therefore around him he did allow to seep an aura of smugness – the smugness that comes from having taken charge of one's life and from having been proved right to have done so.

The putrefying, largely headless corpses of Cross-Bones proved to be the gory sensation Dawes had hoped for. It provided additional public pressure on Fredvie further to escalate the war against the Tay and Waifu. Which, of course, further increased the need both sides had to buy Richardson's weapons of mass destruction.

However he saw or described himself, Richardson was now far too wealthy to be 'summoned' to the Baccanaals. Fredvie therefore invited him there. Minor Minor (it was these days almost needless to say) was also in attendance.

"The emperor has something he has to tell you," Minor Minor

told Richardson, who was heavily involved in scraping muffin crumbs from his beard.

"I've given Mercia all the discount I can," Richardson replied.

"That's so ever so not it." There was a pause. Minor Minor looked to the emperor, who studiously examined the rubies on the uppers of his Arabian-styled slippers.

"Well?" the baron asked eventually.

"There's so ever so not an easy way to tell you this," Minor Minor faltered.

Richardson went ghostly white. "What is it?" he asked coldly, dispassionately, trying to check the dread, stop it from surfacing.

"The Crown Prince of Belgiss," Minor Minor said. "We've found him. I'm so ever so ever so sorry."

Richardson put down his tea-cup. (The emperor always served tea to the Belgics. It was his way of being thoughtful. No Belgic ever complained.) The colour was returning to his cheeks. "Okay," he said.

"Okay?" Minor Minor asked.

"How much?"

"I'm not with you," said Minor Minor.

"To unfind the prince. How much?"

The emperor and Minor Minor exchanged a silent look. Was this a bribe worth pursuing? "I'm afraid," Minor Minor finally said, "you don't understand."

"At the end of the day," Richardson countered, "it's only money which talks. So? How much?"

"This is the Crown Prince, Baron."

"I know it won't be cheap. You know the flak I'll get from Nancy, though? If suddenly she's not going to be Queen?"

"We so ever so can't unfind him, Baron."

"Ah!"

"Ah?"

"Leamore and Dawes."

"Well ..." Minor Minor conceded tentatively.

"They want the prince on the throne."

"'Want' so ever so doesn't come into it, Baron."

"I can't pay more than they can." Which was the point at which Fredvie returned to his slipper scrutiny.

"His Imperial Majesty, Baron, recognises it will be ever such a disappointment."

"Disappointment!" Richardson snorted.

"His Imperial Majesty is prepared to compensate you. Handsomely."

"Oh?"

"His Imperial Majesty wants the lid to remain on this Pandora's box."

"And the compensation?"

"There's a shipping charter available: the exclusive right to moor in Mercia's ports."

"And the emperor would want how much for this concession?"

"That is ever such an unworthy thought, Baron Richardson," said Minor Minor. "His Imperial Majesty would, of course, seek nothing for himself. However, if your perspicacity is such that you recognise ever such a debt of gratitude to His Imperial Majesty then His Imperial Majesty might feel ever so constrained to accept, with diffidence, some sort of permanent ex gratia payment."

"Of?" asked Richardson.

"The largesse from His Imperial Majesty is ever so large. The gratitude, it would be appropriate, should be commensurate."

"Fifteen percent?"

"Twenty-five?"

"Twenty?"

"Done."

"To the Rasbox Shipping Line, then," said Richardson, stroking his beard as if he expected it to start purring. With his other hand he raised his teacup in a toast.

"Rasbox?" asked Minor Minor.

"Short for the Pandora's Box we're going to keep the lid on."

"Maybe so ever so slightly obvious?" suggested Minor Minor.

"Pando, then?"

"Perfect," said Minor Minor.

Like many rich men, Richardson, albeit a fool, was not an idiot. If the young prince were discredited, if somehow he could be proved to be an impostor, a pretender, then, not only could he rule the mercantile waves, but his wife could also be Queen.

That, as a picture, was as wide as it got.

Chapter 55

For all that it used a language familiar to the prince, Mercia had never felt like 'home' to Charming. Even the home he'd felt amongst the Waifu was that of being enormously comfortable, but in a *second* home. The smells around the Waifu were not the smells of home, the air was not home-like, the bond between him and them was spiritual not genetic, and had, at least, as much to do with hope as with reality. For all that the Azrian tongue was *unknown* to him, the prince, immediately he set foot on its soil, felt considerably more at ease than he had throughout his non-Waifu stay in Mercia. To say that he felt he had *come* home would be to overstate the case. But he certainly knew he was travelling towards it.

Mounted on a sheening Peggy, his own features bronzed, his body hardened but his eyes still those of a poet, the prince was an attractive sight. Young women, whose disciplined modesty was usually absolute, found themselves gawping after him – and in a fashion their chaperones would have dubbed 'brazen' were they not doing exactly the same.

It was without difficulty that he found out the whereabouts of Cordelia's house. But it was not without difficulty, his strikingness notwithstanding, that he got into it. The sentries manning it would not let him through the gate, would not even send a message to Cordelia to say her half-brother was there. They wouldn't even allow the prince to wait in the lane for Cordelia's carriage (as one day it would have to) to pass.

The prince went round to the back of the mansion, used Peggy's back as a springboard to jump over the huge fence which surrounded it – only to be caught on the other side by yet more sentries. Who likewise refused to consult Cordelia before summarily, and bottom-bruisingly, booting him out.

It was (maybe appropriately) bootless, the couple of days Charming then spent mooching around the town in the hope that somehow or other his path might cross Cordelia's or Antonio's. He was getting hungry. He returned into the countryside, cut himself a length of wood from which he could whittle a bow, cut other shafts which he shaped into arrows. Peggy fed lushly off the local vegetation. And Charming caught a hare – from which he was able to eke out three meals.

As importantly, he now had a bow and arrows. If he could make contact with Syun that way, why not Cordelia?

Finding a bit of suitable bark he used some charcoal from his fire to write on it: 'Hi – your ½bro.' (This form of letter-writing was not one which encouraged eloquence.)

He returned to that part of the wall he'd scaled previously. It was memorable for the enormous walnut tree, which seemed to snuggle into it. Again the prince clambered atop of the wall. God, it was a long way from the wall to the house. He doubted an arrow would make it. No, he *knew* it wouldn't. How then was he to make contact?

As he was puzzling over this, Cordelia's children (Charming supposed) rounded a corner of the mansion and came out into the garden before him, presumably to play. If they found an arrow, their innate curiosity (so Charming's rationale told him) would ensure they took it to Cordelia, if only on the basis of "Look, Mummy, what I've found".

But he didn't dare fire the arrow. Arrows have no brain ... and no conscience. All missiles – arrows, darts, bullets – strike indiscriminately the good and the bad, the blameless and the guilty. He pulled a green kernel therefore from the walnut tree. This he cast expertly in the direction of the young boy. So 'expertly', it missed by a good few yards.

He adjusted his mental 'sight' and cast another. This time it was close enough for the lad to see. But he paid it scant attention. Until *its* arrival was closely followed by that of another. Funny sort of a storm, raining walnuts. The boy started looking around him.

On top of the wall, Charming was gesticulating like a semaphorist with a stutter. Eventually the boy saw him. Charming quickly put a finger to his lips, indicating to the boy that he should not make any sudden noise. He then indicated the arrow, and mimed its path with his hand. He also mimed to the boy to watch its flight.

Then he fired the arrow straight into the air, judging (correctly) that it would land far enough away from the two children as to constitute no danger to them. He had also judged correctly that the children's reaction would be to take the arrow straight indoors. Please God, to their mother. Please God.

Charming crouched behind the arras of the walnut tree. He could still be seen, but only if you knew where to look. He had imagined that within five minutes his sister would charge out onto the lawn, desperate to see her brother. Ten minutes went by. Twenty. Half-an-hour. Charming had grown quite slumbrous.

Eventually, almost testily, Cordelia did emerge. Antonio was with her, quite as testy as she. Her son was almost forcibly dragging her, it seemed. He pointed to that part of the wall where Charming had been. And then looked about him, as the absent-minded professor would who has 'lost' the spectacles now perched on his forehead.

Charming needed to check that the coast was indeed clear; that there weren't any unpleasant surprises – in the guise of guards or sentries – just about to spring on him. Finally he figured that Mummy's temper with her son was of a testiness that outlawed patience: A few more moments and she'd return inside.

He loosed off another arrow.

Perhaps the definition of a cliché is that it is a term where overuse has changed its meaning. If that is right, it was not clichély that Cordelia could not believe her eyes, but actually.

When she first caught sight of Charming she waited for the apparition, for the *hallucination*, to disappear. When, after a few seconds of staring, this had not happened she made a couple of faltering, almost drunken, steps towards it.

The children had sensed that something momentous was occurring, and that it involved their mother in a way which would preclude her tending to them. They had therefore trotted, clumsily, to their father. Who was also gazing fixatedly at the apparition. Instinct urged him not to intervene, advised that the scene unfolding was for two actors only.

Charming stared back at Cordelia. He had the advantage of knowing he had never died, of course, and therefore of having no concerns about the reality of what he was seeing. But his head was suddenly jostled also by a thousand thoughts and memories, like a pack of cards feathered through by a conjuror. There was a consciousness of fifty-two cards, but they passed before his eyes too quickly for any one card to have an identity – they were blurred images, no more, of a Diamond or a Spade, a King or a Knave.

He stared till he stopped seeing woozy memories and hazy portraits. He stared till he started to see her. And in the present. As she was today. He stared at her and stared. And his heart suddenly wanted to burst. Because the stare told him that Cordelia loved him. He suddenly realised he'd never been sure. Not till then. Since the murder, all the time there'd been a doubt nagging at him, finger-wagging at him: Had she indeed killed them, Philly and Horatio? And if she had, was it in trying to poison him?

"Who the Hell do you think you are?" finally Cordelia said to him. "Humpty Dumpty? Stuck on a wall like that? We don't, clot, have any king's horses here, or men, so if you *do* have a great fall …"

He had sprung down from the wall. And he was running towards her, his arms outstretched. Just for a pace and a half she allowed him to come to her. Then she also ran to meet him.

They collapsed into each other's arms, hugged – as only those can hug when one has returned from death. She held onto him, subconsciously feeling the blood pour through him, checking the pulse, the surge, the life-force.

She held him and closed her eyes.

She held him and opened her eyes, checking that the trees were still where they had been, that the sun had not turned purple.

She closed her eyes again and held him. And then she squeezed him. A melon, to see whether it was ripe enough. And then she pushed him from her. And she gazed into his eyes. And she smiled. Then didn't. Then smiled angrily. Then squashed her smile. Then smiled broadly. Then she frowned. And then she slapped him.

"What's that for?" he asked, stunned and wounded.

"You're supposed to be dead."

"Sorry," he said.

"So I should think," she said and smiled again, biting her lower lip as if to anchor it to her face, for fear that the smile would simply grow wings and fly away. It was at this moment that her two children came to grapple at her knees.

"Sebastian," she said, "Viola, this is your uncle. Probably the best-looking ghost you're ever going to meet. Also a ghost with a Mercian accent. That we will have to do something about!"

Antonio made also to hug the prince. But Cordelia wouldn't cede him enough space for him to be able fully to do so. She'd lost him once. Never would she do so again.

These were moments Charming would cherish well into his old age.

The returning do not need calves to be fatted in order to feel welcome, they just need joy to be unfettered. The English encourage understatement. The Belgic royal family had noted this trait, had thought it sophisticated, and had largely sought to emulate it. As a literary device, it can have merit. *Emotional* understatement, however, can easily be mistaken for indifference, even coldness.

Cordelia on this occasion was not prepared to use understatement. The joy, the happiness and delight fountained from her, poured from her. It gushed from her. It was evident in the way she stood or scooped a loose hair behind her ear; in the way she drank a cup of tea or told the cook what to prepare for dinner; in the way she ran a bath for the children or tossed Antonio's dirty laundry into the basket.

France's Louis XIV famously remarked: "The state, that's me." Those seeing Cordelia in those days could have parodied that. "Joy," her whole being proclaimed, "that's me."

Three nights after Charming's arrival, Cordelia was in her bedroom. Her husband was preparing for bed. She was writing a letter.

"To whom?" Antonio asked casually.

"Nancy," Cordelia replied. *Her* voice was not casual.

"Oh," said her husband. Antonio never folded his breeches, always left them where they fell. Now he folded them very carefully; carefully laid them across the back of a small chair of a damson velvet. It was also slowly and methodically that he donned his cotton night-shirt.

"I have to do this," she said slowly, almost apologetically.

"I know."

"When it was just me, it was one thing."

"Yes."

"Now there's Charming."

"Yes."

"It *makes* it another thing, Antonio."

"It does."

"You don't agree?"

"That it makes it another thing? How could I not agree? It'd be like trying to say that a glass of water mixed with whisky is the same as it had been before the whisky was added."

"I *will* be all right, dearest," she said, again in that same slow, almost apologetic tone she'd used previously.

"No," he said, "you won't be."

"I have to do it, Antonio."

"I know."

"It's the right thing to do."

"Then don't do it, Cordelia."

"What?"

"If it's the right thing to do, don't do it."

"It's the *only* thing to do."

"You know that's different?"

"I *have* to do it."

"Yes." Antonio had leadenly clambered into bed.

"Say you understand."

"I don't understand, Cordelia." She sighed in exasperation, her shoulders slouched and she let the quill she was holding simply drop from her hand. "But," he added, "I do love you."

She rose from the desk, rushed to the huge four-poster bed, sat on the freshly turned straw mattress. She took both his hands in hers, and kissed him. She could write to Nancy, she decided, the next day. Tonight there were important matters to attend to.

Chapter 56

"The cheek!" Nancy exclaimed. "The unmitigated cheek!"

"That's five syllables," Richardson replied, who had stopped marmalading his toast in order to count.

"What?"

"'Unmitigated': five syllables. Isn't there a law or something banning five-syllable words? At least, before breakfast?"

"This is serious, Baron."

"So is breakfast, dear."

"Cordelia is coming home."

"Before breakfast?"

Nancy tutted loudly, and explained as if to an obtuse child, "She's bringing Charming with her."

"Ah!"

"Ah, indeed."

"Isn't he dead?"

"Apparently only temporarily."

"Ah!"

"'Ah'? Can't you, Baron, think of anything more sensible to say than 'ah'?"

"Interesting."

"Interesting?"

"The complications."

"I despair of you, you know that? Despair."

"That's awfully energetic of you."

Nancy emitted a low-pitched gurgling "uh!". "She wants me to pave the way for their return."

"*Their* return?"

"Hers and Charming's. Wants me to tell papa."

"Oh, I wouldn't do that."

"She thinks it might soften the shock."

"It's awfully good, this marmalade."

"Why wouldn't you do that?"

"Mmm?"

"When I said Cordelia wanted me to tell papa, you said, 'I wouldn't do that.'"

"Did I?"

"Yes."

"Ah!"

"Why wouldn't you tell him?"

"I wouldn't tell your father anything."

"That's not what you meant."

Richardson pushed his chair back from the table. He brushed the crumbs from his fingers. "Okay, breakfast's clearly over. Business can begin." He looked firmly at Nancy. "Don't worry about it," he told her seriously.

"It's my crown we're talking about here. *My*," she emphasised, "*crown*," she emphasised.

"Don't worry about it, Nancy," he told her. "It's good news, in fact. In fact, *great* news."

"How is my losing the crown of Belgiss 'great news'?"

"You won't lose the crown. You're in a stronger position now than you ever were. Is Cordelia going to write to Fredvie?"

"Fredvie?"

"Does she mention writing to him in her letter?"

"What are you going on about, Baron?"

"She won't be writing to Fredvie. She wouldn't think there was any need to."

"What has ...?"

"Wider picture, Nancy. Just hear me out: Fredvie will be sending his pretender across the seas, more or less at the same time. Whoever gets here first will be like England's Lady Jane Grey – a nine-day's wonder. Pretenders are like negatives, Nancy. Two of them together cancel each other out. Once the second pretender arrives, both will be discredited. Let me put it another way: Both *can* be discredited. If there are two pretenders, one clearly *has* to be an impostor. If one, why not both? The difficulty would have been to convince the king that *one* was an impostor. With *two* Charmings about to arrive, that job's been done for us."

"You sound very confident."

"I *am* very confident."

"And the crown *will* be ours?"

"It'll be yours, my dove."

"And now I should ...?"

"Do nothing."

"Cordelia's letter?"

"What letter?"

"We'll have to have one of the servants flogged. For having mislaid such an important letter."

"A small price to pay."

"In the wider picture?"

"No. Just a small price to pay."

***

Elsewhere in Wodinton, HM was also taking breakfast and reading her mail. This included a letter from Winny informing HM that she and the look-alike prince were on the point of leaving Biga-buga. Such was the communication of the time, that receipt of the letter had to mean the *Enterprize* was already close to Blefton.

***

This was a titbit of information proffered by the Mercian ambassador to Naitly at a breakfast meeting the former had organised. It was the only titbit on the menu. Indeed Naitly was considerably less surprised by the news than he was by the gargantuan size of meal presented to him. There was no way he would finish it, so he protested he'd already eaten and declined even to start.

The thing was, did he tell the king or did he wait?

Did he tell HM?

***

Antonio had chartered the same ship which had brought Charming to Azrac to convey both the prince and Cordelia to Belgiss.

He had insisted she say goodbye to the children at home. He said he didn't want the children subjected to a dockside adieu. What he really didn't want was for the children to see him cry.

Which, as the ship sailed slowly from the quayside, he did. He wasn't weeping. He just let the tears slide in a steady stream down his cheeks. He knew he would never see Cordelia again.

***

HM knew HM's best interests lay in it being she who broke to the king the glad tidings that the *Enterprize* would soon be docking in Blefton and that therefore his son would soon be arriving in Belgiss. She also wasn't frightened of a little indigestion. No sooner had she read Winny's missive, therefore, than she was hot-footing it round to the castle.

Any news, even good news, when broken to King Cole needed to be made more palatable. HM knew of only one way to improve the palatability of news: To mix it with the elixir found within his bowl.

She studied him closely as, with trembling hand, he drank first one draught, then another. His eyes steadied. HM could see they were capable now of concentration. "Your son, sire," she told him, "he's almost home."

Cole looked at her. He didn't understand, to begin with. Then he didn't want to understand. Then he was frightened – oh *so* frightened – of understanding. "Don't tease one, HM," he pleaded with her.

"It's true, sire. The *Enterprize* will be mooring any moment."

"One's son?"

"Yes, sire."

"Almost home?"

"Trust me."

"One's son?"

"Your son, sire."

Cole became all of a-dither. He paced this way, and then that. Went to drink from his bowl, then replaced it on the table. Sat at his desk. Rose. "Does Nose know?"

"Nose, Your Majesty?"

"Does he know, HM?"

"*I* haven't told him, sire."

"Good, good. That means one can tell him oneself. Tell him his master's almost home. His master *is* almost home, isn't he, HM?"

"And, sire, we – you and I – we're getting married."

"Let all the bells in all the land ring out for his return, HM."

"They could, sire, also ring out for our betrothal."

"What?"

"Save the bell-ringers' arms, sire. I mean, one lot of clanking …"

"Clanking?"

"Clanging, knelling, whatever you call it. One lot, sire, more than enough, no?"

"Clanking, HM?"

"Pealing. *Ap*pealing pealing, indeed. Very appealing pealing, Your Majesty. But one lot, eh? To cover your son's return, and our joyous betrothal?"

"One has things to do, HM. Important things. One can't be standing around, HM, dilly-dallying with you. Chit-chatting with you, HM. One has much to organise. One has, HM, Nose to tell."

"Yes, Your Majesty."

"Clanking, HM?"

"A slip, sire, of the tongue."

"Yes." He went.

HM banged her fist hard on the top of the king's desk. She immediately regretted it. It felt like she had broken at least three bones. That was the kind of thing Fredvie did!

Chapter 57

There have been historians less than enamoured of Winny. By those she's portrayed as some kind of cross between Sleeping Beauty's stepmother, Lady Macbeth and the Loch Ness monster. Even if they are right, it's important to remember that no monster is born. Monsters are always created. If the present had been more merciful to Winny, maybe her past would have been viewed more favourably by her future.

And the truth is Winny *wasn't* a monster. Not at this stage. Later ... Well, the later chronicles chronicle what happened later. Then she just wanted her place in the sun. And she wanted to enjoy it.

She'd enjoyed schooling her charge. She'd enjoyed watching the roughneck slave develop into a personable and poised young man. She had even enjoyed the attendant frustration. Frustration comes only if you are striving. The apathetic and lazy do not get frustrated. Winny had realised, coaching the pretender, how unused she was to it. For Michelangelo and Mozart frustration was a mundanity of life. For Winny it was Valhalla: It included an awareness of life, and a hope of love.

She was surprised, frankly, that the 'prince's' arrival at Blefton should have been so pompless and quiet: There were no massed bands, nor a guard of honour. There wasn't even a lone piper. All there was, there was a somewhat succinct note from HM telling her to report (plus prince) immediately to her, HM's, apartments.

Most of the trip from Blefton Winny spent nagging at the 'prince' not to goldfish at all the sights assailing him, not to comment on the smells and sounds. This, she kept reminding him, was countryside which was familiar to him. A tired disdain would be a more appropriate attitude, an ennui which (because he was of the Court and therefore courteous) he would not allow free rein. He was, she nagged at him, to remember the waving lessons she had given him. A good waving technique to a royal is as indispensable as a sense of rhythm to a drummer: Most of the contact he'd have with most of his subjects would be precisely that – waving at them through carriage windows.

There were, furthermore, still wrinkles in his Mercian accent. These needed to be steam-pressed out. Really he wasn't yet ready for public display. But then – and this Winny understood – *really* he never would be.

At Wodinton, Ginny was left to go home to Prim and Prim's new husband (and stepdaughter). Winny and the 'prince' were expected. They were ushered through corridors and up 'backstage' flights of stairs, before being smuggled, via the kitchens, into HM's hospitality suite.

HM was waiting. "Let's have a look," she said by way of greeting them when they arrived.

Truthfully, Winny had not known what to expect. Except that she had been expecting ... *something*. And that she had been greeted with a lack of something hurt her. Not body-blowly, but enough: A wasp sting may not be a mamba's bite, but it still hurts.

For her part, HM was considerably more emotional than she wanted to confess to herself, let alone to demonstrate in public. She didn't delude herself that Winny's actions were not principally motivated by self-interest. But that Winny thought her self-interest lay in confiding to her was the nearest thing HM had received to something that could be construed as an indication of friendship. Within her she felt emotion seeking elbow-room. She evicted it. She *had* to keep things on a *strictly* business footing. Had to. Her whole future hung in its balance. The plot they were embarked on contained risks. Huge ones. If it all went pear-shaped she'd have to have Winny executed. She didn't want to execute what could be the only friend she'd ever had. Better, never to have had her as a friend.

HM inspected the 'prince', first as if she were a buyer and he a slave, then as if she were a general inspecting troops, after that a farmer valuing livestock. And then as a critic assessing a work of sculpture. Finally she looked at him like a choreographer auditioning a dancer. And as the role of inspector changed, so did Winny's as chaperone. She in turn became slave-seller, drill sergeant, cattle-breeder, sculptor. And surplus to requirements.

"Not bad," HM finally told not the 'prince' but Winny.

"Thank you," she replied.

"He's been away some time. That'll help."

"For pity's sake, we didn't have a lot of time, HM."

"I told you, not bad. What more do you want?"

"You want me to come with you?" she asked.

"With me?"

"When you present him to the king?"

HM laughed – she thought delicately. Winny thought the laugh raucous. "No," said HM. "I think not."

Winny was already crest-fallen. This rebuff sent her crest tumbling. "Oh!" she said.

"Go home, Winny. He's not, as I say, bad. If you don't hear from me, you'll know he's passed muster."

"You'll keep in touch?"

"Trust me."

Winny looked at the 'prince', then at the Minister. "It's just ..." she started. She waved at HM to pull her into a congress that was more private. "The thing is ... I was wondering, you see ... You'll have heard of our little arrangement, Fredvie's and mine ... The thing is, for pity's sake, I was wondering when you were thinking of announcing it."

"Announcing what?"

"Our ..." And here she looked around the room lest she could see slippers skulking under curtains. "... oh, for pity's sake ... our engagement."

"Your what?"

"Engagement," Winny replied almost sheepishly.

"Your engagement?" asked HM, strangling her incredulity.

"Yes."

"To the prince?"

"Yes, for pity's sake. Yes, yes, yes."

"To the heir, Winny, to the Belgic throne?"

"Fredvie didn't tell you about it?"

"No," said HM. "He didn't."

"You're thinking we should wait a bit."

"Maybe."

"I could see you were thinking that."

"Very perspicacious."

"One thing at a time, that sort of idea?"

"More or less."

"I understand."

"Good," said HM.

"You'll let me know?"

"Trust me."

"You won't go announcing our engagement or anything …"

"Not a chance."

"… not without letting me know."

"Trust me, Winny."

"Oh, I do, I do. I'll be going now."

"Right."

"I think I'll *just* go, for pity's sake. No goodbyes. No 'au revoir's."

"Simplest is best."

Winny turned to go. "It'd have been nice, you know … Forget it."

"What?" HM asked.

"It's too late. Forget it." Again Winny made to leave. "It would just have been nice … a 'well done' or something."

"You're right," said HM. "I'm sorry."

"It's no big deal, anything like that. It'd just have been nice."

"I was thoughtless. I'm sorry."

"You'll let me know?"

"I'll let you know."

"Right."

"Edwina?"

"Yes?"

"Well done."

Winny stopped in the doorway. She looked at HM, trying to figure out what was meant by the remark. She realised she had a thousand choices, and she'd never know what was the real one. She therefore opted to believe HM was being sincere. "Thank you," she said.

Chapter 58

It was at about the same time that the real prince's eyes – and those of Cordelia – were again gorging on the familiar sight of the Belgic coastline. They had their arms wrapped around each other. This was their home. And together they had great plans for this home. Together they would make of Belgiss the finest home the world had ever known. Not just for themselves, for everyone who lived there.

There was a stiff breeze blowing, but the sun's effortless warmth was still discernible beneath it. It was a breeze which blew away all problems, all set-backs, all haze and fuzziness and cobwebs. It was a wind not only of change, but wherein change was warming and comforting. As inevitable as spring is. And as welcomed.

Together they would change the future from being a scary place to one where bounty was bountiful. For all Belgics. For all people.

***

"Was one not right?" the king asked.

"Sire?" asked HM.

"To have had the prince's toe tattooed? When all the world, all the *Court* was brandishing one a madman, was one, HM, not right?"

"When is Your Majesty ever not?"

"Oh, come now, HM. One has been known to have erred."

"Never, sire, for very long."

"Well?" the king asked again. He took two or three nervous puffs on his hookah and sought to drown his nerves with the bowl's elixir. HM was on her knees some feet before him, examining the 'prince's' foot. A surgeon had had to be brought to start removing the bandage. And then they'd had to wait whilst the formality of his dismissal was played out: The detail of the tattoo, of course, had to remain secret.

"It would certainly appear well, sire. I was just wondering, though: When was it you were thinking of making public our betrothal, sire?"

"Is it one's son, HM?"

"Is it my *step*son, sire?"

"This begins to smell, HM, of blackmail."

"Is Your Majesty trying to tell me he is in love with me?"

"Nose!" the king suddenly exclaimed.

"Sire?" HM asked.

The king went to the door, and said to the guard outside it, "Bring Nose to one."

The 'prince' who had looked extremely uncomfortable throughout the interview now looked nonplussed. Clearly nothing had been done to prepare him for Nose.

HM saw all this and took pre-emptive action, "He's been away a long time, sire. Dogs are not elephants. They only *seem* to have a memory. In reality they have none at all."

"Is that right, HM?"

"Trust me, sire."

"Of course one trusts you, HM. Are you not soon to be one's queen?"

"I would be a good queen, sire."

"And a good wife?"

"A very good queen, sire."

"What is one supposed to do, HM?"

"Do, sire?"

"Do we embrace him? Shake hands with him? What?"

"The ... announcement, sire, of our nuptials?"

"Tomorrow? What do you think?"

"I think, sire, that between now and tomorrow the most appropriate reaction will occur to you."

There was a knock at the door. And the guard brought Nose to the king. The 'prince' the dog just ignored, as he also ignored HM. HM mimed to the young man that this was his long-lost mutt.

"Ah, my dog," exclaimed the 'prince', about as convincingly as the unsuccessful alchemist trying to persuade an investor that the brass before him is indeed gold. HM signalled him to approach the dog. Which, tentatively, the young man did.

Nose snarled very quietly, very menacingly. The 'prince' retreated.

"You mustn't rush it, sir," HM rushed to say to the 'prince'. "Nose hasn't seen you in several years. Give him time, sir."

"You bet," the 'prince' said unBelgically.

"If one knew whether or not you were one's son, one could say to you, 'Son, give him time.' But, of course, one doesn't so one can't."

"You bet," the 'prince' said again, with a magnanimity he would have considered real princely.

"The Mercian accent," HM shrugged, "awfully infectious, sire. If Your Majesty will excuse us ..." She made to go.

"Why? What do you have to do?"

"The ship of state, alas, sire, does not steer itself."

"The ship of state steered itself quite satisfactorily for some years, HM, without the prince's help."

"He is required for debriefing, sire."

"Debriefing?"

"Yes, sire."

"Bit uncivilised, isn't it? Bit British public schools, HM?"

"Sire?"

"Taking someone's underpants off them? Not the act of a courtier."

"Not that kind of debriefing, sire. He lived in Zanoria for a time."

"That's a place, is it, Zanoria? Oh, do what you want, HM. You will anyway. You will be with one tomorrow, one takes it."

"For the announcement?"

"Of course for the announcement."

"I wouldn't miss it, sire, not for the world."

"Go."

"Yes, sire."

Both she and the 'prince' took four backward steps, then let themselves out of the door.

"We've got to get rid of that mutt," said the 'prince'.

To which, both mimicking him and not, HM replied, "You bet."

***

Cordelia and Charming were riding towards Wodinton. Charming was riding Peggy. Cordelia sat side-saddle on a horse she'd brought from her stable, Sparkel. What for Peggy was a gentle canter, for Sparkel was a full gallop.

Not that either of them (who knew nothing yet of the pretender's place at Court) was in a tearing hurry. The reward for the returning traveller is not the sights that confront them, not even the smells: it is the feel. The feel of the air and the water, the feel of the streets and the people. It was this feel that was infusing into them, as the taste of tea infuses into boiling water.

It would have been to this that they ascribed their unqualified happiness. Maybe abetted by the joy they had in the rediscovery and in the company of each other. Far deeper than either was prepared at that stage to delve was also the realisation, the almost *divination*, that they were embarked, ineluctably, on the road which was their destiny; that, after years enmeshed in a thorny labyrinth, they were now on a sun-warmed boulevard; and that that boulevard would lead them directly not only to where they wanted to be, but also to where they *had* to be.

***

"He's an impostor, sire," Richardson said. He tried to ignore the six empty bowls and the sixty sticky bowl-rings dotted around the bedroom.

"One's tired, Baron. So, so tired."

"Sire?" the baron asked, unable to see the significance of what the king was saying.

"What one's saying is: at the end of the day, does it matter?"

"The man is an interloper, sire. He will deprive your own flesh and blood, sire, of her rightful inheritance."

"Goneril is dead."

"Nancy, sire."

"Nancy's dead?"

"She could inherit."

"Goneril's dead, Baron," the king said testily.

Richardson tried another tack. "Nose?"

"Nose?"

"What did Nose do, sire, with the so-called prince?"

"Dogs aren't elephants, Baron."

"No?"

"One has it on the best authority."

"And who might it be, this 'best authority'?"

"All the best authorities, Baron. HM for one."

"HM?"

"She's confiscated him, you know?" said the king

"Who?"

"Who?" the king replied blearily, blearily watching the baron.

"Whom, sire, did HM confiscate?"

"Nose. Do listen, Baron. One finds it tedious always to be repeating oneself."

"And where is he now?"

"Who?"

"Nose?"

"Nose?"

"Nose."

"Nose. Do listen, Baron. One finds it tedious always to be repeating oneself." The king shook his head, believing he had just experienced a moment of déjà-vu. "'Evening, Baron," he said to Richardson. "And what can one do you for this evening?"

Chapter 59

"We're so close, Nancy," HM told the princess. "*So* close."

"Richardson thinks you're going to betray me. *Us*," she added hastily.

"Why would I? I've nothing to gain. We, on the other hand, Nancy – you and I –, we have *everything* to gain. And we're so close to gaining it. So *very* close. It's just a question now of holding your nerve. 'Just screw your courage to the sticking-place', Nancy, 'and you'll not fail'."

***

The feel for Cordelia and Charming was no longer one that was Belgically familiar. It was now Wodintonly so. Apparently even Peggy felt it. Charming was having to rein in the horse quite energetically.

Brother and sister smiled at each other, squeezed each other's hands.

Soon be home.

***

"'Just screw your courage to the sticking-place', Lord Chancellor, 'and you'll not fail'," HM advised him.

"The ambassador wants us to endorse the prince."

"Of course he does," HM replied.

"I don't understand."

"No."

"Not helpful, HM."

"Mercia wants us to have power without power. You want that?"

"Power without power?"

"You want that? Not gold but fool's gold?"

"Fool's power?"

"Quite," said HM.

"No."

"'Screw your courage to the sticking-place', Lord Chancellor …"

"I do wish you'd stop saying that."

"Then start screwing, Baron. You've been screwing the country for years. You should be getting rather good at it."

***

Perched atop Wodinton's highest hill, its castle was a magnificent and awesome sight. Charming and Cordelia needed a moment of still just to absorb it, and to bask in it.

They knew that, in reality, most of it was cold, draughty and cheerless. It was a lot less attractive to its residents than to its sightseers. They had never before been a tourist, and they'd never before gloried in its sight.

Great architecture, they both realised as they marvelled, is truly the most democratic of the arts. Because great buildings are not only accessible to everyone, but (in a very real sense) they are owned by everyone.

***

"Your Majesty," said HM. "'Just screw your courage to the sticking-place …'"

"And one'll not fail?"

"You cannot, sire. Nor can we."

"Where's Nose?"

"I thought it prudent, sire, to lock him away. Just till the announcement's been made, just till we know whether or not the young man is, indeed, the prince."

"Are all in attendance?"

"Breaths are bated, sire. All are aware of big news. No-one is sure of what that news comprises."

"Big news afoot, eh, HM?"

"Now, Your Majesty promised me he wasn't going to use that joke again."

"Bit corny, is it?"

"Or that one, sire."

There was a rumpus outside the door. HM was on her way to investigate when the door flew open.

Into the inner sanctum walked Charming and Cordelia.

***

It was a dilemma, all right. In fact, it was a dilemma kerneling an enigma wrapped in a mystery.

And, to be fair to Cole, the dilemma was a real one. Seen together, there was almost nothing to distinguish one young man from the other. The pretender was a whisker taller than the real prince, whose hair was (if studied carefully) a touch lighter. In Belgiss the accents of both sounded contrived. Indeed maybe that of the real prince twanged a touch more Mercianly than the pretender's.

But, the lapse about Nose notwithstanding, Winny had done her job well. Had done it brilliantly, in fact. There were aspects about the prince's childhood which the pretender remembered better than the real prince.

Cole insisted both were dressed identically lest, somehow, sartorial considerations were to prejudice his final decision.

A decision which, he knew, would require the wisdom of Solomon. He knew of only one place where such wisdom could be found. It wasn't therefore that he dipped into his bowl, but rather that he plumbed the depths of it.

***

"I cannot stress too much," Naitly not not-told HM, in a private conference with her, "how deep is my love for you, HM. How much I have always not unloved you." Canoodling is a skill like any other. Naitly's canoodling skills were roughly those of the elderly Beethoven for piano-tuning.

"I don't not love you too," she told him. He went to kiss her. "But we'll have none of *that*, thank you."

"Sorry."

"Not till I've married the king."

"No, of course."

"I'm a respectable unmarried woman."

"Of course you are."

"Queens, on the other hand, are expected to have lovers."

"Right."

"You'll have to be patient."

"I'm not too good at patience."

"It's very simple, Lord Chancellor: the Queen goes on the King …"

"And the Knave goes on the Queen?"

"Quite."

"And the Joker?"

"The Joker, Lord Chancellor, is *always* wild."

***

"You're drunk, papa."

"One is most certainly not drunk."

"The future of your whole country hangs in the balance, papa, *my* whole future too," exclaimed Nancy, "and you go and get yourself drunk."

"One is not drunk. One is nervous. One's nerves need steadying."

"Oh, and alcohol is so good for steadying things. We see how much more steadily the drunk walks than people who are sober."

"When your mother nagged at one, Nancy, it was intolerable enough. Isn't there a commandment about honouring fathers? One will not be lectured at by one's children. It goes against the natural order."

"'Natural order'!" she snorted.

"Just like it does, losing a son. And then finding two."

"I want to be Belgiss's first ruling queen. Is that too much to ask?"

"One doesn't know any more, Nancy."

Nancy softened her tone. "Papa," she said, "you know, don't you, that they're *both* impostors?"

"How does one know, Nancy, that you're not?"

"What? You think I'm some kind of double? That one night a bunch of extremists came in, kidnapped the real me, replaced me in bed beside my husband, and no-one ever noticed the difference? You've been reading Dawes's gazettes again, haven't you? Or listening to Naitly's speeches. The threat from outside, papa, is only there to keep the public in order. Please try and remember that."

"If there are two impostors, why not three?"

"Maybe there's nothing but impostors."

"Maybe one is *also* an impostor," said Cole petulantly.

"If not an impostor, papa, certainly impossible."

"That is the lot of the powerful."

"No, papa. That is the lot of the drunk."

***

The Mercian ambassador was not a happy man. Now he had Naitly trotting to him any time there were things to talk about, he'd thought his life was organised. When Fredvie had heard, though, that another pretender to the Belgic throne had turned up, the emperor had turned Realrichly incandescent with rage. It was not only that he had gnawed at the carpet, but that the consequent froth had also cleaned them. (Wonderfully, it should be added.)

The Mercian ambassador had, in no uncertain terms, been told to get his substantial posterior round to HM's place, and to ensure that the joker knew what was expected of her.

"You are, I take it, real aware," the ambassador told her, "that it's not a question of your knowing which side your bread's buttered on?"

"Oh?" HM asked simply.

"Without Mercian support, there *is* no butter. No bread neither. On both the wheat and lard front there is, in fact, joker, just a big fat zero."

"I am, Your Excellency, a senior government minister of a sovereign state. You will not refer to me as 'joker'."

"Oh, Jeez, have our delicate little sensibilities been touched? Oh dear. *Mercia* is so sorry. I, joker," he said pointedly, "am so sorry." His sarcasm ceded to venom. "At this level, *joker*, you play the full nine innings."

HM's eyes froze so that what normally would be a twinkle became an ember, one burning with hatred. And then she relaxed. She started gently to laugh. "You know why, Your Excellency, Mercia will never truly be a super-power?"

"Oh, certainly, *that's* why I'm here: to listen to lecture on international politics from the Court jester!"

"You have power from the end of a gun. That's not power. That's ceding power, in fact, to the gun. And that is an abuse of power.

"Throughout history, Mr Ambassador, those with power have abused it. We have survived for as long as we have because there is an innate understanding in the people – in those whom you like to think powerless – that civilisation is a better idea than barbarism.

"Christianity has survived not because of the Church, but despite it. Civilisation *will* continue, Mr Ambassador, not because super-powers hold double-barrelled muskets to our heads, but despite that. Guns are not the indication of civilisation but the indication of a *lack* of civilisation.

"Oh, civilisation *will* survive, Mr Ambassador, because eventually governments and guns will be overcome by something more powerful than either. It will survive because – finally – whether in Orismine or Zanoria, in Biga-buga or Wodinton, there are considerably more good people than bad ones. More people want to help a blind man cross the road than shoot the head off a stranger; more people want to rock a baby to sleep than to sell it into slavery.

"Coercion as an instrument of power is poor and short-lived. Like paper it burns brightly and fiercely, but it burns itself out quickly.

"In thinking about Belgiss's future, I had thought to include Mercian interests in my considerations. Mercia is, after all, a part of the globe – a *part* of it, Mr Ambassador, not (as Mercia appears to think) the whole planet. But then I realised that the last person you want as an ally is someone so determined to commit suicide he antagonises every two-bit thug, every would-be assassin around him.

"Mercia has so much going for it. *So* much. No other empire in the history of mankind has had the chance to do so much good. It is a tragedy – literally of global proportions – that it should be so blind as to where its true interests lie that, rather than seeking to do good, it has opted to do incalculable, irreversible, and irreparable harm."

"You will regret, madam, having spoken in that way to Mercia."

"And that you fail to understand the irony of what you've just said, Mr Ambassador, only underscores the tragedy. Trust me."

"I shall inform the emperor that you have chosen to defy him. You will last precisely three days."

"If you inform the emperor thus you would *mis*inform him. I shall not defy him. Not deliberately. His wishes will simply not figure in my deliberations. As to my longevity ... My removal might provoke the need to expose Mercia's plan to put a pretender on the Belgic throne. It would be a scandal not even Dawes's gazettes could afford to ignore."

"What I'd expect from a Court upstart: blackmail."

"If Nero had ever been brought to trial, he would have accused everyone in the courtroom of malfeasance. The serial killer always blames others for his crimes. It is only the truly great, the really super, who start by examining their own offences. I think it was someone called Jesus Christ who suggested we might do that."

"You just signed your own death warrant, joker."

"If you will excuse me, Your Excellency ..." HM said and left. She shut the door and burst into laughter.

For HM the whole thing, her entire career from joker's school forth, had only ever been a game. She had merely wanted to see how far she could take it, and how far she could go with it. She always knew the game would end in her death, but then a life which had had no game in it would also have ended in death. This way, at least, she'd had a few laughs along the way.

None more so than now.

She left the 'audience' determined she would put the real prince back on the Belgic throne. That would be *such* a poke in their arrogant eye.

And then she stopped.

There is no powerlessness quite so absolute as the illusion of power. If she put the prince on the throne, she would – transparently – have outplayed them. But the victory, almost for that reason, could be Pyrrhic. If, however, she put the *pretender* on the throne, then not Fredvie, not Leamore nor Dawes would ever know if that had been because HM had actually obeyed them, or because she was only *seeming* to obey them until the time was ripe for her to show her true colours.

Oh, they wouldn't stand for that for too long. HM had no doubt of that. But for as long as they were struggling to find a way to oust her, HM would enjoy their discomfort.

Not only on her own behalf.

She would enjoy it on behalf of all the robbed, the cheated, the abused, the humiliated, the impoverished, the disenfranchised, the subjugated ... on behalf, in other words, of the vast bulk of humankind.

And because the numbers on whose behalf she would enjoy it were so vast, she was determined she would enjoy it vastly.

***

Cole would show Nancy who listened to whom! He'd show her alright. "Two impostors," she'd said. "There might be two impostors."

He ordered both to be arrested and to be cast into the deepest dungeon. He forgot to add that they should be cast also into *separate* dungeons. By the time HM found out, the two 'princes' had been together for over a day.

Chapter 60

Wodinton Castle was abuzz. At least one head would roll that day.

The throng gathered outside the railings had swelled to such numbers that the authorities had feared deaths by crushing, and had therefore opened the gates to the hoi-polloi.

The axeman was already standing by his block. Useless Eustace stood behind him, ready to pass him the axe, or to step in to fill any breach should his boss feel tired or have been bribed too little.

Within, the Court was assembled, including most of the players of our drama – those, anyway, who were still alive.

Fredvie, of course, was ensconced in the Baccanaals, rapidly forming an addiction to carpet-chewing. Leamore and Dawes were developing several scenarios to exact their vengeance on both HM and Belgiss – most of which are chronicled in the second volume of the prince's life: 'Too Charming!'

Antonio was still in Azrac; Syun in her village; Squeers in Zanoria, still Protectoring it (as he would be for some time to come). He was getting more and more entrenched in an ever more bloody war with the Waifu and the Tay. Prim and Ginny were at home house-training Prim's most recent husband and his extremely dreary daughter.

But Winny *was* in attendance. HM felt her loyalty should be rewarded by letting her attend the unmasking of the pretender.

Winny was still (hoping against hope) waiting for the announcement of her engagement to the Crown Prince. She hoped-against-hope today might be *the* day.

The king had come out onto the balcony, holding HM's hand. Naitly was a pace behind them. The king was, he told the crowd, delighted to introduce to them his bride-to-be: HM. And he raised her arm. The crowd had cheered their approval, with that under-exuberance which usually greets the supporting act before the main event.

As they turned back to go inside the throne room, the king allowed himself to peck his fiancée lightly on the lips. "Happy?" he asked her.

"Delirious," she replied, and kissed him back, extending her left hand, as she did so, to Naitly. Who surreptitiously squeezed it, and as he allowed his also to be squeezed.

Not one of the Court came forward to congratulate the royal couple. And that, for some time, would rankle with HM. But, at that moment, she had other things on her mind ...

The Mercian ambassador was in attendance; likewise Richardson and Nancy; Cordelia. And, of course, the two vying princes.

HM wondered whether Winny could distinguish the real from the phoney. She knew *she* couldn't. Peas in a pod, by comparison, were Adonis and Quasimodo.

She still couldn't make up her mind which of the two it would best serve her interests to be the impostor. She knew that the consequences to Belgic history would be significant ... no, enormous. Frankly, though, she was more concerned about the consequences to her own.

Charming was nervous. The more so as he was standing right next to a Cordelia, whose nervousness was so great it was *feeding* his – and, consequently, was also being *fed* by it. Both siblings had expected to be clutched to the royal bosom. And both were aware of how bad a sign it was, the total lack of any such clutching.

Charming looked at his doppelganger. They'd spent a day together. He even rather liked him. One of them would be dead within half-an-hour. The other would one day be king of Belgiss. The pretender appeared to be relaxed. But he was gently gnawing at his lower lip.

"I'd never really thought about the after-life. Any of that," King Sebastian told me. "Not even when Philomena and Horatio had died. I still thought I had had time. I *had* to have time, I was a young man. But Horatio and Philly, they too had been young, for God's sake. For *God's* sake? Where was God *then*? Why hadn't God been protecting *their* young lives? And if He hadn't protected theirs, why should He protect mine? For God's sake. They'd been even younger than I was. And they too, for God's sake, had had destinies to fulfil.

"I suddenly felt myself *enraged* at God.

"Enraged that He so clearly didn't exist. And enraged that it would be so prematurely that I'd meet Him."

Charming did not want to die. Charming, in fact, was terrified of the whole thing: of death, of dying, of the block, of the walk to it. He found he could not even imagine a Charmingless world. He *couldn't* die. Who would return for Syun, if he didn't? Unrescued, she would spend her life never forgiving him; at her death she would feel he had betrayed her. He couldn't bear that idea.

These and a thousand other sensations were all cascading through the prince as he was also noticing, almost in slow motion, the thousand and one things happening around him:

Nancy's right hand splaying as it sought out Richardson's left; her *left* hand rubbing the fold of her dress at womb-height. He guessed (correctly, as it turned out) that she was pregnant. He noticed that the guard standing right behind her had a pronounced mole on the side of a bulbous nose, and that there was a smear of some kind of grease smudging the waist of his breast-plate.

He noticed his father's increasingly frail walk, and that his barber had missed a tuft of stubble on the far side of his neck. He noticed the extravagant ring on HM's finger and that her hands had been more carefully manicured than he had ever previously seen them.

He noticed dust beneath the curtains, noticed that certain heads of the gladioli were dying, that there was a loose thread on the arm-rest of the throne, that there was a money spider scuttling towards one of the latticed windows.

And then he saw HM pointing at him. And his ears opened again to hear what she was saying.

"... is clearly the impostor. Which means, sire – and I cannot tell you the regret with which I say this – that your daughter, Cordelia, must also be an accomplice in this deception."

"NO!" screamed Cordelia.

"No," screamed the pretender. No-one ever understood why. Charming said nothing.

"Too late now for remorse," HM told the princess.

"What are you getting out of this, HM, huh?" Cordelia asked. "What? You know this is a lie, that it's a travesty."

"Take them away," HM told the guards. Who immediately moved towards Charming and Cordelia.

"Don't you understand, papa?" wailed Nancy. "They're *both* impostors. Both so-called princes, I mean."

The young pretender shot her a glance which made her understand that he had heard what she had to say, and that it had registered. He stepped forward, and knelt before the king.

"Sire," said the young man, "today is a joyous day. You have announced your betrothal to this beautiful woman. ..." HM could not stop a gentle blush from leaping to her cheeks. Naitly mused, not for the first time, about the vanity of women. It was Naitly's vanity that never did he muse about the vanity of men! "... I have been returned to my rightful place as your dutiful son and most humble heir. ..."

"Oh, well played," Charming thought to himself.

"... This is not a day, sire – not a day, *Father* –, for shedding blood." HM looked aghast. Naitly was decidedly unhappy.

"All impostors," Nancy insisted. "Just as I said. Which one of *us* would make a speech like that?"

Cole looked to HM for guidance. She seemed to be lost in too much reverie to notice his appeal for help. "The clemency of your spirit does you credit," eventually His Majesty told his 'son'. "It augurs well for the realm's future. However, not everything – as you yourself will discover – ..." Was there threat contained in these words? "... is within the sovereign's gift. An act of high treason has been committed. For high treason there is only one penalty possible. Even if one wanted to, one cannot commute it. One's hands, my son," he told the pretender, "are tied."

"His hands are tied," HM confirmed. She could feel Naitly's smirk boring through the back of her head.

"Sadly," Cole told Charming and Cordelia, "you have to die. Take them away," he told their guards.

The pretender stood and he started to turn around.

Charming fully expected the face, when it was completely shielded from the king's gaze, to be wreathed in smiles. But it wasn't. There was real sadness etched into it, profound sadness. Charming even found a part of himself feeling sorry for the young man. They were both being manipulated by forces way beyond their control, both prince and pretender. The pretender was not in fact his enemy but his co-puppet.

The pretender could not sustain a look to the prince. He cast the merest glance in his direction. But in that glance too was the recognition that the prince was his colleague, that their situations could so easily have been reversed, that they were both no more than minnows caught in a gigantic net. In that glance both asked forgiveness. And both thought they had extended it.

"God forgive me," yelled Winny at that moment. And she fainted.

Chapter 61

Now that sentence had been passed, Naitly wanted Cordelia and Charming removed with the minimum amount of fuss. The diversion caused by Winny's fainting was exactly what he needed: At the same time as courtiers administered, amateurly, to the stricken nanny, guards (on Naitly's insistent nod) dragged the two of them away.

The Lord Chancellor and the king's fiancée would oversee the executions. Cole, it was suggested, would be better off in his inner sanctum: Treason or not, it was his daughter who was about to lose her head.

As if to confirm which, the king sighed expansively as he signed her death warrant and that for her accomplice. Sometimes it was a lousy job, ruling a country. To recompense himself for which lousiness he ordered that several of his all-time favouritest bowls should be brought to him – immediately, if not sooner.

HM wanted to feel better than she did. After all, if there was a winner in all of this, it was certainly she. She'd outplayed them all. The king, of course, was no competition. Nor was Fredvie. But she'd beaten expert players – 'seeds', they'd be called in tennis: Naitly and Dawes, Leamore and Goneril. It was winning Olympic laurels, golden spurs, world championships. It was the ultimate win.

Soon she would be queen. She would shortly afterwards bear the king's child. Boy or girl, she'd swat away 'Charming' or Nancy, and her child would become the monarch. She'd by then be married to the Lord Chancellor. Whom she would, of course, allow to remain the figurehead, whilst holding the real power herself.

It wasn't just the culmination of her dreams, it was the culmination of dreams she'd never *dared* to dream. And yet ... never in her life had she felt more empty. As if some archangel had invisibly scooped all her insides out. It wasn't even that she felt unhappy, or unfulfilled; it was that she felt utterly void. Eviscerated. A shell without a snail, a beeless hive.

This feeling started off by flummoxing her. Then it led to it disorientating her. Which yielded to dizziness, and that to testiness. The proverb came to her mind: 'If the gods want to punish us, they give us what we pray for.' Was it that? *Was* it that?

In the corridor Naitly sought to snuggle close to her. "Happy?" he asked her, his own grin dwarfing that of the canaried cat.

"Delirious," she again replied. But the tone was one whose sarcasm was citrusly acid. As was the peck she budgerigared on his lips.

***

Cordelia and Charming were preparing to die.

Cordelia had surprised herself by wanting to pray.

"And I surprised *myself*," King Sebastian told me, "by continuing *not* to want to. There was so much I wanted to say, and to so many people. And it wasn't all right that I left it unsaid. It wasn't. It wasn't all right either that all the things I had to do would never now be done. There were things in the world which needed to be done, which *had* to be done. And those things, because I was not around, wouldn't be.

"I found myself raging at Quifah. Who the Hell did Quifah think he was? If I hadn't listened to him, I'd now be safe and living with him. My bloody 'destiny'. 'Yes,' I chortled unhappily, almost aloud, '*literally* that, apparently: my *bloody* destiny. Bloody Quifah.'

"No, of course I wouldn't be living with Quifah, what was I thinking? I'd have run away with Syun. We'd now be together, working together, maybe in Biga-buga. Maybe with a homestead in Phillizelda. Happy together. I wouldn't be just about to die.

"I *wasn't* going to die. It wasn't going to happen. I was too *young* to die, for God's sake. And Cordelia too. She was too young to die. And Cordelia had children, for God's sake, who were *far* too young for her to die. Neither of us was going to die. God, for God's sake, would simply not allow it. The king would sign the amnesty – damn what HM had said.

"And damn HM. HM knew she was lying. She *had* to know she was lying. Her conscience would get the better of her. She'd recant. A huge reconciliation would be effected. The king would sign the amnesty and we would be freed. Not executed, anyway. Imprisoned, maybe, for a week or two. Till the mess got sorted out. But not killed. Not beheaded.

"FOR GOD'S SAKE."

***

Having prayed, Cordelia felt calmer. Maybe, like the hurricane, the first onslaught of rage had blown itself out. It was now still – regathering its strength, preparing for the second attack.

The guards had left paper and quills for them both. Cordelia had two important letters to write: to her husband and their children.

Charming also had letters to write. To Syun and Quifah. But he'd never seen Waifu written down. To Syun he could, of course, write in Belgic, but what would he use as an address? Unable to communicate by writing, therefore, he took a candle into a corner of the room, knelt before it and spoke into its flame.

Charming may have had the eyes – maybe even the soul – of a poet. But he did not have a poet's words. Nor did Cordelia. Their goodbyes were touching but predictable, the words hackneyed and the sentiments … sentimental.

The prince had finished a while before Cordelia.

Charles I is remembered by history as being the only king executed by the British. He was beheaded on a cold day and asked for a second vest lest the crowd mistake his shivers for nervousness. Charming too was shaking. But shaking with rage. An entire haberdasher's stock of vests would not stop that shaking. It was not that he was *just* shaking: He was *quaking* rather. Quaking with the injustice of it all. And with all the injustice.

There was then too much injustice for one person to be able to absorb it all, let alone to quake from it all. But in quaking from the injustice being meted out to *him*, Charming also shook for that of which Cordelia was the victim – and Antonio, their children; Gretel in her exile; that to which Syun and Quifah were being subjected, the entire Tay and Waifu nations; the injustice the orphans were suffering in Biga-buga, or the slaves in Mercia or the good-as-slaves in Belgiss and Azrac.

Cordelia had not yet finished writing when the key to their room rasped in its lock. It was, the guards didn't need to say, 'time'.

Cordelia had been struggling to find variations on the theme of 'I love you'. She had finished the sentence she was writing. She added 'I've got to go now' as if she were popping to the shops for a loaf of bread. And signed the letter – 'Always remember that I love you, Mummy'. She put three 'x's' afterwards which, in Belgiss as in Britain, signified kisses. And she shook sand from a shaker to blot the ink.

She gave the letters to the most senior of the guards. "Would you please make sure," she said to him, "that these get to my husband and children?"

"Of course," said the guard and put them into the inside of his tunic. He was to find them there some days later, and, because he couldn't see the point of sending them, then to throw them away. He looked to Charming for any mail he might have.

"I don't have a husband and children," the prince told him, with a smile almost as feeble as the 'joke'. He'd resolved, if he was going to die he wasn't going to do so without a bloody great struggle.

He still had one card up his sleeve.

Chapter 62

There was nothing ghoulish about HM. She hated being there on the balcony. She knew it was really unfair, what was happening to Cordelia. Whom she liked and admired. As for Charming ... well, she saw herself as Yorick to his Hamlet. Except that, in this version, the jester outlived the prince. 'Alas, poor Charming ...'

It was a shame – a real shame – that the saga had to end with these two deaths. She'd racked her brains to find an alternative, knowing as she did so that there was none. And that, even if there were, Fredvie and the others would not allow it, that they'd insist that the exorcising from their flesh of these two thorns was a permanent one.

Cole not being there was just as well. His bowl consumption had passed the point where his legs necessarily obeyed his brain: Wobbliness might be perceived by the crowd as squeamishness, and squeamishness as an indication of a guilty conscience. Cole's absence might excite conjecture. Better by far, though, that the gossip centred on what might be causing his absence than the guilt of his conscience.

The king nevertheless did have to be represented. He was the state. And the executive too had to be represented. Hence Naitly's presence. Both he and HM were on the king's balcony, extremely visible.

Invisible and in the throng were Nancy and Richardson. She just wanted to make sure the execution really did happen. With one Charming out of the way, she only had to dispose of the other before the crown was hers. As for Cordelia ... She'd convinced herself again that, over and above the highness of her attempted treason, she clearly *had* been an accomplice in the murder of her son, and that her execution was therefore *doubly* justified.

Also in the crowd was the pretender, still dressed exactly as the prince was. He'd ambled blindly into that field of numbness where all is just beyond reach, including your own senses. He didn't even know quite what he was doing there. He just knew there he had to be.

Around him there was the muted roar that comes with expectation. We are all children sometimes on our way to a birthday party. And there is also in most of us – hard though it may be for us to admit it – the ghoul.

"We do not become better people by ignoring the ugly aspects of ourselves;" opined King Sebastian, "we become better people only by finding the courage to deal with those aspects. You cannot deal with them until you allow yourself to acknowledge them."

"Sire!" I exclaimed impatiently.

Suddenly the whole throng fell eerily quiet.

On the dais there was stir. The axeman looked round to Useless. It was to check that all was in readiness. He folded his arms over his huge barrelled chest. His masked face looked pointedly at the wooden door within the stone-clad walls.

A slow drum beat started.

The door creaked heavily open. HM and Naitly, who had been sitting, rose from their chairs. All eyes centred on the door.

Through it emerged, first, the drummer. Two guards followed him, then another two. The Court chaplain next, reading from a Bible. Behind him walked Cordelia, her long hair dancing in the gentle breeze, their electricity causing a few strands almost to stand on end.

The crowd drew in a communal breath.

Coming to in one of the castle's bedrooms, Winny heard that breath being held. She held hers. Then started to choke. The coughs from which soon gave way to tears. And these escalated even more quickly into howls.

Those howls could vaguely be heard by the crowd. But they melted into all the other background noises: the rumble of distant cart-wheels on cobbles, the flap of the canvas around the base of the dais, the odd cough, birds' songs. Most of all, the slow boom-boom-boom of the lone drummer.

After Cordelia came the prince. And every female heart gave a flutter of despair: It wasn't as though Belgiss were exactly knee-deep in good-looking men. How could *anything* that beautiful be destroyed?

Behind the prince came another four guards.

A way opened up before the condemned and their escort. There was no need for cordons or crowd-controllers, a path just formed itself that led directly to the scaffold.

No sooner had Charming emerged through the door than he let out a very high-pitched and piercing whistle. He then craned his neck to try and see above the crowd, in the clear expectation that some force would emerge behind it – and which, presumably, would effect his escape.

The anticipation in the crowd grew tenfold. Only, when no such rescuer revealed himself, to fall into a sulky sense of anti-climax.

Even as he climbed the scaffold's steps, Charming continued to look about him expectantly. But the crowd no longer believed him, some even started hooting.

Cordelia was clearly irked by him, and thought he had injected a wholly inappropriate note of either facetiousness or frivolity into what should be the most solemn of occasions.

What none could see was that, in the royal stables, Peggy was thrashing around like a horse gone mad, trying to break through the wooden stalls which penned it.

Nor could anyone in the square see that buried deep in the dungeons, Nose was frantically chewing at the bottom of an already frayed wooden door, desperate to widen the gap to one big enough for him to scramble through.

Cordelia passed her cloak to Useless. She went to Charming, kissed him on his cheek. She smiled up at HM in the balcony. She passed the axeman the ten doubloons necessary to ensure a clean decapitation. He touched what would have been his forelock had it not been hidden by his mask.

She looked up at the sky, looked over the crowd, then into it. There was a baby suckling her mother's breast. Desperately, desperately Cordelia held onto that image. She knelt before the block. The drumming stopped. She laid her head on it.

The axeman glanced quickly up to the royal balcony. Both HM and Naitly gave the curtest of nods. The axeman didn't even acknowledge these, but brought his axe up over his head.

And swung it down.

Chapter 63

Still Nose was gnawing at the door, scratching at the impacted earth beneath it. Still Peggy was kicking at the wood of its stable.

And still Charming was aware of neither.

He'd turned away from his sister's execution. There was no element of it which did not appal every element of him.

He was observant, however, *aware*, in a more general way; more sharply aware, in fact, of his body's sensations than ever he had been. More acutely aware of everything around him. He grasped onto every tiny detail as if it might be that the rope which would yank him to safety.

He kept waiting, the prince, not for divine intervention, but for divine in*spiration*: A flash which would imbue him with the wisdom of understanding what the Hell the whole thing had been about.

The drum had started again. Boom, boom, boom. It was an echo of the heartbeat he'd soon have no more. Boom, boom, boom. He kept expecting some kind of angelic prompt, telling him some wonderfully poetic last words to say.

Boom, boom, boom.

He kept wanting to feel suddenly old and accepting of the fact that his life was over ... boom, boom, boom ... but nothing came.

And he pouted in a sort of stoic cynicism that such is life and why – boom, boom, boom – should he expect its end to be different from any – boom – other – boom – part of it?

Boom, boom, boom, boom.

He was wearing no cloak so had nothing to pass to the senior guard. He saw Useless pass a fresh axe to his boss. He looked up at HM, smiled defiantly at her. He found the pretender in the crowd. Smiled malevolently also at him.

Boom, boom, boom.

He was relaxing his knees, preparing to kneel. Suddenly, from the back of the crowd, a rumpus did break out.

Chaos broke out.

Peggy was avalanching towards him, rearing and bucking, its huge hooves scooping a path before it, as if it were digging a furrow. It was determined to beat a path through them, the mob. Which gave before it just as quickly as their jam-packedness would allow.

Women started screaming, trying to protect both their own heads and those of any infants in their charge; men made idiotic "shoo"ing noises; the older children were worming their way through human crannies. It was borderline panic, and approaching that border rapidly beyond which people were going to be badly hurt, if not killed.

The axeman had glanced away from his appointed task to see what the fuss was. The prince used that momentary distraction to grab hold of his axe. Even through his mask the man looked startled; more startled yet when the prince hit him with the axe handle and knocked him out.

Peggy was now only yards away. But the crowd around the dais was even denser. Those pinioned there were trying to get away by diving under it. But that was taking time. The shrieking and the screaming grew in intensity; and underlying both were a rumble and whoosh of primeval fear feeding on itself, about to create a monster. There was no sense of fun now, nor of carnival. All was fear.

The prince whistled again to Peggy. Which caused the beast to redouble its efforts.

Well below them, Nose also heard that second whistle. It re-injected heart into his gnawing.

So great had the clamour now become that Cole himself had wandered onto the balcony to see what was happening. HM and Naitly urged him back inside. But the king wouldn't hear of it.

From the corner of his eyes the prince saw Useless sidling towards the supply of axes. He moved threateningly towards the deputy executioner. Who, in the blink of an eye, decided that heroism was not his thing and backed away.

The *prince's* eyes were *not* blinking, but ablaze. He wielded the axe above his head. It would have killed anyone who came close.

He scanned the crowd for the pretender. This way he looked. Where was he? Then that. He had to be somewhere. He had to be …

He saw him. Cowering. Cowering by a cart, close to Peggy's bucking path. Cowering next to a woman in a faded pink shift, holding a dirty-mouthed infant with a squashed nose.

The pretender's attention was completely on Peggy's hind legs hurtling menacingly into space only inches from his face. In the midst of the mayhem, though, accident had it that, for the merest moment, their eyes met. In that look an encyclopaedia of information was exchanged. And from it the prince knew he had to kill him. The only way that the prince would be recognised as being the rightful heir would be if there were no pretender. It was, quite literally, the pretender's life or his.

Peggy was now about three ranks of hysterical people away from the dais. The horse wasn't going to get any further. The throng was wedged so tightly the prince thought he could make it to Peggy by scuttling from one shoulder to another.

He jumped from the platform and did exactly that. Scuttling, scurrying, scrambling. He did just make it, capsizing gratefully onto Peggy's back. His thoughts were of escape. He wheeled his mount around.

No.

Before escaping, there was a little something else he had to do.

Still all around was chaos and screaming. The soldiers were trying to restore order. Being, in fact, quite brutal so doing. They had to be. They had to take order – and now – or people would die. A lot would die.

The prince wanted no-one to die. He didn't even *want* the

pretender to die. He knew the pretender had to, that was all.

Peggy was now becoming frightened itself. When the prince started to try and force it in the direction where the pretender was cowering, Peggy was reluctant to obey him. Bareback and bridleless, to get it to do his bidding, the prince had to use every inch of his horsemanship.

All around was still screaming, and jostling and clubbing and bludgeoning. Pain and panic ... swords and screams and soldiers ... and blood. And more blood.

There was the pretender. There, there.

The pretender had seen in the prince's eyes his murderous intent. He needed to protect himself. The squashed-nose infant had vanished, but the woman in pink he now held before him, almost as a shield.

She'd run, the prince was sure, she'd run before the axe struck. She *would* run. The lethal axe above his head, Charming pushed Peggy towards the pretender. Move woman, *move*.

The woman bit the pretender's hand. He "ow"ed cursed and let her go. She fled: The prince had him. He *had* him.

A soldier swung his sword at Peggy's throat.

The horse died instantly, crumpling into a heap, throwing prince and pretender together.

Soldiers came, grabbed both. These looked from one to the other, trying to work out which was the condemned man and which their future king. But there was suddenly no longer prince and pretender, there was only prince 'a' and prince 'b'.

Now that the rampaging beast had been felled, calm re-established itself amongst the crowd. Bruises started to be rubbed, cuts licked, truant children regathered. The calm shifted into an almost cathedral-like reverence and quiet. There was a consciousness that this was a historic moment, and that those present were part of it.

The woman in the faded pink shift was still shaking from the shock. But even she, who had so nearly been murdered by one for protecting the other, stopped for a moment to compare the twins in the courtyard's centre. Both, of course, continued to insist on his own innocence and the guilt of the other.

Cole looked to his fiancée. "Your call, one thinks, dearest," he said.

HM knew she had to be decisive. If she were seen to waver, then the assumption would have to be that she *also* couldn't distinguish between the two. And the inference of *that* would be ... possibly difficult, politically. Potentially awkward. Maybe even very awkward.

On the dais the axeman was slowly coming to, and Useless was busy making himself really important by checking the axe-rack yet again.

"Both of them impostors, papa," Nancy, despite her husband's frantic attempts to "shhh" her, yelled again from within the crowd. "Both, *both* of them. Can't you see that? Are you blind, papa? Both impostors."

"The one on your right, guards," HM announced. "Take him away."

"No," said the prince on the right, as he on the left allowed a large grin to meander across his face. "No, you've made a mistake. A terrible mistake. You want *him*. You want *HIM*. Not me. NO!!!"

Kicking and struggling, the prince was dragged to the dais. The axeman had been handed the axe by Useless, who stood with another in his hand, more as a symbol of office than a tool.

So much did the condemned prince struggle that he had to be manacled, and then his arms held. Those holding him forced the young man to his knees, simply by kicking the back of his knee-caps. "No," he kept shouting, kept screaming. "No, it's not me you want. Not me. You want him. Him. You want him. Father, listen to me. People of Belgiss, listen to me. NOOOOOOOOOOOOOOOOOO!!!!!!!!!!!!!!!!!!!!!!!!!!!!!!!!!!!"

The soldiers holding the condemned's arms used them as a

lever to place his head on the block.

The axeman grinned malevolently. This low-life had knocked him out cold. Well, pay back time, my friend! *One* blow? He should cocoa.

Which thought gurgled where it stood. The entire of the axeman's body at that moment froze. Before he let out a large and vibrant: "YEOOOOOOOOOOOOOW!"

Nose had hold of his thigh. He let go. But only to snarl at him, to let him know he was ready to take *another* chunk out of him.

In a gesture that was completely out of character, Useless moved forward and with one swipe took off Nose's head. Blood was also pouring from the axeman's leg. "*You* do it, lad," he told Eustace. "You do your worst. I do mean your *worst*, Eustace."

"Oh, I really don't think … " Useless started to say.

"Just do it!"

"WAIT," Cole bellowed from the balcony. He'd seen Nose's death and had been deeply moved by it. Tears were streaming from his eyes. Behind him Naitly and HM looked at each other uncertainly.

Useless wasn't sure whether it was he who was being addressed and therefore continued to raise the axe.

"Wait, one said," the king roared. "If the prince's dog was trying to save the prince, then it's clearly the prince he was trying to save. Therefore, my dear," he said, addressing HM, "you were on the point of executing the wrong man. Guards, seize that pretender in the crowd. And you, one's son," he said to the young man still on his knees before the gory block, "come immediately to this balcony, so that one might welcome you back to Belgiss, to your future crown, and to one's arms."

"Noooooooooooooooooooo!" screamed the young man in the crowd. "Noooooooooooooo!" he screamed again.

"Nooooooooooooo!" he screamed until the very end.

***

"Thus finally justice was done," King Sebastian said.

"Right," I said, for want of anything brighter to say. I was waiting for another homily.

"A sort of justice, anyway. A sort-of-justice is usually as much as any of us can hope for. Not too much justice for Cordelia."

"Or mercy," I added, "for the pretender."

"As you say," 'Charming' agreed. "King Cole – I said this before – was desperate that I marry," he continued, anxious (it felt) to change the subject. "Poor Winny still thought it was *her* right to be my bride. That number with the glass slipper? That was a device Cinderella worked out. It added spice to Cinderella's revenge. She wanted her step-sisters humiliated. She knew nothing would stop them, Ginny and Winny, poor things, from trying to squeeze their size twelves into it.

"In all Winny's calculations, in her wildest conjectures, never had it even occurred to her that it might be this rather dreary step-sister of hers who would end up at the royal altar. She thought Fredvie would stand by the commitment he had made to her. I wasn't the pretender, I had to remind her, I was the prince. And she had tried to kill me. Oh, I didn't mind. That, after all, is politics. I felt sorry for her, actually. Still do. I mean, how naïve can you get?! As if Fredvie even understood the concept of standing by a commitment!"

"And the others, sire?" I asked. He didn't seem to understand. "Well, did they live as 'happily ever after' as the story tells us? Did *you*, for that matter?"

"*Happily* ever after? I suppose most of us were moderately happy. At least, most of the time. Some of the time, anyway. That time, that after-Cinderella time, that is the second half of the story. A book all by itself. *Ever* after? *Is* there such a thing?"

"I suppose we must like to think there is," I ventured.

"Oh more than that, I think, my dear." If he only knew how fingernails-on-blackboard that condescension was! "I think we're *desperate* to think there is."

He stopped. He was making a decision. "Before I started talking to you I had to weigh that in my considerations," he said, finally. His words felt draped in sackcloth. "A much cleverer man than me once said, 'Man cannot take too much reality' … something like that, probably expressed better. And he's got a point. But Man has got to start learning to cope better with reality.

"Ours, my dear, is a world which prefers myth and fantasies to truth. It is from myths that Dawes sells his gazettes, Leamore keeps his money, and Fredvie his power. And so determined is our world to believe in the myth, that it demonises not those who make, and profit from, the myths but those that expose them.

"Oh, it's not one myth, of course, or fantasy, it's an agglomeration of them, a mixture of them. Almost the core myth, though, is the happy ending. That myth, the happy ending myth, has become the bedrock of our society. And it is not only the central myth, but the greatest – it is *so* great a myth, in fact, that it is suitable *only* as the coda to a fairy-story.

"To believe that myth is to build our house on the sandiest ground there is – to build it as near as dammit on *quick*sand. To rest not just our own house, but the whole of our *society* on that quicksand ... well, there are no words to describe that danger. That is *so*, so dangerous.

"And yet it is precisely that myth which we do believe. Or, at any rate, that we have allowed ourselves to be seduced into believing. Sadly, harmless ogres are, again, the stuff only of fairy-stories. And believing ogres when they insist, deep down, they're really good guys is to believe three bears would talk to a little girl about porridge.

"Me, I'm popular, I know that. But only as a figure of fantasy. As a real person … you know, I'm really not too sure.

"To be honest, that was part of my ambivalence about telling you my story … 'coming out,' I suppose that'd be called today. It's not easy for me to admit this – it's quite painful, in fact – but … my popularity was important to me. I had to face that fact. I had to come to terms with that vanity in me. And – take it from me – that wasn't easy.

"You see, there is a part of me – I'd love to say there *was* but it isn't a 'was, it's an 'is' – which is envious of Cinderella. I mean, *hugely* envious of her. In the traditional telling of our story, what *am* I? Barely a bit player: I get one scene at the ball as a callow and moonstruck youth – when a pumpkin and some mice get considerably more attention than I do –, another scene as a sort of out-of-work and itinerant shoe salesman … and the wedding … In which all I do is say 'I do'.

"That, though, is no longer the point, my envy, my petty-mindedness, whatever the Hell it is. What *is* the point is that my vanity got me to thinking about that in others, about the hankering we most of us have for some sort of posterity, to leave our mark on history – like a wolf marking its territory, almost. And, like the wolf too, savage if our territory – our place in history – is invaded.

"Oh, don't misunderstand me, that hankering has, I'm sure, led to some of humankind's most glorious achievements. I'm prepared to bet there was more than an element of it in the creation of the 'Mona Lisa' or 'King Lear' or 'The Magic Flute'.

"And yet, so often a healthy hankering for a life-after-death has developed into an unhealthy obsession, and one which wreaks havoc on the lives-before-death of so many more … wreaks a *savage* havoc on them. How many were killed building the pyramids? Or China's Great Wall? Or St Petersburg?

"Should not a lesson be from the past that the cost of one infinite future can be the annihilation of ten thousand presents? A hundred thousand? In the cases of some tyrants, literally millions of presents?

"Should not history be warning us that one man's yearning for posterity can become an obsession threatening the lives of countless others? *Countless* others?

"In my opinion, Naitly sent young men to be massacred in

Orismine not – as is supposed amongst the cynics – to keep on the right side of Fredvie, not even for Orismine's mineral rights. Oh, both were certainly a bonus, but they were neither of them the main point.

"The main point was that Naitly wanted his place in history. And hawks appear to take up more space in the history books than doves. To this day, Alexander is gloried more than Aristotle.

"History is thus distorted, of course – and the wise would do well to remind themselves of that and to tell their children of that: Aristotle was far more important to the good things in our lives today than Alexander. And the wise would also do well to ask themselves *why* there is such a propensity to distort history. But, for the likes of Naitly, history's distortion is not the issue. It is their *place* in it which is.

"And the Naitlys of this world hate us, the royals, hate us with a passion – and for that reason. Royals take up space in the history books. Not only that, they do it without even trying! The republicans, the anti-monarchists are right, a hundred per cent on the button: Without lifting a finger, we royals have status, wealth, fame … and, most important of all, immortality.

"Know what, though? That's how those who *aren't* royal see it, not those of us who are.

"In my experience, most of us royals have spent our lifetimes trying to prove to the world that we *were* worth those things. And many of us succeed in doing so. Even our opponents have to concede that. But you know whom, almost without exception, none of us ever convinces? Ourselves. I know of not one single member – one single *healthy* member, I should say – of any royal family who, at the level of his soul or hers, believes they are due the reverence afforded them. Certainly I haven't persuaded myself that I am.

"What I *have* persuaded myself of, however, is that fantasy is a curse. And that the fantasy pervading the world is one which, unless it is treated, will destroy it. Surgeons do not cure their patients by pretending they are not sick. *If* we want to survive – and, apparently, that is a big 'if' – , it's time for us to stop sugar-coating our situation, and to start taking whatever medicine we need to in order to live – however foul, however unpleasant, unpalatable, even painful. It's time we started facing reality.

"Our children have to know the horrors we have perpetrated, often in their name! They have to know that so many who portend to protect them don't.

"All the time we warn them against accepting sweets from strangers, and yet – somehow and bizarrely – we encourage them to swallow strangers' lies: the lies of politicians and clothes manufacturers, the lies of fast food venues and soft drinks suppliers, those of gazetteers which frighten them and of historians which delude them … the lies of books which tell them good people live happily ever after. The *hugeness* which is that lie.

"We vilify and imprison paedophiles, yet those who thus abuse our children we enrich and honour. Abuse is no less real or painful or damaging for being intellectual abuse or emotional abuse … or an abuse of a child's potential.

"It was that which finally persuaded me. The telling, the reliving, that has all been painful for me – in fact, enormously painful – but pain that saves others pain is pain that has a point," the king continued, "and pain which has a point, *its* sting is in the past. The pain of the present, the pain you can *never* get rid of, is the pain which serves no purpose, the one from which no-one learns, the mistake which we make over and over and over again, apparently from one generation to the next, ceaselessly, remorselessly."

The king leant forward on his chair. He tapped me on the knee, almost as if beating out Morse code. His whole demeanour seemed to have changed. "There's one question I never get asked. You know that? It's always intrigued me why I don't. It's the most obvious question of all. Know what it is?"

"No, sire."

"Can't you guess?"

"I'm not too good at guessing games," I tetchily confessed.

The king laughed and leant back again into his chair. "'How can we be sure, sire,'" he mimicked the hypothetical questioner, "'that it was the *pretender* who was executed?'

"After all, if the real prince (as the history books say he did) *had* been educated in San Pedito, would I (as a pretender, pretending to be the real thing) not have had to invent a story similar to that you've just heard? Despite my twenty-four hours with … my rival, I'd scarcely have the type of detailed knowledge about school in San Pedito which would have stood up under pressure. If I were a journalist, know what I'd ask: 'How can we be *sure*, sire, that the pretender, that's not in fact you?'?"

I was surprised. But by myself. It wasn't that I'd been muzzled: I didn't work for Dawes, my editor still believed in things like free speech. To my shame, the question – frankly – simply hadn't occurred to me. Why hadn't it?

"And how, sire, would you have answered that question?" eventually I stammered out.

The king looked at me, his gaze more rigid than at any other time in our interview. "*Would* you have answered it?" I asked.

'Charming' held my glance for a beat longer.

And then he started to laugh. Not a sad laugh, this, but a full one. That laugh was his answer. Laughing, he left the room.

Was he laughing at himself, I wondered, at the absurdity of his situation, of *our* situation? Was he maybe laughing at the absurdity of life in general?

Or was it, that laugh, the last laugh?

And was it then on us?

*** The End ***